PRAISE FOR WISH

"Wish is so unique and unlike anything I have ever read before. It is a riveting, fast paced read, one where we never quite know where it's going to go next, which makes it a real page turner."

Jaclyn Kot | @jaclyn.kot

Amazon Bestselling Author of *Between Life & Death*

"Wish hits all the right spots with its unique blend of rich cozy world building and characters in every shade of morality, ranging from pure goodness to the most bone-chilling evil you're likely to encounter. Fantastical magic and raw human emotion make up in equal measure the thread that weaves this unique page turner. Truly excited to see what Sara has in store for us next."

J. M. Rose | @thatwriterjess

"This book kept me hooked, beginning to end! By combining Fae and genie magic into Wish, Sara truly created a unique world and magic system that I have never read before, but one that blew me away!"

Kaitlyn | @kaitlynhillebrand

"Not only does Wish have EVERYTHING I love in dark fantasy romance, it delivers a unique heart wrenching experience. Wish has a genie, fae, blood magic and evil evil villains that will leave you feeling a little murderous right alongside Mora."

Maryann | @maryannaugerbooks

"FMC, cursed as a wish granting genie, with a major chip on her shoulder? Yes, please! The rage you feel emanating from our main girl lends to Sara's fantastic ability to bring you into the scene. Her stunning visuals shake you up... right alongside Mora's latest victim. Morally dark with a side of fated mates *chef's kiss. Anxiously waiting for more!"
Mary | @_thebookdragon_

"Be careful what you WISH for... It may lead to a: W: Whimsical Deadly Quest, I: Insidious Keeper, S: Stabby Snarky Genie, H: Hot as Hell Warrior."
Alexis | @thepaperback_girl

"Atmospheric and sexy, WISH is impossible to put down. With a badass antiheroine and impeccable world building, Sara weaves a story that will have you by the throat from start to finish."
Hope A. Brookes | @spinecracker_

"Wow. wow. wow. wow. This was so good and hit all the sweet spots for a good novel - makes you feel, cliffy ending, and a plot that is woven with the characters and relationships. This was well and truly dark. It was perfection and I want to read more LIKE THIS."
Courtney | @floofymoosereads

Villainous FMCs are so much fun to get to know. Mora's reasons and motives only make her a more complex character, one that you can't help but love.
Rachel | @rachelelysebooks

"Wish was truly a unique story and I loved every minute of it! It had everything I need in a 5star read. A gripping story, interesting characters, creative magic and an ending that leaves me wanting more!"
Vee | @readswithvee

WISH

THE ONYX MIST SERIES
BOOK 1

SARA FLANAGAN

Wish

Sara Flanagan

Copyright ©2024 by Sara Flanagan

Editing by New Ink Book Services

Proofreading by Veerie Edits

Sensitivity Reading by Ritika and Lwazi Vazhure

Cover Design by Hey Gigi Creatives

Cover Flask Rendering by Covers by Jules

Formatting by Sara Flanagan

Map, Chapter Headings and Original Flask Design by New Ink Book Services

CONTENT WARNING

Wish contains mature themes and is intended for an adult audience. This book is a dark fantasy romance with subject matter that may be triggering to some. Please visit saraflanaganbooks.com for more details.

PLAYLIST

Oblivion – Neoni x Zayde Wølf
Eyes Don't Lie – Isabel LaRosa
Lethal Woman – Dove Cameron
Make Me Wanna Die – The Pretty Reckless
Demons – Hayley Kiyoko
Snakes – Miyavi & PVRIS
Lovely – Billie Eilish, Khalid
Enemy – Tommee Profitt Feat. Beacon Light & Sam Tinnesz
Vampire – Olivia Rodrigo | Rock Version by Rain Paris
Dead Man – David Kushner
We Go Down Together – Dove Cameron & Khalid
Dying Star – Ashnikko
What Could Have Been – Sting
Shadow – Livingston
The Death of Peace of Mind – Bad Omens
How Villains are Made – Madalen Duke
Lips of a Witch – Austin Giorgio
Shameless – Camila Cabello
Who's Afraid of Little Old Me – Taylor Swift
You Make Me Sick – Ashnikko
Rise – Katy Perry

FIND THE SPOTIFY PLAYLISTS AT SARAFLANAGANBOOKS.COM

TO THOSE WITH MONSTERS IN THEIR
HEARTS AND FIRE IN THEIR EYES.

AND TO ADRIEN, MY LOVE.

PROLOGUE

MORA
300 YEARS AGO

*T*he pain was excruciating, rising and cresting in agonizing waves as her entire being unraveled. Mora grit her teeth so hard she feared they may crack under the pressure. Pulling in what air she could, she realized she was panting, thick spittle dripping down her chin. Stubbornly, she held off the impending transformation with all her might. This must be what dying felt like.

And yet this was not her ending. No, no, death would be too kind. She now knew, without a shred of doubt, Dother didn't have a speck of kindness in his frigid, black heart. Instead, he'd gifted her a long, harrowing existence at his side. Finally, he owned her, in a way she never could have anticipated. Her throat burned with bile as she grappled with that repulsive idea.

As if her thoughts summoned him, Dother stepped out from the shadows, a diabolical grin contorting his handsome features. Kneeling in front of her, he grabbed her chin and forced her to look into his eyes. They sparkled with his triumph.

He leaned in as he ran his thumb over her bottom lip, smearing drool across her mouth, and whispered, "Did you honestly believe I'd let you go, Treasure?"

Despite herself, a strangled sob escaped her lips. The pain continued to expand, clawing its way through her body. There was no escaping. This would be her downfall. Her will only delayed the inevitable.

Mind racing, she desperately sought a way out. But she could barely breathe through the agony. It was inevitable... she would be his. His will hers to execute, his desires hers to fulfill. There would be no running from what happened next.

Mora seethed as her strength waned and she felt a sudden tug in the center of her chest. It was as if someone pulled on a thread, unweaving her form into something more pliable. Smoke oozed from her pores, slowly enveloping her in a cool caress. It crawled and slithered down her body toward the ornate crystal flask discarded at her feet.

Squeezing her chin uncomfortably tight, Dother chuckled before releasing her and sitting back on his haunches. He wanted to watch what happened next. Delighted in her destruction.

But Mora didn't watch. Instead, she glared deep into his azure eyes, bestowing him with a silent promise. He may very well be responsible for her undoing. But she would be his end.

CHAPTER 1

MORA

Pain bloomed in Mora's palm, an intense sting that pulsed along with her frantic heart. She squeezed her clenched fist tighter, focusing on the sharp ache. Willing it to pull her from the darkness in her mind. It was a struggle to breathe—she sucked in the cool spring air in quick gasps, which did little to fill her lungs. Little to free her from the citrus scent that assaulted her senses when she revived the herb garden.

Damn lemon balm. It summoned memories of *him*.

I will haunt your every breath.

Mora shook her head as if it would silence the echo of Dother's voice. Digging her nails into her palm, she flinched as the sting intensified. It was as if she were stuck; unable to move, unable to break free.

Eyeing the sprawling garden, she tried to focus on the symmetry of the herb and flower beds. Each was a perfect mirror to the one across from it, cut by a narrow walking trail. They were surrounded by manicured hedges, rose bushes, and a cluster of trees encircling a lake whose surface still clung to thin pieces of ice, unwilling to leave winter's embrace. Everything straddled the line between death and life, waiting to awaken now that spring had found Berwick.

A light breeze danced through Mora's long, dark brown curls, tickling her round cheeks and cooling the sweat beading on her brow. She took a slower, deeper breath.

Gods, her bodice felt too tight, its clutch on her rib cage fighting against her efforts to fill her lungs. As she ran a hand down the golden boning she scratched at the soft, turquoise fabric, imagining honing her smoke into claws and tearing herself free. Sadly, the lord's wish wouldn't allow it. Try as she might, she couldn't find a tear-your-dress-off loophole.

Focus, Mora.

It helped that an interesting afternoon awaited, considering the note she'd found tucked under her chamber door this morning. A disruption in her day she already appreciated. Though she wasn't sure what to make of it.

All she could do was imagine for the time being. There was much to do in the gardens.

It took weeks for nature to explode into a kaleidoscope of vibrant colors, each leaf and flower unfurling in their own time. The nobles weren't known for their patience, and Mora's Keeper was desperate to impress. One simple wish and nature's schedule no longer mattered.

Mora could rush life. She could do almost anything. As powerful as she was, she was powerless—other than turning to smoke on a whim, she couldn't use her own magic freely. She was bound to her Keeper's wishes, and whatever loopholes she could create. Whoever held her flask compelled her to do their bidding. For a time. Though they could only make three demands of her. Once they'd uttered their third Wish, they could never be Mora's Keeper again.

Except Dother.

From the moment he'd first laid eyes on her, Dother never intended to let her go. The curse he'd spun bound her to his bloodline. Made it so he could ask for anything, as often as he liked.

And his favorite thing to ask for was...

Mora's muscles tensed, a torrent of panic and fury churning in her belly.

He's dead, he's dead, he's dead.

She chanted the reminder, over and over, hoping it would help ground her in the present and fight off Dother's lingering hold on her mind.

The midday sun glinted off the bay windows resting at the back of the sizable manor, bouncing into Mora's amber eyes. She hissed. Raised her hand against the blinding light and realized what she'd done. In her terror, Mora had grasped a rose bush, squeezing so hard its thorns buried themselves deep.

What a beautiful mess she'd made.

Pressing against her skin, Mora gritted her teeth, wincing as she encouraged the thorns to surface. It was unnecessary—the wound would heal the moment she untethered herself and became a being of glittering onyx mist. But she found she liked the distraction—her mind became blissfully quiet.

As she tossed the last thorn to the earth, she eyed the blood seeping from the wound, coating her warm brown skin. It pooled in her palm, red and gleaming with the finest streaks of gold. She couldn't help her fascination as it dribbled down her fingers. The warm droplets splashed against the long, gold-tipped sleeves of her turquoise gown, rolled over the leather pouch at her hip and dripped to the ground.

It was a rare thing, to feel physical pain, to spill her own blood. Perhaps she should have been more careful... though she was already cursed. What more could someone do?

Mora squeezed her fist tightly and took a twisted pleasure in the intensifying throb. More red liquid seeped through the cracks in her fingers. She failed to notice what rose in its wake. The earth was grateful for her offering, and in return it gifted curious, gilded daisies, sparkling at her feet.

They stretched their golden petals, catching each sanguineous drop, soaking up the rare magic saturating her blood, until Mora picked up her skirt and moved through the gardens. The hard soles of her black leather shoes fell upon them, snapping their stems and crushing their petals.

As quickly as they had risen, they wilted, returning to the clutches of the earth, where they would once again wait for the call of Mora's blood.

Thick black smoke glittering with the slightest hints of gold spilled from Mora's fingers and seeped onto the ground. It approached the gardens like a ravenous wave, caressing every plant in its path. When it reached the rose bushes, beautiful pink rosebuds appeared in its wake, blossoming and greeting the warm sun. It continued onward, crawling up the manor wall, enticing green ivy to follow. The leaves adopted the most incredible shades of viridian, beautifully framing the manor's red bricks.

When the garden was perfect, Mora faced the trees. She allowed herself to come undone, pulling on the ethereal thread in her chest and exploding into a cloud of inky fog.

Curling and flowing through the grass and among the trees, she felt at one with the earth. It sparked a warm current of joy, the delicious feeling spreading like wildfire in her heart. Three hundred years ago, when she was a princess with a secret and a need to pave her own path—before... Dother—she hadn't felt overly connected with nature. Now she relished any opportunity to use her magic to be at one with the earth.

It was rarely demanded of her—her current Keeper hadn't exactly requested it. But he hadn't *not* requested it either. And considering his ask, this made sense. How could she pass up the opportunity to self-indulge?

Everywhere Mora's smoke touched, nature awoke. The earth was eager to please her—she'd created acres of plant growth no land would see for weeks if not for a touch of inexplicable magic.

Landing in the middle of the garden like a twirling mass of shadows, the smoke came together into the shape of a woman with glowing amber eyes peeking out through the darkness. Until it faded and Mora rematerialized—it was like the onyx mist never existed at all. Though the long, trumpet sleeves of her turquoise gown billowed as if battered by a phantom wind, before calming to a flutter, thanks to the gentle caress of the spring breeze.

The sweet aroma of roses hung heavy in the air and a weight lifted from her chest. She was free from the citrus poisoning her mind. Mora plucked a flower, grinning as she brought it to her nose. Its deep pink tones complemented her dress perfectly, so she carefully broke off the thorns and tucked the stem in her hair.

It was time to return to the manor. Mora dawdled as she made her way to the servant's door tucked into the western corner. Letting her imagination run wild, she dreamed she was a creature of the Forbidden Forest, hiding among her glorious flowers and trees.

Oh, to be Fae, unable to lie but skilled in deceit. They'd enjoy her ability to bend her Keeper's wishes to her will. Mora chuckled, imagining the monstrous games they could play together—she felt an odd sense of kinship with them, though she'd only met one. Briefly. A memory she'd prefer burned along with the Fae who'd crossed her.

Fae sightings were rare—no one entered their forest. After the Exodus centuries ago, the woods wouldn't allow it. A wall of ominous trees stood strong in central and western Berwick, flanked by bramble and shrubs so thick entry was impossible. It was rumored the trees themselves moved, blocking the path of any who tried to pass through.

Few dared to enter before when one needed to leave an offering in exchange for passage. Fewer still were found worthy. And those who passed through the tree line never returned. Until one day every human and Halfling fled the woods, a massive storm at their heels. As if the forest itself chased them out. And life in Berwick was never the same.

A minority of Halflings, human-Fae hybrids born in the woods were gifted with powers, the likes of which Berwick had never seen. They faced hell when they were discovered.

The Laws of Confinement.

Labeled as the Forbidden, even those with the weakest magical abilities were imprisoned. Kept in cloisters, studied and, sometimes, if their powers were of use, gifted to noble houses as Indentured.

Some ran and attempted to hide. When they were caught, they paid with their lives. Those among the Halflings without magic were spared, but when they had a child with abilities, they were required to hand them to the King's Guard.

None returned to the embrace of the forest. They were no longer welcome.

The Exodus was a time before Mora's birth. A horrific spot in Berwick's history. One her parents knew well—they grew up in the chaos that followed and did their best to reign in its wake, creating chaos of their own when they attempted to save their daughter from the Laws their parents enacted.

All she knew of the Fae, all anyone knew, were stories from the Forbidden who had been captured. Stories that were stolen by guards, and weaved woefully into their art. Many noble houses featured glimpses of Fae in their architecture. Halfling tales expertly carved in wood and blended into paint. Made by the Forbidden.

Things weren't much different today, despite her parent's and... Dother's efforts.

Mora's stomach churned as his name echoed in her mind—no, she wouldn't think of him again.

Pushing bitter thoughts aside, Mora examined her work one final time. Pride swelled in her chest and she beamed as she took in the parade of living adornments. The Forbidden Forest would be foolish not to welcome her into its bosom. She'd created a glorious haven of life, beckoning to all who may wish to take in the greenery.

And if Lord... what was his name? Gods help her, Mora wasn't sure. Plucking a leaf from the ivy, she toyed with it while she searched her mind for the answer. It was hopeless.

In truth, she didn't care enough to memorize their names. Her Keepers all blurred together over the centuries. Although she had fond memories of the deaths of those who'd earned it. Their pleas, their apologies, the moment they realize their incessant blubbering wouldn't convince her to stop... it delighted her in a way little else could.

Still, she couldn't be bothered to remember what most of them called themselves.

Regardless, if this lord had his way, there would be a large gathering of Westmont's nobles tonight, and perhaps more if the wealthy from the rest of Berwick deigned to make an appearance.

This Keeper was lanky, ruddy-haired and suffocating under the weight of his insecurities. While he hadn't explicitly told her, his wish for her to *make him memorable* said enough. He recently inherited his lordship. And in one sentence, he'd shared his weakness—he was desperate to be accepted. A weakness she intended to exploit. While Mora had yet to decide how, humiliation was the clear course of action.

A warm shiver ran up her spine, and motion caught her eye. The trees... they bent oddly, the movement almost purposeful, as if they were reaching for something behind them. The canopy she created blocked out the sun, shadowing the spaces between the trees. But there was something there, something calling to her. Whispers of the most beautiful song she'd ever heard danced through the winds, beckoning to her and promising heaven. Without thought, she took a single step forward.

When she squinted, she could have sworn she saw...

Within a blink, the trees bent back into shape, and the apparition was gone. Goosebumps trailed up her arms, and she tore open the servant's door, scrambling into the cramped halls. But something warm pulsed in her chest, begging her to run to the trees and never look back.

CHAPTER 2

MORA
300 YEARS AGO

"May I have this dance?" A dashing rogue with blinding blue eyes and tousled hair the color of the most decadent milk chocolate extended his hand.

Mora bit her lip, eyeing his sun-kissed fingers, her palms sweaty and shaking.

Someone in the far corner played the fiddle so fast she wondered how the woman's fingers could move that swiftly along the strings. She'd never seen the likes of it, having grown up only around music her mother deemed respectable. The angelic tones of the harp, calm notes of violins and piano keys soothed into a harmonious melody. Though they never had the stamina of the tavern's fiddler.

And oh, the fit her mother would have if she witnessed how they danced. The closeness of their bodies, the unpracticed, unwieldy way they moved. But her father would be eager to join the revelry.

Nearly the entire room danced, lost in the joy of the music, feet stomping and slipping along the worn wooden floor sticky with spilled ale. This was the kind of fun she'd snuck away to enjoy.

Philip, her personal guard, would be furious when he found her gone. She could picture his red, freckled cheeks now, and the wrinkle on his forehead that made an appearance when he was mad.

But she couldn't stand another night filled with talks of civil unrest and marriage prospects. She practically gagged at the thought.

"You wound me," the man said when she didn't move to join him. His eyes glittered with mirth as he pouted. He pulled his hand away, running it down his dark green breeches, and she followed the movement, her eyes still trained on those tanned, callused fingers. He tapped them against a red journal bound by leather straps that looped around his belt. It hung low, beneath a dark brown leather pouch, the silver buckle glinting in the candlelight along with an odd ring adorning his pointer finger.

Metal curled around a large, pearly white gem. As he moved his hand, it twisted in its casing, and she found herself staring at an obsidian void that looked too much like an iris. Mora's stomach tightened. Was it watching her?

"I..."

"Do you always overthink, Treasure?" When she didn't give him her eyes, he brought the same adorned finger to her chin, pushing gently until their gazes met. "Dance with me."

This time it wasn't a question. But she nodded anyway.

The moment she acquiesced, his hands found the curve of her waist, hesitating for a moment before he lifted her in the air. She squealed as he twirled them around the slick floor, his booming laugh music to her ears. As they spun, she was engulfed by his intoxicating scent—the sweetest splash of citrus sprinkled with fresh herbs, an aromatic blend of lavender, sage, and thyme, and something she couldn't quite put her finger on. Copper?

The simple gray dress she'd stolen from Rosemary, her favorite lady-in-waiting, twirled with them, albeit less than any of her magnificent gowns would. The fabric felt stiff, tickling her ankles and scratching her silky skin. She'd be squirming if she had any mind to pay attention to the strange texture. But she was too busy getting lost in those crystal blue eyes.

A brilliant smile encompassed her entire face, her cheeks aching, and she chuckled as she wondered what her mother would say if she could see her now. And the earful she'd receive when she returned home.

The feel of his taut muscles against her as he held her firmly made her heart flutter, and her breath caught when he allowed her to slide slowly down his body until her feet returned to the floor. She swallowed, her hands lingering on his hard chest as she eyed the hair peeking out between the loosely tied laces of his white tunic.

He led them in an unhurried dance, so unlike the rhythm of the music. He was less clumsy than she anticipated, his movement almost as smooth as a waltz, and she flushed when she wondered if he were skilled in a different sort of dance.

Smug amusement glittered in his eyes when he leaned down to whisper, "May I have the fortune of knowing your name?"

A shiver skittered down her spine as his beard tickled her skin. It was well kept, trimmed yet scruffy enough to tease her cheeks. She could feel his warm breath kissing her ear and found herself swaying in its direction.

A name. Oh gods, she hadn't thought to prepare a false name. "Gentlemen first," she said, shifting uncomfortably.

She tried to step back, but he grabbed her hand, pressing it back against his chest before she could move. The calm, steady beat of his heart greeted her, and she wondered if anything ever made him nervous.

"I believe it's ladies first," he responded before lifting her hand and gracing her knuckles with a soft kiss.

Her breath caught in her throat as his lips lingered. When he straightened, he graced her with a sly smile. The bastard knew what he was doing.

A name. A name. Think of a name.

"Morrigan," she blurted. It tasted off in her mouth, but she couldn't think of anything else.

The man snorted. "All right, Morrigan."

Hell, he knew she was full of it.

Playfully, he tugged on one of her dark curls. "I'm Cillian. And I'm very pleased to meet you."

"Cillian," she repeated. She wondered if he spoke the truth. Though, all things considered, it hardly mattered.

"How old are you, Treasure?"

Mora didn't think twice about giving her true age. "Twenty-one."

He smirked. "Twelve years younger than me, though I'm certain that won't be an issue." Entwining their fingers, Cillian pulled her toward an empty table. She didn't know how they'd converse in such a loud, crowded space. But she was excited, nonetheless.

They were greeted by a pile of abandoned mugs, one of which had toppled, lying in a golden puddle of ale. She eyed her dress, wondering if Rosemary would be upset if she returned it stained. Though she hadn't asked to borrow it—Rosemary wouldn't be pleased regardless.

The hell she'd face when she returned to the castle was inevitable. Why not live for the moment? Besides, she could give Rosemary one of her older gowns to make up for it.

Mora reached for the worn, splintered chair when shouts erupted behind them. She barely had a moment to startle before she was pressed behind Cillian's back, his stance defensive. Rough fingers grasped the sides of her dress, pinching her skin. She hissed at the bite of pain and attempted to pull away, but Cillian's hold was firm. Every muscle in his body tensed, ready for a fight.

Peeking over his shoulder, reality reared its ugly head.

Two brutes pummeled each other for gods knew what reason. Mora winced as a battered fist landed with a loud crack against a weathered face. The attacker pulled back, revealing his victim's now crooked nose. Blood gushed from his nostrils. With shaking hands, she touched her own nose, running her finger down its long, elegant bridge and wincing as she imagined it broken.

The second man grimaced as he wiped the blood on his sleeve. It smeared across his cheek and stained the dark fabric of his shirt. But that didn't give him pause. He launched forward, grabbing the other man around the middle and knocking him off his feet. They landed on the table, close to where she'd almost sat, weak wood imploding under the pressure.

Cillian moved back, herding Mora away from the growing crowd as splinters flew through the air. A small piece nicked her skin and blood trickled down her arm.

A symphony of voices overtook the room, cheers erupting in hysterical fervor. It made its way through the crowd like a contagion, clinging to the drunk and rowdy. And soon more fights broke out.

A new wave of sweat gathered in her palms and her heart galloped in her chest. What was she doing here?

The spell was broken, and now she took in her surroundings without a wistful twinkle in her eyes. The unruly crowd grew ravenous, eager to consume her and Cillian at a moment's notice. And the tavern was a cramped, crowded mess. Too many rickety tables were pushed against the walls, covered in stains and abandoned half-drunk mugs. The bar at the far end was manned by someone who clearly wasn't concerned with the safety of his patrons. He wiped sweat from his brow with the same filthy rag he used to clean the bar top, eyeing the brawling miscreants with disinterest. And while the fiddler continued to play passionately, a few drunks surrounded her, pressing too close and trailing greedy fingers over her worn, yellow dress.

Mora's lips trembled as her gaze darted madly about the room. The dancing, the flirting, the joys of being anonymous, all faded away. While Cillian still gripped her dress protectively, the crowd worked to engulf the tavern—it wouldn't be long before her back was pressed against the wall with a charming stranger shielding her from the mayhem.

"I'm s-sorry," she stuttered at Cillian's back, not sure if he'd heard. Mora tore herself free from his grasp and pushed her way through the throng of disorderly patrons. Panic painted his features as she slunk into the masses. He reached for her, but she was too quick.

"Wait!" Cillian's call sounded desperate, loud enough to rise over the cacophony of music and voices. But she didn't look back as she made her way to the door.

Mora leaned against the building's rock façade, eyes closed and palm pressed against her chest. The hard surface dug into her back with each hurried breath, but the shadows of the alleyway held her in their embrace, calming her racing heart.

What had she been thinking, sneaking into a tavern? This was her most reckless adventure into Moldenna—Philip could never know where she'd gone. No one could.

A warm sensation bloomed in her chest and she rubbed the spot above her heart, her brows furrowing.

Something pulled at her focus and her eyes flew open in time to catch the dark figure towering over her. A black hood hid his face, but she could make out a thick patchwork of scars along his lightly tanned, muscular forearm as he reached for her.

"Oh gods," she murmured, shrinking back.

He gripped the front of her dress, long fingers curling over the stiff fabric as he pulled her forward and slammed her back against the wall. Her lungs screamed as the air was forced from them, and a grating pain reverberated throughout her chest.

She'd barely had the chance to blink before he pressed a cool blade against her throat, sharp metal kissing her skin. Stilling, a whimper escaped her lips, and she wheezed, struggling to fill her lungs. Tears pooled in her eyes, but she willed herself not to tremble.

A deep, rumbling voice washed over her. "Hello, Princess."

CHAPTER 3

MORA

Mora leaned casually against the counter, watching the hustle and bustle of the kitchen while savoring a stolen piece of chocolate truffle. The hard shell melted on her tongue, enveloping her mouth in the decadent, bittersweet flavor she loved. She stifled her moan when she got to the soft, creamy ganache filling. Gods, she could live off of these.

Plucking another chocolate from the tray, she popped it in her mouth as her eyes roamed the room, searching for someone.

Her steely gaze landed on a gentleman with wide brown eyes. Flour peppered his linen apron and clung to his long, brown sleeves—he'd managed to get a sprinkle in his dark hair. He paused, his hands pressed into a sticky ball of dough, and stared at her. Mora winked, daring the baker to say something as he watched her swipe another handful of chocolates, depositing them into the leather pouch at her waist. A treat she intended to indulge in later. But he paled and looked away.

Mora grimaced, a spark of ire simmering in her heart. Most of the staff scurried away when she came near, avoiding eye contact or doing their best to pay her little mind. This was typical. They feared magic on principle, and Mora's power was strange. Not to mention, she wasn't exactly... personable.

Snatching a final handful of confectionaries, she shoved them in her pouch. May he be the one responsible for making a new tray.

With a sigh, she pushed off the counter and wandered deeper into the kitchen, crumpled note tucked in her clenched fist. The room was loud and hectic. A concert led by the endless rhythm of knives cutting through vegetables, water bubbling in various pots, steam wafting, and oil popping in pans. A sticky heat hung in the air, clinging to everyone's skin. But the woman she searched for should be easy enough to find among the madness.

Observation taught her one thing about the cook in question. If you were looking for Lillian, follow the cursing and you were headed in the right direction.

Mora prowled forward, eager to discover what enticed the woman to summon a monster to her aid.

CHAPTER 4

LILLIAN

"Fuck," Lillian cursed under her breath. She'd nicked her thumb with her paring knife. The slice was small, but it stung and blood oozed from the wound, staining her ivory skin. Sucking on the stinging flesh, she eyed the potato she'd been torturing instead of properly peeling. Chunks were missing from the tuber—wasted white bits clung to brown peelings sitting in a pile on her worn wooden cutting board.

"Good job, Lillian," she muttered, too damn lost in her own thoughts to deal with the madness of the kitchen today. She wished she could close her eyes and go back in time—two months ago she didn't worry about... fuck, she couldn't think about it. Nausea clawed at her throat and she had half a mind to find a bucket, just in case.

Bowing her head, she tuned out the voices and sounds around her and took a deep breath. The savory aroma permeating the air did little to soothe the churning in her belly. Strands of sandy blonde hair tickled her sweaty forehead, the stubborn pieces unwilling to stay slicked back in her ponytail.

I can fix this, she thought, clinging to hope. But the darker parts of her mind chattered away, intent on convincing her she was doomed.

Lillian nearly jumped out of her stool when a crumpled note dropped onto her cutting board, rolling down the moist pile of peelings. Water saturated the paper, but she recognized her writing peeking out between the folds.

"You called?" A woman with eerie, glowing amber eyes stared down at her, her head cocked to the side, dark brows raised. Lord Frederick called her Mora. A Forbidden, apparently capable of anything, but, according to the lord, not Indentured. Whatever that meant, it hadn't sat well with many of the staff.

"You scared me half to death," she hissed, baring her teeth.

Smirking, Mora examined her nails. "Your note asked me to meet you in the kitchen. I'm here. Did you not expect me to come?"

"I didn't expect you to sneak up on me like some demon."

Mora chuckled. "Demon. I like that."

Lillian leaned back in her seat, her stool creaking in protest. She watched Mora warily—there was a wistfulness to her tone, as if she truly liked the idea of being a demon. Something was off about her. Not that she hadn't known before. But she hoped...

Was this a mistake?

You don't have many options.

As Mora smoothed her thick, turquoise skirt, the gold detailing on the trim caught the light. She looked beautiful, her luminous brown skin made all the more radiant wrapped in those lovely colors. It hugged her hourglass curves and Lillian found herself envious—she could never fill out such a fancy gown. Though she supposed it was fine—clothing like that was completely out of place in the kitchen.

Mora quirked a brow and Lillian quickly looked away. "You called, and I came," she said, her tone sharp. "I'm quite busy, Lillian. What do you need?"

Lillian frowned. Busy indeed. Everyone was busy. All the damn time. Unless you were one of the nobles, born with a silver spoon up your ass, you worked tirelessly, making the world run for them. Even Lord Frederick, whom she enjoyed working for, needed a large staff of servants to help him along. More than most, she imagined, since he had no Indentured on his staff.

Time was finite. When you wanted to do something, you *made* time. Lillian desperately needed to convince Mora to make time for her.

"I know you're busy planning Lord Frederick's banquet, but I need your help. Can we speak in private?"

Mora stared at Lillian, silently assessing for what felt like eons. She couldn't help but fidget under her scrutiny, her fingers twisting in the stained linen fabric of her apron. She had a mind to tell her to forget it. But before she could open her mouth, Mora nodded once and flitted her hand out, signaling for Lillian to lead the way.

Where the hell should she go? Lillian cursed herself for not thinking ahead…

The pantry?

The kitchen was stocked and everyone was on task, preparing for the lord's guests. No one would need the pantry.

Lillian pushed away from her station, grimacing when her stool screeched along the checkered tiles. While she'd like to say she exuded confidence, her shoulders curled inward, and her head hung low. She prayed to whatever Gods listened that Mora could help.

It took mere moments for her to usher Mora into the cramped space, closing them inside. It wasn't the best spot for a meeting. The room was a mess of shelves full of root vegetables and pickled foods. Garlic braids hung from every corner, onions were overflowing from a bowl in the back, and a few stray bulbs littered the floor. There was barely enough room for two.

It smelled like dirt. But Mora's scent of burning embers, lavender, and pine curled through the air, a pleasant aroma, though an odd choice of perfume.

"While I'm flattered, I didn't think you'd be propositioning me today, Lillian." Mora cocked an eyebrow as she leaned against the shelves in the back, playing with a garlic braid.

Lillian snorted. She'd played this conversation out in her head many times, and yet she hadn't anticipated this. "As lovely as you are, I'm not here for that."

Amusement sparkled in Mora's eyes, even as she pouted, and Lillian realized she briefly forgot her anxiety. Had the demon done that on purpose?

"Promise me you won't share this with anyone." Picking at a stain on her simple brown dress, she spoke the next words carefully. "Is there some sort of magic that binds you to secrecy?"

Mora's face darkened. "You ask for my aid in one breath and distrust me in another." Her fiery gaze flitted to Lillian's apron and the smear of blood left behind from her cut. "You should be more cautious with your wounds. A drop of blood in the wrong hands and you may find *yourself* bound to something undesirable."

Was that a warning or a threat? Fear of the Forbidden was normal; they could be dangerous. But they were rare and the Crown's system kept them under control. Except for Mora, it seemed. "You're the only Forbidden here. Do you plan to steal my blood?"

What could she possibly accomplish with a few drops?

Mora's features contorted in anger. "You aren't my Keeper. I can't help you."

"What the hell is a Keeper?" Lillian muttered, her brows scrunching. Mora tried to push past her, but Lillian moved to block her path. She gulped when Mora curled her hands into fists. "Is it that you can't help me, or that you won't?"

The accusation hung heavy in the air. And by the way Mora's eyes narrowed, Lillian knew her words were a mistake. She tried to step back, but Mora moved with her, unwilling to allow Lillian's escape.

Mother was right, you're a halfwit.

"I'm many things, Lillian. But a liar is not one of them," Mora seethed, voice low. "I'm bound to the lord's will. My magic is his and, unless your problem relates to tonight's festivities, I can't help you."

Lillian shook her head slowly, unable to look at anything but the worn leather shoes she'd thrown on this morning. "This has nothing to do with tonight."

Mora's gaze was cold. "How desperate are you?"

While the demon's face was impassive, there was excitement in her tone. Lillian wasn't sure she wanted to know why. But she couldn't keep her fucking mouth shut. "I'm sorry?"

"You need my help. Would you be willing to steal for it?" She took another step closer, forcing Lillian to stumble back.

Her mouth felt dry, her palms clammy. What had she invited into her life?

The silence curled around them, smothering them in discomfort. It didn't help that Mora's fiery gaze bore into Lillian the entire time, as if she thought she could glare her into... into doing what?

With a heavy sigh, the demon finally looked away, disappointment flittering across her features. She bumped Lillian's shoulder, pushing her out of the way as she made for the door.

I'm fucked.

"Wait, please, stop!" Lillian practically dove on Mora, her hand landing hard on her shoulder. The demon stilled, her muscles tensing under Lillian's touch. The shadows in her eyes gave Lillian pause, and she jerked her hand away, unwilling to discover what haunted memories she'd unwittingly brought to life.

Mora took a few deep breaths, flexing her fingers, but she hadn't moved to leave again... that had to be a good sign?

"Are you saying you'll help me if I steal something?"

That, it seemed, was the right thing to say.

A small smirk graced her lips, though it didn't reach her eyes. "My flask. If you get your hands on it, I can do anything you ask of me."

Was everything a riddle with this woman? "I don't understand."

Rolling her eyes, Mora grabbed Lillian's chin, fingers digging in somewhat painfully. "You don't need to understand. You want my help, fine," she spat, leaning closer. "You've insulted me, accused me of blood magic, called me a liar and yet I'm still here. I'm intrigued, Lillian. Do you know how often I get to make my own choices?"

Lillian shook her head as best she could in Mora's steely grip.

"I *want* to help. I'll take you to my flask and bind myself to secrecy once you have it, if that's what you wish. Do you want this or not?"

Her stomach lurched, but she swallowed against the bile crawling up her throat and, like an idiot, Lillian nodded.

The demon released her grip and stepped away, revealing a slow smile. The room spun and Lillian's knees buckled—she stumbled, gasping when her back hit a shelf. Glass clinked as pickle jars toppled to the ground—soon she'd be standing in a mess of brine and shards of glass.

Lillian closed her eyes, waiting for the jars to shatter.

The crash never came.

When she opened her eyes, she was greeted by glittering onyx mist and a handful of jars, floating in its embrace. They hovered in the air for a moment before the smoke shifted, returning them to the shelf.

The unnerving smoke leaked from Mora's outstretched hand, spilling out from somewhere within her. When she was done, it curled around her fingers and up her arm, twisting over her long, delicate sleeves until it seeped underneath and was gone.

It was unlike any magic Lillian had seen. Unlike anything she'd heard of.

"We may need those pickles for the banquet," Mora said with a wink. "Let's go. We don't have much time."

She turned to leave, but Lillian didn't follow. Leaning against the shelf, she stared at the ceiling, wondering what the hell she had gotten herself into.

CHAPTER 5

MORA
300 YEARS AGO

*T*he press of the dagger against her throat stung, and the tavern's hard stone veneer dug into her back. Mora struggled to focus on anything else. She did know her attacker hadn't followed her from the tavern. There wasn't a hint of alcohol wafting off him—his scent, however, was almost intoxicating. She could get drunk on the refreshing aroma of mint wrapped in the cool embrace of a summer rain with hints of pine.

He's holding you at knifepoint, Mora, snap out of it.

Worse still, he knew who she was.

There was a way out of this. But was it worth revealing her power?

"What do you want?" she hissed when she found her breath.

"What do you have to offer?" His voice was a low rumble that made her shiver.

Mora swallowed and felt her skin give to the edge of the blade. One wrong move and he'd slit her throat. Even her mother, with her love of propriety, would want her to defend herself, regardless of how it may affect the crown.

Gathering her courage, she reached for the edge of his dark cloak and gripped the soft fabric. "Is it gold you're after?" she asked, voice trembling.

"Is that all you think the people of Berwick need, Mora?" It was more of an accusation than a question. And while she couldn't see his face, she imagined he had an intense gaze that bore into her soul.

When she didn't answer, he pressed a bit harder against the blade. "Nothing to say?"

"I'm not sure what you want to hear."

He shook his head, jostling his hood, and she caught a glimpse of perfect, downturned lips. "Of course you don't think for yourself."

There were many things she wished to say in return, thousands of retorts bubbling on the tip of her tongue. But she kept her mouth firmly shut.

Mora knew what she had to do, but she hesitated—the material of his cloak felt heavy in her hand. Her fingers curled, and she took a slow, deep breath, staring up at him with pleading eyes.

Don't make me do this.

While he didn't move the blade, his hold on her loosened when he turned to look toward the mouth of the alley.

It was now or never.

Pulling from the well of power within, she encouraged a flame to build in her palm. Smoke tickled her nose as fire licked up the fabric, climbing toward his chest.

The dagger clattered to the cobblestones as her attacker jerked back, his yelp echoing through the alley. "You little witch!" he hissed while he desperately smacked at the fire. It didn't matter. Mora kept her hand outstretched, using her magic to feed the flame.

As he stumbled back, his hood fell, revealing elegant, pointed ears, short raven-black hair, and a devastatingly handsome face. Mora's power sputtered when she took in his beautiful, endless black eyes, wide and horrified.

"You're Fae?" she whispered, utterly confused. What was a creature of the Forbidden Forest doing here? What did he want with her? And how did he know who she was?

Dumbstruck, she attempted to grab him. Before her fingers could grasp his burning cloak, rapacious hands wrapped around her waist and pulled her back onto the main street.

"What's happening? Are you ok?" Cillian stilled when he took in the burning Fae, now rolling on the ground behind her. She winced when he bellowed, guilt punching through her chest and warring with her racing heart.

It helped to remind herself she no longer fed the flame—it should go out soon enough. But then what? He knew her secret. And she had given him every reason to seek revenge.

"I need to leave."

Had Cillian realized what she'd done? Would he harm her?

His grip on her arm tightened, and she wondered if she'd wake up to bruises in the morning. He looked left, then right, his azure eyes fixating on a drunk who'd paused near the door to the tavern. The look on Cillian's face became monstrous, and the man gulped audibly before he turned and wobbled back inside.

"I know what you are, Treasure. We're one and the same." His voice was quiet, but his features softened and she felt, well, not safe, but calmer somehow. "Let me get you out of here."

He held her firmly against his chest before reaching his free hand into the leather pouch at his belt and pulling out a small, translucent orb. Something fluttered inside, clinking against the glass, and Mora twisted in his grip, attempting to gain a better view.

A hazy, black substance writhed within the orb and she thought she saw fluttering wings and tiny hands pressing against the surface. Cillian pulled out another with a dark blue essence splashing inside.

"I've got you," he promised, clutching the back of her neck and stroking his thumb over her soft skin. He smashed the first peculiar orb at their feet before throwing the blue one into the alley where her would-be attacker still whimpered and burned. Darkness exploded from the sphere the moment the glass erupted against the cobblestone, surrounding them in a cloud of onyx. It fluttered against her skin, tickling her arms, and blotted out the moonlight.

Grabbing her hand and twining their fingers, he yelled, "Run," before pulling her forward. His legs were long—she could barely keep up—but his grip was solid and somehow she knew he wouldn't let go.

They remained hidden in his mist like they were ghosts clinging to shadows. It was as if the entire town of Moldenna faded into an undulating cloud—Mora couldn't see a thing. Somehow, Cillian navigated the streets with ease, running at full speed. He took so many dizzying turns, she wondered if she'd ever find her way home again.

Eventually, they stopped, and he fiddled with his pouch once more. Hands on her knees, she wheezed, directing accusatory eyes up at her companion. Her entire body ached and she could hardly catch her breath. Had they run the length of the entire Kingdom?

Somehow his breathing was even, and an impish grin pulled at his lips. Asshole.

Narrowing her eyes, she playfully slapped his shoulder. "You're not winded at all, are you?"

"Does that impress you?" *He wiggled his brows, a mischievous glow in his blinding blue eyes. Mora giggled but said nothing. It did impress her, but she didn't wish to feed his ego.*

"Do you think that... man will be ok?"

A muscle feathered in Cillian's jaw. She wasn't sure what to make of it, but he quickly schooled his features.

"He attacked you. I don't think you need to worry about what happens to him."

Tearing his gaze away, Cillian pulled out an empty glass orb and placed it in the center of his palm. His breath quieted as he focused on the glass.

The murky smoke receded, gathering around the glass and pressing against the container. Mora's mouth fell open. She had little experience with magic, but this was unlike anything she'd imagined. It pushed and pushed until there was a small popping sound and the vapor was trapped within the confines of the trinket.

An uneasy feeling sat heavy in her gut when tiny hands pressed against the glass. She found herself reaching for it, aching to set the little creature free. But before her fingers could reach it, Cillian gently closed his fist, pulling away and shoving the orb in his pouch.

"*What* is *that?*" *Mora asked, clenching her fist as her gaze bounced from his eyes to his pouch and back again.*

"*Enchanter's secret, Treasure,*" *he replied. Stepping closer, he ran his palm along her cheek, his heavy gaze imploring her to understand. She shivered when his ring dragged along the curve of her jaw. "It's nothing nefarious. Simply a little binding magic.*"

"*And what do you need to trap shadows for?*" *She laced as much authority into her question as she could and crossed her arms.*

He winced, running his free hand through his silky, brown hair. "Trap is a heavy word. It's a shadow sprite. They're basically insects from the Forbidden Forest. And I'm glad I have one. How else would I whisk you away from danger?"

Mora scowled in response, pulling from his grasp. She'd never seen a sprite before. Knew nothing of them, or binding magic. But seeing it trapped like that... it didn't sit right with her.

Was she overreacting? She knew almost nothing of magic—her parents weren't certain how it got into the royal bloodline, and her abilities were her family's best-kept secret. Mora had few opportunities to explore.

Enchanting was the biggest mystery—there were few among the Indentured, and thus little knowledge of them. It was believed such magic was rare, but perhaps they were better at hiding their abilities. Elementalists, Naturalists, and Aegists were the most commonly caught. Mora had a bit of an understanding of her own ability to manipulate fire and had watched Naturalists coax plants to life in the royal gardens. She'd never seen Aegists create near-impenetrable shields. There had been some Indentured to the Royal Guard services prior to the overturning of the Laws. But Mora spent little time with the guards, other than Philip.

Putting some distance between her and Cillian, she turned and sauntered away. She needed a moment to breathe. To think.

A fresh, sweet breeze twirled in her long, dark brown curls and the world was quiet, but for the crickets singing their lullabies. He'd led them to a field outside of town—she was far from home. Unkempt grass tickled her ankles and fireflies danced between the blades. But it was the endless, sparkling skies that stole her breath.

An abandoned barn stood tall, watching over the field. As she got closer, she noted the chipped red paint and how the door hung at an awkward angle. She couldn't decide if she was relieved or horrified to be lost and alone with a stranger.

A stranger who followed her like a shadow.

"You're bleeding," Cillian said, voice thick with concern as he trailed a finger down her arm, leaving goosebumps in its wake. He frowned when he noted another trickle of blood on her throat, a small gift from the Fae's blade. "Let me take care of you."

He pulled a handkerchief from his pouch and cleaned the blood away from Mora's wounds. His touch was gentle, and she found herself closing her eyes, swaying in his direction.

"You're one of the Halflings," Mora breathed. Using one's power freely and publicly was illegal until recently.

"As, it seems, are you, Morrigan," he responded, sarcasm dripping in his tone. "An Elementalist. You've surprised me." He shoved the sullied handkerchief back in his pouch before backing her against the weathered barn door. He cradled her cheek, radiant eyes searching. For what, she couldn't be sure.

Magic was rare. And until her parents overturned the Laws of Confinement, those who had it were kept in cloisters or Indentured to noble houses. Public opinion remained low and to reveal your power was dangerous. If anyone found out the crown princess had power...

It was incredible she and Cillian found each other at all. And they'd shared their secret.

Cillian snaked his other arm around her lower back and pulled her close before leaning down and pressing his soft lips to hers. He'd moved so quickly Mora hardly had the chance to react. When she gasped, he used the opportunity to deepen the kiss, his tongue exploring her mouth. She stumbled back. But he held her tighter, as if he needed to consume her whole. The feel of his hard body overwhelmed her, and she found herself frozen.

The door was as unprepared as Mora—it creaked open and she squealed as she stumbled back, tumbling into an abandoned pile of straw with Cillian landing on top of her. He braced his arms by her sides, caging her beneath him.

Nibbling along her jaw, he whispered, "You're like no other. I knew it the moment I laid my eyes on you." She found herself burning hotter than any flame she'd summoned, and yet her heart slammed against her ribcage. Did she want this? This was happening too fast...

Cillian, on the other hand, had no qualms. His fingers found their way under her dress, trailing along the curve of her thigh, working ever higher. And he stared at her as if she were the most precious thing in the world, an avaricious gleam glittering in his eyes. If she were being truthful, it frightened and excited her in equal measure.

With shaking hands, she grabbed his tunic and pulled him closer, gracing him with a soft, hesitant kiss. He groaned and kissed her harder before running his tongue over her plump bottom lip.

"Oh, Treasure," he purred as he pushed his fingers beneath her undergarments, "you're the answer to every prayer I've uttered to the Gods. I'm keeping you."

Keeping her? He didn't know her. They'd likely never see each other again after tonight.

Her mind blanked when he circled the sensitive bundle of nerves at the apex of her thighs. She jerked and whimpered at the sensation while he moved his fingers agonizingly slowly, teasing the taut bud.

"Tell me you want this."

Mora gulped, hesitating. It sounded more like a demand than a question. There was a weight to his stare as he waited for her answer.

Cillian's clever fingers moved faster, and she moaned, her thighs shaking. "Tell me."

"I want... tonight," she sighed, her breath fluttering against his lips.

Mora nearly cried when he pulled his hand away, her unsated body sagging against the straw. It was difficult to ignore how it scratched her skin, digging in harder with each nervous inhale. But it didn't last long. Cillian untied his breeches, slipped them down his legs, and kicked them off with shocking speed.

Before she'd caught her breath, he'd pushed her skirt up and shoved her undergarments to the side. She jerked as he glided his length over her sensitive folds, slipping through her arousal. "You're beautiful," he whispered reverently, notching himself at her entrance.

"Cillian," Mora said slowly, suddenly a ball of nerves. What was she doing, lying with a stranger in a barn?

She didn't have the opportunity to finish her thought—Cillian entered her in a powerful thrust that had her back arching. His hand squeezed her rear as he pulled her closer, working himself into her, *before sliding his rough fingers down her leg and wrapping it around his lower back.*

"You feel divine," he moaned, his lips finding their way to her neck. He nipped at the sensitive flesh there before kissing the small ache away.

Mora shuddered as he moved, her hips driving up to meet him. This was the last thing she anticipated when she snuck out tonight, the last thing she'd ever imagined herself doing. And yet, with each swivel of his hips, she found herself melting further against him.

"That's it," he breathed when she muttered a mixture of pleas and prayers, gasping and crying out as he filled her perfectly.

The groan in her ear when she dug her nails into his back nearly undid her, and she found herself pressing her lips to his shoulder, stifling her moans. It was a shame they were still mostly dressed—she ached to feel his skin against hers. To see all of him, to taste every inch of his body.

Slipping his hand between them, he rubbed that aching bundle of nerves again in slow circles, the gentle motion at odds with his rough thrusts.

"Cillian," she sighed as pleasure blossomed in her core. She was deliciously close to the edge, longing for the fall.

"I love my name on your lips," he breathed against her skin, working her harder.

It felt as if she were coming undone. And she loved it. Loved being surrounded by him, enveloped by the sweet scent of citrus and herbs, and overwhelmed by the bliss he gave her.

Oh gods, oh gods, oh gods.

Mora felt her inner muscles flutter, and she screamed as the most divine feeling erupted within her. It took her a moment to realize she had bitten his shoulder, her muffled cries still echoing through the barn.

"Yes," he groaned, his wet fingers grabbing her hip and repositioning her to fuck her more deeply. Their lustful moans invaded her ears, like a carnal song she'd never forget, and he returned his attention to her throat, his nips more brutal with each punishing thrust. There would be marks come morning, marks she'd need to keep hidden.

It hit her then that they were unprotected. What had she been thinking?

"Cillian," she said, smacking her hands against his firm chest, "Cillian, you can't."

He grumbled but pulled away, thank the gods. Their eyes never left one another as he wrapped his hand around his cock, groaning with each pass of his clenched fist. Knowing she brought him to the edge, that in this moment she possessed his mind and owned his pleasure, gave her a satisfying sense of power.

It wasn't long before his body jerked, his own release barreling through him and soaking the hem of Mora's dress.

When he stilled, he stared down at her unabashedly, panting softly. A splash of pink stained his cheeks—Mora reached up and trailed a finger over his cheekbone and down his jaw, enjoying the scratch of his beard.

For a moment, they watched one another, their shared breaths twisting together in the air. Once he'd caught his breath, Cillian collapsed on her, his lips finding hers as he pulled her to his chest. They rolled in the straw until she was splayed on top of him, trapped snuggly in his arms while he lazily explored her mouth.

When he pulled back, he smiled, the soft expression lighting up his face. His fingers found their way to her curls, pulling gently at the *ringlets. The most delightful, warm feeling spread through her chest and part of her wished this moment would never end.*

"I think the Fates are smiling down on us," he said, tired voice wistful.

His eyes gleamed with a yearning that made her heart ache. She didn't have it in her to bring up the inevitability of their parting, so she snuggled closer and closed her eyes. They may not have a future together. But the least she could offer him was tonight.

CHAPTER 6

MORA

Mora bounced on her feet and hummed an ancient song as she made her way back to Lillian's station. The rhythmic clicking of her heels on the tiles brought the music to life. It pulled on her heart and pushed her back to a time she rarely allowed herself to remember.

When she closed her eyes, she could hear her mother singing, her soft voice bouncing off the opulent white walls of Castle Berwick's great hall. Mora ran her finger over the soft petals of the rose she'd tucked in her hair. Her mother loved flowers—fresh blooms covered every inch of their home. For once, the memory didn't cause an ache in her chest.

She turned to offer Lillian a smile. Except... Lillian wasn't there.

The song died on her lips and the darkness inside rose up and devoured that tiny sliver of joy.

Could she not have this one simple thing?

Choosing a Keeper. She ached to have the luxury. Even if it meant strong-arming the woman into it.

Had she come on too strong? Grabbing her was a mistake, but Lillian said *yes*. And Mora intended to hold her to it. Perhaps that was wrong. But she couldn't find it in herself to feel any semblance of guilt. Lillian needed help. What did it matter if Mora forced things along for her own benefit?

And yet, it did matter. Because Lillian hadn't followed.

Frustration wrapped around Mora in suffocating coils and she clenched her fingers into tight fists, her knuckles aching under the pressure. The thunderous beat of her heart pounded in her ears and her breathing quickened.

She pivoted before she could think better of it, marching back toward the pantry door. As the voices of the kitchen staff faded and the pantry neared, Mora hesitated.

Calm yourself or she'll run.

Gods be damned.

The cramped hall was as good a place as any to stop and clear her mind. Mora leaned against the wall and tipped her head back, taking one slow, deep breath. And then another. And another.

It helped to imagine her frustration dripping from her pores like smoke, pulling away from her flesh and dissipating into the air. With each steady breath, the pressure in her chest eased and her heart slowed to a reasonable pace. For now.

Donning what she hoped was a convincing smile, Mora made her way through the pantry door.

Lillian stood at the back of the pantry, a faraway look in her moss green eyes. Pink bloomed in her ivory cheeks and her fingers twisted in her apron—Mora frowned when she noted the blood stain once again. It was little more than a smear soaking into the off-white fabric. But, when an Enchanter was skilled in blood magic, a drop or two could go far... For people who claimed to fear magic, they knew little about the real dangers. Fools.

Despite her greater height, Lillian looked small, huddled by the jars Mora saved.

You've broken her already...

Clasping her hands in front of her stomach, Mora ran her thumb over the gold detailing that followed the seams of her bodice. She could fix this. She had to.

"Lillian," Mora said in the gentlest voice she could muster. "Are you coming?"

Lillian's startled inhale did little to soothe Mora's concerns. And her wobbly smile... it was over before it started.

Her uncertain gaze found Mora and narrowed slightly, like she was trying her best to solve an impossible puzzle. There was a tightness in her face, regrets likely coursing through her mind. Worse still, the woman said *nothing*. The silence pressed against her, filling the empty space between them. It was too thick—Mora felt as if she may drown in it.

Risking a few steps forward, Mora ran her hand down Lillian's forearm, in what she hoped was a soothing gesture.

"We have lots to do and little time." Mora hated that she sounded desperate. Detested the heat darkening her cheeks.

Please. She raised her wide, pleading eyes to Lillian. *Please let me have this.*

"I want to help," she said, her voice quiet. "Once you have my flask, I can help." She stopped herself from explicitly promising to make things better. Promises were foolish dreams cast out callously into the waiting palms of the unwise. It would be a lie to make a promise. Mora had to believe Lillian would grasp onto hope and follow along willingly.

Lillian leaned against the shelf, her brows furrowing with worry. "I don't want any trouble."

"It seems trouble has already found you," Mora replied, keeping her voice soft.

Would she notice that Mora, again, made no promises? She had no idea what Lillian needed. Trouble could be an inevitability.

Perhaps the kindest thing would be to walk away. Mora had once been kind. But that was a long time ago. And what good had it done her?

She kept her firm hold on Lillian's hand as she turned to leave the pantry, pulling the woman along.

Mora plucked the sorry excuse for a peeled potato from the cutting board, frowning as she turned it around in her hand. It was as if it offended the person cutting it—there was barely any potato left. She cocked an eyebrow and looked to Lillian. "I hope this isn't your best work," she said with a snicker before handing it to her.

"What now, demon?" Lillian's eyes widened when Mora snatched the paring knife off the counter.

Mora smirked, twirling the knife idly in her fingers as she surveyed the room. "Shh."

Everyone worked hard to pretend they weren't paying attention.

The baker kept his eyes downcast as he spread softened butter on a flat piece of rolled out dough. But he peeked at her when he reached for a cinnamon-sugar mixture he'd prepared in a small bowl.

The spit-boy, a tall, lanky thing no more than a day over eighteen, if that, sat on a short stool by the stone fireplace, a pile of dry oak logs burning inside. Sweat pooled on his brow and he turned the spit, a half dozen chickens cooking along the metal skewer. Though he'd shifted in his seat, placing Mora in his peripheral.

And a woman in the back, the saucier if she remembered correctly, held a dark gray mortar and pestle. However, her hand stilled. The sternness etched into her face made Mora wonder if she'd ever learned to smile.

She knew they all wondered why Lord *Frederick's* Forbidden was lollygagging in the kitchen with Lillian.

"Act natural," Mora whispered, handing the knife over.

Lillian, however, did not take Mora's advice. Her hands remained extended, as if she were presenting the blade and battered potato to Mora as an offering. "I'm sorry?"

Mora couldn't be bothered. Instead, she plucked at the thread that bound her to her Keeper's demands and pictured her intentions.

Frederick will be pleased if things move along a little faster. If he has the opportunity to test the meal and make sure his guests will like it.

Mora reasoned with the wish, bracing herself for a sting of pain if the magic rebounded, unhappy with her attempt to work around the demand. But it didn't.

The tension in her shoulders eased and Mora smiled wide, her steely gaze landing on the baker.

Cool onyx mist kissed her warm, brown skin, like drops of dew caressing late summer leaves. She coaxed it to life, until it spilled down her arms and slithered to the baker's station. He yipped, jumping back as his work disappeared in a blackened cloud. Mora snorted. All the attention in the room shifted and a sea of gasps rose in the air. *Perfect.*

"Make sure no one's watching you before you leave," Mora said, voice low. "Meet me at the stairwell in the eastern hall."

Not waiting for an answer, Mora exploded into a thick mass of ebony smoke and descended upon the kitchen. The space was assaulted by a symphony of shrieks. Some froze in place, their expressions a mixture of fear and awe. Others backed away until they were pressed against the wall, trembling as a living shadow weaved around every station, enveloping everything in its wake.

Mora hoped Lillian managed to slip out unnoticed.

Rematerializing in the center of the room, Mora landed gracefully on the checkered tiles and surveyed her efforts.

The chickens were now roasted, cooked through and juicy with crispy skin. They were plated and surrounded by apples, caramelized onions, and sage. Everything paired well with the apple cider gravy she'd readied in the saucières. Potatoes were mashed with a delectable blend of garlic, herbs, and butter—steam wafted from the pot, teasing Mora's senses with the savory aroma. She ached to try the cinnamon rolls, their tops browned and covered in a sugary glaze.

Though she hadn't replaced the chocolates.

With the exception of the mossy green gaze of her now favorite cook, all attention was once again upon her. While that was the goal, Mora was miffed that none held a glimmer of gratitude. Or dared to look directly into her glowing amber eyes.

She'd saved them *hours* of work. And this was her reward.

"You're welcome," Mora spat, scowling.

Grabbing a plate, she stalked through the room, scooping up samples of each dish. That pounding feeling in her chest returned as she shoved her way through any who didn't have the mind to move. Why bother with politeness? They'd made up their minds.

Once the plate was full, Mora turned and left without a word. Lillian was waiting. But first, she needed to fool the lord.

CHAPTER 7

MORA

The sweet, pungent scent of old tomes nuzzled Mora's nose, and she found herself admiring the library's comfortable surroundings. This place felt like home. Massive shelves cradled endless sources of knowledge, some aged enough that she wondered if they were purchased during her youth.

Mora ran her finger over the books' smooth spines and listened to the quiet voices up ahead where Frederick's desk sat.

"I'm sure you've heard about my half-brother. It would mean a lot to both of us," someone said. He sounded haughty, with an annoying air of self-importance. Mora could only assume he was a noble, too used to getting his own way.

Frederick—Mora smirked, she'd have to thank Lillian for reminding her of his name—did his best to sound firm, but his voice was too soft. A timidness weaving its way through his words. "I'm glad you found each other, Lord Halvard. And I can relate to how much your brother's life must be changing as he steps into his new role within your family. You have my support. But I can't make any promises."

Mora shook her head. The lord was too kind for his own good.

"We came all the way from Baith. Surely we can come to an agreement," Halvard said, unable to hide his frustration.

"I'm glad to have you both here," Frederick sighed, a slight tremble saturating the sound. "Thank you for traveling all this way. We can talk more after the banquet, but I can't guarantee anything."

Halvard was quiet for a moment before he muttered, "Fine."

When he rounded the corner and saw Mora, his gray eyes widened. Mora swept her bored gaze over him. His light complexion was unblemished, like that of a porcelain doll—had he spent a single day under the sun? Mora nearly rolled her eyes. Typical lazy noble. Though she had to begrudgingly admit he had style. The man wore a gorgeous, tan velvet coat with light blue tailored trousers, and had swept his dark auburn hair into a sleek bun.

Halvard froze in place, gaping, so she sidestepped him and made her way toward Frederick.

While the library was pristine and perfectly organized, Frederick's desk was chaotic. Papers, ink, and quills littered its surface, crowding the globe resting on the corner. And a crooked pile of books sat terribly close to the edge. Mora's fingers twitched, aching to straighten them and push them further onto the desk's surface, where they'd be safe.

She crossed her arms, waiting for Frederick to notice her. Already, he'd dove back into his studies, those forest green eyes darting along as he read. How could someone be this unaware of their surroundings?

The lord was handsome, she had to admit. The splash of freckles dancing across his youthful face added a certain charm. Though his ruddy hair was a mess—it stuck up at odd angles, like an unkempt mane in desperate need of taming. Beautiful red hair like his was rare. It made her think of a different man from a different time. A man she'd cared for deeply. A man she couldn't bear to remember.

You're a monster.

Mora squeezed her eyes shut, willing Philip's voice to quiet. He had been right. And she'd embraced it over the centuries. But hearing him say it... it awoke an old ache in her heart.

A lump formed in her throat and she did her best to clear it, inadvertently startling Frederick.

The lord jumped, nearly falling back in his chair, his dark green eyes going wide. "Oh, uh, hello, Mora." He closed his book and placed it on his desk before awkwardly rubbing the back of his neck. Mora spied the title—*The History of Berwick's Noble Houses*. Interesting.

While he was studying his guests, too many of whom were as snobbish as Halvard, there'd be more to learn. Like the gory details of the infamous coup that ended the Royal Althenis family line. Her family.

Though it wouldn't mention her involvement in that or Castellan's civil war that followed. Ending Dother was... cathartic. Though she regretted her mother's fate more than anything.

Would there be a family portrait in Frederick's book? Did she want to see it? Part of her would give anything to stare at their once happy faces. But that ever-present ache opened its eyes once more and Mora rubbed her chest. No. She couldn't.

"When did you get here?" Frederick asked sheepishly.

He almost looked nervous. What would he look like later, when she crushed his dreams and humiliated him in front of his peers? A thrill shot through Mora at the thought.

"Just now, my lord." Mora smiled, doing her best to look kind. She plucked the rose from her hair and placed it on his desk. "I wanted to give you an update. Your gardens are in full bloom, months ahead of the rest of Berwick. I'm sure your guests will be awed."

Frederick's face lit up as he grabbed the flower. "I can hardly imagine it," he said, running his fingers over the delicate petals. "You're Gods-sent, Mora."

"Thank you, my lord." She curtsied, enjoying the feel of her skirt's soft fabric under her fingers. Her turquoise gown was extravagant. Memorable. That's what allowed her to create it, a treat for herself as she fulfilled the lord's wish. Frederick, on the other hand, had no sense of style. His ivory poet shirt, despite its delicate lace collar and loose sleeves that cuffed at the wrist, was not fitting attire for a lord who intended to entertain this evening. Halvard must have been appalled. She made a mental note to make Frederick his outfit for tonight.

"Are you hungry?" Mora raised her hand, revealing the stream of smoke that spilled down her arm. With a flick of her wrist, a dark cloud came closer, carrying a plate piled high with the food she'd prepared. "I thought you'd like to test tonight's meal."

Frederick blinked, a touch of red painting his cheeks. "I... yes. I'm actually starving."

Obsidian smoke crawled up Frederick's desk, consuming everything in sight. Mora expected fear to cloud his eyes. Instead, he chuckled and leaned closer, watching in awe as it cleaned and organized his desk. She cocked her head to the side, observing him. His fascination was... odd.

When the desk was cleared, she placed the plate in front of him. The smoke broke apart, snapping back and twisting up Mora's arms until it disappeared. Remnants of its cool caress echoed on her skin and she shivered.

"I assume you'll be studying for a while?"

"Yes." Frederick nodded as he eyed the mashed potatoes, licking his lips. Mora found herself salivating as well. The savory aroma teased her senses. Why had she not grabbed herself a plate?

Ah, yes... because Lillian was waiting. And, while Mora could be cruel, she wasn't cruel enough to sit and eat while the poor thing waited. Or perhaps she wasn't foolish enough to think she'd wait that long.

"I suggest you take some time to relax and enjoy your lunch. And perhaps partake in better reading material."

If she and Lillian were lucky, this would buy them time.

Frederick practically melted in his chair when he enjoyed the first bite. "Mm," he moaned as he tasted the chicken. "This is wonderful! I'm in your debt."

Mora frowned, her brows furrowing. In her debt? Did he think she did this because she wanted to? That she had a choice in the matter? She was spelled to do his bidding—the nature of her curse meant he owed her nothing in return.

"Thank you, Mora." He spoke with gentle sincerity, kind eyes boring into her own.

Mora's eyes narrowed as she examined his face. He seemed genuine. But... no. This had to be a trick. Some attempt to sway her favor. For what purpose she couldn't be sure, but it was the only thing that made sense.

The silence grew awkward as he waited for her to say something. Mora kept her mouth shut. She couldn't tell him he was welcome because it would be dishonest. No one was *welcome* to make a wish.

Frederick sighed and ran his fingers through his hair, mussing it up further. "I'd forgotten to eat. If I'm being honest, I'm anxious about tonight."

He stood, stretching out his back, before he rounded the desk. To Mora's utter confusion, the young lord offered her his hand. She stared at it, then looked up at him, eyes wide.

Frederick shuffled his feet, his hand hanging in the air between them. "Sincerely, thank you for all your hard work. I appreciate it." He hesitated for a moment, a small smile playing on his thin lips. "I'm not sure what we would have done without you."

Mora opened her mouth and then shut it, unable to find any words. Instead, she grabbed his hand, shaking it in two quick jerks before she dropped it and backed away.

"See you tonight," she mumbled. Before Frederick could speak another word, Mora turned and fled the room, praying the lord wouldn't follow.

CHAPTER 8

MORA
300 YEARS AGO

*M*ora *curled into herself and shivered as a cool breeze caressed her skin. Something creaked, and she startled, her eyes flying open. Warm morning rays leaked through the cracked roof, spilling over the rafters, and the crooked door squeaked again as the wind pushed against the wood.*

How dare the wind steal her warmth and startle her awake? She rolled over, hoping to huddle against Cillian, but the space beside her was empty.

Sitting up swiftly, Mora looked around, wondering if he got up to stretch his legs. All she found were empty stalls, scattered straw, and a musty scent she hadn't noticed before.

Because you were too caught up in Cillian.

Mora grimaced as she looked at the night through a new lens. Cillian was relentless and made the oddest declarations. It had given her pause—she'd imagined this morning would be awkward as she untangled herself from his arms.

But she'd also anticipated a goodbye.

The faint scent of citrus still clung to her clothes, but the straw beside her was cold. He'd abandoned her hours ago. That prick.

Mora screeched, tossing a handful of straw across the aisle. It barely made it a foot before fluttering back to the ground, doing little to satisfy her growing ire.

She wasn't sure where he had taken her, or how to find her way home.

When Mora peeked out the barn door and across the rolling fields, she could make out the townhouses of Moldenna standing proud in the distance. Their dark slate shingles bathed in the morning sun, under the watchful eye of the gray stone castle towering over them.

Mora heaved a sigh, tired already. She was in for a long trek home.

A handcart rolled over the cobblestones and Mora cringed, tipping her head down and allowing her hair to fall over her face. She caught glimpses of the few who rushed to morning worship, and she prayed that no one would look her way. Why anyone rose this early when they had the choice to remain in their beds was beyond her. Thankfully, most of the people of Moldenna chose to rest until a more reasonable hour.

She hoped those who passed didn't recognize the Crowned Princess Mora Althenis-Diera, making her way to the castle in a disheveled dress, her long, dark curls a horrid, frizzy mess. They were still covered in straw—no matter how hard she tried to pluck each stubborn stem from her ringlets, more remained.

While no one paid her any mind, Mora felt like she was being watched. Her eyes darted to every shadowed alleyway. A few balconies were occupied, but she hadn't noticed any watchful eyes.

And yet Mora felt *a presence.*

She needed a hearty breakfast. And a nap.

The castle's outer gate neared and Mora mulled over her choices: sneak through the secret passage, increasing her trek and risking the discovery of her preferred escape route, or walk through the gate. She'd use the servant's entrance to avoid too many eyes, but the guards would see her, and that wouldn't sit well with her mother.

Each step caused more discomfort than the last, blisters no doubt peppering her heels.

Curse these worn leather shoes and Rosemary's too large feet.

Consequences be damned. Mora made her way to the towering gatehouse. Pushing her hair back, she smiled as the sun kissed her face, bringing out the golden glow in her tan skin. Her shoulders shifted, and she stood taller, adopting the posture of a princess.

"Where have you been?"

The hiss of Philip's furious voice made Mora stop dead in her tracks, shoulders drooping. Her guard's black boots crunched over the pebbles that made their home between the cobblestones. A redness stained his cheeks, matching his hair. And those dark blue eyes bulged under furrowed brows. She was in trouble. The forehead wrinkle said it all.

A spark of guilt twisted in Mora's gut when she took in his disheveled appearance. A baldric hung crookedly over his broad shoulder, but the silver-encrusted scabbard was empty—had he forgotten his sword in his chambers? And while he wore a beautiful tunic of royal blue and silver, her family's house colors, it was wrinkled. Not to mention his hair, which he usually slicked back without a strand out of place, was horribly unkempt. It unsettled her—she'd never seen him look anything less than perfect.

She'd prepared herself for her mother's fury. But Philip... she hated upsetting him.

Mora swallowed. "I went out."

"It isn't safe for you to visit Moldenna alone. And look at you." He gestured to her dress, her hair. "I can't bring myself to ask where you went."

Mora's cheeks heated. "You're right. It's none of your business."

"I thought something happened." Philip's voice lowered, as if he spoke more to himself. He rubbed his brow, and for the first time she noticed the dark circles under his eyes.

"I always come back, Philip," she said gently.

He dropped his hand to his side, his frown deepening. "Normally I find you before your mother notices you're gone."

Mora was an ass for putting him through this.

And her mother... it had been inevitable she'd discover her daughter missing. Mora knew what she'd face when she'd made the decision to leave. Expecting something and knowing it had come to fruition, however, were two different things. She gulped at the prospect of facing her mother, her pulse fluttering like a frightened bird in her chest.

Queen Aedlin Althenis-Diera, the Crown of Berwick and a master of the games of court, would not suffer her daughter's absence when presenting a new potential husband. What had she told them when Mora was nowhere to be found? She'd need to ask Rosemary—her mother definitely wouldn't share many details.

"Would it help if I said I'm sorry?" Mora asked, clasping her hands in front of herself and offering a small smile.

"It would help if I knew you wouldn't disappear again."

Mora gave him no answer. She couldn't make such promises. Last night had been a disaster, her companion less than gentlemanly—her upper lip curled at the memory, and she was once again aware of the straw clinging to her clothes, scratching her skin—but it was worth the adventure.

Though she wouldn't return to the tavern. Some lessons you only needed to learn once.

"I best get to my rooms and face her," she said instead, before making her way toward the servant's entrance. Philip's lips thinned, but he stayed quiet and followed dutifully behind.

As she slipped into the hall through the servant's stairwell, hoping to make it to her rooms before the admonishments began, she found her father waiting. King Kalyan Diera. He leaned against the wall, adorned in a loose lilac silk top, the collar and sleeves intricately embroidered with silver thread. It matched his breeches, a blend of casual elegance her father preferred.

Mora froze, eyes glued on her father as he took a bite of his apple and smirked, as if to say caught you.

"Your majesty," Philip said reverently, bowing low. Kalyan offered a small nod, but Mora recognized the way his lips twitched into a minute frown. All these years, and he hadn't grown used to the pageantry that came with his title.

A simple silver crown encrusted with gleaming diamonds that accentuated each point sat heavy on his dark brown curls. He'd recently grown them longer—his ringlets reached his strong chin. Mora was his mirror in all but her amber eyes, a gift from her mother.

The two of them watched one another, waiting for the other to speak. Much to her father's dismay, she also inherited her mother's stubbornness—they could stand here all day; Mora had no intention of speaking first.

A gurgling sound interrupted the silence, and it took Mora a moment to realize it was her stomach. Traitor.

Kalyan chuckled and broke the distance between them. "Eat, pumpkin, you'll need the energy." A glimmer of amusement sparkled in his deep brown eyes as he extended his hand and offered her what remained of his apple.

Mora took a bite and reveled in the sweetness dancing on her tongue. There was nothing royal about the way she mumbled her thanks, mouth obscenely full.

Moving a hair away from her face, her father's brow arched when he found an errant piece of straw. "I hope whatever you were up to was worth her wrath."

"It was worth it, papa," she promised. Though, if she were being honest, she wasn't sure. What would her father think if he knew? The tavern, the fight, the Fae who'd threatened her, and the man who'd wanted one thing—the thing he'd warned her many men would quest after, with care for little else. A lesson she'd already learned. Though, apparently not well enough.

Years of practice helped her maintain a convincing smile. Though it wavered when she looked up to find her mother.

Aedlin stood outside Mora's rooms, framed by a new garland of greenery—white lilies and pink roses hung around the thick, silver door frame. She'd dressed to match her husband—her lilac ball gown made of silk tulle so soft the voluptuous skirt appeared to float around her. A silver crown, twin to her father's, rested atop her head. And her light brown hair was piled into a perfect bun.

A tinge of pink bloomed on her fair cheeks, and she crossed her arms, frowning deeply. Those furious amber eyes widened as she took in her daughter's appearance. Mora did her best to smooth out her skirt, but as she fidgeted with the wrinkled, gray fabric, she knew it accomplished nothing.

"Good luck," Kalyan whispered, leaning down to kiss Mora's cheek.

Nausea churned in her stomach and the last thing she wanted was food. She handed the apple back to her father and followed him to her doom as Philip trailed silently behind.

When they arrived, Kalyan stopped with her and reached for her mother's hand. They shared a look, and he tipped his head, a silent request for Aedlin to go easy on their daughter. Aedlin's features softened, and she cupped the king's cheek, raising to her tippy toes to kiss his lips. Mora hoped she calmed. The glare she received when they broke apart destroyed that dream.

"We will discuss your shortcomings at length later, young lady," she huffed, eyeing the sorry state of her daughter. "There's a suitor here to meet you."

For the love of the gods, another?

Who would be seeking her hand today? This was the last thing Mora wanted. But she bit her tongue and followed her mother, leaving her father and Philip outside.

They passed through her sitting room, and Mora stared longingly at the soft white chaise near the glass balcony doors. Sunlight beamed into the room, bleeding onto the royal blue cushions, and she longed to curl up there with a good book. With a sigh, she looked away, silently promising the bookshelves against her walls she'd return to them.

The plush off-white carpet in her bedroom felt divine, even with Rosemary's shoes still chafing the skin off her heels. Soft scents of lavender curled in the air, flowing from her bathroom. Was her bath cold? If she needed to entertain another boring noble, she deserved the embrace of warm water first.

"Would you like me to help you out of your dress?" Mora looked up to see Rosemary waiting, her hands behind her back and her posture perfect. Her voice was steady, but there was a clear accusation in Rosemary's tone. She pushed an errant strand of brown hair behind her ear, the color so much like Mora's Mother's.

Mora swallowed. "Please."

"I can't believe you," her mother muttered as Rosemary helped her undress—gods, Mora hoped she didn't notice a certain stain on the hem. Her help wasn't needed, but this was their norm, and her lady-in-waiting appreciated the distraction from Aedlin's wrath. Mora flinched when her mother slammed her armoire shut, a slip of a red gown catching between the doors. "Abandoning dinner last night was offensive enough, Mora, but to return in this state? Where did you go?"

Mora ignored her question as she stepped out of Rosemary's clothes. Her skin itched and scratches marred her arms and back, likely from being prodded by straw throughout the night... but Cillian left a few marks of his own on her neck. She prayed her mother wouldn't notice.

"I asked you a question, young lady."

With a sigh, she turned to face her. "Who's here to see me, mom? There were to be no more visitors after last night."

"A night you missed," she growled, making Mora's pulse skyrocket. Rosemary took a step back, doing her best to disappear.

Mora tried to sound dignified, despite her state of undress. "Have we not run out of undesirable noble sons to parade around the castle?" she asked as she sat on her bed. She knew what her mother would say, couldn't bear to watch her say it, so she fiddled with the lace canopy.

"You will marry, Mora." Aedlin paused, attempting to soften the blow. But Mora memorized the script weeks ago. "And if you don't pick a suitor soon, I'll be forced to choose one for you."

Mora rolled her eyes, her fingers curling around the delicate white fabric. "I don't wish to marry unless I find love, mother."

Aedlin sat on the bed beside her daughter and rested a gentle hand on her shoulder. "I know, sweetheart. I didn't want to marry either. But look at the love I have with your father. Look at the beautiful life we've created together, and the good we've done for our people. You need a champion by your side for the day you take the throne."

Mora couldn't hold back her shriek. "I don't need a man to help me rule!"

Aedlin did not deign to respond to her daughter's outburst. She stood and swept her hands across her gown, smoothing out the delicate fabric. "I expect you not to dawdle. Lord Dother has traveled all the way from Eldenna. He's owed a proper introduction."

Mora snorted at the prospect of a noble traveling across the sea to a small island nation for a woman he'd never met. "What's his full name? I'll be sure to show him proper etiquette when I offer my rejections."

The hardened look in her mother's bright amber eyes was a warning to behave. "You will address him properly. But if you must know, his first name is Cillian."

Aedlin let herself out and Mora fell back onto her bed. She traced Cillian's love bites, wondering if he'd be the one seeking her hand. Had he known who she was? Her heart fluttered in her chest and Mora couldn't decide if it was excitement or apprehension that held her in its grasp. What games was Cillian playing?

CHAPTER 9

MORA

Absolute silence greeted her in the hall. It was almost jarring, but she had picked this spot for a reason. Other than Frederick, few came this way, and his rooms weren't far from the top of the stairs. Mora couldn't help but grin—stealing from him would be easy.

But where was Lillian?

Absent-mindedly, she fiddled with the buckle on her pouch, wondering if she'd need to hunt her down. If Lillian left, Mora would find her and drag her up these stairs herself.

But there would be no need for dramatics. When Mora made it to the stairwell, she found Lillian slumped against the wall, lost in whatever hell clung to her mind.

"Chocolate for your thoughts?" Mora asked as she pulled a couple sweets from her pouch.

Lillian gasped and jolted upright, a pink blush blooming on her cheeks. "You need to stop fucking doing that."

Mora shrugged. "You knew I was coming. It's not my fault you weren't paying attention." She held out one of the chocolates in offering. "Take one before I change my mind."

Lillian accepted, but her eyes widened when she looked at the confectionary. "Did you steal this from the kitchen?"

"Maybe." She flashed a devious grin, then tossed her piece into her mouth. Closing her eyes, she moaned in delight as it melted on her tongue. "Chocolate is the solution to most problems."

"If that were true, I damn well wouldn't need you, now would I?" She frowned when Mora pulled another piece from her pouch, but that didn't stop her from taking a bite of her own. And then she smiled. It was small, but impossible to miss.

"See? I was right,"

"They're perfect," Lillian mumbled around the dessert. Her eyes wandered to the pouch on Mora's hip. "How did you prevent these from melting, demon?"

Mora followed her gaze and grimaced. Of course she'd have to ask. She cleared her throat and attempted to sound casual. "It's an enchanted pouch." Any hope she had of avoiding further discussion withered and died. Lillian perked up and Mora swore under her breath, though not quietly enough, judging by the way Lillian's brows quirked upwards. This was the last thing Mora wanted to talk about. But if she wanted Lillian's trust, she'd have to be somewhat forthcoming. Right? Why did that have to be right...

Mora blew out a sigh. "If you must know, it keeps things in a sort of stasis. Which is useful, since it could be years before I eat all of these."

Surprise flared in Lillian's light green eyes. "Years?"

A bitter chuckle escaped Mora's lips. "Comes with the territory."

"I have so many questions... I—"

"*I* would prefer you not ask any of them." Pity softened Lillian's face and Mora couldn't stand it. She tore her gaze away, distracting herself with the polished banister. "Have you ever found it funny that you're raised to hate the *Forbidden*, and yet the nobility keep them as Indentureds and display art depicting the Forbidden Forest?"

She trailed her fingers over the smooth grooves in the wood. Each baluster featured impeccable carvings of flowers and pixies playing gaily among them. It all came together on the newel post, where there were two Fae holding hands and gazing lovingly at one another. Mora assumed they were mates.

According to Halfling stories, the magic of the Forbidden Forest sometimes bonded two souls so intricately they could hardly breathe without the other present. It sounded horrific. Though it seemed rare, thank the gods. Or at least there were few among the Halflings who claimed to have such bonds. When separated, they became violent, lashing out at the King's Guard or harming their lords. Most were deemed unstable, a danger to Berwick, and were executed.

Lillian eyed her warily. "I don't know what you want me to say."

"Of course you don't think for yourself," Mora mumbled under her breath, remembering a deep male voice and the threat of his blade at her throat.

"Excuse me?"

"You've reminded me of someone, that's all." Endless black eyes haunted her mind and she could almost feel the soft fabric of his cloak trapped in her grip. Smell that intoxicating scent. Mora cleared her throat and shook her head, as if it may dislodge the memory. She smoothed out her skirt, avoiding Lillian's gaze. "You should hurry, there isn't much time. If you aren't quick, I won't be able to help you until the banquet's over." Mora didn't spare Lillian a glance as she stepped around her and made her way up the stairs.

A silence settled over them—even their footsteps were muffled by an emerald runner. Lillian's fingers twisted in her apron, her dread so palpable Mora could taste it. "May I ask about your pouch?"

A quick breath of air rushed out of Mora's nose as she leashed her annoyance. Gods help her. "What would you like to know?" She clenched her teeth so hard she was surprised the words were capable of escaping.

"Did you make it?"

"No." That was all the answer Mora wished to give, but a pregnant pause sat heavy in the air—Lillian wanted more. Why had Mora shared anything at all? Of course Lillian was intrigued; this was likely the first enchanted item she'd seen. Mora swallowed. "This pouch was a... gift." Bile crept up her throat with the words, her belly churning.

"Holy hell," Lillian breathed. "That's quite the gift. I assume it was from a lover?"

Those words had teeth. They stung when they found Mora's ears, tearing and burrowing through her mind. She stopped abruptly in her tracks.

He's dead, he's dead, he's dead.

Mora clenched her eyes shut and curled her fingers into painfully tight fists, nails digging into her palms. She took a slow, deep breath, desperately clinging to some semblance of calm.

Minutes passed while Lillian waited in silence. When the thunder in her head quieted, she turned to face her. Whatever Lillian saw in Mora's glowing eyes had her taking a single step back. But Mora shook her head and held up a hand. "This pouch was from someone I had mistakenly grown to trust. A mistake I intend not to repeat. That's all I'll say on the subject."

She spun on her feet and continued up the stairs faster than before. Lillian had no idea how right she was. And Mora hated it.

CHAPTER 10

MORA
300 YEARS AGO

"I made this for you." Cillian grinned and held out a dark brown leather pouch. "It's a twin to mine."

Mora eyed the pouch warily. Knowing Cillian, this was no ordinary pouch. To wear a magical object... It felt like courting disaster. While she hadn't been part of any political discussions, Mora heard whispers of unrest.

Last week, a child in Reverie suspected of having Halfling blood was murdered. A neighbor swore the boy called upon the winds, barraging the town in a harsh torrent on an otherwise calm day. There were no prior records of the child's family among the Crown's Forbidden. And he was too young, regardless, to manifest power—most Halflings discovered their abilities around puberty. That hadn't mattered to the man who stole his life.

The murderer's execution did nothing to staunch the flames of hatred that festered like a gangrenous wound in all of Berwick. More needed to be done.

The family recently settled there, and people were distrustful. A common issue since the Laws of Confinement were overturned. Fear of magic bubbled into something dangerous. And the nobles hadn't helped—despite her mother's best efforts, their support for the crown waned. Mora wondered if their real issue was the loss of their Indentured.

If they knew the Princess of Berwick caused this change, there would be riots, and wearing a magical object could lead to too many questions. It would be foolish.

Cillian, however, wouldn't hear it. He had righteous beliefs, a dream of a changed Berwick where all were equal. And he saw their union as the answer.

Despite her trepidations, considering their meeting, they'd been courting for months. Her mother was overjoyed. Counting the days until their engagement. While Mora hated to admit it, her heart fluttered whenever he came near. Often, she lost herself in those bright, azure eyes, and found herself enamored with his passionate heart. Philip would be furious if he knew how often Cillian snuck into her chambers—they spent their nights tangled in her sheets, with Cillian slipping out before the sun crested over the horizon.

Though she couldn't help but wonder if he cared more for her or the power that came with her hand. Their chance meeting was a gift from the Fates, according to him. Proof their joining was Gods-blessed, as well as an opportunity for them to come to know one another outside of the pageantry that came with her title. It was a beautiful notion. But, in the quiet moments, Mora wondered if it was too good to be true.

"Do you like it?" he asked, his voice adorably soft.

Cillian was always sure of himself. When he wanted something, he made it happen. He charmed her, her parents, and many of the nobility, an impressive accomplishment considering the state of affairs. Though, when he had doubts or anticipated resistance, he bit his left cheek. A minor tell. Mora spent enough time staring at him to recognize it. It created a sweet divot on his face. She held herself back from poking it and teasing him—he was a hard man to read, and she planned to keep this little tidbit of knowledge hidden away in case it became useful.

Mora cleared her throat and ran her finger over the silver buckle at the center, the metal cool to the touch. What magic are you hiding, little thing, she wondered. He pressed it into her hands, the soft, grainy texture tickling her skin. "Thank you, Lord Dother," she said cautiously, searching her mind for the right words.

Closing the distance between them, Cillian's fingers found a stray curl that had fallen out of her loose braid. Their chests nearly touched, and her back pressed against her armoire's hard, wooden doors. The sweet scents of citrus, fragrant herbs, and copper curled around her nose as their breaths mingled. Mora inhaled it greedily. Cillian tucked the curl behind her ear before trailing his fingers down her neck, and she tried to ignore the warm metal of his ring, pretending she didn't feel its eerie, endless stare.

"How many times have I told you not to call me that, Treasure?" He placed a soft, lingering kiss on her cheek. "We're far too familiar for bothersome titles."

Mora hummed in response, always a moth to his flame once he had her in his embrace. It was easy to call his name when they came together in the night. In public, a certain decorum needed to be followed. Lord Dother was the appropriate option, and she found it hard to call him anything else, even in private, during daylight.

Cillian pulled back, eyes searching hers as he chewed on his cheek. "Do you like it?"

Mora hesitated. "Yes."

There was more to discuss, many things she needed to say. But her yes was all Cillian needed.

"It has a special enchantment, I'm excited to tell you all about it!"

Those luminous eyes bore into hers, sparkling with excitement, and she didn't have the heart to deny him. "Tell me, Lord Doth... Cillian."

He squeezed her neck gently in approval. "You'll love this." Cillian smiled as he released his hold on her and took a step back, gesturing for her to take a closer look at the pouch. "Firstly, I've created a stasis within it. Whatever you place inside will stay pristine. It prevents decay and any wear and tear, no matter how much time has passed."

Mora looked down at the unassuming leather with wide eyes. "How?"

Cillian chuckled. "Enchanter's secret, Treasure." He unbuckled the pouch at his hip and riffled through it, his red journal bouncing against his thigh with the movement. "Secondly, it can hold far more than you can imagine. While it isn't infinite, I doubt you'll ever manage to fill it."

Mora shook her head in disbelief. "That's impossible."

He paused his search and looked at her, lips quirking upward. "With the right reagents, I can make anything possible."

"Could I put a horse in it?"

Cillian snorted. "Could you fit a horse through the opening?"

Mora shook her head and pouted. "I'm disappointed."

"I'll be sure to enchant something for horse storage later, Your Highness," he said, sarcasm dripping over each word. He pulled out

a matching, dark brown leather belt. It was breathtaking, featuring hand-carved daisies, branches, and leaves.

"That's beautiful! Did you make it?"

Cillian ran his hand over the belt, his expression unreadable. Something odd gleamed in his eyes. In the span of a breath, his delighted smile returned. "Of course I did." He held his hand out in a silent demand, and Mora handed her pouch over. "Thirdly, Treasure, it will always be light, no matter how much you store in it."

"Is there anything in it now?"

He finished threading the belt through the looped leather straps attached to her pouch, then popped the buckle open. Mora's heart sank as he pulled out a glass orb full of writhing shadows. When he rolled the object back and forth in his palm, she spied flapping wings among the darkness, and tiny hands that plinked against the glass in a desperate attempt to steady itself. "I gave you a handful of my sprites. They're bound to my blood, so they won't be as compliant with you, but you'll get one use out of them."

Mora shifted uncomfortably on her feet. Cillian knew she hated his trapped sprites. Their little forms pressing against the glass were haunting. She opened her mouth to protest, but he didn't allow her the opportunity to speak.

"Lastly," he said, a harsh edge to his voice. "All you need to do is think of what you want, reach inside, and it will find you." He shoved the sprite back without sparing the poor creature a single glance, then held the pouch out. "Try it."

The one item she knew to summon was a sprite, and he knew it. His eyes narrowed when she hesitated. "Go on, Treasure."

Mora's upper lip curled, but she did as he said and imagined the poor thing pressing against the glass in a bid to break free. The cool sphere brushed against her skin and she shuddered. Cillian beamed when she pulled it from the bag, which made her stomach drop further. "I don't want this, Lord Dother."

He took a step closer. "Call me Cillian."

Mora ignored him and focused on his horrific ring. It flit back and forth, its attention split between her and the sprite. Mora tensed when Cillian reached for the creature, but before he could grab it, she smashed it on the floor. Fluttering shadows enveloped them, blotting out the light. But, unlike the last time, she could make out a hazy outline of the room.

Cillian crowded her, those blinding azure eyes shining in the darkness. "Why do you insist on being difficult?"

"It deserves to be free!"

"It's little more than a bug," *he gritted out.*

Mora crossed her arms and leaned against the armoire. "I don't like it."

His frustration was palpable, though the darkness swirling around them shadowed his face. "You're refusing my gifts?"

Mora couldn't stop the exasperated sigh bubbling in her chest. She raked a hand over her face, her body tensing. "You know I shouldn't carry magical items. There would be too many questions. I might be discovered."

The leather squeaked as his grip on it tightened. "And? The world should know you're a gifted Elementalist. You shouldn't be ashamed of what you are."

Pushing past Cillian, she thanked the gods she still wore shoes when glass crunched beneath her feet. Rosemary wouldn't be happy to pluck the little shards out of her carpet. Mora took a deep breath and began to pace—moving helped her think when irritation clouded her mind.

"I'm not ashamed. I know you have your own thoughts on the matter, but we've talked about this. There would be riots—"

"And whose fault is that?" His hand wrapped around her forearm and he tugged her back into his chest.

"Don't!" Mora hissed, twisting in his embrace. What he'd implied... he was right, and she knew it. Hated it.

Cillian pulled her along, ignoring how her feet dragged on the floor, flipping up her carpet. The darkness moved with them, as if pulled along by an invisible string. Cillian didn't seem at all blinded. He avoided her bedpost, passed her dresser, and swung the door open, stopping when they reached her sitting room. "I know your parents overturned the laws, Mora. But they did it because of you. And they've done nothing to make things better for our people. They've been left with two choices: hide or die. It isn't much different than before."

Our people. *He always spoke as if those with magic were their true subjects. It was incredulous, the deep connection he felt with Berwick's Halflings. His family fled to Eldenna after the Exodus—he had no ties here.*

"You know it's not that simple."

"It doesn't need to be complicated. Imagine the difference we'll make when we marry and ascend to the throne."

Mora swallowed. He was certain of their path. But all he'd managed to do was water the seeds of doubt festering in her heart.

Cillian knelt in front of her and looped the belt around her waist, the deep brown blending well with her dark purple gown. "The people love you. I've already won a handful of the nobility. Once we reveal our true natures, things will change. We can make *things change.*"

"Cillian..." She paused and winced when he cinched the belt a little too tight. He adjusted it, looping the leather so the remaining length hung down her waist.

"I know you don't like to talk about it, but you need to recognize your privilege. You avoided the Laws of Confinement. You weren't forced to live in a cloister. Never gifted to some noble prick like you were little more than an object."

"And you were?"

Cillian's eyes flared, and he gave her a look that stilled her tongue. "You don't know what it's like to run, fearing death if they find you. Or to hide, living in squalor because that's the best you can hope for. Our people suffered and died because of laws that were overturned to spare you."

Mora's pulse pounded, and guilt sat heavy in her chest. Yet it wasn't enough to change her mind. "And you don't think they'll be angry too, if they discover what I am?"

He admired the way the belt highlighted her hourglass curves, hands lingering on her hips. Then he rose and leaned in for a quick kiss. "They may. But I can fix it."

Mora closed her eyes and shook her head. "Sometimes I think you're too sure of yourself." No matter what Cillian thought, revealing herself wouldn't solve the problem. It would further feed the flames of turmoil burning across Berwick. If the people discovered their princess was a Halfling and her parents spared her... they'd revolt. People would die, her family potentially among them. Something had to be done, Mora knew, but Cillian's idea was misguided.

She nearly melted when he cradled her cheeks. "Look at me, Treasure." Her eyes snapped open, and he brightened. "Together, we will make an incredible difference for our people."

When he leaned in for a kiss, he took his time, savoring the taste of her soft lips. He groaned when she kissed him back and slid his hands down to her waist. They stumbled back a few steps before he fell onto the soft cushions that lined her chaise, tugging her down with him. It felt easy, losing herself in him like this. To drown in his delicious scent, cuddle into his warm embrace, and pretend things were simple. But they could never be simple.

Mora pulled away, blinking when the shadows dissipated. It was hard not to grin, knowing the sprite must be free, but there were more important things to discuss.

"I'm not ready to marry." The words rushed out of her, as if spitting it out could save her from the discomfort. Cillian recoiled. A muscle in his jaw feathered, that divot appearing on his left cheek. Tears gathered on her lashes, but she held them back. "I want to marry for love, not politics."

"And you don't think I love you?"

Mora bit her lip and looked away, wiping furiously at her watery eyes. "It's too soon."

Cillian laid her on one of the pillows and stood, giving her his back. He ran his fingers through his hair, pulling at the roots as he silently seethed. His cheeks reddened, the color much brighter now that his tan faded. Mora eyed her bedroom and wondered if she could live with the embarrassment that would come from bolting into her room and locking the door. Though Cillian would catch her within two steps.

Fisting her dress, she focused on the feel of the soft fabric slipping between her fingers and took a calming breath. Cillian turned to face her, a dangerous gleam in his eyes. A rift formed between them; she could feel the shift as surely as she could see the way his nostrils flared.

But his features softened and his eyes gentled, and Mora wondered if she imagined things.

"Then we'll wait until you're ready." His lips twitched into the whisper of a sad smile when he offered her his hand. Mora swallowed past the lump in her throat as he helped her up and pulled her close, resting his chin on her crown. "I want what's best for both of us. Take all the time you need, I know you'll choose me."

Mora snuggled into his firm chest, her voice muffled by his soft gray tunic. "And if I don't choose you?"

"You will." He gave her braid a gentle tug, forcing her to look up at him. "We're fated, Treasure. When the smoke clears, you'll know beyond a shadow of a doubt you're meant to be eternally by my side."

Mora ached to roll her eyes at his declaration, but that would reignite the argument. At least they could move on to more pleasant things. Cillian could hold on to his dreams of eternity. And she'd wait and see if she desired the fate he offered.

CHAPTER II

MORA

Mora rapped her knuckles against the ornate wooden door that led to Lord Frederick's chambers, much to Lillian's dismay. The poor thing looked like a ghost, her eyes bulging from her face.

"You're fucking mad," Lillian hissed.

Mora snorted. "I've been told that a time or two." She knocked again, for the heck of it. Unlike Lillian, she knew Frederick wouldn't be inside. Though, perhaps they'd find someone. A maid or a lover tangled in the lord's bedsheets. Mora shook her head. No, Frederick didn't seem like the type to fall into bed with someone and then hide them in his rooms. While it was best to be cautious, she'd rather rile Lillian up a little after her questions on the stairs.

Cold, trembling fingers encircled Mora's wrist and pulled her hand away from the door. Mora rolled her eyes. "Calm down. I'm making sure no one's inside." She pressed her ear against the cool hardwood, but Lillian didn't let go.

"And if someone happens to come to the door? Then what?" Lillian's lips pressed into a firm line and her face hardened, but her voice wobbled.

"You're going to have to trust me eventually, Lillian. I would have come up with something." Narrowing her eyes, she listened for any movement inside. Perhaps now would be a good time to tell her Frederick was preoccupied in the library. But where was the fun in that?

When she was certain she heard nothing, she straightened and nodded. "You worried over nothing."

Mora made no effort to be quiet as she threw the door open. She waltzed in like she owned the place, dragging a stunned Lillian past the threshold. Rolling her eyes, she closed the door silently and gave Lillian an exasperated look that screamed, *Happy now?*

They were greeted by a spacious sitting room. A deep emerald and ivory tapestry decorated the far wall. Matching green chairs sat near the window, their plump ivory pillows beckoning for someone to cozy up for a nap. A low burning fire crackled in the fireplace, glowing embers waning but still lending some semblance of warmth to the room. The subtle scents of smoke saturated the air, mixing with a soothing blend of cinnamon and cloves.

Mora looked back at Lillian, chuckling when she found her with her mouth wide open. "It's not *that* impressive in here." She turned toward the next chamber, tossing the door open with little care as she pulled Lillian along.

The room was dark, save for the late afternoon light streaming in through the multi-paned arched windows. A soft rug cushioned their feet as they neared a massive bed with a gorgeous ornamental canopy. Every piece of fabric the same dark emerald. A rumpled tunic tangled with Lillian's feet and she squeaked when she stumbled, but she still clung to Mora and managed to right her footing.

Mora rounded the bed and tugged Lillian in front of her before she gestured toward the bedside table. Its wooden legs had a corkscrew pattern, and it housed a small drawer with intricate swirls and whirls carved into the wood. "My flask's in there."

Furrowing her brows, Lillian took a tentative step forward, darting questioning eyes Mora's way. Mora hoped her smile was encouraging. She nodded, her penetrating gaze unwavering, but she couldn't help but drum her fingers against her thigh.

Lillian reached out and grabbed the cool metal handle. "Once I steal this, you'll help me?"

"We've been over this, Lillian." Mora's lips twitched, but she held back her grimace. "Once you have my flask, I can do anything you ask of me."

The wood emitted a squeak as Lillian coaxed the drawer open. Nestled in a bed of papers, trinkets and coins was a strange, teardrop shaped crystal flask. An almost ethereal glow emanated from the bottle and its bottom half was decorated with delicate golden filigree shaped like daisies, leaves, and vines. Strips of golden bark covered the neck, tied in place with gilded thread. And a golden stopper sat on top, its design reminiscent of a piece of wood with an array of rings on top, as if it displayed the lifeline of a tree cut down in its prime.

It was beautiful. So beautiful in fact, it took Lillian a few breaths before she reached out and ran her fingers over the golden flowers.

As soon as her hand curled around the bottle, an icy cold feeling skittered up her spine, making her gasp.

Mora placed a hand on Lillian's shoulder. "Keeper of the flask," she said, smiling softly. "My power is yours to command."

"What kind of gods damned nonsense is this?" Lillian shook the flask as she spoke.

The smile died on Mora's face. Could nothing be easy with this woman? "What exactly is your problem?"

"Are you pulling my leg? You drag me all the way up here, to a place where I'm not welcome by the way... you have no idea the consequences I'd face if I were caught—"

"Oh, I'm well aware of the consequences, Lillian." Mora's tone dripped with annoyance. "I made certain the lord would be occupied."

Lillian cursed under her breath as she squeezed the flask tighter. "You could have told me that before your show at the door." She began to fidget, her free hand twisting in her apron. "You drag me into the lord's personal chambers with the promise to help me if I steal something for you. You scare me shitless, many times over. And all for what?"

"To help you," Mora grumbled. Her methods may be... unorthodox. But, for the most part, this was all about helping Lillian. Her selfish reasons hardly mattered.

Lillian narrowed her eyes and shook her head. "Whatever you say, demon. *Keeper of the flask.* What the fuck does that even mean?"

An exasperated sigh spilled from Mora's lips, so heavy it was nearly a growl. "I made myself clear, Lillian. Steal the flask and you'll have my help. You are now my Keeper and my *power* is yours to command."

Mora paced and ran her hands through her thick curls. This was more frustrating than she imagined, yet she wanted it more than she'd wanted anything in a long time. A Keeper of her choosing. "So long as you are the Keeper of my flask, I can help you three times. And before you ask, no, I can't change the past or bring someone back from the dead. I can't make someone love you. If you're looking for a fortune teller, look elsewhere, the future is as much a surprise to me as it is to anyone. Don't expect me to create something out of thin air, that's a ridiculously common notion. Though, with the right materials, I can pretty well do anything. And, as you can see, I'm not above stealing if needed. You seem impatient and time is an issue. Can we *please* move on?" Mora stopped and looked back at the cook, glaring daggers. "Or would you like to remain in these chambers asking questions until the lord finds us?"

"What about the banquet? I doubt me touching a fancy bottle changed your priorities."

Mora rolled her eyes and returned to her pacing. She wanted to shake her. To demand she make her wish now. That wouldn't go well, so she wore a path in the carpet instead.

"I wouldn't call it a personal priority, but it still stands. Once a wish is made, I'm compelled to fulfill it. Anything short of the wish maker's death can't stop me, even if someone else grabs the flask. And, no, you can't undo their wish with another. Contradictory wishes won't take hold. So, unless you'd like to wait until tomorrow for my help, I suggest you hurry. Or we could kill your precious lord. That would buy you lots of time." She didn't think it was possible, but Lillian paled further. Mora's expression turned monstrous. "Not a fan of murder?"

Lillian shook her head and backed away as Mora approached.

"Then get on with it." She maintained a comfortable distance, her eyes flicking to her flask. "You can take my flask with you. Though I recommend you leave it in the drawer, so the sweet lord is none-the-wiser." Mora hesitated, then shrugged. "But do as you will. If he picks it up, you won't be my Keeper any longer. And if I'm not near and you need me, you'd have to hold the flask and call my name."

"This bullshit is too complicated," Lillian mumbled.

"It isn't. Make a wish. Make three wishes if you'd like. Until someone else touches the flask or you've used all your wishes, I'm yours."

"You're mine?" Lillian parroted.

"I'm cursed, Lillian," Mora seethed. "How is that not clear? I'm bound to the flask you now hold, which means I'm yours to command."

Lillian looked down at the flask with a frown, and the pity Mora hated once again painted her face. She opened her mouth, but Mora interrupted. "Don't." She cleared her throat and straightened her skirt. "You asked if I could bind myself to secrecy. I give you my word I won't say anything. But if you'd like to waste a wish, now would be the time."

Lillian took one last look at the flask before she placed it back in the drawer. She fiddled with the drawer's handle and kept her eyes averted as she spoke. "I do wish for you to keep this to yourself."

A frigid sensation skittered up their spines, winding around their bones. It felt strange and came with a bite of pain, but Mora had grown used to it over the centuries. Lillian, on the other hand, was woefully unprepared. She slapped her hand to her chest and leaned against the table, her eyes wide. "What the hell was that?"

"Your wish taking hold." Lillian, however, hadn't specified *what* she wanted Mora to keep to herself. There was a lot of wiggle room for her to play with. Foolish girl. "Now, for the love of the gods, please tell me what you need."

Lillian righted herself and swiped a small glass trinket from the bedside table. She watched it roll around in her palm, still unwilling to give Mora her gaze. "A few weeks ago a lord visited the manor... and he..." She shook her head as if it would chase away the memory. "I'm pregnant."

A familiar unease crept up Mora's throat, and she narrowed her eyes, focusing on Lillian's trembling hands. On the tension in her face. The tears beading in her eyes. Sweat slicked Mora's palms, and she knew... saw visions of her old self, huddled on Dother's bed, clutching his lavish black sheets as her own hands shook.

"Who did this to you?" Mora gritted her teeth as she spoke, her voice low and deadly.

Lillian clenched the paperweight, her knuckles turning white. "It doesn't matter. What matters is he never finds out. That this is undone."

Mora could have sworn she felt Dother's breath against her neck as he whispered in her ear. *Undress me, Treasure.* She shivered and clenched her eyes shut. *It's a phantom, Mora. A memory. He's dead.*

As he deserved to be. As Lillian's assaulter needed to be too.

Mora flexed her fingers and swallowed the lump in her throat. No matter how easy and familiar it felt, now was not the time for violence. "Do you wish to end your pregnancy?" Mora asked, her voice thick.

There was no hesitation—Lillian answered with an emphatic, "Yes."

"Make a wish and I'll be glad to make it happen." And Mora meant every word. She had no desire to twist this wish—no one should be forced to carry an unwanted pregnancy.

Lillian placed the paperweight down on the table with an audible *thunk*. She took a deep breath, her shoulders straightening as if she felt lighter. "I don't want to be pregnant. I wish for you to end this."

She didn't flinch this time as the wish took hold. Instead, she closed her eyes and sighed, a soft smile spreading on her youthful face.

Mora held out her hand and was delighted when Lillian didn't hesitate to take it. It didn't take long, however, for her calm demeanor to crack. Her screech bounced off the walls as Mora enveloped her in a mass of glittering onyx mist.

CHAPTER 12

LILLIAN

A torrent of obsidian descended upon the gardens, wrapped in the arms of a phantom wind. It landed on the gravel path that cut between flower beds and undulated in place before shrinking back to reveal Mora, her curls wild and her amber eyes aglow. And the woman who clung to her, face ashen.

Lillian released the demon woman as if she burned her and backed away, mouth agape. She blew unkempt, loose strands from her ponytail away from her eyes before taking in the hedges, flowers, and leaves that rustled as the wind died down. They were in Lord Frederick's chambers. But in the span of two breaths she was outside, surrounded by a world in full bloom... how?

The memory of the cool caress of onyx mist lingered on her skin. Scents of burning embers and pine clung to her clothes. Lillian shivered and rubbed her arms. It had been dark, except for glints of gold glittering all around her, as if she'd fallen into the night sky and floated among the stars. She had been alone but *felt* Mora's presence.

"What in the blazes was that, demon?"

Mora shrugged. "We're fulfilling your wish."

That explains nothing, Lillian thought with a frown. Yet she kept her mouth shut. Getting information out of Mora was like pulling teeth. She was learning to pick and choose which questions to ask. This didn't feel worth the potential backlash, and besides, she knew enough. Mora was cursed, bound to a fancy bottle, and could grant wishes to those who held it. Oh, and she turned into smoke. Nothing weird about that.

You were right to call her a demon. Lillian chuckled half-heartedly under her breath.

Mora furrowed her brows but said nothing as she made her way through the garden, expecting Lillian to follow. They walked in casual silence, and with each step, Lillian's chest felt lighter. The nightmare was almost over. She took a deep breath, appreciating the refreshing spring air. The green glow and perfume of fresh roses were a calming boon—she was grateful Mora brought her here.

Lillian opened her mouth to thank her, but Mora was no longer there. How the fuck had she lost her already? She spun in place, her mind racing. Was this all a strange ruse? Oh gods, she could already feel her heart fluttering as nausea churned in her stomach. Without Mora, she was screwed.

But then she saw her and the panic ebbed.

Mora had abandoned the path and wandered closer to the thicket of trees leading down to the lake. She stood stock-still in the grass, her eyes closed and hands extended, as if in a trance. This was the calmest Lillian had seen her.

Black mist spilled from her palms toward the ground, pooling at her feet. At first, nothing happened and Lillian found herself fidgeting, her fingers curling in her apron as she imagined clawing the invasion from her womb. She wanted to ask Mora how long it would take. Instead, she bit her tongue and allowed the woman to work. She could be patient. Maybe.

The smoke pulled back, green stems rising from the ground in its wake. Fern-like leaves with saw-toothed edges sprung up around them. Each plant held a small, round, yellow flower that reminded Lillian of buttons. It was odd, yet incredible to watch.

Mora gazed upon her creations before lowering herself to the ground. The flowers bent toward her, reaching for her outstretched hand, and as she ran her fingers over their tops, a soft smile rose on her face. Lillian found herself smiling too, wondering if she should offer to help. But then Mora fisted a large handful and squeezed, more of her strange smoke oozing from her palms and curling around the plants.

What in the blazes...

The flowers in her hold withered and rotted, turning an unsightly brown. Their leaves curled inward, a few breaking from the stems and falling to the earth. And the button tops were consumed by black rot. They curdled before disappearing altogether.

Lillian's mouth hung open, but she remained silent, watching. It made no sense to her how Mora could look calm and joyful as she created life, and yet completely unaffected as she destroyed it.

With her other hand, Mora ripped a living handful of flowers from the earth with such brutality the roots tore from the ground. Clumps of dirt broke away and tumbled into her lap, but she paid the mess no mind. More raven smoke twisted around the stems, sucking the life from them. They withered and dried out, much like the herbs hanging in the pantry.

Once she seemed satisfied, she plucked leaves from both bundles and placed them in her lap before brushing the dirt away. She reached into her enchanted pouch, an incredible thing Lillian couldn't believe Mora owned, and pulled out two small sachets. In one, she crumbled a handful of leaves. From the other, she pinched a strange, yellowish powder and sprinkled it into the mix before putting it away.

Mora hesitated for a moment, then gazed around the yard until her eyes landed on a rose bush. With the flick of her wrist, a length of dark mist appeared and slithered to the plant. It crawled through the brush, leaves rustling in its wake. Then it snapped back to Mora's hand and disappeared into her skin.

A sharp thorn now sat in Mora's palm. She stared at it for what felt like eons, her expression impossible to read. Lillian found she could no longer remain silent. "Did you need anything, demon?"

"Is there magic in your bloodline?"

Lillian arched a brow. That was the last thing she expected Mora to say. "My great aunt was a Forbidden. I never met her. They took her when my grandmother was a child."

Mora cringed but nodded along, still eying the thorn. "Then it's possible you have something?"

A shocked laugh escaped Lillian's lips. "Fuck no."

"Because it would be awful to be like us," she seethed.

Lillian recognized the glint of rage in Mora's golden eyes. In an attempt to ease the tension, she held her hands up and kept her voice soft. "I didn't mean to offend you."

"I suppose it hardly matters," she said, more to herself. She seemed to have calmed. Thank the gods. Lillian released a breath and lowered her hands. Then Mora closed her fist and squeezed the thorn. Blood dribbled out from between the cracks, laced with fine streaks of gold.

"What the hell, Mora?" Lillian hissed, but Mora shushed her. It must have hurt. Though there was no hint of pain on her face.

She opened her palm, eyeing the liquid crimson, then tipped her hand and allowed a drop to drip into the sachet. It disappeared into the crushed leaves. With little care, Mora tossed the bloodied thorn to the ground and went to work, tying off the small bag. A sparkle caught Lillian's eye, like a piece of treasure hiding among the flowers. The golden glow pulled her focus and Lillian found herself unable to look away as a gilt daisy bloomed where the thorn fell, its golden petals reaching for the sun.

Another pushed through the soil, glinting in the sunlight. She moved closer, glancing to see if Mora noticed. But her attention was on the sachet. New wisps of smoke bled from her fingers, twisting through the mixture inside. When Mora nodded, satisfied with whatever she'd accomplished, it shrank back into her skin.

"What *is* that?" Lillian asked, glancing back at the daisies, but Mora said at the same time, "It's ready."

It was ready. Lillian's lips parted as she stared at Mora's offering, the flowers forgotten. Mora stood and grabbed Lillian's hands.

"Take this," Mora said as she placed the bag in Lillian's palm and gently closed her fingers around it. "Treat it like tea. But be thoughtful about when you drink it because you may experience some bleeding and pain. This is an enchanted blend of dried golden bitters with a touch of death to help grant your wish, and a drop of immortality to protect you. The powdered ginger should help with any nausea and discomfort."

Lillian's throat tightened, and a tear ran down her cheek. She'd barely held herself together for weeks and finally felt like she could breathe. Clutching the herbs to her chest, Lillian asked, "Is the drop of immortality your blood?"

Mora nodded.

"I thought that was dangerous?"

"You don't have magic. And if you did, what are you going to do, Lillian? Bind me to a flask for eternity? Oh, wait..." Mora chuckled, but there was no humor in it. "You should know it goes both ways. If I wanted to, and I had access to my magic, I could bind you to me once you drink my blood."

Mora spit the words out like they were bitter, and Lillian wondered if she spoke from experience. "A curse that binds you... one involving your blood and the blood of another? That's what happened?"

Mora's amber eyes narrowed, but she ignored the question. "Who did this to you, Lillian?"

"Did what?" Lillian's stomach clenched and a sour taste flooded her mouth. She didn't want to remember. Didn't want to think about *him*.

"You know what. I support your choice, but... we can't let him get away with this. What if he harms you again? Or hurts someone else?"

"... I..." Lillian couldn't bring herself to answer. It was exhausting, lying awake night after night fighting the horrific memories, dreading that he'd do it again or hurt another. She lost many hours of sleep worrying. And when she found out she was pregnant, it consumed her mind, brought her lower than she imagined possible. Had Mora not agreed to help... she wasn't sure she could have survived this. She trembled, her fist tightening around the sachet. It felt like a lifeline.

Mora shocked her by pulling her into an awkward embrace. Her movement was stiff as she ran her palm up and down Lillian's back. It seemed Mora wasn't quite sure how to provide comfort. Her efforts were calming, nonetheless, and Lillian found herself clutching her back as she inhaled a shuddering breath.

"You're safe," Mora whispered, holding her tighter. "You don't need to talk about it if you don't want to. You don't owe me any details. But I *can* protect you, Lillian. And I can make sure he never hurts anyone ever again."

Lillian whimpered. "He's dangerous."

"More dangerous than me?" Mora pulled back, rage flaring in her eyes. Lillian found herself shivering as she held her stare. A demon truly lurked behind that lovely face. One that should never be unleashed upon the world.

"I don't want to harm anyone."

Mora tilted her head to the side and Lillian felt as if she somehow saw all the way to the depths of her soul. "I understand," she said, and Lillian hated her serious expression. Hated that she continued to push. "But don't you wish he were incapable of harming anyone else?"

"Damn it, Mora," Lillian yelled, throwing her hands up in exasperation and shoving Mora away. "Of course it's my greatest wish he never hurt anyone again!"

Lillian tremored as a torrent of anger and fear clawed up her spine and wrapped around her ribs like a frigid fist. She shivered. Could still feel the press of his body on hers. Her lungs screamed at the memory. He'd nearly crushed her under his weight and Lillian had wondered if she'd survive the night. Then came the agony of discovering she was pregnant... he had no heirs. What would happen if he found out she carried his child?

Mora grabbed Lillian's shoulders, her touch gentle and kind. "Shh, it's ok."

Lillian felt lighter, like some of the pressure lifted off her chest. She leaned into Mora's embrace and closed her eyes, willing her racing heart to still.

"Gregory will *never* be a problem again," Mora said, a deadly edge to her voice.

... how did she know his name?

Lillian's head snapped up, and she was horrified by the cruel smile on Mora's face. It made Lillian's skin pebble.

It took her a moment to realize what she'd done, the hell she'd unleashed. That discomfort in her bones, it hadn't been her emotions overwhelming her... Lillian had given Mora exactly what she wanted and made a wish.

Lillian turned wide, pleading eyes to Mora. "Please, I don't want you to kill anyone."

The demon shook her head, that horrific smile never faltering. "Then you should have been more specific when you made your wish."

Lillian reached out and clutched Mora's dress, as if she could somehow stop her. Within moments, all she held onto was a clump of cool, glittering smoke. The dark cloud trickled through her fingers, no matter how tightly she attempted to hold on. She watched, powerless, as it twirled around her and flew up into the bright afternoon sky before disappearing over the horizon.

CHAPTER 13

MORA

The Golden Ox, a local tavern, was more crowded than Mora anticipated. Did these people have nothing better to do with their afternoon than drink? A few couples danced as a bard belted a tune and strummed the lute, while others drank, ate, and chatted. All dressed in their finery.

The tug of Lillian's wish led her there, but she wasn't sure where to find him. Lord Gregory Palmer. The moment she'd tricked Lillian into making the wish she knew. His name echoed in her mind, along with flashes of muddy brown eyes and long, graying brown hair slicked back into a bun. And a smug face that needed to be bloodied. Flexing her fingers, she made her way through the crowd.

The hardwood floors gleamed, and Mora spied bottles of fine wines and high-quality liquor behind a pristine bar with a dark marble top. The bartender wasn't hard to look at either, dressed in a black suit, with skin the shade of deep mahogany, short, tight curls, and kind hazel eyes. Though there was an innocence to him Mora didn't like. Life hadn't yet stained his soul. One night with her and he'd be ruined.

She wasn't too far from Frederick's manor and, judging by her company, this tavern was a place for the upper class to unwind. Something unheard of in her time. Nonetheless, being here tugged on the threads of memories she'd rather stay buried.

Mora's eyes roved over the tables until they landed on Gregory, sitting alone with a full mug of ale trapped between his grubby hands. Shadows clung to his corner of the tavern, granting him what little privacy someone could hope for in a public place. They couldn't protect him from Mora. He may hide in the shadows. But she could *become* them.

At a glance, he appeared to be a fine gentleman, dressed lavishly in a bright red tunic and black waistcoat encrusted with what she assumed were rubies and other precious gems. Upon closer inspection, a monstrous gleam hid in his eyes. One that would be easy to miss, unless you'd grown accustomed to seeing the demon hiding behind someone's stare. He watched a group of women that drank and laughed across the room with far too much interest.

Mora gritted her teeth, her jaw cracking under the pressure, but she schooled her features as she approached.

"Hello, handsome," she purred, smiling innocently when his attention snapped to her face. His repulsive gaze roved down her body, appreciating the tight, maroon gown Mora created before entering the tavern. It hugged her ample hips, leaving little to the imagination. It had been easy to recycle her turquoise gown and steal the dye from the curtains of a carriage. Though she imagined the owner wouldn't be pleased with the now bleached material.

The bodice swooped low, revealing a generous serving of cleavage. She wondered what her parents would have thought of her wearing something this scandalous. Mora smirked—she didn't have to wonder. Aedlin would have been appalled, and Kalyan would give her the *you knew this would upset your mother* look. Gregory, however, licked his lips in appreciation as he stared.

"Charmed," he said, standing and extending his hand, though his eyes never left her breasts. Mora kept her grimace at bay as she accepted and curtsied. Or, at least, attempted to—the dress made the motion difficult. "I don't recognize you. What's your name, Lady?"

"Morrigan."

"Morrigan." He slowly shook his head. "I haven't heard of you. Where are you from, Treasure?"

Fury erupted in Mora's chest, clawing at her ribs as if it ached to crack them open and break free. It took everything in her to leash it. Hearing that word... she wanted to tear out his tongue and shove it down his throat. But a man like Gregory deserved to sit with his sins and beg forgiveness. And she hadn't had her fun yet. Her fingers twitched in his grasp, but she stopped herself from crushing his hand and forced herself to be pleasant. "I've recently arrived in Westmont. I hail from Moldenna."

He released her hand and sat, leaning back in his chair. The sleeves of his red tunic strained against his muscular arm, and Mora could tell he was flexing. Pathetic. "What brings you to the north?"

"Hopefully good company." Mora slid her fingers along her collarbone and gave Gregory a questioning look.

He grinned and patted his thigh, firelight glinting off his platinum wedding band. Did his wife know she married such a disgusting man? "Please, join me," he said, his grimy voice full of wanting. It slid over Mora's skin like sludge and she swallowed against the bile crawling up her esophagus.

Mora settled onto his lap, leaning into his embrace. The overwhelming scent of his cologne flooded her lungs, and she nearly gagged on the pungent smell. She took shallow breaths and kept her composure. It would all be worth it.

Playfully, she ran her hand up his chest as she leaned closer and whispered, "I'm looking forward to our time together." Despite the wrongness of his touch, Mora wasn't lying.

The demand of Frederick's wish curled tighter and tighter around Mora's bones. It wasn't enough to fracture... yet. But with each breath her ribs ached—she was running out of time. The evening was coming and Lord Frederick's banquet began soon. His wish needed her attention. Soon denying its call would be agony.

While she hoped to whisk Gregory away from the prying eyes of the tavern's patrons, it had been harder than she'd imagined. He ordered a variety of dishes, insisting they take their time savoring the rich spread of food and that they fed each other. Was this foreplay or a pathetic attempt to impress her? How she restrained herself from biting off his fingers, she had no idea.

Mora dipped her fingers into the warm pile of mashed potatoes and dragged them through the dish. "These are my favorite."

"Really?" Gregory asked, his greedy eyes following her fingers back to her mouth. She sucked them clean as she nodded.

"Mmhmm," she hummed in earnest. They were well seasoned and, if she had the time, she would have enjoyed a larger portion. "I think they need a little butter, though. Don't you?"

Of course Gregory nodded. The oaf would agree to anything she said, in the hopes of getting his hands in her undergarments.

A butter crock sat in the center of the table, but her fingers grazed the cool handle of the knife when she attempted to reach it. Gregory gripped her hip harder, holding her to him as he leaned forward and grabbed it for her. After he buttered the potatoes, he made to put the knife back, but she shook her head and slid her hand down his arm until her fingers encircled his wrist.

"I want more," she said, taking the knife from his hand. Gregory watched her lick the remnants of creamy butter from its blunt edge. When the blade was clean, she gently trailed it up his neck and whispered, "I have a confession."

"Oh?" he asked, closing his eyes and enjoying the feel of the cool, dull blade sliding over his skin.

Mora traced his square jaw. "I knew who you were before I approached you."

Gregory opened an eye, smirking at her innocent expression. "Someone was telling stories, were they?"

"A friend, actually."

"Is that so?"

"Yes." She nodded slowly, trailing the butter knife up his cheek like a lover's caress. "Would you like to know what she told me?"

"Of course I do, Treasure. What did she say?"

Mora stilled, her grip on the knife's handle tightening. The pressure of her power bubbling under her skin was overwhelming, but the timing was perfect. Leaning forward to mutter what he assumed would be sweet nothings in his ear, Mora directed a trickle of smoke to spill from her calves and wrap around his ankles, securing them to the chair. More weaved around his center. Not tight enough that he'd notice, but ready to cinch the moment she commanded it.

"She told me you're a pathetic waste of flesh and she hopes she'll never have to withstand your repugnant presence again. I'm inclined to agree."

Gregory stiffened, his eyes widening in shock before they narrowed in fury. He attempted to stand, hoping Mora would topple onto the floor, but she was ready. Those dark tendrils of mist snapped him back into his seat, binding him in place. They were as strong as steel—he couldn't escape unless Mora allowed it.

Gregory thrashed, but it accomplished little. "What the fuck are you doing, Forbidden scum?"

Mora squeezed her fist and her power followed suit, pressing him into the chair until the wood groaned. An anguished wheeze escaped his lungs, and he thrashed harder. "Ah, ah, ah," Mora tsked, "I'm afraid there'll be no escaping my judgment, Gregory."

"I'll petition for the king to give you to me. I'll make your life hell if you don't stop." Gregory spoke quietly between clenched teeth. She supposed that was all he could do under the pressure of her smoke. *Oh well*.

Mora donned a cruel smile as she pushed the butter knife into his cheek until she could feel the pressure of his teeth against the metal. Finally, she could drop the mask. A thrill shot through her when he shrank back. The monster prowling behind her cold, amber eyes was all he could see now when he looked at her face. Pity that monsters rarely learned to look for those who were more monstrous. Arrogance and hubris were their downfall.

A cold sweat swept across his brow. "What do you want?"

"Ask me to stop."

"What?" Gregory frantically searched the room for help, but no one paid them any mind. He'd picked a shadowy corner table for a reason. The privacy it created worked well in Mora's favor.

"Ask. Me. To. Stop."

He hesitated, so Mora shoved harder against the blunt knife until blood pooled at the tip. "Stop! Please!"

"Hmm." Mora tapped a finger against her lips as she pretended to think. "Did that work on you when they asked you to stop?"

Gregory gulped. "I don't know what you mean."

Mora rolled her eyes. "We *both* know you do."

His legs shook and Mora snickered as her dark vapors crawled up his body and curled around his arms. This was the part that broke him—he bucked wildly, almost unseating her. "Help," he screamed, despite the pressure of her smoke against his chest. "Help me! This Forbidden whore is a lunatic!"

The melodic tone of the bard's voice halted, and the patrons became silent. Gregory's cries created a vortex that attracted their attention. Mora hadn't wanted a spectacle, but it seemed unavoidable. "You had to have an audience, didn't you?"

"Hey!" someone shouted, and Mora turned to see a bulky man pushing his way through the crowd as he marched toward them. He was manning the door when she entered. And he was *huge*. With shoulders so broad the buttons on his shirt likely screamed in agony as they held on for dear life, their threads straining under the pressure. Even his forearms were muscular, veins bulging against his skin. If he came between her ending Gregory and fulfilling Lillian's wish, she could take him out too. But she was in a hurry, and Gregory deserved all her attention.

With a sigh, Mora lifted her hand and allowed a new wave of obsidian smoke to leak from her flesh. The man ran toward them, but he wasn't fast enough. Within a breath, they were shielded by a dark, impenetrable cloud. Though Mora could feel the fists banging against the other side and heard the muffled demand she let Gregory go. Too bad for them, she had no mercy to spare.

Turning back to her prey, she clicked her tongue and shook her head. "Did I not promise there'd be no escape?"

They were in their own world now, with nothing but a few flickering candles to keep them company. Gregory wept and gave her the predictable spiel. She'd heard it many times before. While Mora sat still in his lap, fingers gripping his jaw tightly enough to bruise, butter knife digging into his cheek, he offered riches, begged to know what she wanted, promised her power.

Blah, blah, blah.

Mora yawned. "Are you done?" Gods, she hoped he was. The pain of Frederick's wish pulsed under her skin.

Gregory finally accepted his words were useless. Fat tears rolled down his cheeks and soaked her fingers. It took him a few shuddering breaths before he had the courage to ask the one question that mattered. "Why?"

Mora's upper lip curled and Gregory flinched at whatever he saw in her eyes. She trailed the knife further up his cheek, stopping below his left eye. "Lillian says hello."

She bellowed as she lifted the blunt butter knife and plunged it into his eye with all her might. Gregory screamed, the shrill sound bouncing in her ears, making them ring. But she ignored the pain.

When she pulled the knife out, hot blood bubbled up from his socket. It dribbled down his cheek, painting her fingers red before soaking her lap and puddling on the floor. The man shrieked and thrashed against his bindings, more blood gushing with each useless attempt to break free.

"Please," he begged. "Please stop!"

Mora pouted. "But I'm having fun." She lifted her arm and plunged the blade in once more before pulling it out swiftly. It made a horrific squelching sound as it came free. Gregory gagged, and she hoped he wouldn't vomit. Blood she could handle. Someone else's bile in her lap? No.

A sharp pain thrummed in her chest as Frederick's wish contorted around one of her ribs. The bone cracked, fissures spreading through it like furious roots. There was no time left to play.

"Good riddance, Gregory," she hissed before plunging the butter knife back into his eye.

Again.

And again.

And *again*.

Mora smashed it through his bloody socket a final time, pressing against the handle until the knife pierced his brain. Gregory's struggles became sluggish, his legs twitching until he stilled, one final moan escaping his lips. The man slumped in the chair, blood staining his face, his neck, his chest. It covered Mora's hands and forearms, and flecks scattered across her face. She reveled in it—the splatter of an enemy's blood soaking into her skin made her feel powerful in a way little else could.

It was a good thing her gown was maroon. Turquoise looked horrendous spattered in red.

Mora wiped her hands on her skirt before she stood and admired her work. The knife remained where it belonged, sticking out of Gregory's eye socket. Sweat gathered on her forehead and her palm stung. It was shocking how strenuous that had been, though she supposed she was to blame. A butter knife didn't make for a good weapon. But it felt more personal than the wrath of her obsidian mist. A fitting end for a man like him.

Flexing her aching wrist, she massaged the area as she called back her smoke. It soaked into her hot skin and she found she enjoyed its cool caress. Her head fell back, and she closed her eyes, taking a slow, deep breath. Savoring a rare lightness in her chest. She hoped Lillian would feel the same and Gregory's death became something cherished. A soothing balm when memories and panic threatened to pull her under.

When Mora opened her eyes she was met with a hushed crowd. It seemed the entire room gathered around her smoky dome. The bartender and the bulky doorman stood in the front, the former's hazel eyes widening, blood draining from his face. He turned and vomited, bile splashing against his shiny, black shoes. Then he ran, pushing through the crowd until Mora could no longer see him.

Mora snorted. *It seems he only needed to be* near *you to be ruined.* Shrieks and gasps filled the silence and one of the Ladies Gregory had been watching fainted. Mora opened her mouth to tell them they were better off without a rapist in their midst, but the doorman grabbed her, his huge hand wrapping around her forearm.

"Murderous, Forbidden filth," he spat as he dragged her away. Bruises bloomed under his crushing grip, but Mora didn't care. She didn't fight or offer a snarky retort, too focused on a pair of wide, mossy green eyes. Lillian stood in the doorway, sweat and tendrils of sandy blonde hair sticking to her brow, a pink flush staining her ivory cheeks. Her chest rose and fell quickly, like she'd been running for hours, searching for Mora and Gregory. As if the man deserved her concern.

The look of horror on Lillian's face made Mora's cheeks burn. But she lifted her chin and offered a cocky sneer, pushing against the discomfort. "You're welcome," she mouthed, a cold look in her eyes, before she exploded into a cloud of sparkling onyx and raced back to the manor.

CHAPTER 14

MORA

The room smelled divine, swathed in the refreshing aroma of roses, lilacs, and apple blossoms—there were flowers everywhere, from the bouquets on tables, to the garlands hanging on the walls. Though the apple tree behind the head table was Mora's favorite. Its flowering branches created a stunning canopy of pink blossoms she couldn't wait to sit under. Whoever dragged in the cement pot she'd grown the tree in, however, had her pity. Perhaps she should have offered to do it herself.

Oh well.

Mora leaned against the wall, sipping on wine and spying on the nobility. They seemed to enjoy the soothing music trickling down from the minstrel's gallery. A few swayed as they listened. It was a shame there wouldn't be a ball. The low candlelight flickering in the iron chandeliers gave the banquet hall an almost romantic feel, perfect for dancing in the arms of another.

Regardless, Mora was successful—Lord Frederick would be remembered fondly. She considered being kind and not humiliating him. Which surprised her. But killing Gregory scratched that itch. And, as much as she hated to admit it, Lord Frederick seemed innocent enough.

As she surveyed the nobles, she couldn't help but wonder who would be her next Keeper. She sized them up. Made mental notes in case she later found the information useful.

Knowledge was power. Especially when crafting someone's downfall.

Their chattering voices echoed throughout the space as they drank and nibbled on hors d'oeuvres and desserts. They were particularly fond of the chocolates, plucking them from the platter and returning for seconds after a single taste. The baker made another batch after all. Though perhaps not enough. Mora snickered and wondered if she could get away with emptying the plate.

Never mind, she thought with a sigh as the man from the library stumbled into the table. Though he looked impeccable, dressed in a knee-length, maroon dinner jacket, he was drunk. *Extremely*. He nearly tipped over but caught himself by smashing his hands onto the plate, crushing the desserts. Judging by the snide looks everyone made before returning to their conversations, this was a common occurrence. When he straightened, he stared at the mess he'd made and chuckled before wiping his hand on the tablecloth and sauntering away.

Mora's gaze traveled over his half-lidded gray eyes and the redness blooming on his cheeks. Would he be easy or difficult to destroy if he managed to snag her flask? He didn't seem phased by the judgment of his peers. Though he clearly had a problem. And like a rotten tree with gnarled branches and bleached bark, his problems had festering roots she could exploit.

Somehow, his cheeks grew redder when another man approached. Apparently, he cared about *someone's* opinion. Perhaps this was his half-brother?

The newcomer gave Mora his back, but she admired his royal blue waistcoat and the silver detailing along the trim. The colors reminded her of her family and a home that lived on in her memories. He'd rolled up his black sleeves to his elbows, displaying sun-kissed skin and corded muscles she found herself admiring. And there was a lovely shine to his chocolate brown hair. If only he'd turn around...

An arm snaked around her shoulders, and she stiffened. "Enjoying the festivities, Mora?" Lord Frederick asked.

"Yes, my lord." Mora tried to sound pleasant, but her words were flat. "Are you pleased?"

"Very much."

While his smile was anything but confident, Mora made certain he dressed handsomely. She'd crafted him an emerald tunic with delicate gold embroidery. The color brought out his green eyes—they practically sparkled. And he looked like the handsome noble he longed to be.

Swathed in a matching gown with gold beading along the bodice and a full, layered skirt, Mora was his perfect counterpart. It made a statement. One she wasn't too fond of as guests would interpret it as Frederick displaying his ownership over her. But it fulfilled his wish to be memorable. And she couldn't pass up another opportunity to wear something lavish.

Frederick released her from his hold and she almost sagged in relief as the tension bled from her shoulders. Her next breath felt fuller, the air more refreshing.

"My staff and I couldn't have done it without you." Frederick's voice softened. "Thank you, Mora."

Mora blinked. *What was with this man?* Her eyes roved over his face, looking for any sign of insidiousness, but she found none.

She managed a slight smile but said nothing.

When the silence grew awkward, Frederick cleared his throat and rubbed the back of his neck. "We'll dine shortly. I'd like to greet everyone first. Will you join me?"

Would she join him? As if she had a choice? He offered his arm and Mora took it, but she couldn't help but frown.

It had been a blur, parading around the room with Frederick. While Mora noted gleams of interest in many eyes, few bothered to bid her more than a polite hello. She knew what he was doing, showing her off. To those who knew of her, being Mora's Keeper was a sign of power, a declaration he belonged among them.

Temptation to drag her feet nipped at her heels, but she begrudgingly ignored it and remained obedient as he pulled her from guest to guest. She'd been a part of this song and dance many times, even *before*. The longer Mora lived, the more she understood her father's distaste for pageantry. The endless wave of haughty arrogance made her nauseous.

"And this is the lovely Mora," Frederick said after the necessary, hollow flatteries. He spoke highly of her, praising her work. But many introductions were followed by a barrage of grins, eager stares, and a mockery of purposeless questions directed at Frederick as if she weren't standing *right there*. Sometimes, greedy fingers clutched at her emerald skirt. Thankfully, those who dared to touch her never clung long. All it took was a glare, and they'd release her and step back.

It was funny how people explained away the stories in the hopes of gaining power. Those who were aware of her either assumed the hardships or deaths that befell many of her Keepers were coincidental or believed they could control her. Fools.

While it was no surprise everyone stared, Mora hated it. As she moved through the room, the weight of their eyes on her back clung to her like cobwebs. The more she tried to ignore it, the more the feeling stretched and expanded, seizing her senses. Her skin crawled, a wave of goosebumps skittering over her flesh. A bidding war had undoubtedly already begun.

What would they be willing to trade to get their hands on her? What would Frederick desire in return? It made her want to hate him. And yet she doubted she'd have a Keeper kind enough to thank her again for many years. Nor one who wished for things as simple as banquets and good connections.

And the next Keeper wouldn't have a Lillian. Mora pressed her lips together—Lillian would be pleased to see her gone.

She found herself wishing to stay. At least for a while. To spend her days ransacking the kitchen for sweets. To perhaps foster a friendship with Lillian if she could convince the woman to forgive her. It was unlikely, but the challenge would be interesting.

And, oh, to laze about the gardens or spend her nights curled up in the library, reading until her eyes ached. Wouldn't that be marvelous? A wistful sort of longing wrapped around her heart in tight coils. Though it wasn't heavy enough to distract her from the fury burning in her belly.

Frederick, despite all his kindness, would hand her over like she was nothing.

By the time they were seated, her feet ached and exhaustion threatened to drag her to the floor. She'd talked herself in and out of humiliating Frederick several times over. Mora sighed and fiddled with her fork as she stared at her plate. Roasted chicken and mashed potatoes swimming in gravy and greens drizzled with lemon demanded her attention. She'd outdone herself. The decadent, savory smell was inviting. But her mind was too loud; she couldn't focus on her hunger.

Frederick leaned in and whispered, "I'm sure you know there are many here who'd like your help once our time is done."

How Mora managed to hold back her grimace, she didn't know. Somehow she plastered on a hollow smirk and nodded instead.

Frederick smiled that sweet smile of his in return. "Let me know if there's someone you'd prefer. Or, if you'd like, you're welcome to stay."

Mora blinked several times, and her fork clattered, forgotten, on the table. She played back his words in her mind, over and over.

You're welcome to stay.

Welcome to stay.

Stay.

Frederick silently watched her, those kind, green eyes giving her visions of forest canopies and the welcoming scents of spruce and pine... was this real? Had she imagined it? Mora gripped the table-cloth, needing an anchor. "I—why?"

Placing his hand atop hers, Frederick's smile gentled. "You've been a huge help, Mora. I'd be happy to repay you. Think about it. We can discuss things further tonight."

Mora's gaze dropped to her plate, but she saw nothing at all as she attempted to process everything Frederick said. "I want to stay," she whispered, but the words were so quiet *she* barely heard them. And Frederick's attention had already been drawn elsewhere.

He'd pulled a note from his pocket, eyes roving over the scribbled words before he placed it on the table, stood, and cleared his throat. Clutching his goblet like a lifeline, he trembled, the wine nearly spilling. As he gazed at the crowd, his face paled.

From their seat at the front, they had the perfect view of the many circular tables around the room. No seats were left empty. Mora supposed it was a big group, though she'd seen bigger. She imagined Frederick hadn't and doubted he enjoyed being the center of attention. Or perhaps she was wrong. Perhaps a fear of failure had him standing there, frozen. Regardless, if he didn't wish to appear weak, he needed to either sit or speak before someone noticed.

Mora took a swig of her honey wine before she grabbed her fork. Clinking the cutlery against the goblet, she nudged Frederick. "Our lord would like to make a speech," she called out. His eyes widened, redness staining his pale cheeks, but she admired how quickly he schooled his features.

Facing the crowd, he took a quick, steadying breath and began to speak. "Thank you, esteemed guests, for gracing me with your presence. In six short months, I've been fortunate enough to form strong bonds with many of you. I hope to have the opportunity to form more. You've welcomed me into your community and it is my sincerest wish this gathering serve as an offering of gratitude and friendship—"

Frederick droned on and on, his speech too sincere for the crowd of vipers he'd welcomed into his den. In all his earnestness, he'd told them he desired their acceptance, something they could exploit for their own gains. Clearly, Frederick didn't know the rules—to bare your soul was to court your downfall. While he may buy himself some respect tonight, if he didn't harden his heart they would eat him alive.

Tuning out his dull, driveling speech, Mora took in the crowd. It was a relief, being free of the weight of their attention. And she was fascinated by how much the fashions evolved over the centuries. While some things never changed—Mora noted the way many women pinned their hair back in delicate buns, no different from her mother's preferred style—their necklines dove deeper and deeper by the decade. She took mental notes, dreaming of the next gown she'd create.

The inebriated man from earlier caught her attention. He sat in the back. Well, sat was a generous way of putting it—he slumped forward, his head resting on the table, eyes closed. Mora almost pitied him. Whoever sat beside him drummed their fingers on the table, the flickering candlelight glinting off their ring. It almost reminded her of...

Mora's stomach dropped as the pearly white gem swiveled inside its casing until it revealed a horrific pitch-black void she knew all too well. It locked onto her and the blood drained from her face.

Her eyes roved up a muscular arm, barely glancing at the royal blue waistcoat she'd admired earlier, until they landed on what she already knew she'd find. What she dreaded more than anything.

Blinding azure eyes.

An imposing smile graced his lips as he watched her fall apart.

He's dead.

Frederick's voice was far away, and the edges of her vision blurred. The man raised his eyebrows in challenge and Mora felt the room shrink, walls pressing in on her. She summoned the memory of Dother's blood dripping down her arms, soaking her hair, her dress, his sheets. It usually calmed her, pulled her from the misery haunting her mind. And yet...

He's dead.

Those bright blue eyes ensnared her, a ravenous gleam sparkling in their depths. Chocolate brown hair tickled his forehead. The same color as...

HE'S DEAD!

He tipped his cup in a silent cheers for the things to come and Dother's voice boomed in her mind.

You'll never be rid of me, not truly.

CHAPTER 15

MORA

Mora curled her shaking hands into fists as panic twisted around her throat and squeezed, leaving her gasping. She wheezed with each labored breath and felt Frederick's eyes shift to her, concern painting his face. But she couldn't pull her gaze away from those horrific azure eyes, couldn't stop the flood of memories that came with that stare.

You're finally understanding, Treasure. You were always going to be mine.

Oh gods, no. She couldn't do this. Couldn't stand the memory of his voice. Couldn't endure one more second trapped under the weight of his stare. And if he touched her... *please, no.*

He'd come for her. And Dother would stop at nothing until he got what he wanted.

But... was it him? It couldn't be. No one could survive what Mora had done. There was so much blood. She could still feel it cooling on her skin, his death enveloping her like armor. That night saved her and damned her all at once, and she'd do it again, a thousand times over.

It had been *centuries* since she'd watched him take his last breath. Yet, there he was, Dother's Ghost in the flesh, with an avaricious grin while he twisted his ring around and around his finger. Savoring every second of her misery.

He couldn't have her. Not again. Never again.

It was overwhelming, the urge to run—her limbs shook with the surge of adrenaline. But running was pointless. Mora wouldn't get far. Not with Frederick's wish shackling her to this room. She could force herself to endure the agony of a wish tearing her apart, blood, bone, and flesh, until she heeded its call, but it hardly mattered—she was bound to her flask. And it wouldn't be difficult for someone to find, stashed in the lord's bedside table.

Mora flinched when Frederick's hand landed on her shoulder.

"Are you all right?" he asked, brows furrowing. His words were muffled, as if she had been plunged under water, drowning silently while *he* watched.

If she managed to avoid his clutches tonight, he'd come for her. Frederick could refuse to hand her over—he would if she asked, she felt it in her bones. But the lord's days would be numbered—Dother's Ghost would kill him to get to her.

Unless...

If I end Dother's Ghost, Frederick will be memorable, she reasoned, but the wish disagreed. Frigid tendrils of smoke bubbled under her skin and crawled along her chest, slipping between muscle and sinew, until they curled around her ribcage. In a blink, they'd cinched themselves tight, crushing everything in their ethereal grasp. The little air she'd managed to inhale was forced from her lungs. Mora winced, gritting her teeth until her jaw cracked under the pressure. Of course it couldn't be this easy. Black spots crowded her vision and her lungs burned. Until the wish's furious hold eased. Gasping for air, she stumbled until she slammed her hands on the table to prevent herself from falling.

"Mora!" Frederick cried as he tried to steady her. Her palms slipped through hot gravy and mashed potatoes, squishing between her fingers. She stared at the mess, chest heaving. While the lord rubbed her back, she came to a sickening realization.

Mora managed to glance at Frederick's face, admiring the splash of freckles along his cheeks and over the bridge of his nose. And that beautiful red hair... like Philip, he was a good man. He deserved better than this. But she was monstrous enough to pay any price.

A branch from the apple tree seemed to sense her trepidation—it swayed toward her, tickling her cheek with its soft blossoms. Mora closed her eyes and inhaled the sweet, floral aroma. Frederick continued to rub her back, ignorant of the power thrumming within her, eager to be released upon the room—it took no issue with this plan. And she saw no other way.

If Dother's Ghost lived through the night, he'd walk away knowing that to hold her flask was to court his demise.

Mora prayed that would be enough.

Trickles of cool smoke flowed from her palms, slipping through the mess of food and spilling onto the floor. They slithered toward the apple tree, creeping up the onyx pot until they splashed onto the damp soil. Mora felt when her mist curled around the tree's roots, coaxing them to grow. They stretched in the dirt, pushing deeper and deeper, until they pressed up against the cement. Cracks spread over the pot, bits of soil leaking to the floor below as ferocious roots forced their way through.

More onyx mist curled around the trunk, racing up into the branches. Wood stretched, like a babe awakening from a restful sleep, and reached for the ceiling.

The tree creaked as it expanded, startling Frederick. His hand stilled on Mora's back, and he turned in time to watch the pot shatter.

"Mora... what's happening?"

Mora's face hardened, and she smothered the flickers of empathy threatening to erupt in her heart. "I'm granting your wish," she said flatly.

Frederick's eyes widened when the voracious branches began to claw at the high ceiling. "I don't understand?"

The structure groaned against the intrusion, earning a gasp from the crowd, and fissures skittered across the beams. Within a breath, chunks of wood rained down, plopping onto their plates. Bits of food splattered on Mora's dress, sullying the emerald fabric. Frederick shrieked and jumped back, but the tree's now massive trunk gave him little space to move.

"Mora, stop!" Frédérick shouted. She offered him no answer and instead lost herself in the cool caress of her smoke. It rose up from her pores, enveloping her in its chilling embrace. Frederick finally saw her for the monster she was, wrapped in writhing shadows, amber eyes aglow.

The ground beneath their feet rumbled under the weight of the ever-growing tree, and Mora stumbled as it dipped toward the trunk. But a branch swooped down and steadied her.

Odd. She hadn't asked it to do that...

The music stopped, but screams bounced around the room, creating a new sort of melody. One that sang to the rage living in Mora's heart. Panic flooded the air, thick enough that she tasted it with every breath. Chairs squealed over the white tiles as people jumped from their seats and ran to the door. Some would live to *remember*. But many weren't fast enough.

More debris fell from the ceiling, and Mora watched a large chunk strike a woman's head, blood spraying from the wound. She fell to the ground, motionless, mouth open in a silent shriek, before she was trampled by the frenzied crowd. Hot wax rained down on them as the chandelier tipped—it wouldn't be long before it fell. And vicious roots broke through the floor, curling around a few unlucky ankles.

Fractures raced across the tiles, slabs shifting before breaking apart. The center of the room became a voracious maw, swallowing those who were unfortunate enough to be stuck there. Loud, wet thuds reverberated through the space as bodies hit the cement floor below.

"Dear gods, Mora!" Frederick wailed, his grip biting her shoulders. He shook her, begging her to stop, but she pushed harder against her magic. "Why are you doing this?"

A sardonic smile tipped up Mora's lips, and she shrugged. "You asked to be memorable."

"I didn't ask for this," Frederick cried, a tear spilling down his cheek. His pleading eyes found hers, but she wouldn't be moved.

Another slab of wood crashed down on the crowd, followed by more screams. Those who remained were trapped, boxed in by debris and the hole in the floor. Mora couldn't find Dother's Ghost among them. But she *felt* his eyes, watching, assessing, and knew if she looked, he'd be standing at a safe distance in the doorway. *Gods be damned.*

Frederick whimpered when the tree trunk reached them. "I wish for you to stop this, now!"

Mora clicked her tongue and shook her head. At this moment, she had no Keeper. The last person to touch her flask was Lillian, and she'd already made three demands. "You're not my Keeper anymore, Frederick. There will be no more wishes."

"What?" The blood drained from his face.

"Someone else grabbed the flask since you last made a wish. You should have hidden it a little better."

Plump apples rained down all around them, wet pulp exploding as they smashed against what remained of the floor. Mora reached out to flick a piece of apple pulp from Frederick's cheek, but he recoiled. "But you made your wish, and I'm fulfilling it. They will always remember you. Isn't that what you wanted?"

Mora wasn't surprised when he pushed her and scrambled over their table in a fruitless effort to escape. Before her back connected with the rough bark of the trunk, she tore at the thread in her chest and released herself to the smoke.

Flying through the room, Mora circled the chandelier, giving it the last push it needed to tear from the ceiling. It landed with a deafening crash, crushing a table under its weight. Bodies lay mangled beneath, half buried in rubble, while trapped bystanders backed further toward the wall, wailing. Flames from the chandelier's candles caressed the ivory silk tablecloth, creeping over the fabric, eager to devour.

Frederick crawled on the floor, bits of wood and broken tableware slicing his palms, his manor falling apart all around him. A slop of meat, greens, and apple pulp stained his breeches. The floor shook, groaning as the foundation shifted, and Frederick sobbed along with it.

Mora swooped down, surrounding him in a sea of glittering darkness. Icy smoke curled over his limbs, tethering him in place. She could feel him shaking beneath her ethereal grip.

"Please stop," he cried, pulling against her with all his might. It was of no use. Red patches painted his tear-stained cheeks and his ruddy hair stuck to his sweaty forehead. "Please, please, Mora. Don't do this. Please let me go," he begged. "I'll do anything."

The tree continued to expand, consuming the great hall. Its roots found purchase in the earth, and the canopy tore through the upper floors until it found the sky. Moonlight shone down on the chaos, the soft light at odds with the horror Mora created.

A plague of embers licked up the walls, fumes billowing into the night sky, and rubble tumbled downward like a furious hailstorm. Frederick flinched as pieces of debris crashed to the ground around him. Otherwise, the room quieted, and Mora wondered if she and Frederick were all that remained. But she could still feel the weight of those azure eyes.

Thick, coarse bark scratched against Frederick's shoes as the enormous trunk reached them once more. He twisted and tugged against his bindings, screaming when they wouldn't give. The tree's surface was crawling with smoke that sang a song only it could hear, coaxing it to grow bigger and bigger. With a thought from Mora, it stilled and the rumbling floor settled. For a moment, it seemed the madness was over.

Frederick took one sharp, shuddering breath. Then another. And another. A mass of glittering onyx came together into a vaguely human shape, and Mora's piercing amber gaze peeked out from the shadows. He stared up at it, watery eyes wide and pleading. Her heart panged, and she hesitated, her grip on him loosening.

A spark of hope lit up his face. "Mora, please."

Mora pushed back against the scraps that remained of her humanity and adjusted her grip before lifting him from the ground. He dangled in the air, feet kicking against an apathetic wall of smoke. Obsidian claws formed along the mist covering the tree trunk and dug into the bark. They gripped its surface, straining until the trunk peeled open, revealing the heartwood nestled at its center.

Snot and tears ran down Frederick's face, and his entire body shook. "Why?" he asked, voice hoarse. He was met with a cold stare.

Frederick's back smacked against the heartwood as Mora shoved him into the tree, peeled bark marring his skin. His bones groaned under the pressure and he hissed out a pained breath. The bark curled around his body, knitting itself back together. His mouth fell open, but no sounds escaped as he watched his feet disappear into the tree.

Returning his haunted gaze to the onyx smoke undulating in front of him, Frederick pleaded once more. "Please, please no!" He hiccupped between sobs but forced himself to go on. "Oh gods, Mora, don't do this!" Frederick's fingers curled around the bark, trying desperately to pull himself free, but black mist tightened against his wrists, pressing him deeper into the trunk. Bark met his neck and his wails grew louder.

Goodbye, Frederick.

His whimpers echoed through the room until they were consumed by a sudden, horrifying silence. But there, in the trunk of a giant apple tree, was the outline of a man, face contorted in an endless scream, hands pushing hopelessly against the wood.

Mora flew up the tree, curling over the bark and twisting through the branches. Only time could claim the tree's life. It would fall to no axe, succumb to no fire, and Frederick would be remembered. By those present today. And by those who would come to discover his arborous tomb.

Like he wished, Mora thought. But for once she took no pride in what she'd done.

CHAPTER 16

LILLIAN

It took Lillian five long minutes to convince herself to move. She stared up at Lord Frederick's manor, her eyes wide despite the ash tumbling from the sky like fat flakes of black snow. It coated her hair and stained her cheeks. There was already an ache in her lungs and an acrid taste coating her tongue. Yet she stood, frozen, wondering if she were dreaming.

An inferno devoured the building, eating away at her home, her work, her mother fucking life. That alone was enough. But of course there was more. Because standing tall and proud, watching over the flames, was a tree. A giant, gods damned apple tree. Bigger than an apple tree had any right to be—it had torn a good portion of the manor apart. Large pieces of the roof collapsed inward, along with a chunk of the top floor's brick façade. Between the thick wisps of billowing smoke, she could make out glimpses of the mess that awaited her inside.

There could only be one reason for this madness... Mora.

Lillian clutched her apron, twisting the fabric around her fingers. She'd be a fool to go inside. But...

She barely had time to turn her head before she vomited in the grass, bits of bile staining her dress. Coughing against the burn in her throat, she tried to push images of Gregory aside. The bloody socket, the butter knife, the chunks of eye that...

Nope.

Lillian gagged once more and spit out the sour saliva flooding her mouth.

Foolish or not, she couldn't let a demon like Mora hurt anyone else.

Shit. I'm really doing this.

Lillian forced one foot in front of the other, ignoring the way her legs shook. She must have been in a daze because she hadn't registered the garden as she neared the servant's entrance. The door swung open, cracking against the brick, and Lillian stumbled as a sea of panicked people raced through the exit. Some wept, fear shining brightly in their eyes. And the words she picked up among their terrified chattering had her aching to turn back.

She's a monster!

She killed them! Oh gods, did you see? She fucking killed them.

Did Frederick get out? Has anyone seen him?

Why had the Fates placed *her* of all people in Mora's path? They must have been having a laugh. Lillian was a nobody. A cook from a small fishing village no one bothered to think about. The need to turn and run was overwhelming. She trembled like a leaf clinging to a tree on a late autumn day. But she couldn't live with herself if she did nothing.

They barely acknowledged her as she pushed through them, until Ren's deep brown eyes landed on her face. He grabbed her arm, staining her sleeve with flour, and pulled her with him toward the exit. "Lillian! When I didn't see you, I thought..."

"Crap," Lillian muttered under her breath. She pulled against his steely grip. "I have to go inside." Her tone was far too harsh, but there was no time for pleasantries.

Ren staggered back, nearly swept away by the crowd. "Are you mad?"

Probably, she thought, with a bitter chuckle. Instead, she said, "I'll explain later, I promise. You have to let me go."

He gave her an incredulous look and shook his head, but his hold loosened. Lillian didn't give him, or herself, a moment to question her decision. Pulling away, she waded through a sea of workers and nobles alike, wondering if she'd ever see him again.

Lillian rested her hands on her knees and coughed, but it did nothing to clear her lungs. Each breath invited a thick, bitter smog into her airway. If it weren't for the outside air swirling through the upper hall, she would have suffocated by now. She winced when the ceiling groaned and forced herself to push ahead. Each step felt more and more foolish than the last. It didn't take long for her to find the curve in the hall that led to the lord's chambers. To think, it had been mere hours since Mora dragged her there and knocked on the door like a maniac. It felt like a lifetime ago.

Her stomach dropped when she reached Lord Frederick's rooms. The ceiling had partially collapsed, pushed aside by ravenous branches. It blocked half of the damn door. As if today hadn't already been enough of an ordeal.

Lillian crawled on the emerald carpet, blinking against the sweat dripping down her forehead and into her eyes. The space between the debris and the door was big enough she could fit her arm through. It would be a tight squeeze. But what choice did she have? She took a breath, ignoring the way her hands shook, and eased her arm through the crack. A flash of pain made her gasp as sharp pieces of broken wood sliced through her sleeve, tearing at the skin underneath. Blood welled up and soaked the torn fabric.

"I swear, if Mora says a word about this," she mumbled to the air. Not that Mora gave two shits if Lillian protested.

When her sweat-soaked fingers found the knob, she nearly cried. The hard part was almost over.

Or perhaps this is the easy part, her anxiety whispered. Damn those whispers to hell.

Pulling herself into Lord Frederick's chambers, she bolted through the foyer and into the bedroom. Funny, it didn't seem daunting now. Her heart ached when she spied his rumpled poet shirt tossed onto the bed. Did he make it out?

Lillian shrieked as she tore the drawer open, tears streaming down her cheeks. She told herself they were a side effect of the smoke, but she was lying. Coins, papers, useless trinkets and a worn journal fell to her feet, along with that fucking flask. Lillian stared down at the empty vessel, chewing her bottom lip.

Mora killed a man because of her. Gregory's blood would always be on her hands. What he'd done to her was unforgivable, but this wasn't what Lillian wanted... Mora, however, reveled in it. When she'd emerged from that cloud of cursed darkness, she was at peace. Eyes closed and at ease as blood dripped from her fingers and splattered onto the gore at her feet. Until she saw Lillian's disapproval. In a blink, her face hardened, rage glinting in her eerie eyes. Had that fueled Mora to do more? Did Frederick's blood stain Lillian's hands too?

No. Mora did this. Lillian wouldn't carry her fucking sins.

Lillian picked up Mora's flask, scowling at the filigree. Moonlight glinted off the gilded daisies, the golden petals sparkling. They almost looked real. Something that housed a murderer had no right to be that beautiful.

"Mora," she called, shaking the flask. She held her breath and waited for that horrid black torrent to come twisting around her again. Nothing happened. "Mora!" she shrilled once more, glaring at the bottle.

"Fuck," Lillian screamed as she flung the flask across the room. It slammed into the wall, chipping the paint, before bouncing on the carpet and rolling to a stop. "Guess you have no interest in speaking to me now, demon," she seethed. "I wish I never met you."

The manor groaned as it fought to stay standing, followed by the bang of more rubble falling in the hall. Lillian's stomach churned at the sound—she needed to get out. Now. With or without Mora.

At least she had her flask. That would have to be enough.

Lillian released a frustrated breath through her nose and nudged the flask with her foot, half expecting Mora to materialize and torment her. She could already imagine the tense look of disapproval on her face and how she'd corral Lillian, demanding she take back her words. Once again, however, Mora didn't appear. And why would she? She'd already taken everything.

Lillian scooped up the flask and fled the room, praying the manor would stay standing until she was safely outside.

CHAPTER 17

LILLIAN

A sudden gust of wind wrapped Lillian in its chilling embrace, coaxing goosebumps to rise on her flesh. She shivered and hugged herself tighter, ignoring the throbbing sting in her arm. Moonlight skittered over the ice on the lake up ahead, but otherwise, she was shrouded in darkness.

A branch snapped to her right and Lillian spun in the dark, searching for the source. "Hello?" she whispered, clutching the flask tighter. Her muscles tensed, ready to run, but she took a slow, deep breath and told herself it must have been an animal.

"This is the last thing I expected."

"Fucking shit!" Lillian turned and swung the flask blindly. It whooshed through the air, snapping a thin branch in half. But Mora sidestepped the attack and arched a brow.

"Were you planning on hitting me with my own flask?" She smirked, but there was no joy in it. "That seems a bit rude."

Lillian scoffed and stormed toward the lake. The glimmering water felt like a boon, beckoning her forward and promising this would soon be over. Not that she knew what came next. There was nothing to return to. A soft patch of moss cushioned her steps, and she wondered if it would make a decent spot to rest for the night. She was unlikely to find better for a while.

"You don't deserve my kindness."

"After everything I've done for you?" Mora asked with mock surprise.

"After everything you've *done*." Lillian looked over her shoulder, expecting to find an amber gaze sparkling with a simmering mixture of rage and amusement. No one was there. She squinted, searching the shadowy brush for any sign of the demon. Where the hell had she gone?

Fuck it. She wasn't interested in Mora's games.

When she turned back, she shrieked. Mora now stood directly in her path, arms crossed, glittering onyx mist coating her skin. She'd twisted around her in a blink without disturbing a single twig. "Gods!" Lillian pressed a hand to her chest, trying to calm her fluttering heart. "Can you stop doing that?"

"You're being foolish," Mora said dryly as her smoke disappeared. Her narrowed eyes swept over Lillian, assessing. She frowned at Lillian's bloody arm, but if she had any qualms, she didn't speak them. When her focus landed on the flask, Lillian held her breath.

Her grip tightened around the bottle's neck. "I'm doing what must be done," Lillian muttered, steeling herself. The lake wasn't far. She could try to run. Though, if it came down to it, she couldn't take Mora in a fight.

The tension loosened in Lillian's shoulders when Mora nodded and looked away. "I don't care about that." She picked a leaf from the nearest tree and spun it around idly in her fingers. "You gave a demon your back. *That's* foolish."

Was that meant to be a gods damned threat? Whatever relief Lillian felt withered and died. "Why?" A fire blazed under her skin. She couldn't explain what came over her, but she reached out and crushed Mora's leaf in her palm. She was either a fool like Mora said or un-fucking-believably brave. Lillian couldn't decide which. Wasn't sure she wanted to know. But, as she stared Mora down, she hoped she looked somewhat intimidating. "Are you going to kill me too?"

Surprise flared in Mora's bright eyes, her fingers curling into tight fists. "Only if you deserve it."

"Did you kill Lord Frederick?"

"He asked to be memorable," she said bluntly. "I granted his wish."

Something was off in her tone... Lillian took a moment to truly take her in. The emerald gown she wore was opulent, the rich color complementing the golden undertones in her brown skin. But the bodice was sullied with smears of food and peppered with dust. A familiar hardness painted her expression, but she was tense, her gaze haunted.

Swallowing against the lump in her throat, Lillian spoke the words she dreaded but knew to be true. "You killed him."

Mora cocked her head to the side, the motion stiff and animalistic. "Surely you aren't surprised?"

"No," Lillian muttered.

Flashes of a bloody butter knife and a ravaged eye socket flooded her mind, only this time the mangled face was that of the kind lord. Bile burned in her throat and her mouth flooded with saliva. Lillian gagged, but almost nothing came up—there was little left in her stomach. It irritated her lungs, and she found herself bent over, gripping the smooth bark of the nearest tree as coughs rattled in her chest.

A hand gently ran over her back and Lillian closed her eyes. She could still taste the smoke and wondered if it festered in her lungs. If it would somehow linger forever. When the coughing stopped, spittle clung to her chin, dripping in long strings onto the dirt. She stared down at the mess and grimaced before wiping her face with her sleeve. Each inhale cleared her mind, that same steady hand a needed comfort. Mora's hand...

What the fuck was she doing, letting Mora comfort her? She reared back, slipping on the moist earth as she attempted to distance herself. Mora rolled her eyes and reached out to steady her, but Lillian backed away further. "Stay the hell away from me!"

Mora sighed, but she held her hands up and nodded. "Whatever you say."

"You've ruined everything," she spat.

Mora plucked what Lillian assumed were bits of potato off her bodice and flicked them into the brush. "Your world fell apart before I walked into it, Lillian. I believe we can thank Gregory," she said coolly. "Which reminds me, you're welcome for fixing that."

That simmering heat under her skin rose to a boil, and she took one unwise step closer to the demon. She glared, certain Mora could see the fire in her eyes. "I didn't want any of this!" The vehemence in her voice surprised her. It twisted around her words, giving them a harsh edge. Yet they failed to have any bite.

Mora didn't balk. There was no glimmer of surprise or disappointment. She simply shrugged, stone-faced. "You may come to appreciate it."

Appreciate it?

Had she lost her mind?

Memories of the gore smeared on Gregory's face haunted her. There was no future where Lillian appreciated what Mora had done. No possibility she'd be grateful for the blood now staining her soul. "What makes you think I'll ever appreciate this?"

Mora averted her gaze and her voice became soft and quiet. "A dead man can't hurt you."

The sorrow in her words sent a sharp pang through Lillian's heart, dousing some of her rage. She looked down at the flask and frowned. Was this the right thing? A light wind blew through the trees, rustling the leaves and blanketing them in a new wave of smoke. Behind them, the manor burned and fell apart under the watch of a giant apple tree. And Lord Frederick, a kind, innocent man, was dead.

Guilt coated her throat, so thick she wondered if she'd choke on it. If she could handle having *this* on her conscience as well. But Mora was dangerous and something needed to be done.

Before she could say a word, Mora broke the silence. "I know you're going to toss my flask in the lake."

Lillian's jaw tensed. She clutched the flask to her chest, caging it in her arms. There were a few trees standing between her and the water, their thick roots snaking through the earth. She prayed they wouldn't trip her if she needed to bolt.

Before Lillian could shift on her feet, Mora laughed. It was dry and bitter and did nothing to soothe Lillian's nerves. "It's funny you think you could outrun me. If I wanted to stop you, I already would have."

Lillian blinked. Of course Mora could overpower her if she wanted to. Why hadn't she? "You want me to do this?"

Heaving a sigh through her nose, Mora turned her gaze toward the water. "It's for the best."

The golden plants decorating the flask sparkled in the darkness, and Lillian found herself staring at them. An otherworldliness emanated from the bottle and she wondered... was it homey inside? Or would it be torturous to rot behind a wall of glass, stuck to the muck at the bottom of the lake? Because that's what Lillian assumed. Mora was bound to the flask; she'd sink along with it. "Why?"

Of course Mora didn't offer an answer, that would be too simple. Instead, she unbuckled her pouch and grabbed a piece of stolen chocolate. Examining the candy with a smile, she chuckled when a crow landed on the branch above, cawing as if they hoped for a piece. Mora stared up at the creature, before popping the entire thing in her mouth and closing her eyes. The grin on her face was small but genuine, lighting up her soft features.

As the silence stretched between them, Lillian wondered if she intended to speak again. Or if she waited for Lillian to have the guts to toss her bottle into the water.

Mora hummed as the chocolate melted on her tongue. Her fingers grazed the opening of her leather pouch and she pursed her lips before dipping in to grab another.

Lillian cleared her throat. "Did you hear me?"

Mora exhaled a frustrated breath, dropped the chocolate back inside, and closed her pouch. "You have your reasons, I have mine."

"Mine is because you're a monster."

Lillian could have sworn Mora flinched. "You're right, I am. But I promise there are far worse monsters than me."

Careful not to snag her foot on a root, Lillian marched to the shore. "I somehow doubt that," she muttered. Though not quietly enough.

Twigs and old leaves crunched under Mora's shoes as she rushed to walk by Lillian's side. "Who do you think made me this way, Lillian?"

Memories of Mora's shadowed gaze, the tenseness in her shoulders at an unexpected touch, and her reluctance to talk about her past arose. "Who cursed you?"

Together they emerged from the trees and were bathed in the gentle light of the moon. Mora tipped her head up, admiring the glittering night sky. "Don't worry about it." She looked to Lillian, her gaze tired and bleak. "What's important is they never find me."

Lillian fiddled with the flask as she sat on the cold earth. The pang in her heart intensified, but it wasn't enough. She cringed as she spoke, knowing the words to be true but feeling like an ass, nonetheless. "I hope no one finds you."

"Hope is fruitless. Someone always finds me eventually." Mora adjusted her skirt and sat by Lillian's side. "For what it's worth, Lillian, I'm glad our paths crossed. I've enjoyed my time with you."

"I..." Lillian scrambled for the right words. There was something about Mora she liked. Something that compelled her to ask her for help. But now two men were dead and Lillian's livelihood burned at their backs.

"It's ok. I know the feeling isn't mutual. I ruined everything, remember?"

Lillian swallowed against the thickening guilt in her throat. Cold mud soaked into her dress and she shivered, knowing she needed to end this and find a place to curl up and sleep. But she hesitated.

Water sloshed as Mora toed a piece of ice. "I can't say I'm excited about spending gods know how long at the bottom of a lake. I'm sure you've gathered I'll be stuck until the next Keeper stumbles upon me?"

Lillian nodded, unable to meet Mora's eyes.

She shrugged. "It's better than the alternative." She gazed at Lillian, a sad smile gracing her face. "I have no Keeper and the flask is calling. Go ahead, I'm ready."

Before she could think better of it, Lillian chucked the flask as far as she could. Her heart sputtered the moment it hit the water with a resounding plunk, droplets splashing into the air. Dropping her empty hands to her side, she gave Mora an apologetic look. Mora shook her head and gently squeezed Lillian's hand.

Then the demon exploded into a dark, ominous cloud and swirled through the air. Curling around Lillian, she enveloped her in that endless torrent of glittering obsidian, but now all Lillian felt was awe—it was as if, for a moment, she floated among the midnight sky, wrapped in the embrace of a sea of tiny, twinkling stars.

The cool smoke pulled away as it glided over the lake, plunging deep into the depths below. And Lillian found herself utterly alone.

"Goodbye, Mora," she whispered to the night. But this time, no one whispered back.

CHAPTER 18

MORA

T he worst part about months in a flask was the ache in Mora's bones. They cracked as she stretched, tipping her head back and reaching her arms up toward the sky. It was beautiful, painted with a scattering of pink and violet over a deep blue canvas that blackened by the moment. Wispy clouds curled in the atmosphere like playful ribbons. And a cool breeze pushed through the warm air, dampening the burdensome summer heat.

Magic tugged on her chest, demanding she greet her new Keeper. It was strange, warmer than usual, and focused over her heart. Mora rubbed the spot, willing the ache to go away. A slow, deep breath grounded her, and she did her best to school her features into what she hoped was a placid, approachable expression.

"Keeper of the flask. My power is yours to command," she said as she turned to face them. "How may I—" Her words dried up in her throat. "You!" she seethed, eyes widening.

The same lightly tanned, olive-toned hand that once held a blade to her throat clutched her flask so tightly his knuckles were stark white. And those arms... she'd glimpsed them before, but it was worse than she imagined. They were marred by a plethora of scars that clambered over one another, as if eager to mark him. Water dripped from his raven black hair, over sharp cheekbones and down his bare, sculpted chest. Mora's heart fluttered as she watched a drop slide over his hard abs. When it soaked into his black breeches, she shook her head, breaking the spell.

He sneered, sullying his beautiful face, and she hated that she had to hold back a whimper. That, already, he had an effect on her. Mora pushed back against the panic sparking in her belly and marched toward him. Somehow she managed to stare down her nose at him, despite him towering over her. His eyes narrowed as she neared, and a quiet growl rumbled in his chest.

"What the hell are you doing here?" Mora hissed.

The muscles in his jaw feathered, and he pushed his wet hair away from his forehead. It was different, sheared short on the sides with some messy length on the top. But it was him. She'd never forgotten the Fae from the alley centuries ago. The role he played in her downfall.

Oh gods... was Dother's Ghost here?

Mora's eyes darted over the deepening shadows in the trees. An owl trilled in the distance and she startled, earning a mocking chuckle from her Keeper.

"Is he here?" she asked softly. Despite the calming, fresh summer air dancing in her hair and the wide open space, it felt as if the world was shrinking around her, pressing against her flesh.

Breathe, she pleaded with herself. *Don't look weak.*

Mora poured all the fury she could into her stare and glared at him. He raised an apathetic brow before looking away, completely dismissing her.

"I know you were working with him," she spat. The throbbing sting in her palms as she dug her nails into her skin was a welcomed distraction. Though she still trembled—even her legs shook. Hopefully he hadn't noticed. "That night when you... it was part of his plan."

The Fae's upper lip twitched, and he scoffed, the sound low and gravelly. But he didn't utter a single word.

"That's it then? You're going to stand there, brood and say nothing?" she asked, hugging herself tighter.

Those dark eyes raked over her, flecks of glittering gold swirling in their depths. They were like a glimpse of the darkest night sky, beautiful despite the sadness lingering there. "Did you really think I'd have something to say to you, Little Witch?"

Mora stiffened. "Are you kidding me? *I* should have nothing to say to *you*."

"And yet you keep talking." The Fae had the nerve to roll his eyes.

The pounding of her pulse felt like a war drum. Dry mud cracked beneath her shoes as she closed the space between them, but the closeness made her feel smaller. And his mint and summer rain scent... she hated that she loved it. His nostrils flared, and he took a single step back, grimacing.

The Fae's gaze flicked to her flask, and he ran his thumb over one of the golden flowers. "You don't deserve these."

"Excuse me?"

The look on his face became murderous as he bared his teeth, revealing a pair of sharp canines. "They're wasted on you."

Wasted on her? What was his problem?

"I never asked for any of this!" She threw her hands in the air as she shrieked. It was as if he pulled on an invisible thread in her chest. Not the one she was used to, that she could pluck if she wanted to dive into her immense well of power. No, this was different. It was tethered to her heart, tugging her most intense emotions to the surface. Her cheeks felt hot and her hands shook for a whole new reason. His face was the perfect home for her fist.

All he did was smirk and turn toward the trees, motioning for her to follow. What choice did she have but to obey? He had her flask.

As they entered the brush, the trees awakened. Oaks, maples, and pines stretched in his direction, the closest branches gently touching his shoulders. He seemed unbothered. The Fae never wavered from his path and paid them no mind. Over and over again, they attempted to get his attention, stilling when he was out of reach. The darkness swallowed him as he hurried through the thicket. And suddenly Mora found herself alone.

Alone while the shadows crawled toward her as the sun slipped away. Alone with the thoughts clawing at her mind. With the memory of Frederick's screams and pleas for mercy. And the way her skin crawled under the watchful stare of those azure eyes.

The thought of that gaze made her freeze. A few tears slid down her cheeks before tumbling to the ground. She knew every step brought her closer to *him*.

Which meant, in murdering an innocent man, all she'd managed to do was buy herself a season.

Mora wiped at the moisture staining her face and willed herself to be numb. Her stupid heart wouldn't listen. It thrashed in her chest, as if it hoped to escape, with or without her, sputtering when she forced her heavy feet forward. There was little she could do. She followed the pull of her flask, knowing where her Keeper went.

He took no issue with her lagging behind. When she emerged into what was once a beautiful garden, the Fae was nowhere to be found.

The yard was a display of death and decay, swathed in the acrid scent of Mora's sins. It blended with the sickly, sweet aroma of rotten apples. Pieces of the decaying fruit littered the path along with dry stems and blackened leaves, crunching and squishing under her feet. And with each step, she came closer and closer to the manor, forced to face the aftermath of her rashness.

Mora swallowed as she stared up at the enormous apple tree. It seemed to look down on her, shaking off the bits of rubble still clinging to its bark. In the low light, the leaves matched Frederick's eyes. She averted her gaze and kept moving, knowing she deserved whatever came next.

Desperate sobs cut through the silence, slicing a piece of Mora's already heavy heart. It came from up ahead, where she sensed her flask. A loud smack reverberated through the night and the sobbing ceased. It was deafening, that quiet. Because Mora knew exactly who cried in the distance.

They had Lillian.

CHAPTER 19

MORA

Mora pressed against the soot-stained bricks and squeezed her eyes shut. Her stomach was in knots and the world spun—it was an effort not to gasp for air, but she couldn't afford to lose herself to the panic.

She took a slow, deep breath and listened.

Two people bickered around the corner, while Lillian sniffled. She recognized the Fae's voice. It was distinct, deep and raspy, with whispers of melancholy weaved into the sound.

"He told us not to hurt her, Halvard."

"*Lord* Halvard. And I do not remember him giving you permission to order me around."

The man from the library... Mora took another steadying breath. She had many questions. And wanted no answers. If it were up to her, she'd still be in her flask, stuck in the sediment at the bottom of the lake.

"I've told you every-fucking-thing I know. Let me go." Lillian's voice wobbled as she spoke and it was enough to force Mora out of her head. She dared a step forward, pulling away from the safety of the wall.

Lillian huddled on the ground, clutching her cheek. A bright red bruise bloomed beneath her fingers, but somehow that wasn't the worst part. Her hair was greasy and matted, hanging around her face. And her dress, once a simple beige, was dirt covered and stained with splotches of blood.

Mora sucked in a breath through her teeth when she noticed the cuts and burns along her arms. The sound caught Lillian's attention. They stared at one another, Lillian's watery eyes wide with horror. She shook her head, mumbling, "No, no, no, no."

Mora stiffened, hating the hollow tone of Lillian's voice and the devastation on her face. Wishing her magic wasn't leashed by Dother's damn curse.

Halvard cleared his throat. As if he were offended she hadn't given him attention. "Nice to see you again, Mora." He spoke as if they were two acquaintances running into one another at a ball. *What an idiot.* The man deserved little more than an apathetic once over. Mora made sure to look unimpressed. Hoped it insulted him further.

Halvard was out of his element, dressed for a noble function while standing among piles of rubble. He'd likely throw a fit if a splotch of soot stained his knee-length, navy coat. Those intricate flowers embroidering the lapels must have cost a fortune. And the crisp, white tunic underneath was bright enough to blind, even in the dark.

Despite his handsome attire and perfectly styled auburn hair, his face twisted into an ugly sneer. Mora offered a cold smile in return, her eyes flicking to his hand. He cradled it against his chest and she knew he'd hit Lillian. Without thought, she moved closer.

If she couldn't have her magic, she'd use her bare hands to teach him a lesson.

The Fae clicked his tongue. "Don't even think about it, Little Witch." Mora raised a brow in question, but he simply glared, hate glittering in those eyes.

Questions and accusations warred on her tongue, but before she spoke, his head snapped toward the shadows.

Gravel crunched and Mora's blood ran cold as an authoritative voice washed over her. "Halvard, I told you not to hurt her."

Halvard pouted like a petulant child. "She would not stop blubbering."

"You know how I feel about unnecessary violence," the man said before stepping into the moonlight. Those horrific, blinding azure eyes locked on to Mora's face.

She froze, knees buckling.

"I see you've finally found my *Treasure*, Zadriel" he declared, clapping the Fae on the shoulder. And there was that ring, the black iris twisting in its casing to face her.

Mora's heart thundered in her chest.

He's dead.

When he took her flask, she jolted, hissing against the cold bite of magic that made her *his*. Blood rushed through her ears, the sound deafening.

He's dead.

Dother's Ghost tipped his head to the side, smirking like he could hear it.

Why isn't he dead...?

He watched her as he attached her flask to a leather harness hanging from his belt. It jostled the pouch on his other hip, a twin to hers, and the worn red journal strapped beneath it.

Mora swayed when he dismissed her and strode toward Lillian. When had she last taken a breath? When he looked at her, the whole world came to a crashing halt. It was like being trapped in a vortex, twisting around in a sea of haunting memories. She could *hear* Dother's voice, *feel* his touch. It made her want to tear the flesh from her bones, if only to make it stop. Her gaze flicked to the Fae—Zadriel—though she couldn't imagine why. He would offer no comfort. For once, however, she didn't find any contempt. In fact, he wouldn't look at her at all, opting instead to focus on his bare feet.

Mora forced herself to watch as Dother's Ghost knelt in front of Lillian. He pushed his chocolate brown hair away from his face, the cut a little longer than she remembered. When he smiled, it was crooked. Dother had a perfect smile, a weapon he used to charm everyone. A curve graced this man's nose. And his shoulders were broader, arms thicker.

He reached for Lillian's hand, but she flinched away. "Let me see the damage," he said, tone gentle. But it wasn't a question—either she showed him willingly, or he'd make her. Lillian knew it. Learned, like Mora, sometimes it was best to comply, even when every part of you screamed *no*. She gave into him, releasing her grip and displaying an angry red patch where Halvard struck. Blood pooled under puffy skin, forming a painful bruise. Dother's Ghost pressed his thumb into the wound and Lillian gasped in pain.

"Fucking gods," she hissed. Her hand trembled as she returned it to her cheek.

Frowning, he released an exasperated sigh. "I'm sorry this happened." He glowered over her shoulder at Halvard before standing.

"You didn't mind setting one of your fire sprites off on her earlier," Halvard mumbled.

Broken shards of glass dusted the ground near Lillian's feet. Some of the burns on her arms were fresh, while others scabbed over. And a light tan darkened her ivory skin, with angry patches of red where the sun's focus had been too much. How long had they had her? How many times did they hurt her?

Dother's Ghost stood and took three quick, threatening steps toward Halvard. His counterpart blanched, stepping back as he approached. With swift, steady hands, he grabbed the lapels of Halvard's coat and dragged him closer. "That violence had a purpose." His voice was calm and deadly. Mora shivered while Halvard stilled, his eyes wide with fear.

"Thanks to our... persuasions," he emphasized the word, patting Halvard's cheek twice like he was some treasured pet, "we found Mora."

Mora kept her face carefully blank as everyone's attention shifted to her. The cool night air soothed her heated skin and somehow she managed to hold that blinding blue gaze. *It's not him*, she whispered to herself. Though he had all of Dother's things and shared too many features.

Except...

Now that he was closer, it was impossible to miss the patch of bright amber on the bottom of his left iris. Dother hadn't returned from the dead. But the icy bite of magic binding her to his ghost pulsed in her chest and she knew without a doubt they were related. That he could keep her for as long as he desired. Make as many wishes as he wanted. Her new Keeper was *a* Dother. Just not her Dother.

The gentle wind on her face twisted into the memory of his last breath, fluttering against her cheek. That sputtering wheeze, heavy with pain, was the one memory of his voice she didn't abhor.

He'll find you someday.

Somehow, Dother knew this day would come.

Mora rubbed her fingers together, imagining the ash clinging to her skin was his dry, sticky blood. Remembering the way her body sagged with relief when it was over. How the room felt bigger, the air fresher. That was the moment she promised herself anyone who used her would suffer. A vow she'd kept over the centuries.

Dother failed, she reminded herself. *He couldn't bend you into what he wanted. This ghost will be no different.* Though she prayed this man wouldn't be the same. Didn't share Dother's... wants. Mora gulped against the sour taste in her mouth. Could she do it all again? Would there be anything left of her in the end?

What choice did she have but to endure.

"Keeper of the flask," she said, her voice deceptively calm, "my power is yours to command."

CHAPTER 20

MORA

"It's good to finally hear those words," Dother's Ghost declared. Mora clenched her teeth, forcing herself to keep quiet. He released Halvard and straightened his tunic, the fabric a beautiful royal blue with silver thread along the trim. "You can call me Andras. Though I've read you much prefer my last name. Unlike Cillian, I don't care if you call me Dother."

That name festered in Mora's ears, burrowing into her brain and plucking at too many memories. They hummed in her mind, off tune and grating, like a warped melody from a broken lute. Words forced their way through her lips before she thought better of it. "I'd rather call you nothing at all."

Mora crossed her arms and kept her focus on that amber splotch in his eye. It helped, somewhat, to concentrate on the things that made him different.

Who was he to Dother? As far as she knew, he had no living relatives. But the man did nothing but deceive her. This was no different.

Andras tapped the journal with his pointer finger, his ring clinking against the cover. "He said you were defiant." Looking up at the manor, he smiled at the clusters of overripe apples weighing down the branches. "Your tantrum was impressive by the way. I didn't expect such a display, but you were clearly surprised to see me. Do I look that much like him?"

Mora bared her teeth. "Do you know how Dother died?"

"I have a vague idea."

"And you still came for me? You're a bigger fool than he was."

Fire flared in Andras's eyes. "I wouldn't speak so quickly, *Treasure*. Cillian's journal was thorough. I know how to handle you."

Goosebumps skittered up Mora's arms and she tensed. Did he have to call her that? "I'm sure he thought the same," she said, voice low.

They watched one another, two monstrous creatures aching for control. Neither willing to budge. Mora bit her cheek until she tasted blood, but she managed to keep still. To face him without showing the panic pulsing in her chest. A concert of crickets cut through the silence, followed by Lillian's occasional sniffles and Halvard shuffling his feet. Zadriel, however, never made a sound. As if he were accustomed to fading into the background. But she felt his eyes on her, the heat of his fury coating her skin.

When it was clear she wouldn't utter a word, Andras strolled toward her, his confident stride much like his predecessor. Mora froze when he reached out and trailed a calloused finger down her cheek. She tried to turn away, but he grabbed her chin while shaking his head. Gently, he pushed until she was forced to look up at him. "He wrote of your beauty, you know," he said, eyes sparkling. Leaning closer he whispered in her ear, "I can see why he was infatuated."

The sickeningly familiar scent of citrus and herbs washed over her.

Mora sucked in a breath between clenched teeth. *It's not him. He can't hurt you anymore.* She slammed her hands against Andras's chest, forcing him back. Despite the endless pressure in her lungs, she smiled. It was delightful, watching him stumble. Seeing a furious expression twisting his handsome features into something ugly. "I don't care what Dother said in his scribblings. My power is yours, but my body is my own. Don't touch me."

Andras clicked his tongue and slid his hand down her arm. "You have more venom than he described. But I know I can make you do whatever I want."

Halvard had the nerve to laugh, his fingers twitching at his sides as if he were eager for his turn with her.

Mora roared, the sound guttural and animalistic, and launched herself at Andras. They toppled to the ground, the air wheezing from his lungs. Her knees burned as sharp rocks tore at her dress and embedded themselves in her skin. But it invigorated her. As Andras attempted to catch his breath, she straddled him and dug her nails into his cheeks. Blood welled up from the wounds, caking beneath her fingernails.

Reaching out with clumsy hands, Andras scrambled to push her away. But she wouldn't be moved. Mora balled her fists and pummeled his face, laughing when his nose cracked, hot blood pouring from his nostrils. "You. Do. Not. Touch. Me!" Mora emphasized each word with another punch. The violent rage he'd coaxed to the surface was endless.

"Calm yourself," he hissed. Andras slid his hands to her throat and squeezed, crushing her windpipe. Her next breath was little more than a gasp, but she didn't stop. Not when the pressure built behind her eyes. Not as her lungs burned. Not when the edges of her vision became fuzzy and a hoarse, gurgling sound escaped her throat. She'd burst into smoke when she could take no more. For now, she'd show Andras she meant it when she said no one touched her without her permission. The curse may bind her magic to her Keeper's will, but nothing short of a wish could stop her physical assault.

"Zadriel!" he screeched. The pain in her lungs eased a bit when he pulled a hand away and fiddled with his belt. Mora took the deepest breath she could, ignoring the stinging throb in her knuckles as they connected with Andras's face once more.

Something hard struck Mora's temple, and she swayed, her vision filling with stars. A drumbeat began to pound relentlessly in her head. Gold sparkled beneath her and she blinked, attempting to clear her fuzzy vision. It took a moment for her to realize what she was seeing—Andras held her flask tight in his grip. Had he hit her with it?

That second of stillness cost her. The world spun, and she found herself on her back. Beneath Andras. Those cold, blue eyes above her, burning into her soul.

No, oh gods, no.

"Get the fuck off me!" Mora screamed. It had been centuries, but she may as well have been back in that bed, wrapped in black silk sheets. Naked. Trapped.

You're mine, Mora, whether you choose me or not.

That blinding gaze morphed, the amber splotch disappearing in a sea of azure, until it was Dother staring down at her. His smile was triumphant, despite the blood spatter painting his proud face. Mora thrashed in his grip, but it did nothing but jostle her aching head. *Please, let me go.* She wasn't sure if she thought those words or said them out loud. Lillian yelled something in the background, her voice too muffled to make out.

Zadriel's long legs came into view and Dother nodded up at him. He kicked her discarded flask closer and placed something orange and glowing beside it. Droplets of blood dripped from Dother's nose and splashed Mora's face and chest, soaking into the emerald fabric and joining the gravy stains.

"Can you behave?" Andras taunted. Andras. Not Dother. It wasn't actually Dother.

Consequences be damned, Mora slammed her head into his, cringing at the loud crack that followed. The world went white and a wave of nausea surged through her, but Andras pulled away. That was all that mattered. She blew out a breath, trying not to vomit, and fumbled for the ethereal thread that allowed her to dissipate into smoke. It would take the pain away.

But she couldn't seem to reach it.

"I'm disappointed in you, Mora. You've left me no choice."

The sound of glass crunching melded with the ringing in her ears. And a warm sensation bloomed in her chest, flowing over her heart, her lungs, and into her abdomen.

It grew hotter.

Too hot.

Blazing.

Boiling her organs until the blisters bubbled and burst.

The pain was blinding, twisting through her as if she were kindling. Mora's muscles seized, and she rasped out an agonized cry before curling her body into the fetal position and rocking back and forth in the dirt.

Zadriel nudged her onto her back. The light pressure was enough to awaken a new pulse of agony. She yowled. Or, at least tried to. It was more of a gurgle, followed by a mixture of blood and mucus filling her mouth and spilling down her cheeks.

"Does it hurt, Little Witch?" he mocked, his voice a low purr. She reached for his pant leg, hoping to dig her nails into his calf. It wasn't much, but at least it would hurt. The material slipped through her useless fingers, however—her tremoring muscles wouldn't behave.

Mora was vaguely aware of Lillian shrieking, "What the fuck are you doing to her?" Followed by her begging for them to stop. It sounded far away, like they were separated by eons instead of mere feet. There was the distant sound of a scuffle, as Lillian attempted to crawl to Mora's aid, and Halvard muttered a few expletives. Andras watched, the stern look on his face a warning to behave.

Tears streamed down Mora's face, mixing with streaks of blood and saliva. Though it was the maddening crackling churning in her ears that broke her. She could *hear* the flames.

"Have you had enough?" Andras came into Mora's field of vision, the cool leather of his boots soothing her cheek as he pushed her head over. Blood ran down his face, gushing from his broken nose and a sizable gash on his cheek. Something like pride flooded through her and she attempted to smile. The stretch of her skin stung, and she moaned pitifully instead.

Andras shook her flask, rattling the flames in her belly. The bottle glowed, and an orange ember fluttered in its base. Tiny hands pressed against the glass... he'd forced a sprite inside. The fire was a first, but she remembered the last time this happened. Damn Dother and his journal.

There would be no dissipating into smoke. No returning to the safety of her flask. Until Andras decided to release the sprite, Mora burned. Unable to find relief—even the gentle hands of death couldn't reach her, thanks to her curse. Dother claimed he wasn't above sharing if it kept her in line. But he knew the God of Death was greedy, unwilling to return a spirit once it was in his clutches. And no one, not even a god, could have more of a hold on Mora than he did.

Mora gritted her teeth while the pungent flavor of her own smoldering flesh enveloped her mouth. On her next pained breath, smoke spilled from her nostrils.

Crouching beside her, Andras ran a hand through her hair in a bastardized version of a soothing gesture. With his other hand, he pulled a handkerchief from his pocket and pressed it against his bloody nose.

"Are you going to behave now?" He gripped her curls and tugged to emphasize his point, pain radiating through her scalp. When she did nothing but lay there gasping, he spoke again. "Are you?" There was another tug on her hair, the increased force lifting her throbbing head off the ground. Mora did her best to nod. "Good girl," he said, easing his grip and laying her head down gently. Then he patted her cheek twice, the gentle touch somehow agonizing.

Zadriel stood by his side looking down at her, those scarred arms crossed over his chest. Mora hated the hardened look on his face.

Wondered if he felt better after watching her burn. When Andras handed him a spare handkerchief, he sighed, but went to work cleaning the blood from her face. He was rough, chafing her throbbing skin as he dragged the cloth back and forth, unwilling to leave behind a single drop.

Andras pulled a glass orb from his pouch. How many sprites did he have? Were they from Dother's collection? It pained her, knowing there were likely many rotting in the dark depths of his pouch.

Mora watched as he narrowed his eyes and focused on the glass. Fire spilled from her flask and twisted around the orb, and the burning pain tore its way out of her body. It was as if it held her entrails in its blazing fits and refused to let go. Her agonized howl startled the crows hiding among the trees and they joined her, cawing madly.

"Zadriel," Andras barked, "shut her up."

Zadriel pressed his rough palm against her aching lips.

"There's no need for dramatics," he spat.

Mora's eyes flared. Oh, she'd show him dramatics. When the sprite released its hold on her, she took a few rapid breaths through her nose. Zadriel made to move his palm away, but she acted fast, snagging his skin between her teeth. He hissed as she bit down, not relenting until his sweet, coppery blood flooded her mouth.

"Fuck!" Fury weaved through his striking features as he tore his hand away, deepening the wound. The smile on her face was weaker than she would have liked, but she glared at him and licked her red teeth, enjoying the taste. Zadriel's face shuttered. "You're going to regret that."

"What a waste," Halvard muttered, earning a scowl from Zadriel.

Lillian tried to scoot closer, but Halvard stepped on her dress. She stilled and Mora waited for her to cuss him out. Instead, she bowed her head and whispered, "Are you ok?"

When Mora nodded, blisters burst in her throat. She tried her best to hide her flinch, but Lillian frowned and she knew she had failed. Her battered body couldn't take anymore. The temptation to pull on that ethereal thread and dissipate into mist was strong. But she waited for Andras's blessing. Wasn't foolish enough to push things any further. For tonight, at least.

Lillian tugged her knees to her chest and clutched her stained dress. She lifted pleading, exhausted eyes to Mora. "I'm sorry. I tried to keep them from you, but I couldn't take it anymore. And I hoped they wouldn't find you in the lake. You were right... hope is pointless."

Lillian was sorry. Mora squeezed her eyes shut—this was a new low, even for her. She wished she could take it all back. Ignore her note and leave the poor woman alone. "*I'm* sorry," Mora said, her voice raw.

"Can we move things along?" Halvard looked to Andras as he tapped the ornate hilt of the dagger on his belt.

Andras sighed. "Fine..." He hesitated for a moment, chancing a glance at Mora before he added, "Make it quick."

Halvard grinned as he drew out his dagger while Zadriel turned away.

"NO!" Mora bellowed, wincing as her scream tore through her raw throat. She tried to stand but managed little more than a step before she collapsed. "Please. Please let her go." Her hands shook, but she dug them into the grass and dragged herself toward Lillian. Her nails cracked and broke, dirt coating the stinging wounds. It killed her to turn pleading eyes toward Andras. "I'll do whatever you want. Please, don't hurt her."

He cocked an eyebrow and flicked his eyes to her flask, as if to say *you'll already do whatever I want.* A gut-wrenching sob tore its way out of Mora's throat. She choked on her own blood while she cried, pulling herself closer and closer to Lillian. "Please."

Halvard chuckled as he wrapped Lillian's hair in his fist and pulled her head back, forcing her to watch Mora crawl. Silent tears ran down Lillian's face and she shuddered. Those wide, mossy green eyes bore into Mora's and all she could think to do was whisper apologies.

Mora collapsed onto Lillian's chest and wept. "Please, Andras, please don't do this." Lillian clung to Mora's dress, her shaking fingers twisting in the fabric.

"Come now, Mora, return to your flask to rest and heal. I'll call for you when it's time to talk."

Mora watched in horror while mist spilled from her pores, pulling her apart piece by piece. She held it off as best she could, but she had little strength left. Lillian clung to her skirt, knowing it wouldn't be long before all she held onto was a sparkling cloud of onyx that slipped through her fingers. Mora's vision blurred, tears spilling down her cheeks, as she stared deep into Lillian's eyes and murmured, "I'm sorry, Lillian. I'm so sorry."

As Lillian opened her mouth to speak, Halvard plunged the dagger into her throat. All that escaped was a horrific gurgling sound, her shriek drowning in blood. He pulled the blade free and Lillian pressed her hand to the wound. It couldn't staunch the bleeding. Blood spilled through her fingers, staining her dress and puddling on the ground.

When she collapsed, Mora fell with her, little more than a twirling mass of shadows with glowing amber eyes. She watched the blood drain from Lillian's face. Saw every fruitless gasp for breath. Felt the moment her chest stopped moving.

Mora wanted to wail. To shriek. To look Halvard in the eye and tell him all the ways she intended to make him suffer for what he'd done. But she was forced back into her flask, pressing against the glass with no hope of escape.

CHAPTER 21

MORA

The sun chased the moon through the sky day after day after inconsequential day, and Mora couldn't find the ability to care. Had no idea how much time passed since she'd watched Lillian's blood soak into the earth. Warm rays of sunshine kissed her face, but she was numb to the heat on her skin.

And she was so fucking tired.

Sat atop a beautiful, chestnut brown horse with a glorious black mane, she clutched the worn leather reins tightly in her clammy palms. It was an effort to hold her head up—she bobbed aimlessly with each of the horse's determined steps.

Their pace was gruesome, but at least the routine was predictable. Andras led them south, insisting they travel as far as they could by day until they either stopped to make camp or reached a village and found an inn. Then he'd call her to her flask, denying her a comfortable sleep, only to force her to re-emerge the following morning. Why he didn't leave her to rot in her flask, she had no idea.

They slowed as they came upon the Fendu Bay—Mora hadn't noticed until her horse came to a full stop. In the distance, ocean waves crashed against the Esper Rocks, sculpted sea stacks topped with tufts of grass and spindly pine trees. A memory of holding her father's warm hand while they walked through thick, wet sand, eyeing the Rocks and imagining the best ways to climb to the top, washed over her. Now she saw nothing but the ocean patiently chipping away at doomed slabs of earth, and felt a grim desire to lay on the beach until the sea swallowed her whole.

It was too early to camp, but she assumed Halvard made his usual fuss. The man wasn't made for travel. Daily, he'd whine about being sore and tired and demand a break. It led to bickering between the three men, but she tuned it out until the sound blended with the high-pitched seagull caws.

Mora forced herself to focus, her eyes flitting over their small party. Andras cooed at his white and gray speckled mare. There were flickers of kindness on his face as he ran his hand lovingly along her neck. Completely at odds with the monster she knew him to be.

The black stallion in front of her was missing its rider. She barely caught sight of Zadriel before he reached the thick slope that plunged down to the shore. Mora watched with tired apathy, her half-lidded eyes tracking him until she could no longer see the black hood covering his delicately pointed ears. It wasn't long before he climbed back over the hill with a thick piece of driftwood slung over his broad shoulder. The bleached remains of what once was a beautiful tree dragged behind him through thick tufts of beach grass growing in scattered patches along the hillside.

The Fae plunked the driftwood down and fussed until it was positioned perfectly. Without a word of thanks, Andras sat, flipped open his journal, and ran his finger along the yellowed pages. His eyes remained fixed on Dother's writings when he held his right hand open expectantly. *What an ass.* Zadriel already dug through their saddlebags, procuring strips of dried meat to place in Andras's waiting palm.

Something nearby gurgled. It took a moment for Mora to realize it came from her. The spicy smell of Andras's jerky invaded her senses, but even as her mouth flooded with saliva, the idea of eating turned her stomach.

"Where's *my* meat, useless mutt?" Halvard sneered as he settled on Zadriel's makeshift bench, his dark auburn hair tickling his shoulders. As always, he'd dressed impeccably—his loose maroon tunic, made of the finest silk and embroidered with gold, was far too sophisticated for travel. Mora wondered what Andras offered to convince him to leave the comforts of his manor.

A muscle feathered in Zadriel's jaw, but he stalked back to the horses without a word. As he rifled through the saddlebags, he looked to Mora, who still sat in her saddle. When their eyes connected, his gaze narrowed, and he clenched his fists, stretching the scars peppering his warm, olive skin. The shadows in his dark cloak danced on his face, flirting with the sharp angles of his cheeks. But a sheen of sweat coated his brow—he must have been sweltering under that hood.

"Will you not allow your horse a moment's rest?"

As she stared into those dark eyes, Mora felt flickers of anger. Like embers floating on an errant wind. She watched him apathetically, offering no answer.

"Get down on your own or I'll pull you down myself," he spat, stepping closer.

Mora rolled her eyes and slid from her saddle, plumes of dirt puffing into the air around her feet. "Are you happy?"

"What do you think?"

Wordlessly, she pushed past him and sauntered toward the steep hill, trying to appreciate the briny scent hanging heavy in the air. Hints of mint and summer rain filled her lungs as she took a deep breath, hating that she loved it.

Rough sprigs of beach grass caught her linen trousers. The black pants and loose gray shirt she wore felt foreign against her skin. They matched Andras's travel clothes. Mora was his perfect counterpart. *A sign he owns you,* she thought bitterly. She found herself missing her gowns. Missing Frederick.

She didn't deserve to think of him.

When had she changed into these drab clothes? She couldn't remember. Though she knew she managed to keep a single bloody shred of her emerald gown, tucked safely in her pouch.

Her finger slid over the smooth leather. *We are bound,* Dother's memory whispered.

"Not in the way you wanted," she hissed back. At no one. She'd lost her mind, hadn't she? Centuries ago. Would it please him to know a descendant was her Keeper? Perhaps, even in death, Dother ultimately won.

Your freedom dies with me.

Willing her gaze to shift toward the ocean, Mora watched the water rise and consume the beach. Imagined plunging beneath the waves and waiting until her lungs filled and the world went dark. Not that it would matter. She'd wake up in her gods damned flask.

The morose avenue of her thoughts came to a swift halt when a hand clapped down on her shoulder, fingers curling tightly enough to cause a bite of pain. Clamping her eyes shut, she held back the tremors threatening to crawl up her spine, and pulled in a long, slow breath through her nose. When she opened them, Andras's bright gaze was fixed on her.

"Quite the view, isn't it?"

While the Fendu Bay was an incredible sight, she couldn't be sure if he was referencing the ravenous tides... or her. Shifting on her feet, she kept her mouth clamped shut and stared out toward the ocean.

"I know we had an eventful meeting, Mora. I've given you time to process your change of fate. But I don't think you realize, there's no reason this has to be uncomfortable for you."

Mora's jaw cracked as she ground her teeth. "What do you want, Andras?"

He trailed his fingers over her cheek, tucking an unruly curl behind her ear. Every muscle in her body tensed. "I can make things far more accommodating if you choose to cooperate."

Mora's gaze snapped back to him. She'd heard something like that before—*Choose me and I'll set you free.* Locked under the weight of those azure eyes, his face morphed from his to Dother's and back. They'd been cut from the same horrific cloth.

Bile coated Mora's tongue. She tried to focus on the amber splotch in his left eye. Tried so hard not to do something stupid like tackle him to the ground. She couldn't handle the pain of his retaliation again. Not yet. But Andras's fingers still lingered on her cheek and Mora squeezed her fists so hard they ached.

"I lit a fire and prepared some eggs," Zadriel said, drawing a startled gasp from Mora. The Fae's steps were too quiet, like he was built for stealth—she couldn't stand that he was able to sneak up on her. Perhaps she deserved it after Lillian. Mora swallowed, hating herself.

Andras's hand fell from her cheek. He stared at her for what felt like an agonizingly long moment before he stepped away and headed back to the driftwood where Halvard still lounged. Mora sagged with relief, swaying like a leaf on the wind. It took all her power to remain standing.

She couldn't do this again.

Zadriel's eyes roamed her face, his dark brows furrowing when a single tear spilled down her cheek. He opened his mouth to speak, only to clamp it shut and shake his head.

"What?" Mora snarled, surprised she felt another spark of anger. That she was capable of feeling anything at all.

His features shifted into a scowl, but still he said nothing.

"If you're here to berate me, don't bother."

Zadriel shrugged, bitterness coating his tone. "It's better if you don't fight him."

Before Mora could react, he spun on his feet and marched back to Andras and Halvard, leaving her to contemplate the ocean and her muddied thoughts alone.

Mora pulled a chocolate from her pouch and brought it to her lips, only to hesitate. Lillian enjoyed these chocolates. And she'd never eat another. Mora's stomach twisted, and she slipped the dessert back into the bag. She didn't deserve it.

CHAPTER 22

MORA
300 YEARS AGO

"I had them make your favorite chocolate cake. It's for tonight, but we could sneak a slice for breakfast."

Mora peeked out the crack in her door, adoring the mischief dancing in her father's brown eyes. Chocolate cake for breakfast sounded far better than the oatmeal they'd likely serve in the dining hall later. She had no reason to say no. But it was early. And she hadn't expected anyone to come by her rooms for at least another hour.

She'd thrown on a simple white nightdress when Kalyan knocked at the door. If she had more time, she would have chosen one that wasn't wrinkled. At least she hadn't put it on backwards. Hopefully her father assumed her state of dress was the reason she wouldn't invite him in. In truth, Cillian stood silently by her side. Naked. A few inches of wood hid him from Kalyan's eyes.

It didn't feel like enough.

Smug amusement lit his face, and he trailed a finger up and down her arm. It tickled. And the bastard knew it. Mora nearly shook as she withheld her laughter and tried and failed to swat him.

No one could know he'd spent the night. That he spent most nights. "Uhm..."

Kalyan's brows furrowed. "Are you not well, pumpkin?"

"I'm fine, papa. I'll call for Rosemary and meet you shortly.

"I'll fetch her," Philip said. He leaned against the wall behind her father, a knowing look in his eyes.

Fuck...

Mora donned her most convincing smile. "Thank you, Philip. That would be lovely."

"Don't dawdle," her father said with a wink. He leaned down to kiss her forehead, and Mora's hold on the door tightened. Her heart was pounding and her hands were so clammy, she wondered how she maintained her death grip on the wood.

"I won't," she promised. The door creaked as she shut it far too slowly to be casual.

Cillian tousled her hair. "That went well, Treasure."

Mora rushed to her bedroom. "We have to clean. Now!" The bed was a mess, her blankets half on the floor. And their clothes... they were everywhere. She didn't remember being that careless. How was she going to hide this from her lady-in-waiting? "Where will you hide until Rosemary leaves?" Her eyes drifted toward her balcony. It was a chilly autumn morning, but... "I think—"

Cillian's fingers found her lips, and he shushed her. Her eyes narrowed, but he shook his head. "I'm not going to freeze on your balcony. I have my sprites. Though I don't think Rosemary will care if I'm here."

"I don't care what you think." Mora scooped up his rumpled under-garments and shoved them into his arms. "Get dressed."

"You wound me," Cillian said with mock hurt as he put them on. "Your father likes me. I'm sure we could work things out if he discovered us."

"My mother's version of working things out would involve me walking down an aisle."

Cillian shrugged. "An inevitability." He leaned against her door frame and watched her frantically clean.

Mora rolled her eyes. "You're incorrigible." She reached for his trousers, surprised when something soft brushed against her fingers. A strange cluster of purple flowers poked out from his pouch, their uneven petals tickling her skin. It was unlike any flower she'd seen. Before she could examine them further, Cillian pulled his trousers from her grip.

"We better hurry if you truly wish to clean before Rosemary comes."

"What were those?"

Cillian straightened. "What?"

"The flowers. I've never seen anything like them."

Cillian's smile was full of wicked promises. "Enchanter's secret, Treasure." He slipped his trousers on before brushing a slow, gentle kiss on her lips. One that had Mora wishing they had more time.

Noble nonsense nearly drove Mora mad. Their chattering filled the room—complaints about Forbidden magic causing issues in their respective villages, frustrations about how difficult their lives were without their Indentured...

Blah, blah, blah.

Mora rolled a lumpy, orange ornamental gourd back and forth under her palm, listening to her mother's placations. Aedlin was regal, draped in a golden gown with blood-red sleeves. Her light brown hair was piled into a flawless bun, framed by a ruby encrusted crown. As usual, her father dressed to match, sitting by her side at the head of the table. He nodded along as she spoke, savoring a sip of wine.

Cillian listened astutely, nibbling on his left cheek. "We could create paid positions within households that encourage Halflings *to willingly work for you. You'd receive the assistance you're missing, and it would inspire those with magic to be good citizens. Because you'd only hire the best."*

The room went utterly silent, all eyes snapping to Cillian.

Lord Clairmont of Reverie cleared his throat. "Lord Dother, with all due respect, is this something we should spend coin on?"

"Did it not cost money to house them in cloisters? To pay for their food and basic needs? To keep them under constant guard?" Cillian fiddled with his ring, his expression serious. "With all due respect indeed, Lord Clairmont, this is a reallocation of funds. And, might I add, less costly."

Aedlin bit her lip, eyes darting around the table, analyzing everyone's responses and deciding the best course of action. When no one protested, she said, "Lord Dother is correct, we could easily create positions within noble houses to replace the Indentured you've lost." Then she looked to Mora and raised a manicured brow. The message was clear—this is the king you'll need when you take the throne.

"Perhaps we can discuss things in detail after our meal," her father interrupted, lifting his silver wine glass and swirling the pink liquid around.

Thank the gods for her father. Like him, she had no interest listening to the noblemen's endless complaints. Especially before dessert.

Though Mora had to admit, pride bloomed in her chest as she watched Cillian. He'd been born to lead. But did she want him to lead as her king? Mora's grip on the lumpy gourd tightened. How much longer would he wait for her to decide?

"Is something the matter, pumpkin?" Her father's soothing voice pulled her from her thoughts and she couldn't help but smile. He always knew when she was struggling.

She shook her head. "No, papa, just thinking."

"You know what they say about thinking."

Mora rested her head on his shoulder. "What do they say?"

"It often leads to trouble." He took a slow sip of his wine, amusement glittering in his eyes.

Mora donned an innocent expression and pressed her palm against her chest. "Me? Trouble? Never." They chuckled together and her heart already felt lighter.

The delicious aroma of parsley and thyme mixed with savory vegetable stock wafted through the room as the kitchen staff made their way around the enormous table. They placed adorable pumpkins hollowed out and filled with hearty soup on everyone's plates. Mora couldn't get over how cute they were. There was no better time of year than Harvest.

"Thank the gods," her father said quietly, "I'm starving. Cake, it turns out, is not a filling breakfast."

Mora snorted, "I think we needed a second slice."

Her mother leaned closer, her gaze darting between the two of them. "What are you two whispering about?"

"Nothing," they responded in unison.

She playfully pinched Kalyan and the two of them were suddenly in their own world. It wouldn't be long before her father cracked and told Aedlin about their sneaky breakfast.

Steam curled in the air above her meal, but despite the heat, Mora dug in immediately. A sweet, slightly oniony flavor exploded on her tongue while a touch of spices danced along her palate—she couldn't help but moan in delight.

Cillian's hand found her thigh, squeezing her gently. His breath tickled her cheek when he leaned in and whispered, "Save those delightful sounds for my ears alone, Treasure."

Her cheeks burned but she ran her tongue along the seam of her mouth and smirked as those blue eyes tracked the movement. Mora whispered back, "What makes you think you own my pleasure, Lord Dother?"

He tilted his head to the side and smiled knowingly. "We'll discuss this later, when I remind you to call me Cillian." They stared at one another for a moment too long, Cillian's possessive hand still clutching her thigh. Mora imagined he'd crawl into her bed again tonight. Shrouded in his shadows. The man was skilled at sneaking past guards and slipping into her rooms.

When she brought another spoonful to her lips, she moaned lightly once more, chuckling when Cillian's eyes narrowed.

Mora made the mistake of eating her meal too fast. Her stomach nearly burst, but she needed one more bite. One decadent bowl of that creamy, herby soup wasn't enough. Cillian busied himself, chatting with the Lord of Westmont about grain shipments from Eldenna, his food barely touched. She bit her bottom lip, hoping he'd stay distracted as she snuck her spoon into his pumpkin. He didn't glance her way. The perfect crime, *she thought, with a sly grin, savoring one final taste.*

Then Dother squeezed her in silent reprimand.

Damn it!

Mora giggled until she choked. It was anything but regal, and when her father gasped, she assumed he was joining in on the laughter.

Her smile dropped as soon as she looked at him. Sweat beaded on his brow and his typically golden brown skin was ashen.

"Aedlin," he said, his voice quiet. Too quiet. "I don't feel well."

The queen paled, her brows furrowing with worry. "What's wrong?"

"I—" A pained moan spilled from Kalyan's lips and he clutched his chest.

Time slowed. Everything was muffled except her father's agonizing wheeze. Mora stared at his face, frozen.

"Someone fetch a healer," her mother shouted. Within a breath she was kneeling in front of the king. Her hands shook as she touched his forehead, his cheeks, his chest. "What's happening, my love? What can I do?"

The high pitch of her mother's voice forced Mora to move. She stood so fast her chair tipped back and crashed to the floor. Panic consumed the room as people ran to get help. Or, at least, she hoped that's what they were doing. Everything felt far away—all she could see was her father's wild, frantic eyes. And the three steps to his side felt like miles. He was panting, his breath coming out in horrifying, labored gasps.

Kalyan blinked several times. "Mora, I—" He grunted, his free hand smacking against the hardwood table.

The world blurred as tears slid down her cheeks. He looked at her earnestly now, brows raised and eyes wide. "I love you... both. So much," he breathed, wobbling slightly as he tried to push away from the table. The blood drained from his face and a blue tint bloomed on his lips.

"No, papa, stay still," she said sternly as she crouched beside him and grabbed his hand. It was cold and clammy, nearly slipping from her grasp. "Where's the healer? Someone, please, do something!" Threading their fingers, she squeezed lightly, pushing all her love into that one touch. His trembling hand tensed below hers and she swallowed down a helpless wail.

"Help him!" her mother screamed, shaking fingers clinging to her father's shoulder. "Please don't leave me, Kal."

"I love you," he whispered weakly, leaning back in his chair. His labored breaths came fewer and farther between as his eyes slowly closed, and the hand on his chest twitched before falling uselessly by his side. Mora held on tightly to his other hand, failing to notice he ceased holding hers back.

Kalyan's breathing slowed to a stop.

"Papa?" she whispered. Her stomach felt heavy and her eyes stung. She shook his hand, her voice rising hysterically when he failed to respond, "Papa?"

Mora had never heard such an agonizing, deafening silence.

Cillian's steady arms twisted around her waist. He pulled her to him while a healer rushed toward the king, pushing their way through the crowd. But Mora tried to cling to her father. Something in her chest cracked, the pressure clawing up her throat, as her fingers slowly slipped from his. She couldn't bear to watch.

"He's gone, Mora," Cillian said gently, turning her so she faced his chest. "He's gone."

Her mother's sobs cut through the silence and she couldn't take it. It was worse, somehow, than the quiet.

Her father was gone.

She'd never laugh with him again. Never sneak off to eat dessert for breakfast. Or share her struggles. He would never tease her or defend her. Never surprise her at her door.

He was gone.

Mora howled, the sound guttural and broken. It cracked in her throat and thrummed painfully in her ears, but she couldn't stop. Her fingers twisted in Cillian's soft tunic and she leaned further into his embrace. Surrounded as she was, Mora never felt more alone.

CHAPTER 23

MORA

Andras may as well have been conducting mass. The corner table he shared with Halvard was surrounded by a gaggle of people. And someone kept bringing them drinks. Andras barely touched his ale, but a redness stained Halvard's cheeks. Mora envied him. Wanted nothing more than to dive into a drunk oblivion and forget... everything.

She sat by the fire, eavesdropping while she stared at the smoke-stained wall. They shared the harrowing tale of their most recent adventure. Something about retrieving a relic that changed everything. *Mora.*

At least they'd left her alone.

Mora's hand stuck to the bench, so she tapped her finger against the wood, focusing on the sticky feeling. Anything to keep her mind quiet. Someone handed her a plate of oniony flatbread dipped in a brown sauce. She couldn't remember who, barely looked up when she accepted it. The sauce was far too bitter for her liking anyway—she'd pushed it aside after a single bite.

Where were they?

When they arrived, she'd noticed pastures full of horses and cattle, enclosed by ancient wooden fences, each board festered with explosions of cracks and wretched splinters. There were acres of golden wheat and plots of hearty vegetables. And clusters of thatched roofed buildings, with no opulent manor house in sight.

This place was old. And clearly a known haunt to Andras—he'd called it Eden.

Mora knew Berwick like the back of her hand, and Eden shouldn't exist. Didn't exist. On any map she'd ever seen. And yet, here it was, hidden in the southwest. An unknown village cuddled between vast fields and walls of ominous trees.

"Excuse me." A woman with light blonde hair smiled softly as she scooched past Mora, her blue eyes sparkling. She lifted a hand, a flame pooling in her palm. It flickered gently for a moment before slipping from her hold and drifting to the wall sconce.

A Halfling... using magic, out in the open. Without fear of being caught and confined under the Laws.

Mora's mouth hung open as a man with short, black curls joined the Elementalist and they made their way around the room. Together they chased away the darkness. When he turned to kiss her cheek, Mora noticed his bright green eyes.

For a moment, she was back at Frederick's manor, watching the life fade from Lillian's wide green eyes. She clawed at the bench, sticky residue gathering beneath her nails. All she could taste was smoke. All she could see was the hole in Lillian's throat and the blood pooling at her feet.

Mora blinked, and the room came back. But she couldn't breathe. A maddening fire crackled in her ears and burned her lungs. Her foot bobbed against the floor, leg shaking as she fidgeted, eying the exit. Andras was too caught up in his worshipers to pay her any mind. Did they know they venerated a fiend?

Mora couldn't stand to be among them.

She stood slowly and made her way to the bar, eyes darting around the room to make sure no one watched. Bar was a strong word to describe the shabby set up. It was little more than a thick stretch of polished lumber resting on a few wooden barrels. Crooked shelves stood at the back, lined with bottles housing different liquors. From a dark amber she couldn't stomach to a liquid so clear it could pass for water. She reached over and wrapped her fingers around the closest option, a tall glass bottle three quarters full. The colorless alcohol splashed around the glass confines as she quickly pulled it to her chest.

Once outside, she slid against the uneven stone wall beside the building, tucked out of sight. A plume of dirt scattered in the air as her ass hit the earth. It wasn't graceful. Mora snorted—all those etiquette lessons wasted. *Am I still your perfect queen, Dother?*

She twisted and pulled at the stubborn cork, but the damn thing refused to give. It cut uncomfortably into her palm but she carried on with an iron grip. When that failed, she bit into the wood, tugging until it finally came free, before spitting the cork carelessly away.

A sharp, musty odor assaulted her nose, and she winced.

I wish for a kiss, Treasure.

Why did he insist on haunting her mind?

"I didn't grab your favorite drink, prick," she hissed at the darkness.

Mora closed her eyes, steeling herself. The bottle felt cold against her lips, but she tipped it back and chugged.

One mouthful.

Two mouthfuls.

Three.

An unruly cough forced her to stop. Alcohol dripped down her chin and dribbled over her neck. Why did it have to taste awful? An overpowering, burning, bitter flavor coated her throat, saliva filled her mouth, and a queasiness crawled through her insides.

But Mora could still see Lillian's horrified green eyes. Swore Frederick's wails rattled around in her mind.

When she tipped the bottle back once more, she swallowed as much as she could, stopping only when her body revolted. Over and over again until most of the liquid was gone.

Mora rested her head on the gray stone wall and waited for her brain to muddle. A warm, cozy feeling slowly enveloped her extremities and the world around her wobbled slightly as her vision blurred. Would it be enough to quiet her mind?

Apparently not.

Somehow she'd conjured Lillian's ghost—a blurry apparition sat on the opposite wall in her filthy dress. Watching her while blood dribbled endlessly from the wound in her neck.

"You've ruined everything," she whispered.

Mora burst into tears. "Oh gods."

She couldn't do this.

Couldn't live with the weight of her sins or the knowledge she was once again in a Dother's clutches.

Her hand shook as she groped for the bottle at her side, but she found nothing but cool dirt. Where the hell had it gone?

"Looking for this?" Zadriel asked, shaking the bottle tauntingly before tipping it back and taking a long drink. Dressed head to toe in black, his midnight cloak covered most of his refined features, but she'd spent enough time with him to know he glowered at her.

Heat bloomed in Mora's cheeks and she furiously wiped the moisture from her eyes. "Leave me," she muttered, not sparing him a glance. Silence sat heavy between them, save for the woosh of a cool summer breeze twisting through the alley. She reached an unsteady hand out in an unspoken demand he return the bottle.

"I'm afraid only one has the power to make demands of me, Little Witch. And that person isn't you," he said, before taking another swig.

Mora growled as she stood. It hit her suddenly how uncoordinated she was—her head spun and the world tilted around her. The building's rock façade was kind enough to hold her up, thank the gods.

"Return the bottle and fuck off," she spat, though her words slurred. Her cheeks were wet, and she shuddered with every breath. In the corner of her eye she could have sworn Lillian watched on, an amused smile on her cold, dead face. Mora closed her eyes against the vision, praying it would go away.

When she opened them, a hazy Zadriel had somehow moved closer. Glittering black eyes bore into hers from behind his hood, but they softened somewhat. Or maybe she imagined it.

He frowned. "It looks like you've had enough already." After another sip, he turned the bottle, spilling the remnants onto the dirt.

"Fuck you," Mora seethed. She made a sloppy, uncoordinated attempt to kick the wet dirt in Zadriel's direction, but nearly fell.

"Be careful!" Zadriel reached out to steady her but she stumbled back.

"Don't pretend to care."

Mora meandered deeper into the alley, leaving the Fae behind. Damn him and his incessant need to glower. And his delicious scent. Why did he smell so good?

It was difficult to remain upright, so she dragged her hand against the rough stone until she found the back of the building. Letting go was a mistake. A pesky rock hiding in a clump of grass caught her foot and Mora fell. Hard.

Small pebbles embedded themselves into her palms and her cheek hit the earth with a resounding *thunk*. But the sting was a faraway sensation. And the soothing sprigs of grass cooled her heated skin.

The Forbidden Forest loomed in the distance, past rolling hills and blooming fields. Tall, dark trees cast their judgment on the lands, extending southward to the ocean and as far north as the eye could see. What would happen if she tried to force her way in? Would they swallow her whole and spit out her bones? The idea felt oddly comforting.

"Do you want to eat me, scary trees?" she mumbled.

A sudden, overpowering wave of nausea twisted in her stomach and Mora vomited, the force so intense hot bile splashed against her face. She gasped for breath while saliva dribbled over her lips, falling in thick strings to the earth below. The world spun and Mora closed her eyes against it. It helped.

The relief was short-lived as she vomited once more. Bile stuck to her hair and soaked her tunic. It burned her esophagus and a bitter layer of acid coated her tongue, making her gag again. Over and over until she had nothing left to give. Even when her stomach emptied, she retched, spitting up nothing.

When it finally ended, she wiped her face on her sleeve before laying her heavy head down in the grass. She couldn't find it in herself to care that a pile of her own sick cooled next to her face. Or that she'd likely laid her head in some of it and was too numb to notice. Sobs rattled up her body, the noise far too loud when all she desired was to be hidden and alone.

Someone nearby sighed and black boots overtook her vision. They grumbled, "Gods fucking damn it." A heavy exhale curled in the air before strong hands reached down to pick her up. Cradled against a firm chest, Mora closed her eyes and leaned into its warmth. It was the safest she'd felt in days.

"Make him stop," she whispered between hiccups.

"Stop what?" Zadriel's deep voice was softer than she imagined possible.

"Haunting me." Mora's fingers clung to the soft fabric of Zadriel's cloak like it was a lifeline and she continued to mumble incoherent nonsense. Even she wasn't sure what she was saying. Zadriel, thankfully, kept quiet.

Her head spun. She was grateful Zadriel took his time lowering her to the ground. The last thing she wanted was to vomit on him—the idea alone made her want to crawl into a hole and die. He leaned her against a thick tree trunk and held on to her shoulders until he was sure she wouldn't fall over. Dark green leaves fluttering above caught her eye—they sparkled in the moonlight, as if they were dusted with a golden sheen.

"Wow," she breathed.

At the same time, Zadriel muttered, "I can't believe you did this to yourself."

Mora rested her heavy head against the oak and eyed his arms. "I assumed you were well versed in self-harm."

Zadriel snarled and leaned in so close their noses nearly touched. "Many of these scars are because of *you*."

"I haven't done shit to you."

He watched her while their shared breaths twirled together in the air. Too many emotions to count warred on his handsome face. "You're as self-absorbed as you were three hundred years ago," he said. Then he pulled away.

Mora closed her eyes and inhaled deeply. She told herself it was to calm her fluttering pulse. But, in truth, it was him. She could drink his scent like wine, even though he infuriated her.

When he returned, he ran a rag over her face, wiping away the vomit.

Mora swore. Had he never learned to be gentle? At this rate, he was going to chafe the skin from her cheeks. "Do you have to be so rough?"

"I believe the words you're looking for are *thank you*," he grumbled before pulling her hair back and tying it into a messy ponytail with some twine. "Drink this." Zadriel shoved a waxed, cowhide flask into her hand. His serious expression dared her to defy him, and Mora knew... he'd straddle her and force the water down her throat if she denied him.

Surprising them both, she tipped the flask back without argument.

Cool water danced on her tongue and she chugged it down greedily. Unfortunately, her stomach surged against the new intrusion.

She heaved once more, an unsavory mixture of water and bile splattering against the ground by her side. Rough hands rubbed her back awkwardly as she coughed and gagged. When she could speak once more she mumbled, "Why are you helping me?"

It took him an agonizingly long while to answer, his sparkling onyx eyes wary. "I have to." He watched another tear slide down her cheek. Before it could fall, he wiped it away with gentle fingers. "Why are you crying?"

"Seriously?" Their gazes clashed as she glared up at him. "They're dead, Zadriel. Lillian, Frederick... they're dead because of me. And now Andras has me. How long until he..." Mora swallowed against a surge of panic and pressed her hand to her chest. "I can't do this again."

"For what it's worth," Zadriel said quietly, "I'm sorry about the girl."

Something shifted in her chest. It was as if the monster living there opened its eyes for the first time in days. "Don't lie to me!"

Mora bared her teeth, but Zadriel mirrored her. And his sharp canines were far more menacing. Then he tore his hood down and pointed at his gracefully tipped ears. "I couldn't lie even if I wanted to."

No... he couldn't. For reasons she didn't understand, Fae were incapable of outright lies. But that didn't mean they couldn't deceive. She frowned, mulling over his words. Were they too simple to be deceitful or was she too drunk? It made her head hurt, so she gave up.

"Why do you work for him?"

Zadriel sighed as he sat across from her. Their knees touched, but he looked out toward the rolling hills where the breeze played in the grass, rustling the blades all the way to the foreboding wall of trees. A weak, pensive smile attempted to rise on his face before he smothered it. "You're not the only one who doesn't have a choice."

Mora gasped and she pressed her head further into the trunk. Rough bark grounded her spinning mind while she digested his confession. Something still didn't make sense. "You hate me."

Zadriel snorted. "That didn't sound like a question, Little Witch."

"Why?" she asked quietly, almost afraid of the answer.

"Remember setting me on fire?"

"You held a blade to my throat. And you've repaid me for the burning."

Unable to argue, Zadriel was quiet. Crickets sang their tales as fireflies danced in the grass, but there was little joy to be found in their shared misery.

Finally, he looked at her. Pain gleamed in those endless black eyes. "If things had gone differently... I could have gone home."

The weight of his words tumbled over Mora's heavy body and a longing in his broken voice tore at her heart. "The Forbidden Forest?"

"Arcadia," he corrected with a small nod.

Mora bit her lip as she twisted his words in her dazed mind. The world continued to wobble and the taste of vomit overpowered her senses. But she held on, hoping this conversation would stick. Her fingers twisted around the weeds at the tree's base, pulling at their roots while she processed.

Zadriel was cursed. And somehow she'd cost him his freedom. Though she'd only met him once, three hundred years ago. And he'd already worked with Dother. It didn't make any sense.

Whatever happened, he blamed her. And yet he'd tended to her tonight. Felt sorrow for Lillian. Mora wasn't sure what to make of it.

"Are the pets having a soirée?"

Of course Halvard had to interrupt at the worst possible time. His voice grated on her ears, aggravating her already pounding head. She pinched the bridge of her nose, praying he'd move along quickly.

"Mother spare me," Zadriel muttered under his breath.

The man practically marched toward them, his nose in the air. Though he wobbled slightly with each step and his cheeks nearly matched his loose maroon tunic.

Zadriel stood and sneered at the nobleman, burning with an intense rage she recognized all-too-well. A mirror to her own—one she'd been too distracted to see.

Halvard lifted his chin, somehow looking down at the Fae who towered over him. "Put your hood up. What if you're seen?"

Rolling his eyes, Zadriel tugged his dark hood over his ears but said nothing in his defense.

"Find a tree to crawl under or go to your room in Andras's cottage until we have need of you." Halvard flicked his hand in dismissal. Zadriel shook his head, a thick breath leaving his lips before he turned and disappeared into the darkness. His steps were too quiet. Mora's muddled mind couldn't be sure which direction he'd gone.

Another valuable piece of information—Andras had a house here. Was this where he was from? What about Dother? Her eyes glazed over as she searched through her memories. Dother claimed to be from Eldenna. Another lie?

"And you shouldn't be out here either. Go back inside or return to your flask."

The bastard was a fool if he thought he could boss her around.

Mora smiled sweetly. It took more effort than she expected to stand, but she leaned against the tree as she dragged herself up. Unlike Zadriel, Halvard made no attempt to help steady her. He crossed his arms, tapping his foot as he waited. Oh the fit he'd have when he noticed the dirt that clung to those pristine shoes.

"Must I drag you back to Andras?" he asked. His vicious smile told her he would like that. He grabbed her vomit-soaked tunic and jerked her forward. Mora stiffened and dug her heels into the earth, not wanting to tumble into his arms. She had no power or weapons, but all she could think of was how nice it would be to hurt him. Was it possible to gut a man with your fingernails? Mora would love to try.

A maniacal sound burst from her throat, so sharp and sudden Halvard stilled. His face twisted in confusion at her strange bout of laughter as he looked down at her.

"One day, Halvard," she said, snorting. "One day."

"What are you babbling about?" he asked, grimacing.

"One day, you're going to die." A hungry, devious grin slowly twisted on her lovely face. "And *I'm* going to laugh."

Halvard shivered at the murderous gleam in her eyes, but his nostrils flared and his chin inched ever higher. His knuckles cracked as he flexed his fingers. "What did you say to me?"

Mora leaned in closer and whispered, "I said I can't wait to watch the life drain from your ugly—"

Before Mora could finish, Halvard swung. But she was ready. Had purposely goaded his explosive temper. Erupting into a frigid cloud of dark mist, she felt his fist pass through her. He sucked in a sharp breath, but it was too late. Halvard's knuckles slammed against the thick tree trunk with a resounding *crack*.

A pained howl followed Mora all the way back to her flask, that delicious sound echoing in her mind. Tomorrow she'd face whatever came. Tonight she intended to nestle against the glass and savor Halvard's agony. Along with the oddly familiar ember of warmth thrumming in her chest.

CHAPTER 24

MORA

"I wish for you to find the Spirit of the Forbidden Forest, bring it to me immediately, and leave it in my possession. You won't tell a soul outside this room my wish. And you will not interfere with my dominion over the Spirit once you've delivered it to me. Do you understand?"

Icy tendrils wrapped around Mora's spine the moment Andras stopped speaking. The magic sank into her bones until it swam in the marrow. She hissed against the pain—it was worse with Andras than her other Keepers. Much like it used to be with Dother. A reminder her curse was weaved, in part, with his blood.

Flashes of an enormous tree invaded her mind. It made her apple tree look like a sapling. But flames licked up the trunk, racing to a canopy of gilded leaves, and she could have sworn the tree screamed. That the forest screamed with it. Her fingers twitched at her side and she wished she could cover her ears and curl into a ball on the floor—anything to free herself from the horrific sound. Thick globs of golden sap ran down the bark, bubbling under the heat of the flames, and Mora felt the great tree die, its final exhale rattling in her own lungs.

When she blinked, the vision disappeared, and she found Andras watching her with crossed arms. Mora repressed her shudder when she caught sight of his ring. The black void, thankfully, stared past her.

"I understand," she muttered. Behind her, Zadriel slipped from the kitchen, head hung low. His sigh was heavy. It twisted around Mora's heart, but there was nothing she could do. "Am I looking for a tree?"

Andras looked to the kitchen table, where he'd left Dother's journal. "According to Cillian, it comes from an ancient tree with golden leaves at the center of the Forbidden Forest. The Fae call it the Mother Tree. It's the source of all magic."

Mora clenched her fists and repressed the urge to scream. No good would come from this wish. But the magic rumbled under her flesh, demanding she fulfill it.

"I saw it," she said, through gritted teeth. *And watched it burn.* How would Andras react? The scent of her own burning flesh haunted her memories as she imagined returning with an armful of charred wood. It would be better to tell him now. "You should know the wish showed me its death."

Halvard looked up from his seat at the table, his face paling. "What do you mean, it died?"

Mora glanced his way, smiling when she noted his swollen knuckles stained by what must have been a painful bruise. They hadn't healed well—she assumed they were broken. "I don't answer to you."

The man flexed his fist only to wheeze in pain. Mora couldn't help her breathy, vicious laugh. The chair screeched against the worn wooden floor as he pushed away from the table, nearly bumping into the hearth. "You will learn to respect—"

"Leave it, Halvard," Andras warned. The nobleman clamped his mouth shut, but his narrowed gaze promised this wasn't over. Andras shook his head before turning back to Mora. "Tell me what you saw."

"A great tree falling to flames."

His bright eyes roved over her body, a knowing grin playing on his face. "You seem fine."

"Excuse me?"

Andras prowled closer, and it took everything in Mora's power not to shrink back. She bit her cheek until she tasted blood, praying he couldn't see her panic. "You burned alive and lived to tell the tale," he said with an edge of cruel amusement. Absent-mindedly, he trailed a finger down his nose. There was no sign of damage—he'd made her heal him—but Mora wondered if he felt a glimmer of fear. If the pain she'd caused haunted him too. "Even the God of Death can't claim you, Mora. I think you'll find the Spirit is the same."

Mora curled her fingers around her tunic, the soft linen and soothing scent of mint and summer rain a quiet comfort. The morning after she drank herself into oblivion, Zadriel shoved his shirt into her hands, grumbling about not wanting to put up with the scent of bile and liquor all day. Mora had beamed. It hadn't mattered that he scowled back.

Two weeks later, he continued to provide her with a new one daily. Mora practically swam in it—the large tunic fell to her knees. But with her belt cinched at her waist, it felt like a simple black dress. She liked it. A lot. Mora smiled softly as she clutched the fabric. She almost forgot Andras loomed over her. Her heart steadied and her jaw relaxed. She was a fool to press further, but her brave face felt less fragile. "And if you're wrong? What if all I can bring you is its corpse?"

A frown pulled at Andras's handsome features, those bright eyes narrowing. "I'm not wrong."

"What if—"

Andras closed the distance between them, herding Mora toward the wall. There was an uneven slant to the creaky floor and the sloping thatch ceiling was barely tall enough to accommodate his height at this end of the room. When they came to a stop in front of a meager window, he rested his hands on the sill, caging her in. Andras stared past her to the Forbidden Forest, a predatory gleam in his eyes. "You will find it. Alive. And return it to me. Have I made myself clear?"

"I'll bring you whatever remains," she spat, before slamming her hands against his hard chest. He was too close. The sickening scent of citrus made her chest tighten and she couldn't bear it. No matter how hard she stared at the splash of amber in his eye, all she saw was Dother.

He's dead, he's dead, he's dead...

Andras grabbed her wrist and squeezed until she stilled. "Remember what happens when you don't behave?"

Swallowing past a thick lump in her throat, Mora nodded slowly. "Yes," she mumbled, a slight tremble to her voice, her heart pounding viciously against her ribcage.

The pressure on her wrists eased and Mora sagged against the windowpane. "Good girl," Andras said. It took all the strength in her body not to cringe when he patted her cheek twice. "The trees will only part for their kind. Zadriel will escort you there in a few days, but he *must* stay hidden. I'll be shrouding you both in shadow sprites. And he'll need to leave within two weeks' time, with or without you. Once you enter, I wish for you to not leave the forest until you've found the Spirit. And to focus on finding it for the duration of your stay."

"Are you sending *both* pets away?" Halvard whined. He'd kicked his feet up on another worn chair, nibbling on blueberries and watching Andras and Mora as one watched a play.

"Yes," Andras said bluntly. He released Mora, walked to the table and plucked a blueberry from Halvard's chipped ceramic bowl. "I know what I'm doing."

"What if we bring the Fae mutt to the wood's edge? Once the trees open, we can—"

Andras crushed the blueberry between his fingers. "Halvard, I didn't recruit you for your mind. Do not exaggerate your purpose."

Halvard's lips curled downward. He slid his feet off the chair, stomping as he settled them onto the ground. "Need I remind you that you were an impoverished *nothing* before me. One lie about you being my long lost half-brother and I gave you everything." Halvard pointed at Mora. "Including your chance to get *her*." His body slanted forward as he stared Andras down, a challenge in his eyes.

Unfortunately, Halvard underestimated his power. Like most noblemen, he expected it. Felt obedience was owed, simply because of his class. But this wasn't high society—no one here cared about bloodlines.

"Are you done?" Andras's voice was deceptively calm.

"Done? We've barely begun speaking on the subject."

"You've forgotten yourself, Halvard. Perhaps I was nothing, but you were a minor lord with a drinking problem who couldn't earn the respect of his own mother without spending a dime. Now only one of those things is true."

Halvard stood so swiftly his chair toppled behind him. "Excuse me?" A furious blush bloomed across his face and up his ears.

Why don't you compare dicks and get it over with? Mora thought with a sneer. She pulled away from the windowsill and wondered if she could leave without being noticed. Glancing toward the open door off the kitchen, she found Zadriel watching her with those glittering black eyes. He cocked his head to the side in invitation. Before she could take a single step, Halvard's bowl flew past her, nearly hitting her face, and crashed against the wall. Blueberries and sharp pieces of white and blue ceramic rained down onto the floor.

Andras smirked as he eyed the mess. "You need to work on your aim."

"If you expect me to continue to support your interests, Andras, then you need to live up to your promises."

"Calm yourself. I intend to start work on your brooch today. Did you think I'd send Zadriel away before I made it?"

Halvard's brows lowered, but he didn't argue. "Fine." He frowned as he stared at the mess he'd made. "Those were the last of the berries. Can I get more?"

Andras sighed through his nose. "Mora?"

Zadriel's shoulders slumped and Mora stilled. She was so close to the door. "Yes?" she asked hesitantly.

"I wish for you to gather sustenance for the villagers before day's end. Meat and fruit... blueberries. Whatever else you can find in the wilds. It must be safe, edible, and in good condition. Nothing poisonous or rotten. You will ensure neither myself, nor any of the people here are harmed by the food you provide."

Icy tendrils of magic wrapped around her bones as goosebumps trailed up her arms. Gods, Andras was well prepared. Try as she might, she couldn't find any obvious ways to misinterpret his wishes. He was too specific. Thanks to Dother. Would there come a day when he didn't haunt her?

As if he listened from hell, the memory of his voice slithered through her mind. *I will always be your monster. And you will always be mine.*

Mora flexed her fingers, nodding to Andras while she wondered how long she'd need to endure this. Endure him. Endure Dother and the stain he'd left on her soul. *I'm so tired.*

She made for the exit, hoping the fresh air would soothe her nerves and help her think. But the boom of Andras's authoritative voice stopped her in her tracks. "Wait in the next room for a moment. Zadriel can help you once I've finished bleeding him."

A cold wave of horror washed over Mora. They were going to *bleed* him? She turned to face Zadriel, wide eyes roving over the mess of scars along his arms. Centuries of scars. They cut him, over and over again. Andras, Dother... How many years had he endured this? And for what purpose?

Unshed tears stung her eyes and her magic rumbled under her skin, begging to be released. It felt vicious—the tendrils crawled up her neck, pushing against her jaw until her skull ached. It thrashed relentlessly against whatever invisible barrier Dother created when he'd cursed her. But there was no wish to set it free—all she could do was turn into smoke. Which would accomplish nothing.

Mora sank her teeth into her raw cheek and forced herself to walk to Zadriel.

He stood in the doorway, his long fingers curled so tightly against the raw, wooden frame they'd turned white. A flush crept across his cheeks and moisture gathered on his brow. He dipped his chin as his starlit black eyes bore into hers, torturous sadness glittering in their depths. Pain twisted in her heart—she offered a small smile, but tears spilled down her cheeks. Zadriel's hand grazed hers and he gave her fingers a gentle squeeze before pushing away from the door and moving stoically into the kitchen.

"Zadriel. The door," Andras said, pointing with a sharp iron dagger. The daisies carved into the golden handle were a near perfect match to her flask.

Mora jumped as the door snicked closed. The thrum of her heart was deafening, and she was panting, overwhelmed with a need to rage. To tear at Andras's face until those bright eyes were nothing but a sticky, bloody mass beneath her fingernails. To rip the dagger from his grasp and slice the flesh on his arm until it tore away in one long slab. She'd feed it to him and watch as he gagged and begged her to stop. Most of all, she wanted to bleed him until he was nothing more than a mass of agonizing scars.

But she could do nothing.

Slumping against the wall, she slid to the cold floor and covered her eyes with her hands, begging her mind to stop racing. For her magic to calm. Praying the Gods would be kind and she wouldn't hear a thing while Zadriel suffered in the next room.

"I can't do this," Mora whispered to the darkness. She imagined the darkness simply laughed in return.

CHAPTER 25

MORA

The Gods were not kind. Zadriel's sharp hiss pierced through the thin wall, the pain in his voice stealing the breath from Mora's lungs. In response, her magic became rabid, clawing at her flesh and constricting her bones. The pressure had her panting. Clutching her chest in a desperate attempt to hold herself together.

It felt alive, her smoke. Eager to devour. They were on the same page—Mora slammed her fist against the wall when she heard another pained gasp.

"Fuck," she whispered.

Minutes trickled by slowly, as if the God of Time herself were in no hurry to end the torment. And Mora couldn't stand it. A clock *tick, tick, ticked* on the other end of the small space, each second mocking her.

She.

Was.

Powerless.

Mora tapped her foot on the cracked tile floor and dug her nails into her tunic. Zadriel's tunic. Stale, dusty air assaulted her nose—she couldn't help but cough and wheeze against the on-slaught. When Andras's voice sounded from the kitchen, low and domineering, she trembled, while some deep-seated part of her whispered he was coming for her next. She couldn't make out the words but recognized the tone. Dother's voice dipped low like that when she resisted. When he took what he wanted, furious it wasn't freely given.

That Andras dared speak to Zadriel in such a commanding tone while he sliced away at him... she couldn't bear it.

When another pained hiss found her ears, she stood without thought, her tense muscles begging to move. To do... something.

The cramped room somehow grew smaller, the walls pressing against her heated skin. It didn't help that the space was dark, the only source of light creeping in from the crack beneath the door. While she sucked greedily at the air, it wasn't enough—no relief found her lungs as she gasped with each inhale.

Tick.

Tick.

Tick.

Swallowing her shriek, Mora bolted to the source of that incessant sound, nearly tumbling when her knees hit the edge of a lumpy mat-tress. Her hands pressed into a soft linen blanket, hints of soothing mint wafting toward her nostrils. It calmed her pounding heart.

Crawling up the bed until her hands sank into Zadriel's pillow, she laid down and curled into a ball, pulling her knees to her chest.

His mattress sagged in the middle, likely worn from years of use. While she fit perfectly, Zadriel's feet would hang over the end—he was far too tall for such a small bed. For such a small room. This must have once been a pantry.

She could just make out the clock on his worn bedside table.

"I hate you," she muttered, closing her eyes, praying sleep would claim her.

Mora awoke puffy-eyed and parched. Someone laid a soft linen blanket on her as she slept, the warm fabric a soothing boon against her clammy skin. She'd fisted her hands in the sheets and the blanket tangled with her legs, but when she pressed her head back against the pillow she was enveloped by the comforting scent of mint and rain. Her body relaxed as she breathed it in and, for a moment, she felt safe.

"Are you awake, Little Witch?"

Mora jolted as Zadriel's deep voice washed over her. He sounded weak. Tired. She sat up and found him slumped beside the bed, his head resting against the mattress. Thick lashes tickled his high cheekbones—those beautiful, dark eyes were closed, lined with shadows. And a sickly pallor painted his typically warm, olive skin.

Mora whispered softly, "What can I do?"

"Nothing," Zadriel replied, his breathing shallow.

She pulled herself free from the blanket, careful not to jostle Zadriel's head, and slid down to the floor.

Blood soaked through the white bandages they'd secured around his arms. Mora sucked in a breath and clenched her fists in an attempt to calm the magic boiling under the surface. What could she do...

"You need to eat something," she said, more hopeful than certain. Food was one of the few things she had to offer. Reaching into her pouch, she pulled out a handful of chocolate truffles, trying and failing not to think about Frederick or Lillian. She took a deep breath and forced the memories away. There would be time for self-pity later.

"Take this." Mora held her hand out, but Zadriel didn't move. Didn't open his eyes. If it weren't for the soft rise and fall of his chest, she'd think he died. "Are you awake?"

"Yes," he breathed. "I just need a minute."

With her free hand, Mora wrapped her fingers around his wrist, hoping to feel his pulse, but he hissed and flinched away. The way his features tensed caused a panicked flutter in her heart. "I thought your kind healed quickly?"

Soft pants left his mouth through gritted teeth. "Not when injured with iron... or if we've lost a lot of blood." He smirked half-heartedly. "I have the misfortune of suffering both with some regularity."

Mora rubbed her chest, hoping to ease some of the tightness there. "I'm sorry." She looked down at the chocolates in her other hand—they were already melting, staining her palm. "Open your mouth."

Zadriel arched a dark brow. "Open my mouth?"

She heaved a sigh. "Trust me for a moment. Please."

The ass had the nerve to snort. "I'm not sure that's a good idea." While there was no venom in his voice, the words stung.

Could he be more needlessly difficult?

"Will you *please* shut your mouth and let me help you?"

"I thought you wanted me to open it?" Zadriel laughed. It was tired and soft, but musical all the same. The light, joyful sound brought a smile to Mora's face.

She closed her eyes and chuckled along with him. "You really are something." When she opened them again, Zadriel's mouth was open and waiting. "You should know," she said, delicately placing a chocolate on his tongue, "I'm not typically one to share."

A satisfied hum rumbled in his throat as he chewed on the dessert. "What was that?"

"You've never had chocolate before?" How could someone live hundreds of years and not experience chocolate?

"Never," he said, licking the last bits from his lips, an easy smile lighting up his face. Joy looked good on him. It gave him a youthful glow. A glimpse at who he could have been, if not for whatever tragedy led him here.

Mora popped another in his mouth, grinning as he savored the candy. They continued this way until her entire stash was gone. Some of the color returned to his face and Mora nearly sagged with relief. "You have a sweet tooth," she said as she sucked the last bits of chocolate from her fingers.

Zadriel opened a single eye and watched her as she stood. "My mother used to tell me I got that from my father."

"Oh?" Mora looked around for the first time, searching the cramped space for anything that may help him. It was, thankfully, brighter with the door open. And blissfully quiet—Andras and Halvard must have left.

A glass of water sat on the worn, wooden bedside table, beside that incessant clock. It was lucky to be alive, as far as Mora was concerned. The rest of the wall was covered by a dark, warped wooden shelf cluttered with bowls, pots and clear glass jars filled with what she assumed were plants, powders and dried herbs. "What was his favorite dessert?"

"I have no idea. He died before I was born."

The sadness in his tone made her throat tighten. Mora paused and looked back at him. "Did you want to talk about it?"

"There's not much to say. I never knew him, though I feel like I did. My mother spoke of him endlessly. If she hadn't been pregnant with me when he passed, I'm not sure she would have recovered. They were bonded. Mates. A piece of her soul died with him. I hope they found each other in the next realm."

"Your mother—"

Zadriel shook his head, pain and grief flooding his dark eyes. "I'd rather not talk about her."

Mora nodded, her own heart heavy in her chest. "I understand. More than I'd like to." She cleared her throat. "Let's get you something to drink." Maybe she could relieve some of his pain.

Turning back to the shelves, Mora continued her search. Her father often made teas when someone wasn't well and tried to teach her which herbs worked best. She tapped her lip as she took a closer look at those jars. There were some familiar powdered herbs and small bottles of oils. A pale yellow one stuck out, and she reached for it, hoping it was the earthy, woody oil Kalyan preferred. When her hand hit a woven basket, jostling whatever was inside, she froze. Vials upon vials of crimson liquid caught her eye.

Blood. So much blood.

Mora squeezed her shaking fists and forced herself to remain calm. But pain bloomed behind her ribs as her smoke attempted to burrow out. Was this all Zadriel's? Did they take *this much* today? How could they make him sleep next to symbols of his own torture? Her stomach twisted. She couldn't stand it.

She reached into the basket and plucked a single vial. It was still warm. Fresh. What evil did Andras intend to weave with this much Fae blood? Could she somehow use it against him?

Mora peeked back at Zadriel, grateful his eyes were once again closed, before tucking the vial into her pouch. One likely wouldn't accomplish much. But any more and Andras may ask questions.

She forced herself to scan the rest of the shelves, swallowing a shriek. To the right of the basket were jars of horrors. Piles of perfectly preserved eyes and bones, slabs of what looked like skin. There were too many trapped sprites to count, piled into worn woven baskets of their own. Bile crept up her throat when she saw a tiny, purple-haired pixie whose wings had been torn from its back. It stared up at her with hopeless yellow eyes.

"My gods," she whispered, reaching for the jar.

"He'll notice," Zadriel warned. "And he won't be nice about it."

Mora bared her teeth. "Maybe I won't be nice either."

"It's your funeral."

"He can't kill me."

"No. But he'll make you wish you were dead." He swallowed. "He'd probably take it out on me."

The cool glass kissed her fingers—she could grab it now and figure out the rest later... but she hesitated. While it wasn't ideal, she'd be willing to burn again if it meant this creature would be free. But could she condemn another? "He'd hurt you again?"

"I never give him reason to, other than the bleedings. But this is my room, and that's a creature of Arcadia. If the pixie goes missing, he'll assume I did it."

Mora nodded and stared at the pixie, who'd scurried to the other side of the glass. The poor creature was shaking. "I'll try to come back for you," she said, praying she could.

It killed her, turning away. Leaving the sprites and the pixie to rot in their glass prisons. Mora took a slow, deep breath, begging her racing heart to calm. She schooled her features and plucked the jar of oil from the shelf, smiling when that familiar woody, earthy scent wafted in the air. A few drops in Zadriel's water, along with pinches of healing herbs, and maybe he'd feel better. Sadly, there was no sugar and the water was cold—it was going to taste awful.

As she stirred the drink with her finger, Zadriel flexed his wrists and winced, but already he looked much better.

"Can I ask why...?"

"Why they bleed me?" Mora nodded and Zadriel shrugged, or at least attempted to. The weight of his fatigue made it difficult to lift his broad shoulders. "My blood's powerful because of what I am. It helps with their enchanting."

"To hell with their enchanting," she seethed, squeezing the glass so hard she wondered if it would crack. Did Dother do this too? All his talk about the rights of those with magic, and *this* was how he made things. Oh gods... did he use Zadriel's blood to make her pouch? To curse her? What hold did they have on him? "Is your curse like mine?"

"Not exactly. We're both tied to their bloodline. But, while Cillian bound you to an object, his father bound me to their blood. I need to be near them or... it hurts."

Pain like a wish unfulfilled? Mora rubbed her chest, remembering every broken bone, every wheezing breath.

Zadriel continued, "I don't grant wishes. But they have an endless supply of my blood, and... it's easier, and far less painful, to do what they say."

Mora's jaw cracked as she clenched her teeth. "Or they make you obey with blood magic?"

Zadriel looked away as he nodded.

A blood thrall. They were temporary, but the few times she'd witnessed it... Mora shivered. It was horrific, to have an Enchanter bind their blood to yours and puppeteer you. Gods, the Dothers were awful.

"You spoke of him in your sleep."

Mora tensed. "Which one?"

"Cillian. You were thrashing, and you said... I didn't know. I didn't know and..." Zadriel inhaled deeply, anguish flooding his expression. "Mora, I'm sorry."

Mora's eyes squeezed shut, hating that he witnessed her nightmare. That she'd allowed herself to be vulnerable in his presence yet again. When she returned her gaze to his she lifted her chin. "I made him pay," she said, her voice laced with venom.

Zadriel nodded grimly. "When you killed him, I wasn't far. We planned to travel to Arcadia as soon as he was able. He was going to set me free."

"I'm sure he was very convincing," she said as she knelt beside him. Slowly, she brought the glass of water to his lips. Her grip was hard—a violent torrent of rage and sorrow threatened to undo her, and her muscles trembled in response—but she couldn't afford to spill a drop. Zadriel lifted his hand and wrapped it around hers, his touch soft and warm. The monster within her stilled in response. She released a breath, her grip easing, and together they tipped the cup back so he could drink.

Zadriel's face twisted with pain as he moved his arm, but he sipped on the concoction and didn't complain about the undoubtedly horrific taste. Mora hoped it gave him some relief.

When he finished, she placed the empty cup back on the bedside table. Splotches of fresh blood soaked through his bandages and Mora frowned. "He never would have let you go."

"You don't know that!" Zadriel's nostrils flared, but his heated glare focused on something over her shoulder. "Cillian was the closest thing I had to family."

Mora followed his stare to the doorframe. There were divots gouged in the wood with faded names and numbers beside each one. Squinting, she gasped when she realized it said Cillian, over and over again. And suddenly, at around five feet, a second name that began with a Z was added, though the writing was less elegant. Messy. As if written by a child. It became clearer as the heights climbed, until it reached Zadriel's current six-and-a-half foot frame.

"You grew up here together," she breathed. Of course Dother lied about Eldenna.

"We did. Brennan, Cillian's father, founded this village as a secret haven for Halflings. Somewhere they could live without fear of the Laws, right under the king's nose."

How magnanimous of him. Mora doubted Brennan had a single good intention and couldn't care less about Dother's legacy.

"Did Dother bleed you?"

Zadriel shrugged. "It doesn't matter."

"It does matter, Zadriel. You know as well as I do Dother only cared about himself and whatever power he could achieve. His love, if that's what you'd like to call it, was poison. It didn't matter if you wanted it or not... he made you into whatever he wanted you to be. He can't do that anymore. Stop being his pawn." Zadriel tipped his head back on the bed, those black eyes boring into hers. Time slowed as they watched one another in silence. Shivers ran up her spine, but she withstood his careful assessment. "I'm sorry you're cursed and you can't go home," she said softly. "Deep down, you know I'm not responsible for what you've endured. No more than you are responsible for my misery."

Zadriel's throat bobbed as he swallowed hard and he tilted his chin in acknowledgment. Then he pressed his elbows into the bed, groaning as he pushed himself to his feet. The old, wooden bedframe creaked as he slowly rose to his full height. When he wobbled, Mora stood swiftly and attempted to steady him, but the Fae shook his head. "I'll be fine. Andras and Halvard are meeting with the Village Council. He'll expect us to gather food before they come back."

Mora rolled her eyes. She had until day's end. And Zadriel needed rest. But when she studied him she noted the firm set of his jaw, the agony in his eyes. He needed to leave this room. Now.

Mora held out her hand. "I suppose I can cooperate this once," she said. An easy smile warmed his pale face and her chest felt lighter.

Lacing his fingers with hers, he took a few slow steps forward. "Let's go, Little Witch."

CHAPTER 26

MORA
300 YEARS AGO

*M*ora shoved the last piece of lemon tart into her mouth, barely able to appreciate the sweet, citrusy flavor. At least it
mixed well with the taste of wine still permeating her palate. Her feet
wouldn't cooperate and she stumbled into the doorframe that led to her
rooms. Why was it slanted? The whole world spun.

Delicate garland stuffed with peonies, roses, lilies and baby's breath
framed her door. Again. She'd already torn it down three times and
tossed it over her balcony railing.

"I hate you," Mora slurred as she crushed a handful of flowers in
her fist. Petals rained down when she tore the garland away from the
wall. "I hate everything."

The flowers dragged behind her like a living train when she entered
her room. They caught beneath the door after she slammed it shut,
but she couldn't find the will to care. Slumping against the wood, she
hoped Philip hadn't noticed her slip away, or heard the crash of her

door against the frame. Otherwise he'd come running. He always came running. That ridiculous, sweet man.

The fact that they forced her to make an appearance tonight was disgusting. What must people have thought? Would they gossip about the Princess of Berwick downing an entire bottle of wine at her mother's wedding? Mora hiccupped and then giggled—Aedlin wouldn't be happy she had so much to drink. Good. At least they were both miserable.

Kicking off her rose shoes, a color Aedlin insisted on, she moved through her sitting room, ignoring the cozy, white chaise. She'd have someone remove it in the morning. The plush carpet in her bedroom cushioned her sore feet, and she sighed, half considering lying on the floor because her bed felt... wrong. Someone would need to get rid of that too.

The space was a mess, her armoire open, gowns in an array of beautiful colors tossed to the floor. Soon she'd throw her current gown into the pile. A breathtaking corseted pink garment with off-white lace detailing that hugged her generous bust, tapered at the waist and flared out into a thick skirt. It was breathtaking. And she hated it. Rosemary could take her pick tomorrow.

Every letter Cillian—no, Dother—ever wrote was torn into tiny pieces and littered one of her bedside tables. She intended to toss them into the fireplace tonight. Looked forward to watching them burn.

Curling her toes, she took a deep breath, trying to focus on the soft texture of the rug and the relief in her aching heels instead of—Mora growled when her anger flooded through the moment of comfort, crowding her senses. No, she couldn't not think about it.

How could anyone celebrate this ridiculous marriage? They acted as if Lord Dother hadn't been courting the queen's daughter less than two weeks ago. Or should she say King *Dother.*

That fucking bastard married her mother. It all happened so fast.

Those blinding blue eyes boring into her soul as he begged her to marry him still haunted her. And then her mother tried to convince her, told her Berwick needed stability now more than ever. A queen and king on the throne. It had been a mere handful of days since her father...

Tears welled up behind Mora's eyes and she took a deep breath, begging herself not to cry. Grief clung to her like a second skin, sinking deeper into her flesh whenever she allowed herself to acknowledge it. When she tried to ignore it and go on as if everything was fine, it followed her. Sank into her shadow and crawled along the floor, waiting to catch the corner of her eye. Every second without him hurt.

Mora couldn't help but laugh, the sound dull and unamused, as she remembered telling both of them now wasn't the time for a wedding. They disagreed. And made other plans.

Frankly, they deserved each other.

Could Dother not see her pain? Did he not understand she needed time?

Clearly not. At least it answered her question. The man never loved her—he loved her title and her crown. Mora tore the glittering, diamond encrusted tiara from her head. It did horrible things to her carefully braided bun and tore more than a few strands of hair from her head. Thankfully the alcohol numbed the pain. She stared apathetically at the silver crown before tossing it onto her pile of dresses. Rosemary could have that too, for all she cared.

"I loved him," she said to the empty room. "I can't believe I loved him." And she was starting to think he loved her too. *That perhaps they had a future together.*

Mora's blood heated. She'd been so incredibly stupid, letting him sneak into her rooms and whisper such pretty promises in her ear. She could still feel his breath on her neck, his hardness between her thighs, his grin against her cheek when she cried his name, Cillian. *She considered yet another bath, eager to scrub her skin raw once again. But that meant calling for Rosemary. And the look of pity on her lady-in-waiting's face was the last thing she wanted.*

Mora froze. Oh gods, they'd have to consummate their union. Tonight. She gagged at the thought, hating the burn in her throat and the alcohol stirring uncomfortably in her belly. The press of her snug gown against her stomach. She twisted and shimmied in a fruitless attempt to reach the laces and free herself, but it was impossible. "Why is everyone and everything against me?" she screeched. Without Rosemary, she'd be stuck.

"I don't need you, Rosemary," she mumbled to the empty room, slurring her words, "I don't need anyone."

Mora fell back on the bed, her thick skirt cushioning her landing, and stared up at the white lace canopy. Tiny, white flowers had been stitched along the trim. How dare they look so... weddingy.

Aedlin's voice haunted her mind.

I'm sorry.

Please, try to understand.

It will be loveless.

No one could ever replace your father.

This is for the good of the kingdom.

The nobility love Lord Dother.

If you're unwilling to wed and take the throne, I'll do what I must to ensure stability.

Mora barely said a word to her since the wedding was announced. But, as much as she hated to admit it, she missed her mother. Pitied her even. Aedlin was more than capable of ruling alone, she simply couldn't see it.

And Dother—that man had the nobility wrapped around his fingers. Knew them all by name. Somehow formed more connections than she had as the crowned princess. They adored him, looked to him, trusted his judgment. He'd played them all and won the crown.

Damn him.

Damn his love letters.

Damn his handsome face.

Mora struggled as she attempted to roll onto her side, the volume of her skirt hindering her movements. She grunted as she added more force but immediately regretted the decision. When she spun, the world spun with her, and her stomach clenched in warning.

The bottle of wine was a mistake...

Curling her arm around her pillow, Mora nuzzled the silky material, staining the light fabric with the dark kohl she'd used to line her eyes. Perhaps a nap would help ease her stomach and mind. Burning Dother's letters could wait. It would be foolish to play with fire in her state.

Mora was about to close her eyes when something glimmered in the low firelight. A strange bottle sat on the table between her bed and the wall. It was beautiful, a flask adorned with gilded leaves and flowers.

The strangest part—the bottle glowed. It called to her, like a quiet song only she could hear. Before she thought better of it, she reached out, eager to touch its surface.

Something inside of her stilled when she trailed her fingers over the crystal. It was warm and hummed under her touch. Did the golden liquid inside move in response to her fingers? Or was the alcohol playing tricks on her mind?

A note sat folded by the bottle's side and she couldn't help but grumble at the familiar scrawl along the paper's surface. Treasure.

"Why does he insist on haunting my one moment of peace," she said, snatching up the note.

Mora,

I know you're unhappy with my decision. I can't help but be unhappy with how things turned out as well. But I hope one day you'll come to understand.

Consider this gift my apology. A promise to make things right between us.

We're bound now. Not in a way either of us wanted, but I won't allow this to tarnish our bright future.

Yours,
Cillian

Mora shrieked and crumpled the gods damned note in her fist. It took three tries to stand, thanks to her ridiculous dress, and the bedding slid off the bed with her, sheets and furs now half on the floor. Tossing the note into the fireplace, she extended her hand and allowed a spray of fire to spill from her fingers, coaxing the low flames higher. Watching the note burn soothed the weight in her chest, though her heart still

WISH

raced. How dare he call her Treasure or speak of how they were now bound by this ridiculous marriage?

Gods, she needed another drink.

Marching back to her bedside, she swiped Dother's gift off the table, the crystal scraping against the polished wood. Her mother would be furious about the scratch. Good.

The liquid sloshing around inside the bottle was inviting.

Dother collected fancy alcohol and loved to enjoy a glass in the evening. An amber liquid with a sweet aftertaste was his favorite. It was too strong for Mora's liking, but strong sounded good tonight.

If she were lucky, it would help her forget everything, if only for a moment. The idea soothed her. Even if it meant she technically accepted his pathetic attempt at an apology.

Twisting the topper free, she tossed it behind her, unphased when it hit the floor with a loud thunk. A sweet smell invaded her senses—there were familiar notes of citrus and herbs with hints of copper, reminding her of the man she wished to erase from her mind. But there was something else. Something akin to burnt sugar.

Tipping it back, she couldn't help but moan when the delicious flavor bloomed on her tongue. It was unlike anything she'd ever experienced—the sweet taste overwhelmed her senses and she found herself gulping it down greedily. With each swallow she felt lighter—her head cleared—and something else... something strange bloomed in her chest. It felt like the familiar well of fire within her was expanding.

It felt incredible. Liberating. Like coming home.

Until it didn't.

As she swallowed the last drop, something changed.

The bottle slipped from her fingers, plunking on the ground and bouncing off the carpet. Mora gasped and stumbled as something

213

twisted under her ribs. She slapped her hand against her chest, her heart sputtering, and struggled to breathe under the pressure. The power expanding within her grew too large, pushing against her bones so hard she heard a crack.

Then another.

And another.

Mora screamed as her ribs snapped, one after the other as something violent pressed against them, demanding release. It didn't want this any more than she did. Curling her arms protectively around her center did nothing but grant her the horror of feeling her bones twist and break under her fingers.

Something was wrong. Something was very, very wrong.

Mora's legs gave out and she could do nothing to stop the fall. Pain erupted in her head when her cheek hit the ground, but it barely distracted from the agony in her chest. Whatever was inside her was tearing her apart.

An intense sensation bloomed near her heart, the feeling akin to a tug, as if someone attempted to pull a thread. Gritting her teeth, she pulled back with all her might, not certain what she was doing but knowing it was important she did.

Time stilled when an odd wind whooshed through her chambers, snuffing out the firelight and blanketing her in darkness.

A snick sounded in the entryway as someone closed the door to her rooms. "Philip," she cried, praying he heard her screams and came to help. But as the slow, quiet footsteps made their way toward her bedroom, she realized it couldn't be him. There was no urgency.

Whoever it was, they came to watch.

A subtle citrus aroma wafted in the air and Mora knew.

The pull in her chest tugged harder, and she could feel the flask calling to her, its song attempting to soothe and coax her into its suffocating embrace. Whatever was inside her purred in response. It wanted to go to the flask. Mora gritted her teeth, shaking as she denied its call, but she couldn't fight it forever.

Writhing on the floor, she caught a glimpse of his silhouette, standing in the shadows outside her room. He'd done this... bound them somehow. Mora felt whatever magic he'd spun tethering them together and knew she could never deny him. Never be free.

Whatever Dother did, there would be no escape. He got his wish—Mora eternally by his side.

CHAPTER 27

ZADRIEL

An itch skittered up Zadriel's arms as his flesh worked to knit itself back together. It took all his strength not to tear away the bandages and scratch until he bled once more. The Little Witch wouldn't be happy.

Mora was already a handful. He stumbled *once,* and the woman veered off course, pulling him to the stables.

But her soft hand felt warm in his. Grounding. And her tonic, disgusting as it was, worked wonders. Though he wasn't sure how he'd managed to swallow the entire glass without gagging. It tasted like dirt, still coating his tongue. Though it was worth it—Zadriel's pain was little more than a dull throb. And while the black hood covering his ears was too hot for the summer sun, even that felt less burdensome.

Though he wouldn't mind cleansing his palate with another piece of chocolate.

When they neared the stable entrance, Zadriel wondered what Mora had in mind. She marched forward with a single-minded focus, until someone rounded the building.

This should be interesting.

Alina, a freckle-faced girl barely nineteen, didn't look up as she tipped a metal bucket into a trough. The muscles in her thin, sun-kissed arms shook, sweat coating her skin, and she compensated with too much force. Water sloshed against the side of the trough, slipping over the wood and plunging to the ground with an audible splash. Droplets soaked her brown trousers. Alina stared at the muddy puddle, her mouth agape, before running her free hand through her short, blonde curls.

"Gods," she hissed under her breath. But not quietly enough for Zadriel's Fae ears.

He chuckled and Mora flashed him a questioning look. Zadriel simply shook his head, reminding himself not to get lost in that stare. It was unnervingly difficult. Those bright eyes were like buttered gems of honeyed amber. And when her focus returned to Alina, they sparkled with mischief and deadly promises. What was she up to?

When Alina turned to gather more water, she finally noticed them. Whatever she saw when she looked at Mora had the blood draining from her face. Zadriel wasn't surprised. Mora had a... presence. It didn't matter if Alina didn't understand what lurked beneath her skin—the beast behind Mora's eyes made itself known.

Mora released Zadriel's hand and sauntered closer, her shoes crunching over stray pieces of hay. He couldn't help but smirk when she pushed back her shoulders, lifted her chin and said, "Fetch us a horse."

It wasn't a question—regal authority dripped through Mora's tone.

Hello, Princess.

Alina's pale eyebrows lowered as she took a tentative step back, the poor thing already shaking like a leaf. He watched with keen interest as Mora displayed her rage proudly, the weight of her anger wafting around her like some physical thing.

She was a force of nature. A delightfully vicious creature.

Scents of crackling embers, lavender, and pine with a kiss of mint curled in the air—Mora's scent—and he closed his eyes, inhaling deeply. Hating how much he liked it.

"Who are you?" Alina asked, her voice trembling.

Mora scoffed and stepped closer. They were matched in height, but somehow Mora managed to tower over her. "I'm the monster Andras brought back to your..." she paused, eyeing the aged lumber making up the stable's façade. Her stare traveled the length of the pasture and the rickety fence barely keeping the horses in the field, before she returned her gaze to Alina. With a mocking smirk she finished her thought. "...quaint little village."

Zadriel pulled his dark hood away from his eyes and leaned against a wooden fence post, careful not to test its strength with the entirety of his weight. The girl looked to him as if asking for support, but all Zadriel offered in return was a slow smile.

You're on your own, child.

"I can't give you a horse," Alina said, with little confidence. "I don't know you. Andras needs to vouch for you first."

The girl flinched when Mora clapped a hand on her shoulder, tendons standing out so starkly on her throat Zadriel could see her hammering pulse. A dangerous gleam sparkled in Mora's captivating eyes as she asked, "Is Andras your king?"

Alina shook her head. "We serve no king. But Andras is our leader."

"No king, no lord, but loyal subjects all the same," Mora mused, pursing her lips as she trailed her fingers up the girl's dainty shoulder and across her neck until her hand encompassed her throat. She squeezed lightly, pushing the young woman until her back hit the stable wall. "Fetch. Us. A. Horse," she demanded, enunciating each word with terrible clarity. Alina's hazel eyes darted around, searching for aid.

With a sigh, Zadriel pulled away from his perch. The Little Witch was getting out of hand, and as much as he enjoyed watching her aggressive display, he couldn't allow any harm to come to the young woman. Alina didn't deserve it, and Andras would be murderous.

With a shaky hand, Alina pressed her palm firmly into Mora's chest. The cursed woman cocked her head to the side, her expression cold. "I wouldn't bother—"

A blue light erupted between them, smashing into Mora like an invisible force. It tossed her in the air as if she weighed nothing—Mora slammed to the ground at Zadriel's feet, dust and hay floating around them. Dirt sullied the black tunic he'd lent her and stained her dark gray leggings.

"It's best not to assume people are powerless here." Zadriel grimaced when she stared at her bloodied palms. "Are you ok?"

A deranged giggle bubbled up from Mora's chest until she was practically gasping for air. Had she lost her mind? He opened his mouth to ask but couldn't find any words. Crouching beside her, Zadriel ran a tentative hand over her back—that calmed her before.

Mora pushed him away and stood, brushing the dirt from her shoulders. "A little Aegist. Adorable."

Alina trembled and lifted her hands, summoning a shield. Power spilled from her palm and flew through the air, curling around her until she was nestled safely inside a translucent, blue-tinted sphere. When Zadriel squinted, he could see sparks of magic, reacting to the dust particles bouncing against her protective wall. Alina took a steadying breath, tension melting from her shoulders. Oh, she had no idea what she was up against.

Mora narrowed her eyes as she brushed her knuckles over the spot where the magic blasted her chest. Assessing the threat.

Zadriel watched, still crouched on the ground, when something soft tickled his fingers. He looked down to find a cluster of gilded daisies, stained with drops of Mora's blood. They hadn't been there moments before—he reached out, hesitant, wondering if he was losing his mind. A sad smile tugged on his lips when he ran his fingers over their petals, the delicate things as soft as he remembered. He could nearly hear his mother's voice, singing in the old tongue, the language of trees. It made his heart so heavy he could hardly stand it.

Vehsa. He barely remembered her face, struggled to picture her bright golden eyes. But he'd held onto her name all these long years. To how much she'd loved him.

Zadriel's throat constricted, his fist curling around the daisies.

Vehsa had been proud of their purpose, their power. It was her honor, she'd said, to pass down her knowledge. Would she love him now if she knew what he'd become? What he'd done?

Power rumbled within him, the sleeping beast suddenly ravenous. It was almost too much—he rarely acknowledged it existed and was unprepared for its push against his chest. The daisies leaned into his touch as his mother's screams echoed in his ears. Clenching his fist tighter, he tore the golden sap from the flowers, pushing with his power until it bled from their stems. Thick, gilded liquid splashed onto the earth. It twisted in the dirt until every drop gathered into a long strand and slithered toward him. Zadriel didn't want it. He pulled away, willing the sap to crawl into the earth instead—it could feed the plants there or find its way to the great oak. Her oak.

When the blackened husks of the daisies withered and returned to the soil, he released a shuddering breath. It didn't make him feel better. Little ever did.

A whinny drew his focus and he and Mora spun in unison. Lyriah, Andras's horse, neared, because of course it had to be his damn horse. Mora's thunderous expression turned contemplative, and he shook his head. "Don't get any ideas, Little Witch," he said, but she paid him no mind.

Lyriah's speckled white and gray muzzle descended into the trough and Mora's head tilted slightly, recognition shining in her eyes. The most wicked smile appeared on her face. This creature was trouble.

Mora twisted back to the poor stablehand, the young woman slowly moving along the edge of the building toward the gates.

"What's the girl's name?" she asked Zadriel.

Zadriel rubbed his jaw as he weighed the merit of sharing her name. Should he give in to Mora's whims? A name wouldn't sway her from whatever hell-path she'd settled on, but denying her may cause more chaos.

If he needed to, he could subdue her. Exhaustion still clung to his body, but the pain was little more than an echo. And without a wish to unleash her, she was no match. Though he knew she could put up quite a fight.

Zadriel pinched the bridge of his nose—he was in no mood for broken bones today. It would be smarter to force her into a bargain, but he needn't be any more attached to her than he already was. And he doubted he had the skills to outwit her.

"They call her Alina," he answered with a sigh, hoping he chose the easier path. Mora's eyes softened as she watched him and he felt a warm pulse in his chest in response.

"And the horse?"

"Lyriah."

She grinned. "Thank you."

Lyriah watched with interest, swishing her long white tail against a group of bothersome flies.

"Such a pretty girl," Mora cooed as she approached. "Isn't this Andras's horse?" She ran her hand along Lyriah's strong neck and looked back at Alina, arching her brow in question.

Alina stopped dead in her tracks, mere feet from the gates. Her translucent blue shield still pulsed around her—she'd kept her hands raised as she pushed her magic to protect her from Mora. She gulped and nodded, her face ashen.

Mora clicked her tongue. "It would be a pity if something happened to her." She continued patting Lyriah gently while the horse nibbled on stray pieces of hay that littered the ground. "Andras would be so mad."

Glittering wisps of midnight smoke leaked from her fingers and loosely circled the horse's neck.

Zadriel swallowed. "Mora, don't." How was she doing this?

His feet moved before he'd made the decision to intervene. He should have known better. Shouldn't have underestimated her. Mora held up her other hand and a puddle of smoke he hadn't noticed rose up and twisted around his legs. That vixen! The feel of her magic was frigid as he tugged against the vaporous shackles. Their hold was gentle but they wouldn't budge. Of course they wouldn't. Damn raw magic. Damn Little Witch.

Zadriel's lips curled back, and he growled, a deep, low rumble that would send most men running. But Mora stared at his sharp canines, unimpressed. Not even gifting him a flinch.

Mora left him restrained by her cool smoke—a trail of vaporous obsidian followed behind her like an ethereal cape as she approached the girl. Alina pressed harder against her shield, the sphere growing to keep Mora farther away, but Mora didn't balk. She stopped and lifted her hand, tapping lightly against the shield, the full force of her eerie gaze on Alina's face. A zap sounded with each touch, and the tip of her finger blistered.

"Do you know what Andras asked me to do, Alina?"

The girl's knees shook, though Zadriel admired that she held Mora's glowing stare. "No."

"He told me to scour the wilds for food. The way I see it, the difference between this field and the wilds is an old, rickety fence." Her smile widened to a sinister edge that made Zadriel shiver. "One small push and the horses roam free."

Alina's wide eyes nearly bulged from her skull.

"I'm going to give you a choice," Mora said coolly. "Either I cull your herd, starting with Andras's lovely mare, or you saddle her up for us. It's up to you." She raised her hands in mock surrender and took three large steps back.

Alina paled and skirted the building to the door before releasing her shield. The blue orb popped like a bubble as she ran into the stables, straight to the tack room.

Mora's grin was triumphant as she crossed her arms and glanced back at Zadriel. "Can I release you, or are you still intent on tackling me?"

"You're unbelievable," he grumbled.

Mischief glimmered in her eyes as she pulled her smoke back, releasing his legs. "I'll take that as a compliment."

CHAPTER 28

ZADRIEL

"**I** can walk, Little Witch," Zadriel groaned, horrified she'd insisted he mount Lyriah. It felt wrong, sitting in Andras's saddle, the dark, pristine leather in better shape than his own. Mora hadn't joined him, opting instead to hold the reins and lead the way.

They would face hell for this later.

Mora tilted her head up until their eyes met. "Says the man who was stumbling around like a newborn colt thirty minutes ago."

He gripped the saddle horn tightly. "Was it that bad?" He could feel the heat in his cheeks, knew the tips of his ears turned a humiliating shade of red. For once, he felt grateful for the cloak Andras made him wear.

"It was." Mora's tone left no room for argument. Her focus slid away, dismissing him as she sauntered through the unkempt field.

He gritted his teeth when he noticed the carvings on her belt... his mother's belt.

That was Cillian's doing. It was all Cillian's doing.

Zadriel let his gaze wander, admiring the way his tunic hugged her shapely backside and the swish of her thighs as she marched ahead.

It was oddly pleasing, seeing her in his clothes. Matching him.

This was harder than he'd anticipated. It would be easier to keep hating her.

"You need rest," Mora added, stealing his focus. "This is the best I could offer."

Zadriel's sigh was heavy, but he conceded, closing his eyes and tipping his head back. The sun felt nice on his face. And he could smell the fresh soil as the village's Naturalists tended the gardens.

Mora didn't let the silence linger.

"Are you a Naturalist?"

Had she read his mind? "No, why do you ask?"

She gestured toward Arcadia looming in the distance. "Trees react to you. Is it because you're Fae?"

"They react because..." Zadriel trailed off, thinking of those daisies. His mother. Cursing whatever Gods decided his kind couldn't lie. "It's because of what I am."

It was an effort not to sag with relief when Mora accepted his answer and moved on. Perhaps he'd been too quick to curse the Gods.

"Is magic the same for Fae as it is for Halflings?"

"Halflings are limited by the well they're born with."

"And the Fae?"

Zadriel swallowed. "We can be more."

"That's it?" Mora dropped her voice low in an attempt to sound like him. "*We can be more.* Surely there's more to it."

Zadriel ran a hand down his face. *May the Mother spare me.*

"There are many creatures in Arcadia. Not all of them laid with humans, so Halflings don't have their abilities. And the abilities you do have are limited. While you, for example, could control fire, a Fae Elementalist could influence all elements."

"Do you know why Halflings were forced out?"

That was a question he should have anticipated. Zadriel stared at the looming wall of trees in the distance, wondering what could have been. "That was before I was born."

Mora looked back, studying his face. "That's not—"

Zadriel interrupted, changing the subject. "You didn't have to be cruel to the girl."

Her grip on the reigns tightened, but she kept marching them further away from the village. "She wouldn't have given us the horse otherwise."

Zadriel nodded, knowing she was right. They didn't trust strangers here—without Andras's approval, Alina wouldn't have willingly given Mora anything.

With each step, he could feel the tether that connected him to Andras drawing taut. It vibrated in his chest, a warning not to wander far, unless he wanted to feel how the thread weaved around his muscles, his organs... his soul. It would shred them apart, piece by piece, until he lay in agony, coughing up blood. Eventually, he'd drown in it. Only to heal and suffer again, until he crawled back or the Dothers found him.

He learned that lesson when he was eight.

Zadriel bit his lip, glancing down at Mora again. He missed Cillian. Missed the brother who played with him when his father wasn't looking. Who comforted him, grieved with him. Things changed when he embraced the destiny his father envisioned and set his eye on the throne. When he started bleeding Zadriel too.

The things he'd made Zadriel do...

Would Cillian have let him go? Zadriel held on to his promise for centuries. It was easier to blame Mora for his misery than accept... he'd lost his brother long before Cillian died.

What Mora muttered as she thrashed in her sleep... Zadriel couldn't forgive it.

They had to be better, do better.

"Alina's innocent."

Rolling her eyes, Mora looked away, her pace quickening. "No one's innocent, Zadriel."

Zadriel did his best to keep his low voice gentle. "She's not your enemy."

"She lives in my enemy's village, she sees my enemy as her ruler. Doesn't sound like an ally." Her fingers flexed around the reigns, leather digging into her palm.

"She's barely nineteen," Zadriel replied, his voice soft, pleading. "This village has been a safe haven for Halflings for centuries. They've all suffered under the Laws. You can't blame them for clinging to those who've protected them and fought for their safety."

Mora stopped suddenly, her body tensing. Zadriel could *feel* the stiffness in her bones as if they were his own. "Who the hell are you to tell me who I can and cannot blame?" she asked, venom lacing every word. A dark blush flooded her warm brown cheeks.

Zadriel exhaled deeply and rubbed his forehead. This wasn't going the way he'd hoped. "Have you forgotten I'm as trapped as you are?"

Mora continued to give him her back, but her breathing quickened. "I don't know your story, Zadriel, but let me make one thing clear. I won't be kind to the people who worship the family that *protected* them and *fought for their safety* by destroying everything I once held dear. To those who revere a man whose ancestor cursed me, raped me, ravaged and ruined who I once was, and made me into the monster I am now." When she faced him her amber eyes were aflame, raw magic radiating in that ominous glow. "I will burn this village to the ground the moment I'm given the chance."

Zadriel sucked in a sharp breath. "What good will that do?"

"The flames will warm my soul." She smiled, a cold, cruel grin that made him shiver. Told him she meant every word. Or, at least, thought she did.

His lips pressed together in a thin line as his gaze bounced between her eyes searching for... he didn't know what. "No, Mora, they won't. You're mad at Cillian for making you into a monster? Stop being one. I saw the look in your eyes after Lillian, I know—"

"Don't you dare!" she screeched, tossing the reigns at him and storming away.

"Wait!" Zadriel jumped off Lyriah's back, hating that he stumbled, still struggling to heal the damage caused by the iron dagger. "Please stay," he whispered to Lyriah, praying she'd listen. If she disappeared, blood loss would be the least of his problems.

Zadriel was grateful for his long legs when he caught up to Mora quickly. He knew better than to grab her, so he stepped into her path and lifted his hands in supplication. "I shouldn't have brought up

Lillian, Little Witch. It's just... the villagers don't deserve your ire. Andras does."

A deep pain haunted her gaze—his heart squeezed painfully at the sight. Despite the tear sliding down her soft cheek, Mora's voice was steady. "Who are you to speak of misplaced rage? Didn't you blame me for your suffering?"

The guilt slamming against his chest was almost a physical blow. Zadriel stepped back and looked away. It was true... who was he to ask her to be better? "You're right," he said quietly, hanging his head, "I'm sorry."

Mora stepped past him, saying nothing. Within a breath, smoke trickled down her arms like rippling waves of onyx.

"How can I help with Andras's wish?" he asked, hoping, somehow, he could make this right.

The darkness claimed her with each passing second and he wondered if she'd answer at all. When she was more shadow than woman, Mora turned, gracing him with a final look at her lovely face, and said, "Rest. Be free for a few moments. I'll take as long as I can."

Dispersing into mist, she twirled around him, a soft, cool fog that forced his hood back and gently tousled his hair before flying through the wilds like a glorious wraith on the hunt.

As he watched her disappear, Zadriel rested his hand on his chest, soothing the warm ache above his heart. How long could he keep this from Andras?

CHAPTER 29

MORA

W ould Andras be happy when he found two deer, a pheasant, a pile of eggs and massive amounts of berries piled outside his door? No. But imagining the look on his face made Mora's chest feel lighter. It was a small resistance—he hadn't specified *where* he wanted the bounty she'd gathered.

Defiance was power. Andras would come to learn, despite his hold on her, Mora wasn't powerless. If she were being honest, she too needed the reminder. Even if she knew it would cost her.

Exhaustion pulled her into its grip as the sun dipped behind the horizon. It wasn't that her body was tired—the smoke healed everything, from pain to fatigue—it was her mind. One look at her and Zadriel declared it was her turn to rest.

How he talked her onto the horse with him, she wasn't sure. But when she sagged in the saddle, fighting to keep her eyes open, Zadriel adjusted his grip on the reins and curled a hand around her stomach. He pulled her tightly against his chest, and Mora closed her eyes. She liked the feel of his arms around her. And was relieved to see he'd healed, his bandages now removed.

"Why do you smell so good?" she mumbled.

Zadriel huffed a laugh. "I could say the same of you." He ran his thumb in comforting circles on Mora's soft stomach as he leaned his chin on her forehead. Peeling her heavy eyes open, she met his glittering, dark gaze. Felt his breath tickling her skin.

"Sleep, Little Witch."

"My mind won't allow it."

Zadriel pursed his lips, staring ahead as they made their way back. Mora wondered if he maintained a slow pace in an attempt to prolong their moment of peace. "Would you like me to tell you a story?"

Excitement zinged through her and she almost sat up, but Zadriel's grip kept her firmly against him. "Please!"

"I'll do my best," he said, giving her stomach a gentle squeeze. Then he cleared his throat and began his tale.

"There once was a little Fae boy, a child of the trees."

"Arcadia?"

"Yes, Arcadia," he said, wistfully. "He spent his days running through the Forest, dancing with pixies and picking flowers for dryads. The Forest loved him, as it loved all its children. But no one loved him more than Vehsa, his mother. She loved him with all her being. So much she vowed that, no matter what, she'd always be there when he needed her. Vows and bargains are binding to the Fae, much like a wish is to you, so he knew he could forever count on her.

"Ever the explorer, he lived to investigate all parts of his home, loved discovering new creatures. There were so many to discover.

The boy was charismatic and, for such a young age, clever with his words. He felt invincible. Safe in the belly of Arcadia, he may very well have been." Zadriel paused and took a deep breath, his hold on her tightening.

Mora's throat bobbed. Already, she knew where this story ended.

"One day he spied a new creature through the trees. A wolf, roaming the fields. It wasn't of the Forest, it was unlike anything the boy had seen. Though his mother warned him about the danger of wolves, he couldn't help but watch. He watched day in and day out, returning to that spot in hopes of spying the creature. Little did he know, the wolf watched him in return."

Mora's voice was barely a whisper. "Dother?"

"Not the one you knew, Little Witch, but a wolf all the same," he said, his deep voice quiet, heavy. "One day the creature brought him food. A simple gift, but it meant the world to the boy. He laid it within reach, unable to cross the line of trees separating them. His show of kindness made the child wonder if he knew anything about wolves at all."

Mora laid a hand on Zadriel's hard thigh and gave it a gentle, encouraging squeeze. He took a slow, deep breath, and she found herself doing the same.

"One day he brought his pup, the adorable thing almost the same age as the boy." Zadriel stopped suddenly, hissing as Mora's grip on his thigh grew painful. Her nails dug into his flesh, despite his dark trousers. She didn't need to ask—the pup was the Dother she knew. Blood rushed through her ears, her pulse pounding.

Zadriel let go of her belly and grabbed her hand, squeezing gently. Mora relaxed, tension easing from her limbs. The slow, gentle swipe of his thumb over her skin had her melting against him as her grip eased.

Knitting their fingers together, he brought them back to her stomach and hugged her tightly. "They bonded quickly, playing as best they could with the trees between them. The boy knew better than to tell his mother about the wolves he called friends. Knew she wouldn't approve. He found himself caring greatly for them. Grew to trust them implicitly.

"The child gave them his name, ate their food, shared his hopes and fears. It wasn't long before they convinced him to step out from the safety of his trees, so he and the pup could truly play together. The Forest was unwilling to let him go—branches and vines did their best to contain him. But he pushed through until he found himself on the other side."

"Zadriel," Mora whispered, sorrow heavy in her voice. They'd manipulated a child. Convinced him to walk right into their trap. Mora wished, for once, she could revive the dead, so she could kill that man herself, with her bare hands.

Zadriel swallowed hard. "The moment he was away from Arcadia's protection, the wolf grabbed him and dragged him home. The boy begged to return to Arcadia. Cried for his mother. But the wolf insisted this was his home now. That night, the wolf bled him and bled himself, combining the two with other items to make a horrific drink. He forced it down the boy's throat, uncaring when he gagged and choked. That concoction sealed his fate. Made him theirs for eternity."

Mora's chest tightened as Zadriel's hand trembled in hers. She couldn't imagine a child in the Dothers' clutches. The horrors he must have survived. She ran her free hand over his forearm, squeezing her eyes shut when she felt the patchwork of thick scars.

Zadriel's heart pounded against her back and she tensed, preparing for the worst. "He heard his mother's cries when she discovered him missing. She screamed his name for days and wandered from Arcadia in search of him. But the wolves kept him hidden away.

"Bound by the vow, his mother never gave up. For months he heard her call. It grew more desperate with each passing day. The wolves made certain he couldn't make his way back to her. That he could never go home. He tried, only to discover leaving meant experiencing agony like he'd never imagined. Eventually his mother grew desperate, attacking any who approached. Until the wolves banded together to hunt her down."

Mora tilted her head up, her eyes locking with Zadriel's as a single tear ran down his cheek. Reaching up, she wiped the tear away, her fingers trailing delicately against his soft skin. He leaned into her touch. "The day she was ended, they celebrated. The wolves held a banquet and danced around a pyre." Zadriel's voice broke. "But the little boy sat in the dark and cried, the pup his only source of comfort.

"The boy came to love the pup. To cling to him as if they were family. And together they grew until one day, the pup became a wolf. In his blindness, the boy, now a grown Fae, forgot it was best to fear all wolves. Even when his friend bled him, even when he forced him to join great and terrible hunts, he loved him just the same. Because he had no other, and to love a monster was better than being alone."

While they were traveling in a large open field toward the rundown village, back to their doom, it felt as if they were the only two people in the world. The air grew silent around them, and Mora's gaze remained locked on Zadriel's sparkling, midnight eyes, searching the sea of golden stars hidden within them. "What happened to him," Mora asked, cupping his cheek.

"He lost his way. He was broken. The Forest called to him, an endless song beckoning from the distance, but he couldn't return unless the wolves let him go. The pup promised to one day set him free, but death found him first. He was immortal, so the boy found himself alone and unloved, now a monster in his own right." A small smile tugged on Zadriel's lips, a glimmer of defiance shining in that stubborn gaze. "But the story isn't over—I have yet to see its end."

"No, we haven't seen the end yet, Zadriel." She stroked her thumb over his cheek, nearly losing herself in his dark, endless stare. "I vow I will do everything in my power to get us through. And if we are separated, I vow to find my way back to you the moment I'm able."

Something pulsed in her chest as a pleasant, warm shiver ran up her spine. It curled around her bones, almost like a wish. Only this felt right. Wanted.

Zadriel sucked in a breath through his teeth, clutching her hand tighter. "You shouldn't have done that."

Pulling her gaze away, she leaned her head back on his shoulder and closed her eyes, inhaling his minty scent. "I'm not afraid of making vows to you, Zadriel. The wolves took me too. They killed my father. Forced me to leave my mother to face death alone..." Mora trailed off as Zadriel shifted uncomfortably in the saddle. When she opened her eyes, she watched the last of the light drain from the sky. "We'll find our way through this together."

Zadriel was silent for a moment, Lyriah's hoofs crunching against the dry summer grass the only sound keeping them company.

Eventually his deep voice wrapped around her like soft velvet. "Together," he whispered, "I vow we'll find our way through this together."

CHAPTER 30

MORA
300 YEARS AGO

"*W*hy must you be so stubborn, Treasure? Choose me and I'll set you free."

Dother's fingers traced her hip before slowly trailing over her sweaty skin. His seed coated her thighs and there was an ache in her neck where he'd bitten too hard. It hadn't mattered when she begged him to stop. From the moment he'd made her something... other, something that belonged solely to him, Dother hadn't cared about Mora's wants.

Every torturous breath filled her lungs with citrus—she nearly choked. How had she found it pleasant before?

Dother shifted, tangling their legs together, and his gentle touch slowed. "I asked you a question, Treasure."

Mora's chest shuddered but she didn't say a word. Devoted all her energy to holding back the tears threatening to spill down her cheeks.

Suddenly, he pinched her thigh, squeezing so hard she gasped.

"Forcing me to choose you isn't a choice, Dother," she cried.

His grip eased, but his low voice promised violence. "I told you to call me Cillian."

Mora clutched the soft, black sheets, wishing she could crawl under them. "You have the crown, is that not enough?"

"I need the crown for our people. I want you for myself. We're meant to do this together."

A silver crown encrusted with sapphires and diamonds sat on his writing desk across the bedroom, gleaming in the low firelight. Its points were sharp, deadly. Staring at it was a comfort—with each passing day she imagined, more and more, what it would be like to plunge it into his neck. Over and over. Not that he'd ever let her leave his bed—it was always there or the flask.

"What of your wife?" Her mother. Mora nearly gagged. What lies had he spun—did Aedlin believe her daughter ran away after the night of their wedding?

She hugged herself tightly, fingers digging into her ribcage.

Don't cry, don't cry, don't cry.

A quivering breath betrayed her, and she choked on a sob. It had been... she didn't know how much time passed since he'd cursed her. Did he summon her daily? When he'd made her return to the flask in the morning, her awareness became muddled, like watching a strange dream through a blurry window. Voices were distorted, her vision clouded, and her body, or lack thereof, became an empty shell she could barely cling to.

The bed shifted and Dother sat up. "Treasure," he said, voice deceptively sweet. She flinched when he wiped a tear away with his calloused thumb. "It wasn't supposed to be this way."

Silence twisted between them as he waited for her to say... anything. But she wouldn't even look at his face. Instead, her eyes trailed along the pristine, black tiled floor until they landed on her flask. The golden daisies felt out of place, nestled among his disheveled clothes. Clothing he'd made her remove. Mora's lips curled at the memory.

When Dother made a wish, Mora couldn't deny him. No matter how hard she tried. There was only so long she could endure the agony of whatever magic writhed within her, demanding to be set free. Her fingers dug harder into her ribs, the memory of them snapping apart ringing in her ears.

Dother pulled on a stray curl, playfully like he used to. "I'm trying to be nice, Mora."

"You call this nice," she breathed, her voice a quiet whisper. She regretted her words immediately when he twisted her hair in his fist and forced her head back. Her hands shot to her scalp, clawing at his grip. "Dother, stop, I'm sorry!"

"Say my name."

"Dother, please!"

Dother pulled harder, the pain blooming into a horrifying headache.

Mora hated herself for giving in. "Cillian, please."

His grip eased, and he slid his hand down her face until he cupped her cheek. Those crystal blue eyes softened when she finally met his gaze. "Good girl."

Guiding her onto her back, he climbed on top, his lips trailing delicately over her neck. Greedy fingers traced her belly up to the swell of her full breast before pinching her nipple. She squeezed her eyes shut and pressed further into the soft mattress, heart pounding madly in her chest.

"I was going to take you that night in the tavern," he murmured in her ear. "Ransom you to your parents in exchange for a better world for our people. I had my... friend waiting in the alley with a blade. Surely you remember?"

When she said nothing, he twisted her nipple so harshly she yelped. Mora gritted her teeth and nodded, squeezing her thighs together as he pressed himself more firmly against her. Hard and ready once more.

"But you were more than I imagined. You ensnared me. Demanded my affections. When I saw your power, Treasure, I knew you were meant to be mine." Dother's smile made her tremble. "It wasn't hard to get your blood after that. Though I was disappointed I needed to use it and curse you like this." Dother released her breast and slid his hand up to her neck. "Look at me."

Her skin crawled, but Mora knew there was no use denying him. Opening her eyes, she found that bright azure gaze heavy lidded and filled with desire. The only hint of doubt was his clenched jaw and the divot in his cheek.

"You're mine, Mora, whether you choose me or not. I'd much prefer we were making our royal heirs tonight. Because of your stubbornness, you're bound to me like the sprites you hate, trapped in a state of stasis. And I'm forced to lay with Aedlin to fulfill a legacy I'm meant to share with you."

Something inside of her broke in that moment. Something that had been cracking more and more by the day. Rage, like she hadn't imagined possible, twisted in her bones and the wrath in her glare burned into his watchful eyes. Consequences be damned, Mora gathered her saliva and spat in his face, a furious scream exploding from her throat.

Dother clapped a hand over her mouth, the stinging slap echoing through the room. His glare was murderous. But she kicked and twist-

241

ed in his clutches, those muffled shrieks an endless symphony beneath his palm.

"You will behave," he seethed, every word clipped. "I may have cursed you to fulfill my every desire, and that of my bloodline should you not agree to be my queen, but anyone can use you for three wishes. Would you like me to pass you around like a common whore?"

Mora froze, eyes wide. He wouldn't...

As if reading her mind, Dother nodded. "It would pain me, Treasure. But I'll resort to less ideal methods if it teaches you to appreciate what we have."

No. Oh gods, no. She could barely survive being in his hands. Couldn't imagine being forced to fulfill the desires of another. The room felt smaller, the soft sheets too hot against her skin. She couldn't breathe. Gasped for air under his palm.

It wasn't enough.

Dother leaned down and placed the softest kiss on her forehead. It made her want to scream again. To claw at her skin until she couldn't feel him anymore. But he was everywhere. Surrounding her. Living in her lungs.

Mora couldn't take it. She wheezed until the room spun, even when he let go of her mouth. Each gulp of air was tainted. Citrus curled into her lungs until it seeped into her blood.

After he wiped the spittle from his beard, he wrapped his fingers around her throat again, clutching hard enough to remind her he could take her air whenever he desired. She almost wished he would.

"One day you'll say yes to me, Treasure. One day we'll be happy. And we'll change the world together."

When Mora didn't respond, he simply shook his head, before dipping down to taste her lips. There was no better way to describe how he *hungrily kissed her while she lay still beneath him. "Open those pretty legs, I need to feel you."*

Mora didn't listen, but it hardly mattered. Smoke trickled down her arms and pried her legs open the moment he said, "I wish…"

CHAPTER 31

MORA

"Hello again, Alina." Mora crooned at the little Aegist, surprised to find her with Andras in his small kitchen. The poor thing paled, her deep-set hazel eyes wide.

Behind her, Zadriel shrugged off his cloak, sweat gleaming on his long, muscular arms. He hung the dark garment on the hooks by the door. It was hard not to admire the way his black tunic clung to his stomach. Mora remembered what hid underneath. The way the water trailed between all those glorious muscles. Gods, he was beautiful. Though something shifted when they returned to the village—the Fae quieted the moment they'd brought Lyriah to the stables. Back to the broody male she'd traveled across Berwick with.

"Thank you, Alina," Andras said, smiling down at her. But Mora knew the look in his eyes. Recognized the monster lurking beneath the surface. "Why don't you head home? Help yourself to some of the food outside my door." His narrowed gaze slid to Mora. "I'll take care of everything."

"Okay," Alina replied, a slight tremble in her voice. She hesitated, her eyes darting from Mora to the door and back. Mora wouldn't move, cold amusement dancing on her face.

Zadriel rolled his eyes, grabbed the hem of Mora's tunic—*his* tunic—and tugged her out of the way.

"Hey," she spat. But the Fae kept his hold on her, shaking his head.

Alina ran for the door while Mora chuckled under her breath, surprised she hadn't summoned a shield. She looked forward to their next showdown.

When the door clicked shut Andras marched toward her. "What were you thinking!" His voice boomed through the small room.

Zadriel's lips pressed into a thin line. Within a breath, he'd released his hold on Mora and stepped back.

Mora lifted her chin. Focused on the amber splotch in Andras's eye. *It's not Dother,* she reminded herself. She could handle him. Hopefully. Did her heart stutter in her chest as she imagined what he intended for her? Yes. But she knew this was coming. Regretted nothing.

"What do you mean?" she asked innocently.

"Don't fuck with me, Mora," Andras growled.

Mora didn't balk. "What did you expect? You *bled* Zadriel. He could barely walk. I assume you're intelligent enough to understand the simple concept of blood loss and lack of energy. I had to improvise."

"You threatened the stablehand."

Mora shrugged, ignoring the tightness in her chest. "You left me no choice."

"You stole my horse." His quiet voice promised violence.

She squeezed her hands into tight fists and took a step closer to Andras. Willed herself to remain calm. "And I'd do it again."

Rage flared in those dreadful azure eyes. "There's a mess of food outside."

"You didn't say where you wanted it."

"Clearly not there."

"It's not my fault you weren't specific."

Andras twisted that horrific ring around and around his finger as he analyzed her face. Something clicked in his expression and he barked at Zadriel, "Get me a chair."

The Fae didn't utter a word. He simply nodded once, his shoulders tight as he took a few slow steps to the old wooden table by the hearth. Fire crackled within it, flames dancing as they stretched. Would Andras burn her again? Her body tensed as she readied herself for the agony. Already she could taste smoke, though it would be better than the nauseating citrus saturating the air.

Zadriel's lips twitched as he dragged the chair back, the shadow of a frown dancing on his handsome face. It was so minute she wondered if she imagined it. When the chair's legs squeaked against the worn, wooden floor, Mora flinched. Andras smirked, smug satisfaction shining in those too bright eyes.

It's NOT Dother.

Zadriel stopped by his side, chair in hand, unwilling to look at Mora as he waited for Andras's next order.

The room felt too hot, sweat already coating her back. She eyed the window, staring at the darkening evening sky as she tried to remember the taste of fresh air.

"Mora," Andras warned, unimpressed with her lack of focus. He folded his arms across his chest, muscles straining under his off-white tunic. "You are not to threaten my people," he said, calmly, suddenly more composed. Raising an eyebrow, he gave Mora a look that dared her to push him.

"Is that a wish, Keeper?" she asked, unable to hide her disdain.

Andras shook his head. "That's an order." Mora's breath quickened when he closed the distance between them and grabbed her chin. It happened too fast, though she was a fool not to expect it. Behind him, Zadriel bared his teeth, those dangerous canines on display. But he did nothing. Schooled his expression into something neutral within a breath.

Andras's fingers dug into her cheeks, pressing painfully against her jaw. "Zadriel, the chair."

As Zadriel walked to Mora, dragging the chair along, something caught her eye. Over Andras's shoulder, the door on the back left wall stood open and black silk sheets on a large bed gleamed in the low firelight. Mora gulped. Prayed he didn't take her there next.

Do not leave our bed, Dother whispered in her mind.

She didn't watch Zadriel, too caught up in her own nightmares. But she felt when he neared. The calming scents of mint and summer rain with a splash of pine wrapped her in their embrace and pulled her free.

Mora blinked up at Andras, not Dother. At his multicolored eye, the slope of his nose, those broad shoulders.

"Get your hands off me, Andras," she seethed, struggling in his grip. The back of her knee hit the kitchen chair, but it didn't jostle—Zadriel stood behind it, clenching the back in a white-knuckled grip.

247

Mora yelped when Andras clutched her tunic with his free hand, pulling her against his chest and holding her still. "*This* is a wish," he said, unflinching when she wrapped her fingers around his wrist, nails biting into his flesh. "I wish for you to shackle yourself to the chair Zadriel placed behind you. You won't go free until I say so. You will not dissipate into smoke or return to your flask until I give you permission."

Mora's jaw cracked as Andras lifted her off her feet and dropped her into the chair. Icy tendrils crawled up her spine and spread over her ribcage, burrowing into the bone, and she hissed at the pain, glaring up at him with rageful, glowing eyes. But she didn't fight it. There was no point in pushing back against the magic writhing under her skin, demanding release. It would happen, whether Mora liked it or not.

Trickles of onyx mist glittering with faint flecks of gold leaked from her fingertips as her hands shook. It crawled languidly down her body. Softly caressed her skin as it twirled around her ankles and wrists, pulling them against the chair and binding them to the wood. Trapping her.

The memory of a crushing grip snaked around her neck.

Dother's grip on her throat tightened. "You're so beautiful," he said, as he took what wasn't his. His other hand slid down her stomach, then lower still, and she clenched her teeth. Squeezed her eyes shut. Prayed this would end soon.

The room spun. Mora's jaw ached. Her breathing was harsh and jagged. She pulled against her ethereal bindings but, despite their gentle grip, they wouldn't budge.

"What now Andras?" she asked through gritted teeth.

Ignoring her, Andras held his hand out to Zadriel. "Hand me the dagger."

The chair creaked as Zadriel's grip on it tightened. Mora focused on her breathing and stared at a spot on the floor while he walked to the counter. When he returned with the dagger, those golden daisies on the hilt gleamed in the firelight.

The moment Andras's hand closed around it, he unsheathed the blade and moved closer.

"I had a dog once," he said, crouching so they were eye level. He cleaned his nails with the tip of the blade, but his eyes never left her face. "After months of begging, my father had Zadriel acquire him for me. He was a gray, shaggy mutt that growled whenever I entered the room and tried to run away three times." He paused, pointing at her with the dagger's sharp edge. "You remind me of him."

Blistering fury clawed its way through her chest, scrambling over her panic, and the pounding in her ears grew louder. "Are you calling me a fucking dog?"

Andras's attention slid to the smoke binding her wrists. "Are you not my pet?"

"Fuck you," she hissed, jerking against her bindings. A flush of heat swam through her blood.

"Ah, see, you might as well be growling now." Cold metal chilled her heated skin as he tapped the flat of the blade against the back of her hand. "Do you know what I did with my dog?"

Mora locked eyes with Zadriel. He'd moved away to lean against the counter, elbows resting on the stone top. The slanted ceiling grazed his head despite the way he crouched—it was impossible for him to stand at his full height. She hated the way his throat bobbed, that a sheen of sweat coated his brow.

His deep, soothing voice echoed in her mind. *I vow we'll find our way through this together*. Mora clutched those words like a lifeline. Could almost feel a fresh, mint kissed summer breeze on her cheeks when she thought of their vows.

"I doubt you let him go back to wherever you stole him from," she said to Andras.

"Of course not, *Treasure*. Care to guess again?"

"Get to the gods damned point."

Zadriel winced at her words, those onyx eyes going wide. It did nothing to ease the pressure in her chest. She leaned her head back in the chair and forced her breathing to slow.

"I broke him," Andras declared, chin high. "By the time I was done he couldn't piss without my permission."

The blade's sharp edge stung as Andras dragged it down her hand to her pointer finger. He stopped at the nail, tapping the blade against it. With each ping, Mora's jaw tightened.

"Such pretty fingers," he muttered quietly, as he turned the blade sideways and positioned it under the nail.

Mora whimpered when he began to push. She couldn't stop herself from flinching away. With his free hand Andras gripped her, squeezing so hard she thought her bones might break. Then he repositioned the dagger and shoved.

The world went white.

Mora screamed.

Shrieked so loud it bounced off the walls.

So harshly it felt as if it tore her throat.

The sounds of her agony rang in her ears and all she knew was a horrific, blinding pain. It spread through her finger and up her hand.

It crowded her mind. Tears streamed down her face and she cried out again.

And again.

And again.

"Stop, *please*," she begged, voice cracking.

Andras didn't listen.

With a flick of his wrist, he snapped the blade up, peeling the nail away from its bed. Mora sucked in a sharp breath, stomach roiling.

Blood slid down her finger and her nail hit the floor with a *click*. When he pulled away, Mora sagged, her dark curls sticking to her damp forehead. The only things holding her up were her vaporous bindings.

"It's surprising how painful it is to have your nail pried off, isn't it?" Andras sounded amused.

Mora didn't have it in her to respond. No clever words or retorts came to mind. All she could do was try and catch her breath and pray she didn't vomit all over her lap.

When Andras grabbed her hand again, she gagged.

If there are any Gods, please, make him stop.

"That's enough, Andras."

Andras straightened, his attention snapping to Zadriel. "Enough?"

Clearing his throat, Zadriel didn't meet Andras's furious gaze. "You've made your point," he said, a slight tremor to his deep voice. Those long fingers clutched the edge of the counter tighter.

Andras stood, frowning as his focus bounced between Zadriel and Mora. "Interesting," he muttered to himself.

He wiped the blade on Mora's shoulder, smearing her blood onto Zadriel's tunic, then tossed it into her lap. "Hold on to that for me, *Treasure*," he mocked, before walking away.

Slumping back in the chair, Mora's head lolled to the side and her amber stare met Zadriel's beautiful, dark eyes. Silently she mouthed the words *thank you*. He offered her a single nod in return and trailed his fingers over the patchwork of scars lining his arm.

The sound of clinking vials came from his room and they shared a look. Zadriel trembled, and Mora knew...

"Run," she whispered. "Leave me."

Zadriel paled, "I can't." He kept his wide-eyed gaze on his room as he moved away from the counter, backing up until he bumped into the small kitchen table. "Please no," he muttered to no one at all.

Mora twisted in the chair in time to watch Andras walk back into the kitchen. He held up a small vial of Zadriel's blood, the dark liquid splashing against the glass with each unhurried step. "You've never said no to me, Zadriel. Have been nothing but the loyal pet you were meant to be—"

"Andras, please..."

"Cillian expressed the same in his journal. The perfect dog, always ready to do as he's told." Andras sighed. "But he left a detailed explanation of what to do if you refuse to heel." He turned to Mora. "It's a shame I can't do this to you. Cillian wanted a long term binding enchantment that didn't affect your... personality. He felt wishes were a better way to control you. And, if I recall the wording about his disdain for blood thralls correctly, he didn't like the idea of fucking an unresponsive doll."

"Gods, you are divine," Dother groaned, grabbing her hip and repositioning her so he could...

No!

"You and your entire bloodline are a stain on this world," Mora breathed.

"And I will make sure we are remembered, Mora. I'll succeed where Dother failed, with you by my side."

This time Mora's scream wasn't one of pain. The beast within her joined in, screeching at the top of her lungs, the sound one of endless rage. She clutched the arms of the chair, her fingers sliding through her own blood, and seethed at Andras.

He was unmoved. Unconcerned by the monster tethered to his kitchen chair.

Andras grinned as he crushed the glass in his fists and Mora roared again. Shrieked when blood spilled between the cracks in his fingers. Howled when it began to spin around his clenched fist.

Andras squeezed harder, wincing as the glass pierced his palm. More blood seeped through, curling around his hand, and he watched. He was no longer aware of Mora screaming or Zadriel begging quietly behind him. Those two separate streams of blood chased each other around his fist, faster and faster until one dove onto the other.

Enchanter's secret, Treasure, Dother's mocking voice whispered in her ear.

Zadriel recoiled as the blood thrall took hold, knocking over a chair and pushing the table back. A pained moan spilled from his lips and his knees buckled.

An animalistic growl Mora hardly recognized as her own slipped from her throat when he landed on the floor, kneecaps smacking the hardwood with a loud thud. "Let him go, Andras!"

Andras continued to focus on binding Zadriel's blood to his own, the stream around his fist spinning faster. The gem in his ring watched too, spinning around with the sanguinous torrent.

Zadriel's spine arched painfully straight and he gritted his teeth, groaning in agony. Mora pushed herself as far to the edge of her seat as she could, tugging against her bindings, but they didn't budge. The dagger clattered to the ground as she pulled harder. And her wrists burned.

"Mora, don't," Zadriel said quietly, his voice a desperate plea. Tears spilled down his cheeks. Then he slumped forward, his body suddenly stiff, hands hanging aimlessly at his sides.

The blood moved to Andras's wrist, now a single viscous stream, writhing like a living bracelet.

Andras opened his palm and shards of bloodied glass spilled to the ground. He grimaced as he eyed the damage, plucking out a particularly long shard and tossing it aside with a sigh. "Come, Zadriel." The Fae stood and approached with a flick of Andras's finger. His movements were rigid, awkward, so unlike his usual agile gait.

Andras clicked his tongue as he continued to pluck glass shards from his hand. "Look what you've made me do, Zadriel. I'm so disappointed in you."

CHAPTER 32

MORA

Mora's heart pounded wildly, slamming against her ribcage. She almost wondered if it would break free. If the organ was as stubborn as she was, thrashing in her chair, chafing her wrists raw. The wood groaned with each jerk of her arms.

Andras grabbed Zadriel's jaw, tipping his head this way and that. He smiled when the Fae gave no resistance, moving like... she hated that she thought of a doll.

"Much better, don't you think?" he asked Mora as he patted Zadriel's cheek twice.

Condescending prick.

"Andras, I swear to gods I'll—"

"You'll what?"

A low growl rumbled in her chest.

Andras smirked. He released Zadriel—the Fae didn't move at all, his spine so stiff Mora's own back screamed—and strode toward her. Mora tried not to shiver when those blinding blue eyes raked over her body, and kept fighting against her bindings, cursing the creaking chair.

When his foot hit the dagger he bent to retrieve it. Trailing a finger over the intricate vines and daisies decorating the gilded handle, he asked, "Why do you continue to fight me?"

When she didn't answer, Andras came closer. He knelt down so they were once again eye to eye, tucked the dagger under her chin, and forced her to look at him. "Things would be much easier for you if you'd accept your place."

Mora stilled. "You're so much like him."

Those stupid eyes gleamed. "You mean Cillian?"

"Yes," Mora said through gritted teeth as she curled her fingers around the arms of the chair. "Like him, you're foolish enough to underestimate me."

Mora roared as she gave one last hard jerk. A loud crack was followed by intense, radiating pain. Mora ignored it and swung her arm as hard as she could the moment the wood snapped free, slamming it into Andras's smug face and sending him sprawling.

She wanted to laugh. Wished she could taunt him the way he deserved. But all she could do was gasp.

The throbbing pain in her wrist intensified, her fingers oddly numb. Obsidian mist still clung to the broken furniture, binding her in place as Andras wished, but the weight of the wood made her hiss. She gingerly lifted her arm to her chest. Attempted to release some of the pressure. But the limb pounded like it had its own heart, each beat thrumming with a new wave of splintering pain.

Mora tried to wriggle her fingers, only to gag as a wave of nausea consumed her. Bile clawed up her throat, and she knew it was bad. Refused to look. Twisting her head to the side, she spat sour saliva on the kitchen floor, before turning back to eye Andras warily.

I hope you're hurting too, bastard.

He was frozen, lying in a heap near Zadriel's feet. Blood seeped from a deep gash on his cheek, trickling down his neck and staining his off-white tunic. Good. Already the wound was swollen, red blooming around tender flesh.

Andras's nostrils flared. He touched his cheek, wincing, then pulled his hand away to stare at the blood. When his furious gaze found her again, Mora saw nothing but Dother. "Why do you have to make things difficult?" he asked, voice low. Deadly.

Mora's attention flicked to the aged journal on his hip, remembering a time when the red leather was pristine. What horrors had Dother shared inside? Did she want to know? She took a harsh, jagged breath. Ignored the way her stomach roiled and the ceaseless drumbeat of agony.

"You need to do a better job next time you read Dother's scribblings," she spat. "I will *never* make it easy for you, Andras. You can control me, torture me, drag me to the bowels of hell if that suits you. But don't think for a second I won't take you down with me. I'd recommend you ask Dother his opinion, but I can assure you he's *very* dead."

Andras's blinding eyes simmered. There was no graceful way for him to get to his feet, but he attempted regardless, rolling to his side until he could push to his knees. The man steadied himself on his hands as he rose, drops of blood spattering the worn wooden floor.

In the corner of her eye, Mora spied Zadriel, still standing stiffly, limp hands hanging at his side. Those midnight eyes, with their glittering pools of starlight, were empty. Nearly lifeless.

Mora shivered, frigid dread rushing through her. What must he be feeling, trapped in his own mind, unable to do anything but watch?

Andras came at her fast, wrapping his calloused palm around her neck. It scratched her throat as he squeezed. A little tighter and he'd cut off her airway. "I take no joy in hurting you, Mora, but your outbursts leave me no choice."

His focus slithered to her pained arm cradled in her chest. Air rushed through her windpipe when he released her throat, but all she could do was throw her head back and howl as he wrapped his hand around her wrist and pulled it closer to examine the damage.

Ripples of misery spread through Mora's wrist and up her arm. It bled into her skin. Embedded itself into her veins.

Andras dropped her hand back onto her chest and shook his head. "I hope it was worth it."

Mora gasped between clenched teeth. "Next time I'll aim for your eyes."

"You *will* learn to behave."

Sweat dripped down Mora's brow, joining the tears sliding over her cheeks. Her skin was boiling, that incessant pounding in her ears near maddening. But a deadly calm came over her. Her beautiful face became impassive, amber eyes cold.

And she spat on his tunic.

With a heavy sigh, Andras stood, frowning at the glob of saliva dripping down his front. "Have it your way, *Treasure.*"

Mora took a few slow, deep breaths. Attempted to ready herself for whatever came next.

"Zadriel," Andras barked, holding out the dagger. "Finish the job. Left hand only."

Immediately, Zadriel turned, moving with none of his usual grace.

When he took the first step forward she flinched and dug her nails into the remaining hard wooden arm of her chair.

A whimper escaped her lips as he took the next.

Two more long strides and he stood directly in front of her, gripping the dagger.

Closing her eyes, her lower lip quivered when his cold hand grabbed hers. There was no reassuring squeeze, no comforting swipes of his thumb. He ran his hand along hers methodically until he reached her fingers. His grip was harsh as he peeled them away from the kitchen chair's arm and forced them straight.

"... I'm... sorry..." Zadriel's quiet voice was pained as he slowly forced out the words, somehow pushing past the blood thrall.

Mora's eyes snapped open, and she searched his face. His gaze locked onto her hand as he pressed the blade under her left pinky finger. There was nothing there. None of the sadness that typically saturated his gaze, or the disdain she'd come to know during their travels. No hint of the kindness she'd seen since they'd reached the village. His face was relaxed, neutral. But tears spilled from his eyes and dripped into her lap.

"I know," she said softly, holding her breath when the blade pushed under her nail. She trembled as she tried not to wail. "It's ok, Zadriel," she whispered through gritted teeth, jaw creaking under the pressure. "It's ok. I forgive you."

Those were the last coherent words Mora managed before she began to scream.

CHAPTER 33

ZADRIEL

There was fire in his veins. A boiling heat saturating his blood with every shallow beat of his heart. The burn of the blood thrall pushing Andras's influence through him. Each breath was calm. Steady. Nothing like the panic in his mind.

Sticky blood coated Zadriel's fingers. *Her* blood. He'd never forget Mora's screams, the agony cracking in her voice, or the awful thrum of her pain in his chest. It was another scar he'd carry, along with the mess on his arms.

Mother forgive me.

Had Andras seen through him? Did he know? Zadriel shouldn't have allowed himself anything more than the bitterness he'd held onto all these years. What was he thinking?

After he finished... After Andras was done using him to torment Mora, he made Zadriel step aside. All he could do was stare straight ahead at the kitchen table, pushed far too close to the hearth for comfort, and remember the centuries of horrors he'd survived in this place.

"I want to go home."

"You are home," Brennan muttered as he dragged a blade down Zadriel's arm.

It burned. The iron seared his skin, blackening it at the edges. And he knew he'd have a new scar to add to the others Brennan had given him since he'd dragged Zadriel... home.

He wanted his mother. Needed her. Wished he could cling to her and cry. Dreamed of her comforting voice, the safety of their home, the field of gilded daisies he played in while she sang and did her work.

The skin bubbled as it split and Zadriel groaned. Tried not to vomit when the sickly sweet scent of burnt flesh festered in the air. Brennan got mad when he vomited last time. It wasn't good when Brennan got mad.

Blood welled up from the wound, spilling over his arm and trickling into the chipped, ceramic bowl Cillian held. It was blue, like those bright eyes staring up at Zadriel. Redness stained the human child's cheeks and his lips were pressed into a thin line. But the little boy said nothing. Never spoke against his father.

"Your veins are stubborn today," Brennan said with a frustrated sigh before he shoved the dagger deeper.

Zadriel couldn't stop himself from screaming. Crying. Begging for his mother. Flinching and pulling his arm away. The iron blazed on his flesh like a flame, curling through his muscles and sizzling to the bone. And the smell of burnt skin...

He shook as he vomited, thankful he'd turned away in time to avoid the bowl. They would have bled him more to replace it.

Snot dripped from his nose and over his lips as he wept. He wanted to go home. Wanted his mother. Heard her calling for him in the night, desperately searching. Zadriel trembled as he sobbed.

Brennan pulled away, those blue eyes hardening. "If you insist on wailing and making a mess, you know what I'll do."

"Please don't," Zadriel hiccupped, "I'll be good."

His lips quivered, tears still spilling down his cheeks. When Brennan squeezed his arm to draw more blood, he tried to bite back his cry, but couldn't stop it.

Brennan rolled his eyes before running the blade over his own palm, slicing through the flesh. The man didn't wince.

Please, no.

"I'll be good, Brennan. I swear. I'll be good," Zadriel begged.

The iron dagger hit the table with a crack and Brennan's chair screeched against the wood as he stood, shaking his head at the whimpering Fae child. Zadriel clutched his arm, hissing at the burn, his fingers already sticky with blood.

The man dipped his hand in the bowl, soaking up the viscous, red fluid. When he was satisfied he pulled away and eyed his son, beaming with pride.

"Be a good boy, Cillian, and put the bowl on the table for a moment."

Cillian carefully lifted the bowl and slid it onto the round, light-wood table. He'd kept his lips sealed, but the color drained from his cheeks and those bright eyes flicked to Zadriel. They both knew what came next.

Brennan focused and two streams of blood began to chase each other over his fist. The scary ring on his right pointer finger watched with him, that eerie gem inside spinning around and around and around until one stream of blood dove on the other.

Zadriel's heart hammered in his chest and he pressed his back against the rickety chair in a feeble attempt to get away. Invisible tendrils burned through Zadriel's veins, piercing into every cell, commandeering his little body. It squeezed his lungs so tightly he felt he couldn't breathe. Like he'd never breathe again.

"No," he moaned as air was forced from his lungs. His limbs became so heavy he couldn't lift them. He slumped in his chair. No longer whimpering. No longer moving. No longer anything. Silent tears continued to spill down his cheeks.

"Much better," Brennan said with a satisfied grin, admiring the glowing blood bracelet adorning his wrist. He repositioned his chair, uncaring when it scratched the floor, and returned to his spot sitting in front of the Fae boy. With a flick of his hand, he said, "Extend your arm."

Zadriel's arm was pulled by some invisible force, held up straight, perfectly still. The panic in his mind was ceaseless, but those racing thoughts didn't affect the now steady thrum of his heart.

"Bring the bowl here, Cillian," Brennan instructed before returning the blade to Zadriel's skin. With the first touch of the iron's sharp edge, Zadriel's skin boiled. The throbbing pain too much.

But he couldn't flinch.

Couldn't cry.
Couldn't beg for his mother.
He could do nothing but watch.

Zadriel's bones screamed when the blood thrall's hold on him waned and his legs gave out. A new wave of agony washed over him as his knees once again hit the floor with a loud crack. He landed in a heap, but the cold wood soothed his heated skin. Was it odd he felt grateful? Still, he couldn't move. Existed in a body that wasn't his.

He had a perfect view of Mora and the fire still burning in those tired eyes. Eyes that glimmered with raw power. Eyes that beckoned him. Eyes that searched for any way out as Andras neared.

And all Zadriel could do was watch.

CHAPTER 34

ZADRIEL

A prickling sensation clambered up Zadriel's legs, the intensity faint at first. By the time it rose to his stomach, he felt as if thousands of tiny needles stabbed his flesh, over and over until it consumed him.

He groaned. Flinched at the sound. Flinched again when he realized he could. That, at least, was a good sign.

The position he'd fallen into was anything but comfortable—the hardwood floor dug into his side and his bones screamed at him to move. As if he had a say. Worse still, hair stuck to his damp forehead, and he wished he could swipe it away. Scratch the itch.

Testing his control, Zadriel flexed his fingers and rotated his wrist. His lips twitched into the shadow of a smile when they moved. But he couldn't lift his arm. Not yet.

The final dregs of blood magic wore away slowly. While the blood around Andras's wrist was no longer bound to the spell he'd weaved—it trickled down his hand and dripped to the floor, as if from a fresh wound—it still took time for Zadriel to regain control. The reawakening had always been slow, but at least he knew what to expect. Though he'd give anything to never experience the violation again.

"Have you learned your lesson, *Treasure*?" Andras taunted, smiling down at Mora.

The Little Witch stared up at him, exhaustion and pain painting her beautiful face. But that fierce gleam Zadriel admired still shined brightly in her glowing honey amber eyes. Andras hadn't broken her. At this point, Zadriel wasn't sure he could. Judging by the tenseness in Andras's jaw and the redness staining his battered face, he was beginning to wonder too.

May the Mother spare her.

Zadriel prayed he was right. That Mora had more fight in her than he did.

"I asked you a question," Andras hissed and Mora cringed away, a haunted look clouding her gaze. What nightmares had Andras invoked? What had Cillian done...

Andras followed, barely giving Mora the space to breathe. The violence he claimed to detest unless it served a purpose had done nothing to soothe him. The man bared his teeth, his furrowed brows resting over wide, furious eyes. His fingers curled around her bound arm to steady himself, but it pushed the chair back. Jostled the injured arm she cradled on her chest.

More blood drained from her face and Mora gasped, squeezing her eyes shut.

"You have no one to blame but yourself." Andras sneered at Mora. Pushed harder on the chair.

A growl rumbled in Zadriel's chest, the sound faint. He bared his teeth, his lips peeling back before he realized he'd managed the movement.

But he swallowed hard against his instincts and clamped his mouth shut.

Mora already paid a high price for his attempt to protect her. They both had. Blood stained her chair, soaked into her clothes, and pooled at her feet. And his hands... the more he attempted to move them, the more he felt her dried blood crack and peel.

A cold sweat beaded on his back as he remembered what he'd been made to do. He was useless... should have kept his mouth shut. Would she ever look him in the eye again?

Andras slowly shook his head and backed away before peeling off his tunic. The front was spattered with blood, mostly his own. It stained the off-white material and stuck to his skin, red lining the grooves between his stomach muscles. He stared at the garment, lips twisting into a grimace, before tossing it into the hearth.

The pleasant scents of smoke and ash tickled Zadriel's nose as flames consumed the stained fabric swiftly. It reminded him of her. Of crackling embers, florals, and pine. And that new kiss of mint he shouldn't enjoy.

The moment Zadriel could move again, Andras would make him clean the floor and burn the rags. If the man was paranoid about anything, it was his blood getting in the wrong hands.

Andras touched the gash on his cheek. Winced as his fingers traced the split skin. It had stopped bleeding, but Mora managed to jam the jagged edges of the broken chair arm into his face. The wound ran deep—it must have stung horribly. Pride bloomed in Zadriel's chest as he thought of how hard Mora worked to wound him. Though, when he looked at her, he could see she had little fight left in her tonight.

Andras dropped his hand to his side and turned back to Mora. "I wish for you to heal all my injuries. There will be no pain, no scars, no signs the skin was marred."

Mora glared up at him, those unblinking, glowing eyes promising a slow, painful death. It was foolish, considering her state. Though admirable all the same. Dark, ethereal mist leaked from her mangled fingers and curled around him until it reached his cheek. Andras closed his eyes and heaved a sigh of relief while cool wisps soothed his pain and knit the flesh back together.

When she was done, Mora rested her head on the back of the chair. Dark circles stained the skin below her eyes, and beads of sweat ran down her forehead. She was exhausted. Exhausted from what *he'd* done... Zadriel swallowed against the burn in his throat. It hadn't been clean. The sharp edge of the dagger cut into her flesh as he peeled her nails away.

There was nothing he could have done to stop himself... but his stomach roiled and his cheeks burned when he looked at her misshapen wrist. Mora's arm was swollen, raw, discolored, and twisted at an unnatural angle.

Because she'd fought. For him.

Ignoring the pain pulsing in his chest, Zadriel finally dragged himself off the floor, his muscles screaming as he sat up and leaned against the counter. It was an effort, but he raised his arm and looked at the stain tonight left on his skin. He wanted it gone. Now. He shuddered as he stared at the blood and how it caked between his knuckles and stuck in the creases of his palms.

The front door slammed open, smashing into the wall with a loud thud. Zadriel recoiled at the sound, his head smacking into the counter. Hissing, he slowly lifted his hand to touch the tender lump on the back of his head—it took far longer than he'd like, but at least he could finally move freely. The reek of alcohol wafted into the small room and Halvard stumbled in, two women on his arms.

Zadriel recognized them immediately. Chanelle and Mia, two young women born in the village, neither blessed with a drop of power. They'd grown bored of this life and begged Andras to take them with him on his travels. But the man had no interest in playing nanny. Nor did he want them to know how truly brutal he could be—how far he went to protect Eden's interest was between him and the Village Council.

That was about to change.

"Welcome to the humble abode," Halvard slurred. "It's nothing like my chateau in the south." Giggling, he pulled his arm away from Chanelle's shoulders, jostling her long brown hair, only to bop Mia's nose. "I think I'll bring you back with me!"

"What about me, my lord?" Chanelle asked, lifting wide, pleading eyes to Halvard.

"Perhaps," Halvard mused with a hiccup before straightening the brooch on his lapel. The trinket displayed a golden leaf, stained with Zadriel's blood and laid over a bluish-green gemstone, pressed into a small golden oval. Zadriel scowled, wondering what Andras spelled the trinket to do. The new scars on his arms itched the more he stared.

Whatever it was, Halvard was happy. He smiled down at the gaudy piece a moment too long before he looked back to his guests. "Let's see if you impress tonight."

"I'm sure we will," Mia said with a smile, tucking her short, black waves behind her ears. She grabbed Halvard's arm and pulled him into the kitchen. Only to scream.

A flush raced across her high cheekbones, darkening her sepia-brown skin. Chanelle gasped at her side, blood draining from her already pale face. When she swayed, Zadriel wondered if she'd faint.

Halvard took a step forward, shoving past the two women as he surveyed the room. "What do we have here?"

Mora tilted her head, her tangled curls tumbling over the back of the chair. "Oh great, you're here," she breathed. Though she smiled when she caught a glimpse of the bandages wrapped around his right fist.

Halvard's cheeks grew redder. He looked to Andras. "Why didn't you call for me?"

"Get out," Andras hissed.

"Get out? But I've brought friends and I'm willing to share."

Andras took a slow breath and dragged a hand through his messy brown hair. His voice was softer when he turned to the two horrified women. "Chanelle, Mia, I apologize for what you've witnessed. I'll explain shortly. Please, leave."

Chanelle and Mia remained frozen in place, mouths agape, limbs shaking like newborn fawns. Their wide eyes bounced around the room, from the bits of broken wood littering the floor, to the blood-ied woman bound to what remained of a kitchen chair, the Fae collapsed by the cupboards, and Andras, shirtless and covered in blood.

Halvard rolled his eyes. "You heard him. Leave."

When they still hadn't moved, the lord grumbled as he stalked to the door. Once again, it cracked against the wall. "Out," Halvard demanded, before he grabbed the backs of their dresses and dragged them back. Unwilling to step outside himself, Halvard shoved them over the threshold and slammed the door shut. A muffled thud was followed by someone crying.

"Are you happy?" Halvard asked, frowning as he neared.

"Am I happy?" Andras grabbed Halvard's dark green waistcoat and jerked him forward so harshly Halvard's feet couldn't keep up. He stumbled and would have fallen if not for Andras's hold. "Did you use the brooch I made you on *my* people?"

Halvard wrapped his trembling hands around Andras's wrists. "I... you never said I couldn't. And they approached me first, it simply helped move things along."

"That trinket is meant to gain influence among the nobility, Halvard, not fuck two woman at once. I doubt you have the stamina."

The flush on Halvard's cheeks rose to his ears. "Hey—"

"I wasn't finished," Andras growled. "Look around you. Look what you've shown those women."

"You should have warned me, I would have known not to bring them here."

"You should already know not to bring anyone here without my permission."

Halvard nodded and peered over Andras's shoulder. "I can't believe you left me out of the fun."

"This isn't about having fun." Andras released Halvard, unconcerned when the man nearly toppled over, and shook his head in exasperation.

"I've seen the glee in your eyes when you indulge yourself in your *necessary violence*, Andras. At least I'm honest."

Andras's lips curled back. "Mora, Zadriel, leave us."

Wood clattered to the floor as Mora's mist released her. She gasped the moment her arm came free, her face twisting in agony. Sucking a breath through her teeth, her voice was a pained whisper as she said, "I need your permission to—"

"I said leave!" he yelled.

Halvard paled, the redness on his cheeks becoming blotchy, and took a step back.

Zadriel's fists bunched. Could he not give her permission to dissipate and heal? "Andras..."

"WHAT?!" Andras's voice boomed and Zadriel's heart stuttered in his chest. He looked away, hating himself for doing it.

Mora slowly stood, cradling her wrist against her chest as she attempted to leave. But her legs wobbled with each step.

Zadriel rose as quickly as his stiff limbs allowed, hissing against the deep ache in his legs. He pressed on, moving as fast as he could. Mora swayed when he reached her, falling into his chest, and he thanked the Mother he'd made it in time. He couldn't bear to watch her suffer more or be the one to let her down once again.

Curling his arms around her, Zadriel was careful not to worsen her pain. Wondered how best to get her out. But Mora flinched away, those glowing amber eyes widening.

"No," she whispered, nearly slipping in blood.

Something cracked in Zadriel's chest but he kept his hold on her, refusing to let her fall. "It's me, Mora. I won't hurt you."

Her eyes met his, and the horrors of the room faded away. Nothing existed but her, and his need to get her as far away from Andras as he could... if only for tonight.

"Zadriel?" she breathed, leaning back into his touch.

"I'm here," he said as he gently lifted her into his arms and made for the door. "I've got you, Little Witch."

CHAPTER 35

MORA
300 YEARS AGO

*M*ora silently begged sleep to take her. To pull her into its arms and give her some semblance of peace. If only for a moment. It refused, uninterested in whatever she was now that Dother cursed her.

It was quiet. Too quiet. The night seemingly endless while Dother snored softly at her back. His breath tickled the crown of her head. He pulled her closer against his hard chest, his steely grip suffocating. Mora couldn't breathe. The bedchamber was massive, but with Dother's body caging hers she felt like the walls pressed against her skin. Like she would suffocate over and over again, without the sweet release of death. Dother's curse would never allow it.

Sweat slicked her skin, and the sheets were too hot. Mora couldn't risk kicking them away. It would wake him. And that would start things anew. She squeezed the dark, silky bed sheets in her fists, nails pressing against the meat of her palm. The sting helped her think. Helped her feel something other than dread.

It was an effort not to gasp for breath. But she'd endure the pain in her lungs if it meant Dother slept a few hours longer.

The flask lay on the floor, those golden daisies glittering despite the darkness. It rested atop Dother's clothes, rumpled and discarded where she'd left them after he'd made her take them off. She longed to be inside of it. To exist in that strange space between wakefulness and sleep. To be a creature of smoke and onyx, and glittering bits of gold that felt almost nothing.

At least physically.

Mora's mind rarely quieted.

The rattle of her heart was like a frantic song, each thud echoing in her skull. Mora pressed a trembling hand to her chest, begging her pulse to slow. Something else pulsed along with it. An intangible string fluttering in her center with each arduous beat of her heart. It tugged when Dother cursed her and every time he'd made a wish or forced her to dissipate. But she'd never noticed it on her own.

Could she pull it herself?

For the rest of the night Mora tried. When she closed her eyes and calmed her breath, she could almost see it. Wisps of onyx weaving through her chest. They flowed through her veins and twisted around her innards, stark shadows against the white gleam of her bones. At her center, they came together, twirling around each other to form a thread. One she could almost reach...

When the night sky relented to a patch of ravenous navy with the orange glow of the sun at its heels, Mora felt it give. Watched drops of smoke press through her pores like dew on a leaf's surface.

Dother stirred at her back, and she tugged harder, picturing ethereal hands pulling on the twisted strands of smoke. When his thumb twitched against her stomach, Mora nearly roared. Knew it was now or never.

As the thread ripped free, Mora smiled. Then she gave herself to the smoke.

It splashed down onto the mattress and cascaded to the floor below. Mora crawled into her flask, curling in its belly. For the first time in ages—gods, she had no idea how long it had been—Mora felt a flicker of hope.

And for the next few hours, her mind was blissfully quiet.

CHAPTER 36

ZADRIEL

"We're almost there, Mora. I'll need to put you down. Support your arm as best you can."

Mora nodded against Zadriel's shoulder, her chest rising and falling slowly with each pained breath. He found himself holding her tighter. Dreading the pain he'd see on her face when he moved her.

The night was a quiet one, though he'd purposely crept around the back of Andras's house to avoid unwanted attention. Thankfully his kind was quiet by nature—it had never been difficult, hiding in the shadows and making little noise. It made him a decent spy. Something Cillian put to use centuries ago.

When he reached the oak tree, he felt his muscles relax. Took the first deep breath he'd taken in gods knew how long. Cool evening air filled his lungs and his pounding heart slowed. Slightly.

Zadriel rounded the tree so they faced away from prying eyes. Arcadia loomed in the distance, her song curling in the breeze and tugging on his heart. He closed himself off to it, as he often did, and focused on placing Mora down with as much care as possible. It was the same tree he'd brought her to when she was drunk. A great oak whose long branches stretched into a wide, protective canopy. The one place that felt like home in Eden.

He couldn't think of a better spot to take her.

As he laid Mora against a groove in the trunk, the roots groaned. They stretched and moved out of the way—not for him but for her—adjusting so she could rest more comfortably. Zadriel's midnight gaze returned to her face.

Did you see that, Little Witch?

But Mora hadn't opened her eyes.

He took a slow breath and unclenched his jaw. The tree's reaction shouldn't have surprised him, but it reignited an old ache in his chest... and reminded him of the hatred he'd convinced himself he felt for her all these centuries.

It's not her fault. Cillian did this. Made you do this.

Zadriel shook his head, hating the memory. He could still smell the sweet scent wafting in the air with all that black smoke. Taste the ash on his tongue. He took another slow breath, hating that he shuddered.

Mora leaned into the tree's embrace, a sheen of sweat beading on her forehead.

"Would you like some water?" he asked.

"Please."

When he bent down to move a few leaves away, more roots shifted to help. His lips quirked upward as he pulled out the cowhide flask he kept hidden there. Zadriel twisted the wooden cork loose and tossed it to the earth before kneeling in front of her and lifting the flask to her lips.

"Drink, Little Witch," he said gently. Mora nodded, and he slowly tipped the container, careful not to give her too much.

When she pulled away, he looked down at her hands and the gore staining her fingers. There was no way he could draw them into his lap and clean them without hurting her. This night was going to be long if he didn't help ease the pain.

Zadriel bit his lip, weighing his options.

"I can help you feel better, but... there will be a cost."

Mora was quiet for a moment, the silence a heavy, uncomfortable thing. He tried to keep his face neutral, did his best to ignore the flutter in his stomach. When he flexed his hands, he felt the blood—her blood—sticking to his skin. Needed it gone.

"Are you trying to bargain with me, Fae?" Mora asked between gritted teeth. His heart sank at the pain in her voice.

Zadriel shook his head and poured water into his hands, appreciating the bite of cold. Cillian enchanted this flask for him centuries ago—the water was endless and never grew warm. He doubted Mora would appreciate knowing its origins, though she did have Cillian's pouch at her hip—perhaps its value outweighed her hatred for its creator. Now didn't seem like the best time to find out.

"This isn't a bargain," he said softly. He rubbed his hands together, nearly sagging with relief when the blood disappeared from his skin, dirty water dripping to the earth. There was still a weight on his chest—he couldn't stand the sight of her twisted arm or the pallor clinging to her warm, brown cheeks. But for the first time tonight he felt he could breathe a little easier. "Remember when I said you'd regret swallowing my blood?"

"Yes." She nodded weakly, those lovely eyes still closed. He wondered how long she'd remain conscious at this rate. "You were being an ass. I should have bitten harder."

"I deserved it, Little Witch." He'd been awful. Deserved nothing but disdain from her. But... "Next time you can bite me as hard as you'd like."

Mora scoffed. Peeled one eye open to give him an incredulous look.

"How have you felt about me since?" he asked.

Mora snorted. "You've grown on me."

"I could say the same." Zadriel rested his flask against the tree and stood, searching for the right branch. "I spent centuries convincing myself I hated you. That it was better this way. Every time they bled me to make trinkets to aid in their search for you, every time I looked to Arcadia and had to deny its call, I blamed you... Yet there was always this pull, from the moment I found you in the alley. You felt it too?"

Zadriel's hands shook as he ran his fingers over the perfect branch. *Had* she felt it? Or would she be furious at him for suggesting it? The rough bark soothed his nerves, and he looked to the glints of gold in the leaves. They fluttered as the branch pushed into his touch. It made him feel worse for what he was about to do.

When Zadriel looked back, he found Mora staring at him. It was a sharp, scrutinizing gaze boring into the depths of his soul. His heart fluttered as he watched her and waited for an answer. Prayed he hadn't made a mistake.

"I..." Mora swallowed and looked away, her cheeks darkening. "I remember thinking I could get drunk on your scent."

A thrill shot through Zadriel at those words and he smiled, a rare grin lighting up his entire face. "And I you." He snapped the branch free and smoothed a finger over the break in a silent apology. "That pull between us feels like more now, doesn't it?"

Mora's brows furrowed. "What does this have to do with helping me?"

"I'm going to make you a splint. I can't promise it won't hurt, but once it's done, the pain should improve." Zadriel busied his fingers by removing the connecting twigs before cracking the branch in half and dropping the pieces to the ground. He had no idea how to approach his offer. There was so much he couldn't say. Not yet.

"Ok..."

Zadriel reached for his tunic and realized he'd left his cloak inside. *Fuck.* Andras would be furious. The pace of his heart quickened, and he half considered running back to the cottage to retrieve it.

You can't leave her... she needs you.

He took a slow breath. Hoped Andras wouldn't find out.

Many in Eden knew what Zadriel was—it was difficult to keep an immortal being secret when he stopped aging and didn't die over the centuries—but after what happened with his mother, the Dothers demanded he wear a cloak when he left the house. Arcadia was too close. If one of his people saw him, they may cause trouble. And when they traveled throughout Berwick, he needed to keep his identity as hidden as Eden and their magic.

The cloak was an annoyance, especially during this dreadful season when the sun bore down on him with particular fury. If he hadn't known better, he'd think the Sun God was amused by his plight and took a twisted pleasure in making it worse. The alternative punishment for not obeying, however, was less pleasant.

Mora shifted and his eyes roved over her pained face. She endured so much. For her, he could do the same, even if it meant facing Andras again.

Though he may feel differently when the time came.

Zadriel cleared his throat and peeled off his tunic.

Mora's amber gaze wandered down his bare chest before settling on his hard abs. "I wasn't aware I'd be treated to a show tonight."

"Shut your mouth, Little Witch." Zadriel did his best to keep his deep voice serious, but his smile grew.

Mora looked down at her arm and winced at the sight. "Oh gods," she muttered, squeezing her eyes shut. Then asked quietly, "What does a splint have to do with your blood and me not hating you?"

Zadriel's hands trembled once more, so he squeezed his tunic. Begged his heart to slow. "If you'd like, you can drink some."

Her eyes flew open. "Drink your blood?" Her lips curled as she spat out the words. That wasn't the reaction he hoped for.

Why is this so hard?

"Did it not taste good last time?"

Mora ran her tongue over her bottom lip, brows furrowing. "It did..."

His grip on his tunic loosened, and he took a slow breath. "If you drink it, you should be healed by morning. And it will help you sleep. Dull the pain."

"But?"

"But..." Zadriel hesitated, searching for the right words. "It will enhance our connection."

"What do you mean?"

A branch brushed against his shoulder and pushed. If he weren't so nervous he would have laughed. The oak, it seemed, wanted this as much as he did and felt he was going about it all wrong. As he sat in front of her, a gilded daisy tickled his arm—he ran a finger over the petals, marveling at how quickly it grew. Would there be more? Or was Mora's dried, diluted blood less potent?

Zadriel plucked the daisy and tucked it into Mora's curls, a quiet yearning glittering in his midnight gaze.

"It won't make you feel anything you don't already feel. We're connected, Mora. We've made vows. I'm willing to trust you with my blood, but it will bring any feelings you have for me closer to the surface."

Mora's gaze snapped back to his, a fire blazing in those luminous eyes. "Is this a trick?"

"I'm not trying to trick you."

"Blood magic?"

Zadriel frowned. He had no right to ask her to trust him. And... she didn't know it, but this was a monumental step. He was an ass for not telling her everything, but now was not the time to burden her further. If he could help her heal, he'd pay any price. Even if the cost was her wrath.

Zadriel placed a hand on her knee, swiping his thumb soothingly up and down. "It's not that kind of blood magic. I'm not trying to curse you or cause you harm. I want to help. For the Fae, giving your blood like this is rare, we only do it with... people we trust implicitly. And, as you can imagine, I have more reason than most to be cautious."

Mora's face softened. "Ok. I trust you. But if this is some sort of trick, know I will not rest until I've made you pay."

He squeezed her knee, grateful for her trust. It would still be a difficult night, but knowing she would suffer less soothed that sinking feeling in his chest. "Yes, Little Witch. You're very scary, I know."

"I *am* very scary."

Zadriel smirked. He liked that she could be ferocious. Though he'd prefer she not destroy herself in the process.

He moved to her side and brought his wrist to his lips, but before he could bite down Mora inhaled sharply.

"Wait. Will it hurt? Will it scar?"

Zadriel frowned down at the thick network of scars staining his arms. He swallowed against the constricting feeling in his throat, wondering what Mora saw when she looked at him. Did she see him as broken and ruined? Ugly? "No. This won't scar." He forced a reassuring smile. "And it will only hurt for a second."

"Ok." Mora nodded before resting her head back against the tree's massive trunk.

Zadriel bit down, barely noticing the sting when he broke the skin. Warm blood trickled from the wound and he brought his arm to her lips. "Drink, Little Witch." It broke his heart, seeing those mangled fingers as she wrapped her left hand around his wrist. Mora stared up at him, so many emotions glittering in those bright eyes. He kept his voice soft and low. "It's ok. This will help you heal."

When Mora sealed her lips over Zadriel's wrist, he tensed. It felt... right. And Mora clearly felt it too. She squeezed his arm harder—despite the ache it must have caused—and her eyes went wide before she closed them and hummed against his skin. With each swallow, the warmth in Zadriel's chest spread, wrapping itself around his bones like a soothing embrace. Her teeth grazed his skin, sending

285

shivers up his spine. It took all his control not to wrap his other arm around her waist and pull her into his lap.

The world became quiet, as if it were just the two of them under an endless summer sky and the careful watch of an ancient oak with gold glimmering in its viridian leaves. Zadriel closed his eyes. Inhaled her delicious pine and ember scent. Imagined a different world where they were free to get lost in each other with no fear of Andras or whatever consequences may find them should they be caught. A world where they weren't bound by curses and betrayal. Where they could simply be Zadriel and Mora.

Mora ran her tongue along his wrist and his breath quickened. She shifted. Attempted to lift her right hand as if to hold him tighter.

"Gods damn it," she hissed, her head snapping back and hitting the tree. She dropped his hand and cradled the injured wrist she'd momentarily forgotten, new beads of sweat rising on her brow.

"I'm sorry." Zadriel reached for her, only to freeze, unsure what to do.

Mother help me.

Leaves rustled above him before a bough lowered itself to the ground. It found the sticks he'd prepared and pushed them toward him. "I could make your splint?"

Mora took three quick breaths between her teeth before she answered. "Please."

Zadriel nodded and did his best to ignore the way his stomach dropped. She'd have to move her arm in order for him to splint it. She didn't need more pain. He brought his tunic to his lips and bit the dark fabric, puncturing it with his sharp canines, then tore it into strips. "I'm afraid this may hurt," he said as he grabbed the sticks.

"Get it over with," she spat, squeezing her eyes shut.

Sweat slicked his palms, and he struggled to keep his hands steady, but he got to work. Hoped his blood was already helping to dull the pain. Had she taken enough?

Bile burned in his throat when he gently moved Mora's arm and she cried out. "I'm sorry," he breathed. When he wrapped the largest swath of fabric around her arm he hoped he was gentle enough. That the material felt soft against her skin and didn't add to the constant throb of pain.

"Hurry," Mora hissed through clenched teeth.

"I'm sorry, Little Witch. It's almost over." Zadriel used the thinner strips of his tunic to secure the branches in place above and below the injury, careful not to touch the break. "There. How does it feel now?"

"Great," she said with what he assumed was an attempted laugh. It came out more like a wheeze, the air pushing her curls away from her eyes. "A few months ago I was fascinated by pain, if you can believe it."

"Oh?"

"Something triggered a memory of Dother and, in my panic, I squeezed a rose bush. Thorns embedded themselves in my palm, but the pain helped quiet my mind. It had been so long since I'd felt much of anything, I..." Melancholy weaved around her voice as she trailed off.

Zadriel couldn't help but wonder if she was referring to that day in Lord Frederick's gardens. The day he'd found her. As he hid in the thicket of trees by the lake, she'd clung to a rose bush, panic in her eyes.

"You what?" he whispered. A shadow lurked in her gaze. One full of pain he understood all too well.

"I almost find myself missing it." She tilted her head to look at him and smiled softly.

Enthralled, he allowed the silence to sit between them as they watched each other. But he found himself aching to hear her voice. To know her mind. "Missing what?"

"Not feeling anything." A frown pulled at her lovely lips and she closed her eyes tight, heat blooming on her cheeks. "Then I remember."

"Remember what, Little Witch?"

"I was terribly lonely." With her free hand she grabbed his and gently squeezed. "It's nice to have someone I'm willing to hurt for."

Zadriel's eyes fell to the blood still coating her fingers. It made him uneasy, knowing what he'd done and that he may be forced to hurt her again. How could she bear to be near him? He was an unworthy male, from the moment he first laid eyes on her. Shame washed over him, so thick he could hardly breathe. "I will never be deserving of your sacrifice, Mora. Please, don't bring yourself any more suffering on my account."

Mora narrowed her eyes. "Zadriel," she said, her voice sharp, "Did we not make vows? We're in this together, I *will* fight for you."

Zadriel shook his head and huffed out a breath, feigning disapproval. But something fluttered in his chest and he found himself aching to touch her. To wrap his arms around her and surround himself in her scent. Leaning down, he placed a gentle kiss on her forehead, his lips lingering as he closed his eyes and allowed himself a rare moment of peace. A spark of joy arched through him when he felt her lean into his kiss, her breath tickling his neck.

Resting his forehead against hers, he nuzzled her nose gently and breathed the words they both needed to hear, "Together, Little Witch."

CHAPTER 37

MORA

*M*ora *roamed a field of gilded daisies, their shimmering petals tickling her legs. With each step she took, more and more popped through the soil and reached for her. When she extended her hand, Mora gasped. Lines of gold traced her veins, from her fingers all the way to her chest, and pulsed with the beat of her heart.*

She lifted her hands, bathing them in moonlight in hopes of seeing better.

"You're beautiful."

Mora shivered as Zadriel's deep, soothing voice washed over her. He smiled down at her as she turned to face him, a softness caressing his expression, and something else in his eyes she couldn't quite read. But it made her smile back.

Zadriel reached for her hand and entwined their fingers together. As her heart fluttered, gold seeped from her skin into his, crawling through his veins and climbing his arms. Her breath caught in her throat, but Zadriel squeezed her hand and she knew it was nothing to fear.

Mora's white dress, the color pure as fresh snow with glitters of gold along the bust, was soft against her skin. The simple gown had thin straps, a plunging neckline and two high slits in the skirt that ran up her thighs. Zadriel was her perfect counterpart, dressed in a sleeveless crisp white robe, tied at the waist with a gilded belt, with gold dusting the shoulders.

It brought out the flecks of gold in his dark gaze—it was as if she stared into the heavens. As if the Gods themselves kept their secrets hidden in those endless eyes.

Together they neared an enormous tree with gilded leaves and branches that nearly reached the stars.

There was no pain. No fear. No rage coursing through her veins.

Whispers of the most beautiful song she'd ever heard danced in the wind, and a calm like she'd never felt before wrapped her in its warm embrace.

Mora felt it in her bones.

She was home.

CHAPTER 38

MORA

Robins sang their praise to the morning sun, their call gently pulling Mora from the warm embrace of a comforting sleep. She peeled open her eyes, cursing the birds, and blinked against the rays of sunlight trickling through the oak's canopy. It was a shame to wake. To face whatever hell awaited. She was so warm, nestled against Zadriel's chest, his arms gently wrapped around her stomach. If only they could stay like this.

The last thing she remembered was Zadriel's long fingers drawing comforting circles against her skin until her eyes were heavy. "Sleep well, Little Witch," he'd said, before softly kissing the top of her head and pulling her closer.

Then she dreamt of a field of gilded daisies, an enormous tree, and gold pulsing in her veins, bleeding into Zadriel's. It felt real. Too real.

Mora looked down. Gasped at the faint golden glimmers painting her skin.

What's happening to me?

"Zadriel," she breathed, wriggling in his grip.

His breath tickled the crown of her head as he snored lightly, resting against what she learned was his favorite tree. When she nudged him with her elbow he grumbled, his grasp tightening as he nuzzled her hair and sighed happily.

"Zadriel, wake up!"

"Will reality be as sweet as my dreams, Little Witch?" he asked, his lopsided grin showing a single canine. And suddenly she found herself wondering how those teeth would feel against her skin, sliding delicately over her neck as she writhed beneath him...

Now's not the time, Mora.

"There's something wrong with my hands."

Zadriel sat upright, his hand smoothing down her messy curls. Those black eyes widened as they took her in, and a muscle twitched in his jaw. "What's wrong? Are you in pain?" he asked, his voice somehow soft and full of dread.

When Mora looked again nothing was there. "What?" She reached for Zadriel's hand, the movement difficult thanks to her splint, and traced her fingers along his veins and over the raised scars on his forearm, searching for hints of gold. "I... I must have been dreaming."

Zadriel's breathing calmed. "Your nails grew back."

Mora blinked. Flexed her fingers. Realized there was no pain. While her hands were still bloody, each finger had a perfect nail. "They did."

Zadriel hadn't lied about his blood. He'd trusted her and made himself vulnerable, all so she could heal.

Mora swallowed. Felt lighter somehow.

Zadriel placed a hand on her arm, his touch so careful and light. "Do you need the splint?"

When she wiggled her wrist Mora felt nothing. "I guess I don't."

Before she could try to untie the bindings holding her splint together, Zadriel gently grabbed her wrist. "Allow me." He carefully untied the strips of cloth he'd made from his own shirt. "Let me know if it hurts."

Mora nodded, unable to take her eyes off his face. The curve of his strong jaw, the cut of his cheekbones, the tips of those graceful ears. Gods, he was beautiful. She was so caught up in him she hadn't noticed when he reached for his flask. Nearly jumped when the cool water kissed her hands. He used a spare scrap of his tunic to scrub away the blood, his movements slower and softer than before.

"I see you're learning to be gentle," she teased.

Zadriel chuckled. "And I see you haven't learned any manners." When he was satisfied, he lifted her hand and brought it to his lips. Those dark eyes glittered as he kissed her fingers, one at a time. A silent apology for the pain he'd been forced to cause.

"Thank you," she breathed.

"Ah, there they are." Zadriel's grin was wicked and Mora found herself grinning back.

They sat quietly for a moment, watching each other, their faces mere inches apart. And suddenly all she wanted was to eradicate the distance.

Closing the space between them, Mora pressed her lips to his, her kiss soft and yearning. But Zadriel stilled, his breath catching as her lips moved against his.

Had she misread him?

Had the pain she'd felt last night distorted her memories?

Oh gods, what had she done?

Mora pulled back, hating the way her cheeks burned. When she glanced up at him through her lashes a red flush bloomed on his cheeks too. Mora attempted to pull away but Zadriel's grip tightened.

He tilted his head to the side, the movement animalistic. Primal. Then leaned in and inhaled her scent. A joyful hum rumbled in his chest as he brushed his soft lips against hers. At first, Zadriel's kiss was gentle, slow, a sweet exploration of whatever it was that lay between them. The moment she returned his affections he growled and pulled her closer, his fingers trailing up her arm until he was clutching the back of her neck while his other hand splayed against her lower back.

Zadriel's kiss became her delicious undoing. He devoured her, the press of his lips against hers a claiming. As he licked along her lower lip she shivered and gasped, groaning when their tongues met.

Mora needed to touch him. To pull him closer, breathe him in, and be surrounded by him. She ran her hand through his soft, black hair, deepening their kiss. As she explored his mouth, a familiar, warm feeling spread through her chest. This was... right. She *needed* him. His touch, his warmth, his affection.

Pleasant shivers ran up her spine when Zadriel's sharp canines brushed against her lip. He bit down lightly, before running his tongue languidly over the small, delicious ache. Soft fingers encircled her neck—he clutched her throat, holding her in place with gentle, exquisite pressure. Then he forced her head back, his hungry gaze bouncing from her lips to her eyes and back.

"Oh, Little Witch, I can't wait to explore every inch of you."

A thrill rolled through her belly before settling in her core.

"What if I want to touch you first?"

Before Zadriel could answer, Mora ran her hands over his bare chest and down his stomach, loving the way his muscles flexed under her touch. She leaned in and kissed along his jaw. Played with the laces of his breeches. When she trailed her lips down the side of his neck, she nipped him. Felt a strange urge to bite harder. Zadriel bent his neck further, as if in surrender, a deep, satisfied sigh on his lips.

When his laces came free, Mora dipped her hand into his pants and wrapped her fingers around his length. Or attempted to. She could barely get them around him. Gods, he was massive. Zadriel groaned as she gripped him tighter and shifted her hand up and down his shaft.

"Gods," he panted before wrapping her curls around his fist and pulling her head back. Their lips were so close they shared their breath. As he rocked against her, they watched each other, that dark gaze somehow staring through her. To the monster lurking within. To the core of her being. To every scar, every bruise, every stain on her soul. He didn't blink. He didn't look away. Zadriel *saw* her. With awe in those midnight eyes.

Mora broke first, diving onto his lips. Their desperate kiss was a clash of teeth and tongues and somehow she ended up beneath him, with one of his hands pinned by her head while the other squeezed her thigh and pulled it around his waist. She moved her hand faster, reveling in how he bucked against her.

And she realized she felt safe, even cradled beneath his massive body.

"Mora," he groaned against her lips, his body tensing.

Mora sucked on his bottom lip, worked him harder and savored every shaky breath. Found herself moaning between their ravenous kisses, eager for whatever came next.

Zadriel came undone. His head fell to her shoulder as his body jerked, the most delicious groan leaving his lips. He squeezed her thigh tighter, pressed harder against her and bit down on her neck hard enough to bruise, those sharp teeth almost puncturing her skin.

Mora was filled with need like she'd never felt before, her core practically throbbing. She arched her back, their chests pressing more firmly together. She could have sworn their hearts beat in unison.

Zadriel's warm tongue trailed over the mark he'd left, his breath coming out in soft, satisfied pants. "You have no idea what you do to me," he said against her skin. "No idea what I want to do to you."

"Then do it," she breathed as she pulled her hand free. Mischief danced in his eyes and he lifted his head to look at her face. She met that wild gaze, brought her hand to her lips and sucked his seed from her fingers.

Zadriel's nostrils flared, those dark eyes filling with need.

As he trailed his hand over the top of her leggings, she felt a tug in the center of her chest and heard Andras's voice in her mind, calling for her.

The Gods hate me, she thought with a growl.

Mora leaned in for another kiss then pressed her forehead against his, closed her eyes and inhaled his refreshing scent one more time. "I'm being called to the flask, love."

Zadriel tensed. "Be safe, Little Witch," he pleaded, his deep, rumbling voice laced with concern. "I'll make my way back. You won't be alone with him for long."

"Thank you." An uneasy feeling weighed in her chest as the curse demanded she answer Andras's call. It tugged on her bones. Writhed beneath her skin. Pushed until it seeped through her pores.

Mora nuzzled Zadriel's nose, then gave in. Smoke spilled from her pores, enveloping her in its obsidian embrace, and she slipped through Zadriel's fingers. He sat up, staring into the sea of sparkling night she'd enveloped him in.

Mora twirled around him and ruffled his hair. It was difficult to pull away. To leave the moment of heaven they'd carved for themselves, unsure of when they'd have another. As she made her way toward the cottage, Mora prayed they could navigate whatever hell Andras had in store for them. Together.

CHAPTER 39

MORA

Coils of smoke slid into the cottage from beneath the door, flooding the entryway before they curled together in a miniature cyclone. As they dissipated, Mora appeared, her long, dark brown curls bouncing against her waist. Zadriel's tunic hung from her body, the dark fabric stained with her blood.

A comforting throb in her neck surprised her. Mora ran her fingers over it, baffled when it thrummed pleasantly under her touch. Had Zadriel's bruise remained?

Impossible.

Andras cleared his throat and Mora's hand dropped. If the mark was still there, she hoped her hair hid it. Whatever was between her and Zadriel, she didn't want Andras to know. Dreaded what he might do if he found out.

"You called?" she asked sardonically, finally glancing around the room.

At the kitchen's center she found Andras, clutching her flask so tightly she wondered if the glass would shatter... and what would happen to her if it did. Halvard looked up at Andras from the floor, his long, auburn hair a loose, disheveled mess tumbling around his face. A deep red bruise bloomed around his neck. And the lord hadn't changed since the night before. Andras, thankfully, wore a new tunic, the color a bright royal blue with silver filigree along the shoulders.

He never looked away from Halvard as he said to Mora, "I wish for you to leave for the Forbidden Forest. Now. And *Lord* Halvard will be joining you. Right, Halvard?"

Halvard's unblinking eyes stared up at Andras, wide and bloodshot. But he nodded swiftly.

Somehow the room was worse than how Mora and Zadriel left it. A mess of splinters were all that remained of her broken chair, shattered ceramic bowls littered the floor, and the puddle of blood and nails—her nails, she recalled with a shiver—had been disturbed. Sporadic red footprints circled the room, a bloody painting of their disagreement. Whatever led to Andras's decision to send Halvard away, it hadn't been peaceful.

Why would Andras send Halvard to Arcadia? Everything he wanted hinged on Mora finding the Spirit of the Forbidden Forest and, from what she'd gathered, Halvard was here because he helped Andras acquire status and power. *And me,* she thought with a sneer. But there was no trust between them.

Mora didn't understand. Though she wasn't going to risk herself and ask.

With his free hand, Andras pointed to Mora. "Pack. Now."

Something swung in his grip. A pendant perhaps? The sunlight trickling in through the kitchen window glinted off the glass vial hanging from a string of braided hemp, revealing what moved inside. Two sanguineous vortexes twisted around each other in an endless dance. Was that blood?

Could it be Zadriel's?

Magic rumbled under Mora's skin, the pressure nearly too much to bear. One day she'd skin Andras alive and gift his flesh to Zadriel as a symbol of her affection.

Whatever that pendant may be, it was important. Likely enchanted. But to do what exactly?

It took considerable effort for her to pull her focus away, but Mora didn't want Andras to take note of her interest. Forcing herself to focus on him, on the face she abhorred, she couldn't help but notice his chocolate brown hair was mussed. And dark circles stained the skin below his eyes. Her lips twitched but Mora held back her smile. Andras was a man who relished control, and it had only taken two weeks in Eden for Mora to disturb his peace.

So much for Dother's journal.

"What do I need to bring?" She feigned boredom, picking at her nails while she awaited his answer.

Andras gave Mora an exasperated look. When he noticed the golden flower in her hair, his eyes widened for a second before he schooled his features. "Clothing, food—enough for at least two weeks. Zadriel will be with you for that time," he said, holding up the amulet.

It allows him to leave Andras without pain. At least they'd have time away from him. Mora grimaced when she remembered they'd be stuck with Halvard. In Arcadia. It would be two weeks of endless whining and she was exhausted already.

"If you haven't found the Spirit when Zadriel leaves, you'll stay behind. Do not disappoint me, Mora. I expect—" Andras's voice was cut off with a pained grunt as Halvard reared up and punched him in the groin with as much might as he could muster. Andras folded forward, dropping the pendant and Mora's flask to the ground with a clatter. Redness erupted on his cheeks and he closed his eyes, cupping his manhood and groaning.

The moment Halvard dove on her flask, a familiar bite of cold wrapped around her spine. Before she spoke the words Halvard wanted to hear, Mora snatched the pendant from the floor and shoved it in her pouch.

"Keeper of the flask," she said hastily, as she fastened her pouch's buckle, "my power is yours to command."

"Cut the formalities and get me away from him," Halvard hissed, backing away from Andras, who'd already begun righting himself.

Mora cocked her head to the side, a dark promise glittering in her amber gaze. "If that's your wish, Halvard, you'll need to say the magic word."

Halvard's gray eyes widened. They flicked from his brooch to Mora's eyes and back before he squeezed the flask harder and shook it in her face. "Yes, you harlot. I wish for you take me far away from this village, now."

Andras stood swiftly, his gait awkward as he took an unsteady step forward. But the wish took hold, curling around Mora's bones like a vice. She erupted, a torrent of onyx mist barreling so forcefully into Andras he was lifted into the air and flung into the wall with a loud crash. If the wish allowed it, Mora would have torn him to pieces. Sadly, Halvard simply wished to leave. A boring request.

Still, he was a fool who'd learned nothing from his time with Andras. She could take him *anywhere* with a wish like that. To the middle of the ocean. Or a cave full of bears. As long as it was out of this village, there were endless possibilities. He was fortunate Mora had no desire to stray too far from Zadriel.

Halvard yelped as her frigid smoke enveloped him in a dizzying wave. She detested his clammy hands holding her flask. The feel of his body in her ethereal grasp. And, most of all, saving him from whatever horrors Andras would unleash if he'd been forced to stay.

But she didn't have the luxury of choice. And any Keeper was better than a Dother. So Mora twisted around Halvard and envisioned the stables, a reasonable means of escape that hopefully gave her time to find Zadriel.

Gravel crunched under Halvard's feet and he gasped. Stumbled around like a newborn foal, mouth agape while smoke spun madly beside him. Mora had no interest in being careful—she hoped the rocks she flung in the air pelted Halvard's face. Her smoke shrank back slowly, until it resembled a woman made of shadows. When she pulled herself back together, she made for the stable entrance, but Halvard clapped her on the shoulder.

He was a fool not to notice the way her body tensed. Or the flare of horror and fury flashing in her glowing eyes.

"The stables? *This* is what you call escape? Andras could be here in a moment. What kind of wish granter are you?"

"An unwilling one," she spat, slapping his hand away.

A squeak pulled her focus and Mora grinned. "Alina. Lovely to see you again."

The hay bale Alina carried broke apart as it hit the ground. She lifted her arms, hands shaking in a way that made Mora's grin turn wicked, and cast a glowing blue shield. Mora prowled forward, her predatory smile growing wider with each step.

Bits of dried grass flew into the air when they were hit by the Aegist's magic and rained down on Mora and Halvard. The lord sighed as he swiped his hands over his forest green waistcoat.

"I had this mulberry silk shipped from Eldenna," Halvard grumbled.

And the whining begins.

Mora ignored him. "You know what I'm going to ask for, Aegist."

"Stay away, demon," Alina said with as much venom as she could muster.

Mora paused, swallowing against the tightness in her throat. Lillian's voice rose from the ether.

I didn't expect you to sneak up on me like some demon.

What would she think of Mora now?

That you're a monster. That you've always been a monster.

Normally, Mora preferred it that way. Embraced the creature she became to survive Dother and everything that came after. But knowing Lillian thought it... for some reason, that stung.

What other choice did she have?

She's not your enemy, Zadriel's deep, soothing voice whispered in her mind.

Gods damn it. Why did she care what he thought of her? It was easier not to care. But... the thought of disappointing him caused a tightness in her chest. She rubbed the spot above her heart.

"Look, child," she said as she schooled her features into something she hoped was more pleasant. "I need two horses—"

"A carriage," Halvard corrected.

"What?"

"We already traveled across this forsaken country by horse. I'm not doing that again. Get me a carriage."

Mora scrubbed a hand over her face, pushing her dark curls back. "Fine. A carriage and the horses required to pull it," she corrected with a sigh. "As swiftly as you can... please."

Alina lifted her chin and pushed harder against her shield, the blue magic sparking in a semicircle, protecting her front. "Andras told me to come to him if you caused any more trouble."

Of course he did.

"Andras isn't here. You'll need to make your own choices. Would you like to do this the easy way or the hard way? I'm inclined to recommend the former." As if to prove her point, Mora allowed some of her dark power to spill from her fingers. It slithered on the ground, slinking under Alina's shield and crawling up her legs. "Halvard wished to leave and you're standing in our way."

Alina screeched. Kicked fruitlessly against the shadowy mist. The shield flickered when she tripped over her feet, falling onto her ass. Dirt puffed in the air, staining her beige pants, and the shield broke apart with an audible *pop.*

Mora pulled her smoke back and smiled gently. "Give me the horses and carriage, and I'll leave peacefully."

Alina gulped, her head twisting in the direction of Andras's home, as if she wished the man would appear and remedy the situation. If they weren't swift, he would.

"My carriage should be ready, Alina, don't keep us waiting," Halvard said with practiced authority. The gem in his brooch glowed an eerie bluish green and Alina's hazel eyes glowed in response. The tenseness drained from her body and she nodded. Motioned for them to follow.

That's what Halvard's new brooch did? Andras was an idiot.

Did it offer limitless control? Could Halvard ask anything he wanted of anyone? Would it work on *her*? Mora clenched her fists. Studied his lapel and wondered if she could manage to rip the brooch from his waistcoat and destroy it before he could force her to stop.

Though... he made a wish earlier. Perhaps Andras had the forethought to limit who Halvard could control?

"Why didn't you mention you had a carriage waiting?" Mora hissed under her breath.

"I intended to leave today. Everything was to be ready for my departure. Well, almost everything." Halvard cast a look toward Alina that Mora didn't like. Surely he didn't mean to take her. Alina was only nineteen, practically a child, and Halvard appeared to be in his late thirties or early forties. Mora's throat burned as she tried her best not to think of what he wanted from Alina. What Andras promised him. "When I wished to leave, I assumed you'd take me further than the stables." Halvard's gray eyes narrowed as he glared at

Mora. "I also assumed Alina would comply easily once we got here. What did you do to her?"

"Nothing I won't do to you," Mora answered, sweetly. She followed Alina's footsteps to the back of the building. A carriage with two beautiful horses sat ready for their departure. One she recognized—her chestnut stallion from their travels looked dashing in his harness saddle. "Hello, gorgeous," she cooed, reaching up to scratch his neck. He nickered, his soft, round eyes boring into hers. "It's nice to see you again."

"Yes, the horse is very pretty. Get your fine ass up there and get us out of here." Halvard reached for Mora, but she twisted out of the way.

"I don't know how to drive a carriage."

"And you think I do?" He rolled his eyes before marching up to Alina, who cowered at the back of the carriage, nestled in a spherical shield. "Can you drive this, pet?"

Pet? Mora grimaced as she followed. Muttered an expletive under her breath. Alina blinked up at Halvard, those round, hazel eyes wide and horrified. The answer was clearly yes. But there was no way she'd come willingly.

"Be our coachwoman," he said. When she shook her head, Halvard frowned and fiddled with his brooch. "Of course it only works once," he muttered before looking to Mora. "Fix this!"

Mora eyed the road leading to Andras's cottage—had Zadriel made it back? Would he find her before it was too late? Her hesitation cost her. Halvard's wish sank its icy teeth into her bones and a rib broke under the pressure, the crack so loud Halvard heard it. He flinched with her as Mora pressed a hand to her side, gritting her teeth. Gods, she needed to think her way through this. Quickly.

Another rib cracked, the sharp pain stealing her breath. If only Halvard hadn't added *now* to his damned wish, the magic wouldn't be so eager to tear her apart until she gave in.

"So be it," she grumbled before giving in to the smoke.

A wave of darkness descended upon Alina as Mora dove. The poor thing whimpered and her shield sparked, flashes of blue light erupting through the mist. It pierced the darkness, making the glints of gold shine brighter. An oddly beautiful combination. Though, with each spark, Mora felt the Aegist's power burn. It didn't hurt—nothing hurt in this form—but it put up an admirable fight.

Slowly the shield began to crack, like glass under too much pressure. Mora continued to push. Though she felt a pang of guilt over Alina's cries. Sweat dripped down the girl's forehead, the force of Mora against her shield too much to bear—her arms shook and her legs slid back in the dirt. When a crack was large enough, Mora spilled through.

"Oh gods," Alina whimpered, as smoke trickled to the ground and crawled up her legs. It grew dark on this side of the shield as Mora filled the space, like an endless torrent of shadows come to devour her. The shield burst and Alina kicked, punched and twisted in Mora's ethereal grasp. It was of no use.

Whether Alina liked it or not, she was coming with them.

CHAPTER 40

ZADRIEL

"Where is she?" Despite his best efforts, Zadriel couldn't keep the panic from his voice. Hadn't been prepared for what he'd returned to. A wrecked cottage, Andras sprawled on the floor, and Mora... gone.

The room smelled of crackling embers bathed in pine and caressed by mint. It hadn't been long since she'd left. Had Andras hurt her? Had Zadriel taken too long?

An ache burned in his chest, and his heart... it was thundering, begging him to run. But to where?

"Where is she, Andras?" Zadriel asked again.

Andras narrowed his bright eyes at Zadriel's tone. Eyes that, despite the amber in his left iris, reminded him too much of Cillian. Though Andras never had Cillian's charm. The two shared a penchant for cold calculation, but only one could convince you he loved you while he pulled your strings.

"That's none of your concern," he said with a sigh as he brushed debris off of his deep blue tunic.

If Zadriel were thinking straight, he would have nodded. Kept his mouth shut. Pushed against his emotions until everything was so far from the surface he couldn't feel them. But he couldn't think past the thrum of his heart and that squeezing feeling in his chest. He bared his teeth and growled, the sound low and animalistic. His entire body felt like a coil ready to spring at any moment.

Andras gave Zadriel a warning look. "Calm yourself. Halvard has her."

That should have soothed whatever thrummed in his veins, but a new stab of pain prickled in Zadriel's ribs. Something was wrong.

"What do you mean Halvard has her?"

Andras hissed as he pushed himself up from the floor. "I mean he took her. It's an annoyance, but she'll come back to us eventually, thanks to my wish." He pinched the bridge of his nose and sighed. "We'll need to make plans to retrieve the flask."

"They can't be far. I'll retrieve her now."

Andras shook his head. "I doubt they stayed close. I enchanted a pendant for you, so you could leave me for a couple of weeks without issue. But Mora took it. I'll need time to create another before I can send you away."

"Let me go now. If they're nearby, I can retrieve her and the pendant, and then we'll fulfill your wish."

Andras chuckled as he limped to Zadriel and put a hand on his bare shoulder. He squeezed so tightly his nails pinched Zadriel's skin. "You've always been a loyal dog, Zadriel. But never when your precious forest is involved. At least, not since Cillian. He had a good hold on your leash, didn't he?"

A muscle feathered in Zadriel's jaw but he managed not to flinch at the reminder.

Andras continued. "I notice how you shut down when I discuss my plans. And yet now you're eager to help. Why?"

"Is this not what you desire?"

"Oh, it very much is." Andras squeezed Zadriel's shoulder harder, his fingers digging into the muscle and pressing against the bone. Blood welled around the edges of his nails. "But you're showing your hand. While you may want her, you know she's intended to be mine."

"Cillian thought the same—" Zadriel's words were cut off as Andras wrapped his free hand around his throat and squeezed. The metal from his ring dug into Zadriel's skin. He choked out a gasp as Andras stood on his toes and pulled the Fae down so their noses nearly touched.

"I am Cillian's legacy. Where he failed, I will prevail. And, in his honor, I will do so with her by my side. Regardless of how I choose to take the throne."

The pressure built behind Zadriel's eyes as his body screamed for air. And yet he refused to back down. Mora awoke something within him. Something that had been dormant for hundreds of years. It purred in his chest when he stared down at the pitiful man who, physically, was no match for the wild Fae in front of him.

Zadriel pressed into Andras's grasp until their noses met, a feral growl wheezing through his lips. "She. Is. MINE."

Andras barely blinked before Zadriel's fist crashed into his face with a loud crack. Zadriel grinned when Andras's eyes bulged in surprise. Lifted his chin as Andras's mouth fell open. And nearly laughed when the man stumbled back onto the floor.

Andras slowly lifted his hand to his mouth, his face twisting in shock when his fingers came back bloody. Never once had Zadriel denied him, or his father, or his father before him. He'd pay for it later, but he would never forget this moment. Or the exhilaration buzzing under his skin.

Without a word, Zadriel bolted for the door and ran onto the dirt road twisting through the village. His eyes darted back and forth as he searched for any signs of Mora, but he saw nothing unusual. An Elementalist used her gift to pull the water from her laundry. A Naturalist coaxed her strawberries to grow. The street was quiet and calm, so at odds with the panic flooding through him.

Though perhaps Mora went to see her favorite Aegist? If Halvard wanted out she may have gone to fetch him a horse.

Zadriel made his way toward the stables, praying to the Mother she was safe. Not that he had any right to pray to Her.

If you still hear me, please help get Mora away from Halvard and to Arcadia where, maybe, she can be free.

As much as his stomach churned at the thought of being away from her, he had to make sure Andras never got his hands on her again. Even if that meant he couldn't keep her for himself.

How he'd go back to a life of isolation and servitude after experiencing Mora, he didn't know. The village felt smaller as he imagined it. Like a cage forcing him to look through the bars and stare into the heavens, knowing he'd never be free.

The sun's rays felt too hot on his shoulders and he realized he was still shirtless. That he'd have more discrepancies to repent for when he finally returned... *home*, he thought with a frown. Like Brennan wanted.

Zadriel rubbed the throbbing pain in his chest and forced himself to jog faster as he neared the turn in the road leading to the stables.

The Little Witch's vow to find her way back to him would work against them anyway.

Perhaps he could convince her to make a new vow?

Or I could make a wish. Zadriel swallowed at the thought. No. Gods no. He couldn't do that to her.

A carriage nearly ran him over as it barreled into his path. Someone screeched in time to warn him and Zadriel jumped out of the way. Something tickled his skin, and he felt that familiar soft flicker of cold that came with Mora's smoke.

The world slowed as the carriage passed. He caught sight of Alina's wide hazel eyes and the coils of onyx mist holding her in the driver's seat. Leaning out the window, calling his name, was Mora. Those beautiful amber eyes aglow.

"Stop," Mora shouted. "Stop, now. Please!"

Right along with her, in the most grating voice, Halvard called for Alina to go on.

Fucking Halvard.

The carriage sped past Zadriel, and he found himself turning on his heels and sprinting as quickly as he could to catch up.

Alina faltered, and the horses slowed their pace. Yet they didn't stop. As he pushed his body to move faster, Zadriel coughed and wheezed against the onslaught of dust clouding in the air with each beat of the horses' hooves. But he was so close.

Zadriel took a deep breath, pushed harder against his long legs, and launched himself toward the carriage. There must have been a

God or two on his side because his fingers made purchase on the roof, though he scrambled to maintain his hold. He kicked his feet and swung wildly as he tried desperately to reach the carriage step. Rocks pelted his legs and sliced his bare chest, but the pain felt like a distant echo. Something he'd feel later when his mind could quiet.

Mora attempted to scramble over Halvard, her fingers stretching toward Zadriel as if she could grab him and pull him in. For a moment they watched one another, and that warm pulse in his chest expanded. All he saw was her. All he felt was the affection shining in her eyes and the fullness in his own heart fluttering in response.

When his foot caught hold of the carriage step, he took his first steady breath since he'd entered the cottage.

"Mora," he whispered.

"Zadriel," she breathed in return.

Wind whipped through his hair, and the last houses flew by—they had almost left Eden. Zadriel clung to the roof as he pulled a hand free and reached for the door, searching for the handle. Though he couldn't take his eyes off his Little Witch. A flush darkened her cheeks and tears shone in her eyes.

"I'm here," he said. Two simple words, yet he hoped she understood what he meant. He would always be there in all the ways that counted.

While he fumbled with the latch, Halvard twisted in his seat. Zadriel should have known better, should have been watching more carefully. By the time Halvard sank his blade into Zadriel's chest, it was too late.

"Begone, mutt," Halvard seethed as he pulled his hand away, leaving the blade behind.

Iron boiled under Zadriel's skin. It seared through his ribcage and pierced his lung, blisters blooming in its wake. When he coughed, blood splattered into the cabin, droplets raining down on Mora's outstretched hand. He watched her eyes widen with horror. Cringed as she screamed, his ears popping at the intensity of the sound. When Mora tried again to crawl over Halvard, the man held her back, muttering expletives while she struggled in his grip.

One day, Zadriel would make him pay for every insult, every hurt he'd caused her.

A sharp pain pulsed through his chest as Zadriel attempted to breathe. Without thought, he wrapped his hand around the dagger's hilt and pulled the blade free. It clattered onto the ground, disappearing in a cloud of dirt as the horses kept their pace.

Zadriel gagged against the pungent taste of burning flesh filling his mouth with every breath. Each gasp wasn't enough. All he felt was a squeezing pain in his chest. And the heavy hands of exhaustion gripping his shoulders.

The world spun and Zadriel's hand began to slip from the roof. He stared at Mora. Hated that he couldn't wipe away the tears sliding down her cheeks. He longed to hold her and tell her everything would be ok. That he'd find his way back to her, like they'd promised.

"Mora, I—"

Before he could finish, Halvard's palm smacked against Zadriel's chest, and he lost his balance. Mora's horrified face as she shrieked his name was the last thing he saw as he fell to the ground.

Then the world went black.

CHAPTER 41

MORA

The silence was palpable, Mora's harsh breaths the only sound filling the cabin. She stared down at her blood spattered hand, rubbing at the mess until her skin chafed.

I'll find my way back.

Mora held onto her vow. Told herself over and over again Zadriel would live. Because... she couldn't handle the alternative.

She took a shuddering breath. Rubbed her palm over her heart. Something burned in her chest—the pain erupted the moment Halvard plunged his dagger into Zadriel—and magic pulsed under her skin like an endless drum joining the frantic beat of her heart. It took all of Mora's might to maintain a gentle hold on Alina. If she gave into her rage, she'd crush the girl.

Halvard paid no mind to Mora's ire. The man looked bored, his arm resting on the window's ledge as he watched Eden disappear over the horizon. It wouldn't be long before they reached Arcadia's edge. "Why head for the forest? My chateau's in the opposite direction."

Mora gritted her teeth, every word laced with venom. "You never specified a direction."

"Surely you didn't think I'd want to follow through with Andras's plans?"

"Surely you don't think I care about your wants?"

Halvard drummed his fingers against the windowsill and frowned. "But I have your flask."

The flask sat in his lap, the sun's rays glinting off the golden filigree. Mora stared at it, her upper lip twitching as she wrung her bloodied hand harder. "And?"

"You're to fulfill my—"

Mora slammed her palm on the bench, the loud slap reverberating through the carriage. "Let me be clear, Halvard. I may be bound to your wishes, but I will interpret them as I please. And if you think I won't make you pay for Lillian and Zadriel, you're a greater fool than I imagined."

Redness erupted along Halvard's cheeks and he averted his gaze. "I'm no fool."

"We shall see." A cold smile curved up Mora's lips. Though it faltered when her mind drifted back to Zadriel, injured and alone.

Oh gods, she prayed he'd be ok. That they'd find one another again.

Lured by Andras's wish, a tug in her chest led to the forest, the urgency easing as they neared the trees. But something else in her heart led back to Eden. And it stretched taut as the horses pulled them away.

Was it the vow demanding she go back?

The horses slowed and a sinister wall of trees rose to meet them. They nearly blotted out the sun. Before the Exodus, Arcadia's edge was said to be a feast for the eyes, a cluster of tall, glorious trees swaying in the wind, their evergreen needles and viridian leaves beckoning to those with an adventurous spirit. Splashes of colorful wildflowers and mushrooms caressed in a carpet of soft moss once waited on the other side. Now the trees were gnarled. They stretched across the lands, twisted boughs linking together to form an impenetrable wall.

Arcadia hadn't opened to anyone in centuries. Without Zadriel, they couldn't pass through.

Mora swallowed. How was she supposed to follow the pull of Andras's wish if she couldn't make it any further? Was she in for endless agony until she found a way? Or would this be an opportunity to get Zadriel? Her heart fluttered at the thought.

The carriage jostled as they stopped and Alina twisted in her seat, pulling against her vaporous restraints. "Please let me go."

Halvard crossed his arms and donned his typical sneer. "I wish to keep Alina until I say otherwise."

The cold grip of Mora's magic made her shiver. He wanted to *keep* her. Mora squeezed her fists and closed her eyes as Dother's voice boomed in her mind.

Did you honestly believe I'd let you go, Treasure?

Mora needed fresh air. Needed to leave the confines of this space and breathe. She threw the door open and stepped outside, grateful for the crisp, earthy scent filling her lungs.

"I'm not leaving the carriage," Halvard said behind her.

"Suit yourself."

Smoke snaked around Alina's center, the glittering obsidian now fueled by Halvard's latest wish. Bile burned in the back of Mora's throat and she ran a hand down her face. Tried to stop herself from shaking.

There had to be a way to twist Halvard's demand and let Alina go. Mora carried many sins. Took pride in most of the stains on her soul. But she couldn't bear to leave a woman in a man's possession.

Mora took a deep breath and paced, long strands of grass tickling her thighs. As she neared the trees, the world grew silent. Birds quieted, crickets ceased to sing, even the breeze paused, refusing to rustle the leaves. It felt as if the forest watched her. A branch reached for her and Mora lifted her fingers, allowing the leaves to kiss her skin.

The ground shook, a loud rumbling devouring the silence. Mora stumbled, nearly falling over her feet, consumed with memories of Frederick, and the mess she'd made of his manor.

Was the earth going to consume her in retribution?

The forest groaned as it began to move. Ancient trees with enormous trunks and seedlings alike shifted, creaking as they opened to reveal a path into the woods. Arcadia. Zadriel's home.

Hope died in her chest as the forest called to her, a sharp tug in her center begging her to cross the threshold. It was so powerful she found herself stumbling forward.

Until she found the Spirit, there'd be no returning to Eden. No returning to the Fae who'd begun to feel like... home.

Please be ok.

A loud squeal sounded and Mora spun in time to watch as the horses reared. The moment their hooves landed they bolted. Alina shrieked, the carriage jostled and suddenly they were rushing into the forest, dirt flying behind them.

The Fae would not be happy.

"Alina, stop," Mora yelled after them, but Alina was no match for the spooked horses. Exploding into a bundle of mist, Mora chased after them, speeding through the air until she seeped under the crease in the door and appeared across from Halvard.

The man jolted. "You scared me half to death!"

Mora rolled her eyes. "Pity you're still with us."

He scoffed as he drummed his fingers against the wooden seat, the bruise on his knuckles stretching with the movement. "Make Alina turn around."

"Is that a wish?"

"I'd prefer not to waste it."

Mora shrugged. "Then it's none of my concern." Though she cringed inwardly as she thought of Alina. There was little she could do to get her out of harm's way without magic. Mora had almost no experience with horses and Andras's wish demanded she remain in Arcadia.

As they hurtled through the woods, trees continued to shift out of their way and Halvard paled, his eyes darting over the forest's canopy.

What had he seen?

Panic flooded his expression, and he reached across the carriage, wrapping his hands around Mora's tunic. "I'm your Keeper, you do as I say," he spat in what Mora assumed was an attempt at an intimidating voice. As if to further his point, he pulled her from her seat and shook her.

A quiet chuckle was all she gave in response before she erupted, clouds of smoke slipping through his hands. Reappearing at his side, Mora crossed her ankles and leaned back in her seat. "You don't get it, do you, Halvard?"

Halvard ran his hands through his long, auburn hair. "Fine, I wish—" Something whooshed into the cabin, embedding itself into the opposing wooden door. "By the gods!"

Mora caught a glimpse of white hair as someone jumped from one tree branch to the other, running along the boughs. He flicked his hand toward the carriage and another bolt flew through the window.

With a sickening thwack, it embedded itself into Halvard's chest. The man gasped and wrapped his hands around the sharpened branch, twigs and leaves snapping under his grip. "Mora—"

They both nearly fell from their seats when the carriage jolted to a stop. Alina screamed, blue light erupting around her while vines crawled over wheels.

"Let Alina go, Halvard."

"No," he breathed. He stared down at his dark green waistcoat with wide eyes while blood seeped through his wound and stained the fabric.

Mora growled and looked away, peeking through the window. Alina deserved the opportunity to run. Gods damn this pathetic man. She found no sign of the white-haired Fae in the trees, but Mora found a silver-eyed hawk watching them from its perch on a nearby branch.

Halvard's sharp, shallow breaths were deafening as they sat in eerie silence.

"I wish—" Halvard coughed, spittle and blood slipping down his chin. A splotch of saliva landed on Mora's cheek and she grimaced, her stomach twisting as she wiped it away. "I wish for you to heal me." His voice was soft, the rise and fall of his chest slowing with each passing second.

Mora gritted her teeth as his wish took hold. With an exasperated sigh, she placed her hand on top of his and closed her eyes, cringing against the feel of his warm, soft skin. Obsidian fog spilled from her palm, slithering languidly over Halvard's silk top before it dove under the collar and roamed his body.

The frigid wisps dipped into Halvard's wound and he hissed. "That hurts!"

Mora smiled. "Good."

She could feel the projectile piercing deeper into Halvard's flesh with each of his shallow breaths. It nicked his heart and punctured his lung. But the sharpened branch acted like a plug, preventing too much blood from seeping out. Keeping him alive.

Pity.

Halvard's hand flexed beneath hers, those broken knuckles still swollen. She grinned wider, a plan forming in her mind.

"Remember what I told you?" she asked, an edge of cruel amusement in her voice.

Halvard furrowed his brows. "What?"

Her ravenous smoke pulled away from his chest, curling over his hand and enveloping the old wound. As her power healed Halvard's bones, the evergreens outside the carriage bent toward them, their branches scratching against the doors.

Mora pulled away and admired Halvard's knuckles, now free from swelling and bruises. She'd healed him, just as he asked. Simply not where he wanted. "That I'd laugh when your day came."

Confusion, rage and fear all warred on Halvard's face. "You... you bitch." The words barely escaped his mouth.

When she grabbed his hand again, Halvard resisted. He attempted to flinch away, but the pain was too much and he found himself gasping. Mora laughed, the sound low and cruel, as she pried his hand free and admired the branch piercing his chest. She owed the Fae her thanks. Pressing a single finger against the injury, she traced tiny circles in Halvard's blood. A monster glared through her eyes, delighting in the way he shuddered.

Mora wrapped her fists around the branch and pulled. "This is for Lillian," she said as the wood came free, the sharpened edge shining with crimson. Blood spilled from Halvard's chest, and an agonized, gurgling wheeze left his lips. With shaking hands, he pressed against the wound, but it was no use. Blood spilled through his fingers.

"And *this* is for Zadriel," Mora seethed. Her fist tightened around the wooden shaft as she brought it down upon the man. Mora shrieked as she forced it into his neck, pulling it out and plunging it in.

Again.

And again.

And *again*.

A disgusting squelching sound filled the cabin and Mora's hands became slippery. But she didn't stop. Not when blood spattered her face and clung to her curls. Not when it pooled in her lap.

Mora let herself feel it all—the fury she'd carried for centuries. The shame for what she'd done to Frederick. The helpless agony of watching Lillian die. And the endless rage burning in her heart for Zadriel.

Halvard paid not only for his sins, but Andras's and Dother's. And Mora couldn't bring herself to feel anything but smug satisfaction. She continued until the wooden shaft snapped in half and cut into her palm. Until her hands were so slick with Halvard's blood she could no longer pull the branch from his corpse to impale him again.

Her sharp breaths filled the cabin as she closed her eyes and squeezed her fists tight, focusing on the sticky blood cooling on her skin.

I'll find my way back to Zadriel. And when I do, I'll make Andras pay.

Mora's skin prickled with awareness, and magic twirled in her chest. A sweet, earthy scent wrapped in spruce and brimstone curled through the cabin and she knew she wasn't alone.

Her eyes snapped open. A wild, glowing red gaze with streaks of purple bursting from the pupils watched her. They widened when they saw the golden daisy in her hair, then roved over her bloody face.

The Fae's white brows rose as he whispered, "What *are* you?"

CHAPTER 42

THALIAS

Arcadia was ravenous. Thalias felt it in his bones, an urgency that sent him racing through the canopy. Vesryn donned the shape of a hawk and flew by his side, the brown tips of his feathers brushing against Thalias's arm. Whatever hid in the carriage, the Forest wanted it so badly, She let it in.

A wraith-like being covered in blood was the last thing Thalias expected to find.

The vicious creature stared up at him, her amber eyes aglow. Power writhed behind those eyes—it called to him, his own power pressing against his ribs in return. And Arcadia reacted, Her winds picking up and sweeping around them both. It billowed through his white hair and danced in the wraith's dark curls.

Blood slid down her round cheeks and dripped off her chin, but she seemed unbothered. At peace. At least, before he'd interrupted her.

She smelled familiar. Like crackling embers, lavender, and pine, but also... Thalias scrunched his nose against the minty scent, caressed in hints of petrichor. He didn't like it. Though he wasn't sure why. His eyes searched the carriage for another, noting only the cooling body and a strange flask decorated with gilded daisies and golden leaves laying on the floor by its feet. Thalias's fingers twitched as Arcadia urged him to grab it.

"I asked you a question," he said, holding that fierce gaze.

A fresh, gilded daisy sat in her dark curls.

Impossible.

Arcadia hadn't seen the likes of it in centuries.

Roots snaked through the earth, pushing through the soil to cling to the carriage.

The wraith graced him with a sinister smile before flicking the remains of the bloody branch in his direction. "And I've decided not to answer."

Before Thalias could blink, she exploded into a cloud of obsidian. Suddenly Thalias remembered a sickly-sweet scent, the burning pain in his eyes, and the grit of ash coating his skin.

The wraith's vapors filled the cabin, pressing against the walls so hard the wood creaked. Thalias growled as he stepped away, his upper lip peeling back to reveal sharp canines. But there were no fires feeding the violent wave of dark mist. No Mother Tree left to burn.

As if Arcadia felt the pounding in his chest, She moved a nearby tree, its bough bending to rest between Thalias and the carriage. *Thank the Mother,* he thought. Though it wasn't fear coursing through Thalias's veins. The memories made him furious.

The Halfling in the driver's seat squeaked as the vapors released her, the sound so ridiculous Thalias couldn't help but huff a laugh.

Her shield sputtered as she jumped from the carriage and ran, but the Aegist wouldn't get far. Vesryn leapt from the trees, spread his massive brown and white speckled wings, and flew after her.

That strange mist swirled in the air, stretching and undulating in the small space, before twisting toward the floor of the cabin and disappearing.

Thalias blinked several times, silently watching the carriage for any signs of movement. The tension in his body refused to ease. Though all was quiet, except for the incessant whooshing of blood in his ears. He ran his hand over the protective bough in thanks, then stepped around it, approaching the carriage once more.

When he peeked through the window, he found nothing but the dead human and the strange bottle, now filled with the same dark smoke. It undulated inside, glitters of gold visible through the darkness. Thalias felt as if he'd partaken in one of the dryad's special mushrooms. None of this made sense. He rubbed his temples and took a breath.

Why does Arcadia want this creature?

A pixie landed on his shoulder, her fluttering translucent wings tickling his cheek. A frown graced her face and her blue hair blew in the wind, strands catching her little flower crown. Stomping her foot, she squeaked her annoyance, the sound high and lyrical.

"It's not me, little one." Pointing toward the carriage, Thalias furrowed his brow in his best attempt to look serious. "Tell everyone to stay away for now."

She poked his cheek three times as she continued to squawk—it was difficult not to chuckle.

Before he could reassure her, Vesryn emerged from the deep woods. The tall male was no longer in an animal form, his rich, umber-brown skin nearly glowing every time a ray of sun trickled through the canopy. His Druid mate looked handsome in his leather armor, the deep forest green complimenting his warm complexion. Thalias loved that they matched. He let his gaze wander, admiring Vesryn's wide shoulders and thick, muscular arms. Black tattoos peeked out from his sleeves—later he'd trace them with his tongue, all the way to Vesryn's heart.

Vesryn pursed his full lips. Gave Thalias a look that said *what now?* But, for a moment, Thalias got lost in those bright, silver eyes. They made him think of moonlight—the celestial glow in that stare never failed to take his breath away.

Vesryn cleared his throat. "You can stare later, Sapling. What would you like to do with her?"

But I love staring, Thalias said through their bond, the words only for Vesryn. Vesryn raised a brow, but a little smirk graced his cheeks.

He shifted, jostling the Aegist he'd thrown over his shoulder like a burlap sack full of apples. She kicked and twisted in Vesryn's grip, but he didn't flinch. Green vines curled around the girl's legs and wrists—the Forest took her down before Vesryn caught her. Judging by the mud caked on her beige pants, loose gray tunic, and cheek, she'd been caught off guard and fell hard the moment Arcadia decided to grab her.

"Let me go," she cried, a quiver to her voice. Sparks of blue defensive magic danced in the air, a gift from Arcadia she didn't deserve to carry.

Vesryn grunted when one of the sparks hit his shoulder, his muscles tensing. When the girl kicked his chest once again, he sighed and said, "Have it your way." Tilting his body to the side, he let the

Halfling slide off his shoulder and onto his forearm before dropping her to the ground.

Thalias felt it when she landed. The Aegist grunted before struggling to sit up, her bindings forcing her to twist and wiggle into position. Wide hazel eyes stared up at the two Fae. And her lower lip trembled. The pixie jumped from Thalias's shoulder to flit around the Aegist, screeching in her ear before flying off, tiny hands clutching her hair as she continued to grumble. Likely cursing Thalias's name.

The girl's mouth fell open as she watched the pixie fly away. When she turned back to Vesryn and Thalias, she paled. "Please let me go. I'm not supposed to be here."

Bending down so they were eye level, Thalias's expression turned serious. When she attempted to scramble back, he tilted his head to the side. Made sure she saw the beast lurking behind his eyes. "You're right. Which begs to question, why did you enter our Forest?"

"She m-m-made me." The poor thing trembled like a newborn fawn.

Thalias tensed. Assumed she meant the wraith. Arcadia opening for her was a gift, as far as Thalias was concerned. Arcadia opened for no one but Her people. And for this outsider to force others in...

He'd taken care of the human. They were never to enter the Forest again. Yet Thalias was hesitant to end the Halfling, even after all their kind had done. She may be unworthy of her power, but the blood of his people ran through her veins.

"The wraith forced you into Arcadia?"

"I don't know what she is. Please, let me go."

Thalias ran his tongue over his sharp canines, smirking down at the Aegist. "What will you give me in exchange?"

329

The human gulped. "In exchange?"

"For your freedom."

Thalias hadn't thought it possible for the girl's eyes to grow any wider, but he was proven wrong. Those bright, hazel irises drowned in a sea of white and her light blonde curls fell over her face as she hung her head in defeat. "I don't have anything to give."

"Do you have information on the wraith?"

"I don't know anything about Mora. Except she belongs to Andras."

Mora. The wraith had a name.

And she belonged to Andras? As in, he owned her? The Fae knew what happened to Halflings in the human lands. Knew of their horrific laws, confinement and slavery. When they'd been forced from Arcadia, some Fae left with them, unwilling to leave their human and Halfling partners. Most never returned. The few who did brought tales of horror with them.

The wraith, however, was more than any Halfling ought to be.

What is she?

"Unless you have something to bargain with, I'm afraid we're at an impasse. Vesryn, darling, please keep an eye on her." His mate nodded, crossing his broad arms as he looked down on the scrawny Halfling. Vesryn's expression appeared serious to any who didn't know him. But a glint of curiosity glimmered in his moonlight eyes.

He'd never seen a Halfling before. Neither of them had.

They could feel her magic, its gentle thrum under her skin calling to them. Though, unlike the two of them, her power didn't extend into Arcadia's well. The Mother gave her kind a drop and nothing more, as it was meant to be.

A muscle ticked in Thalias's jaw and he stared up into the Forest's canopy. So many things had gone wrong for his people. Nothing was as it was meant to be.

He pushed his white hair away from his face and stood. Made his way to Vesryn. Thalias needed a moment of comfort. He felt the tension bleed from his body when he wrapped his arms around his mate's shoulders and kissed him. Vesryn pulled him closer, smiling against his lips as they enjoyed each other. The moment passed too quickly.

Thalias broke away. "I'll be right back," he said, pecking him once more before marching to the carriage.

Vines followed his steps until they snaked up the door and twisted around the handle. They pulled until the door snapped open, the offensive iron hinge creaking under the pressure. Thalias grimaced as he stared at the metal—iron had no place in Arcadia.

More vines burst through the soil and dove into the cabin, crawling over the floor until they found the flask, their green leaves rustling while they dragged it toward Thalias. The crystal clanked against his knuckles as they tried to hand it to him.

"Patience," he said with a laugh, running a finger over one of the leaves. But Arcadia had no patience today. The vines followed his fingers, pressing against them until he opened his hand and welcomed their gift.

Thalias wasn't expecting a cold bite of magic to rush over him, the feeling like ice coating his spine. Smoke the color of the blackest night sky spilled from the flask and engulfed Thalias until the Forest ceased to exist. Vesryn gasped behind him. Panic thundered in his mate's heart, but Thalias could do nothing but stare into the endless sea of darkness.

Ash rained from the sky and the Forest screamed. Screamed so loud Her people screamed with Her.

Thalias was on fire. The flames so frigid they burned. And yet he closed his eyes and leaned into its cool caress. Smoke twirled around him like a rageful whirlwind, singing to the fury rooted in his own heart.

It was familiar. Though he couldn't understand why.

Goosebumps rose on Thalias's skin as the mist's wrath all but consumed him, his heart pounding against his chest. Until it finally pulled away and he could breathe.

Thalias felt it as Mora's feet touched down on the mossy Forest floor. Heard the crack of her knuckles as she flexed her fingers. When he opened his eyes, he saw her beautiful face, no longer plastered in blood. Those glowing amber eyes narrowed as she spied the flask in his hands, and though she smiled before she spoke, it was anything but kind.

"Keeper of the flask, my power is yours to command."

CHAPTER 43

MORA
300 YEARS AGO

*T*he spicy scent of Dother's drink made Mora's stomach curl.
He sipped it while watching her from his desk, those too-bright
eyes boring into her soul. Mora refused to give him her attention.
Ignored when he drummed his fingers, though the tap of his ring
on the desk's surface made her wince. Instead, she sank deeper into
the plush bedding cushioning her bruised body. Perfect replicas of his
fingerprints peppered her skin, their endless throbbing an echo of his
earlier... attention.

The squeak of his chair when he pushed away from the desk had her
heart racing. Dother's bare feet pattered against the black tiled floor
and Mora clenched the sheets tighter. When he stood in front of her,
she suppressed a shudder. Managed not to flinch as he caressed her

cheek. His fingers trailed down her face to her chin and pushed until she was forced to look up at him.

"Have a drink," he cooed. He pressed his cool glass against her lips and tipped it up slightly until amber liquid danced along the seam of her mouth. Strong fragrance tickled her nose and Mora's stomach revolted. She stared past him to the journal laying open on his desk, refusing to give in. Alcohol spilled over the rim until it dribbled down her neck, leaving a cool, wet trail along her naked body, and soaked his black sheets.

Dother shook his head as he pulled the tumbler away. Swirling the remaining liquid around, he eyed the glass thoughtfully. "I wish for a kiss, Treasure."

The demand sparked in her center—icy tendrils bore into her chest and twisted around her bones. Mora's spine straightened, and she clamped her eyes shut, fisting her hands to stop their trembling. Dother took another generous sip of his drink, finishing it off, before leaning down and pressing his soft lips against hers.

Mora gave in.

Gods, she hated herself. She couldn't handle the pain of denying his wish, even for a moment. Not now. Already she was so tired, and the night had only begun.

When she opened for him a bitter flavor overwhelmed her senses—Dother spat his drink into her mouth before entwining his tongue with hers. Fucking bastard. Liquid slid down her throat and seeped into her windpipe, burning all the way down. Mora tried to push him away as she coughed. But Dother didn't care. Instead, he drew her closer, running his hand along the back of her neck and through her soft curls until he cradled her head. The slap of her palms against his *chest did nothing to move him. He took his time tasting her, knowing his wish forced her to endure.*

His wish for a kiss...

Something dawned on her while her lungs screamed for air. He hadn't specified he wished to kiss her. *Nor did he say* when *he wanted to be kissed. What would happen if she interpreted things differently? Would the wish be appeased? Or would she face the same agony she endured whenever she attempted to deny it?*

It was worth a try. What did Mora have to lose?

A cough rattled in her chest and Dother finally pulled away. Those bright azure eyes glimmering with mischief made her tense, but she could only wheeze against the liquor in her windpipe.

"Are you all right?" he asked as he set his tumbler down on the rosewood dresser.

It took an endless amount of effort not to roll her eyes. Mora wiped her lips on the back of her forearm, coughing a few more times before she answered. "You know I'm not."

"Treasure." He cupped her face. "You know I hate seeing you like this. Be my queen. Let's change Berwick together."

A fire burned in her amber glare, and Mora seethed. Even her power roiled beneath her skin, searching for an out—it stung as it pressed against her bones, but she held her breath and endured. Dother knew her answer. But when he couldn't get what he wanted, he took it. Despite all his talk about creating a better world for Halflings, he was obsessed with power. A crown wasn't enough—Mora was part of the grand legacy he imagined for himself.

She wasn't a fool—Dother never loved her. Mora had the audacity to say no and he couldn't handle it. Even if she gave in, there was no future where he allowed her to be free.

"I will never choose you, Dother."

He straightened to his full height, a sneer replacing his grin. "I've told you to call me Cillian."

Mora stood, before she could think better of it, adrenaline coursing through her veins. There was an edge to her voice she hardly recognized. "And I've told you no countless times. It appears neither of us are good listeners. But only one of us is a monster."

Dother laughed, shaking his head, chocolate brown hair tickling his brow. "I wouldn't speak with such certainty, Mora." He pressed his hand against her chest with enough force to push her back onto the bed and leaned in until their lips nearly touched. "We all become monsters with enough time and the right motivations."

The mattress shifted as Mora leaned back, putting as much distance between them as she could. "I'll never be like you."

"No, but you'll grow to be the perfect queen to stand by my side." He brushed a curl away from her cheek. "I will always be your monster. And you will always be mine. Whether you like it or not."

With an undignified shriek, Mora exploded into an ominous cloud of smoke and dove for her discarded flask. It sat on the floor beside his rumpled, beige breeches. Dother screeched at her to stop before she plunged into the bottle, mist bleeding through his fingers.

It was fruitless. Mora knew it. He'd force her to return momentarily. And likely wish her to stay for the remainder of the evening. But it was worth it, if only for a few seconds of peace.

Mora would never be what he envisioned. What he was trying to make her into. She wasn't clay he could mold in his greedy hands. Though there was little she could do to fight him, this felt like something.

It bought her minutes at best. When he called her from the flask, Mora braced herself for his ire, but was surprised to find him sitting calmly on the massive bed, cradling her flask in his arm. He sighed and ran a finger over the delicate golden leaves gracing the bottom.

"I didn't know these would be yours when I took them. But it's fitting I gift the woman who has my heart with such powerful relics. That I bind us in blood and bless our union with the rarest magic."

Mora furrowed her brows. "What are you trying to say?"

"I want to tie you to me in all ways. Your stubbornness left me no choice but to bind you to me like this. I know you're unhappy, Treasure. This isn't ideal for me either. I want to share our love with the world and our power with our people." He looked up at her, his smile soft. Pleading. "Say you'll be my queen and this ends now."

"I don't love you," Mora shrieked, loud enough anyone passing in the hall could hear. Though she imagined only a trusted few guards remained close to the king's quarters. "Any fondness I had for you is dead, Dother. Destroyed the moment you betrayed me. I will never be your queen."

"Come, sit."

"No."

He sighed, the sound exasperated and tired. "I wish for you to come sit with me and keep me company until I dismiss you."

Mora stiffened. Goosebumps rose on her flesh and the wish urged her to close the distance between them. Her mind raced. Was there a different way to interpret his demand? Her thoughts were dizzying, and with each breath, tendrils of icy smoke burrowed deeper into her ribcage. Soon they would squeeze, tighter and tighter until her bones broke and no air passed into her lungs.

She could think of no way out.

Gritting her teeth, Mora allowed one small step forward, breathing a sigh of relief when the discomfort eased.

Dother clicked his tongue and shook his head. "Your stubbornness does nothing but cause you pain, Treasure. It wouldn't hurt to give in."

Sinking into the mattress beside him, Mora stared straight ahead, her hands resting on her naked lap. She felt his eyes wander her body. Shivered under the weight of his attention.

"Pour me a drink, Treasure." His voice was soft, almost kind. A test—Dother wanted to see if she'd given up fighting.

Mora clenched her jaw, focusing on the bite of pain, and reached for the decanter on Dother's bedside table. There was no point in fighting this. Amber liquid splashed against the glass as she passed it to him. The silence between them became heavy, and Mora found herself scrutinizing his face. Tendrils of unkempt hair fell over his forehead, his beard was no longer carefully trimmed, and dark circles stained the skin beneath his eyes... eyes that snapped to hers as he savored his drink. A weak smile rose on his lips when he caught her watching, but Mora quickly looked away.

When he finished, he handed her the empty glass, silently demanding she return it to the bedside table. As she rested the glass on the wooden top, Dother cleared his throat. "The people are rebelling."

"What?"

"There's unrest."

Mora's eyes flared. "What have you done?"

"I let Berwick know they have an Enchanter King."

Mora ran a hand over her face, hating the tightness in her chest. "I warned you."

What did he mean by rebelling? Her mother told her there was unrest before... everything. Was she ok? Was Philip? Rosemary?

WISH

Mora wished she could leave this room and see with her own eyes the damage Dother had done. "Unless I'm mistaken, you've barely taken the crown. And you decided to tell the people their new king has the one thing they fear above all else? They were already furious with the monarchy for overturning the Laws." The fury burning in Dother's bright eyes gave her pause, but Mora took a breath and continued, "If this is how you envisioned helping your people, you're a fool. Has it even been a year since my father—"

Dother cut her off but Mora couldn't hear him over the buzzing in her ears. Tears welled up in her eyes as she thought of her father. She could still hear his final I love you, *whispered through gasping breaths.*

That morning was the last time Mora felt happy. It made her sick, remembering Dother naked in her room and the way he teased her about marriage as she urged him to get dressed. Or the smile on his face, one she once admired, when she asked about the flowers sticking out of his pouch. He always gave the same ridiculous answer when she asked him anything. Enchanter's secret, Treasure.

Oh gods...

Mora gasped.

"You killed him." The words spilled from her lips before she had the chance to process them.

"Pardon, Treasure?"

A sharp ache throbbed in her palms before she realized she'd dug her nails into her flesh. It did nothing to stop her fists from shaking. Somehow, she kept her voice quiet, the low sound lethal. "You murdered my father."

"Treasure, I—" He blanched when she shrieked. Hadn't expected her to launch herself at him. Dother fell backwards onto the bed, a surprised wheeze on his lips, but he quickly grabbed Mora's shoulders,

flipping her on her back before crawling over her. "Calm yourself and listen to me."

Dother bit his left cheek, that divot she used to find adorable now a satisfying tell. She'd rattled him. Good.

He attempted to grab her wrists, but Mora balled her fist and struck as hard as she could. Pain exploded in her knuckles when they slammed against his cheekbone, but it didn't stop her from hitting him again. The bastard kept talking, pleading with her to listen. Mora refused to hear him.

When Dother wrapped his hands around her wrists and slammed her down onto the bed, Mora thrashed beneath him, cursing every lungful of citrus.

Her breath came in furious pants, but she bared her teeth and spat, "I hate you."

Dother smiled, but it didn't reach his eyes. "For now."

"I will always hate you."

"Your lifespan is now endless, Treasure. And I'll find a way to join you in immortality. Forever is a long time. One day, you'll understand what I've done and grow to love me again."

Mora glared at him, detesting every time his breath tickled her face and fluttered through the messy strands of her long, curly hair. When she said nothing, he shook his head and chewed on his bottom lip.

"I tried. I truly tried to make you choose me. You made me adjust my plans. Envision a future where we change Berwick together. But you wouldn't be swayed quickly enough, and our people need help now. This path allowed me to gain the power I needed. But I refuse to let you go, so I made do." Dother swallowed. "Do you think I like being married to Aedlin? Do you truly believe this is what I want? You gave me no choice."

WISH

Rage coursed through her veins, the pressure near maddening. "Don't blame me for your sick games."

"You still don't understand, do you, Treasure? You've enraptured me. I will haunt your every breath if that's what I must do to be with you."

Closing the distance between them, Dother pressed a soft kiss to her lips. No wish forced her to endure it, so Mora jerked her head away. "Fuck you," she hissed.

Those azure eyes sparkled as he cocked his head to the side, and Mora tensed, regretting her choice of words. She became all too aware of his weight on her body. His naked skin on hers.

"Whether you choose to stand with me or not, you will remain by my side. And I will use every morsel of power you give me." Dother released one of her wrists and tugged on an errant curl, like he used to. It felt like a mockery. A reminder of how perfectly he'd played her. "You get to decide what that looks like."

Mora glared at him, tears spilling down her cheeks. His gaze followed one to her chin before he dragged a finger through it, gathering the liquid and bringing it to his lips. His smirk was triumphant. Until Mora grinned back.

She roared, the sound rumbling through the room, and dragged her nails down his face. Blood welled up and dripped down his cheek before falling onto hers. It mixed with her tears and spilled onto the mattress.

Dother gasped, his eyes widening as he touched his hand to the wound. When he stared at the crimson staining his fingers, his mouth hardened into a thin line. Another drop splashed onto Mora's forehead and she couldn't help but laugh. It bubbled in her chest quietly at first, but soon she was cackling and gasping for air.

I can make him bleed.

She felt weightless. Lightheaded. Euphoric.

Mora ran her fingers through the mix of blood and tears staining her face and grinned wider when she brought them to her lips.

Dother's face twisted into something ugly as she sucked on his blood. His voice was deadly quiet when he muttered, "I'm not above keeping you bound to that flask for eternity, Treasure. *I can be yours or I can be your nightmare. Choose wisely."*

CHAPTER 44

MORA

"Keeper?" the white-haired Fae asked, his voice a soft baritone, like a song twisting through the trees.

He was oddly beautiful. Not like Zadriel, with his high cheekbones, strong chin and glittering black eyes—she ached to find her way back to them—but there was something lovely about this male's face. Hair white as snow tickled his alabaster cheeks, falling just past his pointed ears. And he had a mark on his neck, like a scar made by sharp teeth.

His pale brows furrowed, but the longer she stared the more his lips quirked up into an uneven smirk, creating the whisper of a dimple on his left cheek.

"Yes, Keeper." She lifted her chin. "You have my flask and—"

"I'm not your Keeper, Wraith. We've made no bargains." Those red eyes flared with annoyance, the purple at their center glowing like starfire.

Mora scowled. "Don't ask a question if you aren't interested in hearing the answer."

The Fae huffed a laugh before rolling her flask around in his palm. He stared at it with a reverence Mora didn't understand. "Go on then."

Before she could speak, someone coughed, and Mora and the white-haired Fae turned in unison. Another Fae stood a few feet away, hiding slightly behind the horses.

"Thalias?" he asked, a slight quiver to his voice.

"I'm fine, darling," the white-haired one—Thalias—replied.

Breathtaking silver eyes watched her, the moonlight glow much like those of the hawk she spotted in the trees. His black hair was beautifully weaved into tight braids and bound together in a bun by a loose leather band at the top of his head. She imagined his smile was dazzling, though his lips pressed into a thin line. And he was tall. Perhaps taller than Zadriel. With broad shoulders, thick muscled arms and a solid, round stomach. Yet he cowered behind a horse, as if the animal offered protection.

Too bad *he* wasn't her Keeper. Mora could have fun with his fear. She graced him with her most sinister smile, but it faltered when she spotted Alina, huddled on the ground a few feet away, wrists and ankles bound in vines.

Mora snarled. "Why is Alina bound like an animal?" Her shoulder slammed into Thalias's arm as she hurried to the Aegist. Alina attempted to scramble back and Mora took a breath. Begged the Gods for patience. "I'm sorry," she whispered as she bent down to untangle the vines from her wrists. But the girl only glared, her eyelashes still wet with tears.

"No you aren't," Alina said quietly.

Mora swallowed against the lump in her throat. She *was* sorry Alina ended up here. If not for her attempt to reunite with Zadriel, Halvard never would have made it to his carriage, Alina would have remained in Eden...

And Zadriel wouldn't be alone, bleeding to death on the road.

A crushing pain in her chest nearly stole her breath. Mora paused. Inhaled deeply and imagined the soothing tones of his voice. *I'm here. I've got you, Little Witch.* But he wasn't. All she had left was his tunic, the faint scent of mint and rain wrapped in pine, and an ache in her chest that wouldn't ease.

Mora fisted the vine and tugged harder, unmoved by the way it cut into her palm. She breathed a sigh of relief when it tore free. At least something could go right.

As if the forest heard her thoughts and laughed in response, a new vine burst through the soil and encircled Alina's wrists.

Mora's brows furrowed. "What in the name of the gods?"

A heavy hand came down on her shoulder and Mora froze, the air wheezing from her lungs. *He's dead*, she reminded herself. Mora took another slow breath, soothed by a sweet, earthy scent wrapped in spruce and brimstone. The Fae was nothing like Dother.

"Your Gods have no place in the Forest." Bitterness saturated Thalias's voice, as if he took personal offense to the idea of any Gods but his own.

Shrugging off Thalias's hand, Mora spun to face him. "Let the girl go. She's done you no harm."

"She entered Arcadia without invitation."

Something glinted in his palm, and Mora realized he had Halvard's brooch. Her eyes widened, but she did her best to look away. He couldn't know the power he held.

Mora balled her hands into fists and stepped closer. "Your trees beg to differ, they allowed us entry."

The Fae grinned, his dimple mocking her fury. "They opened for *you*, no one else."

"Then let her leave." Mora spoke slowly, every clipped word a threat.

He tipped his head to the side, eyes roving over her face. Those white brows furrowed at whatever he saw, but it changed nothing. "She entered uninvited and now owes a debt. She'll leave when Arcadia wills it. Unless you'd prefer I take her life in exchange?"

Fire flared in Mora's eyes. "Harm the girl in any way and you'll learn how wonderful it is to be in my company."

Thalias shrugged, the motion pulling at his deep green leather spaulders. They matched his bracers and chest piece—each featured intricately carved leaves with thinly painted golden outlines. Armor would do little to stop her if he didn't heed her warning.

"You have yet to see what Arcadia has to offer, Wraith. I'd be cautious before uttering threats." He dismissed her, showing her his back as he called to his companion. "Vesryn, darling, let's return home."

Branches shifted as he walked, their leaves reaching for him much like they did with Zadriel, and wildflowers sprouted in the wake of his every step. Because of course they did. Their colors were a brilliant array of hues sparkling as they tilted toward their maker. It was unlike anything Mora had seen. She made sure to crush them under her feet as she followed.

Vesryn bit his lips, uncertainty glinting in those moonlight eyes as his gaze bounced between Mora and Thalias. "The horses..."

A soft smile graced Thalias's face before he walked back to Vesryn. "We can free them." He leaned in and kissed a mark on Vesryn's neck. A scar. Much like Thalias's.

Together they undid the buckles and leather straps of the horses' harnesses to let them loose.

"Will they survive?" Mora stepped closer to Vesryn, her hand landing gently on her horse's rump. Vesryn avoided her gaze and ran his hand down the chestnut stallion's neck, admiring his soft fur. It was comical, that apprehension. Mora leaned closer, her mouth tipping up in amusement. "I was talking to you, Vesryn."

Clearing his throat awkwardly, his eyes darted back to hers, those rich, umber-brown cheeks darkening. "That's between them and the Forest."

Thalias waved a hand and grass sprung up all around them, the tall, bright green strands brushing against Mora's knees. "They have plenty of food to enjoy before they make their way to the fields outside Arcadia. Happy?"

Vesryn gave Mora an apologetic look before making his way to Alina. She squeaked as he threw her over his shoulders and headed for the trees, following behind Thalias. The Aegist lifted her head to glare at Mora, fury burning in those hazel eyes.

"Good luck," Mora cooed to her horse, giving it a final pat before she turned to follow.

Alina bounced with each step Vesryn took, her hands and feet still bound. Two pixies spun around her head, weaving Thalias's flowers into her hair. Their iridescent wings fluttered and Mora's stomach sank. The lone pixie trapped in a jar in Zadriel's room would never fly again. Would likely never return home.

And neither will Zadriel.

She rubbed her chest, praying for the pain to ease. Hoping Zadriel would be ok.

The pixies' voices were like music, flowing through the air and curling in her ears. It felt nonsensical. Like a strange combination of gibberish and whistles even the Fae didn't seem to understand. Though, when they giggled, Vesryn and Thalias smiled. Alina, however, grumbled under her breath as they pulled at her blonde curls.

Mora sighed. "You can at least let the child walk, *Keeper*."

Alina scoffed. "I'm nineteen, not a child."

Mora covered her mouth in an attempt to hide her amusement. But when Thalias and Vesryn laughed, she couldn't help but join in.

"Whatever you say, child," Vesryn said as he ruffled her hair. Flowers crumbled under his touch, petals falling to the ground. The pixies hissed, flitting around Vesryn's head, and his laugh morphed into a hearty snort.

"You know better than to court a pixie's wrath, darling." Thalias lifted a hand, and Mora noticed the silver tattoos curling around his fingers and disappearing under his sleeves. The swirls of color pulsed, giving a cool glow to his alabaster skin. Wind swirled around them and flowers bloomed in his palm, their colors as bright and varied as the ones blooming at his feet.

The pixies calmed, fluttering over and snatching the flowers up in their tiny fists. Their musical voices flowed in the air, and Thalias watched them with a small smile on his face, but his tone was serious as he said, "Need I remind you, Wraith, I am *not* your Keeper."

"*We've made no bargains,*" Mora said, doing her best to impersonate him. "Like it or not, Fae, you carry my flask. That makes you my Keeper. My power is yours until you've made three wishes, or someone takes the bottle from you."

"What do you get in exchange?" Thalias asked. Those starfire eyes bore into hers, and the pixies quieted. Watched her along with him.

It was impossible to leash her bitterness. "Nothing."

Thalias frowned, his gaze dropping to the flask hanging from his belt. He ran his fingers over the gold filigree. "I don't like this arrangement."

"That would be a first," Mora said under her breath.

Thalias untied the vine securing her flask and held the bottle out to her. "As your Keeper, I'd be bound to you. Stuck in an uneven bargain. I have no interest in such things, they never end well."

Pixies fluttered around it. They reached out toward the golden plants adorning the bottom, but never touched them. Mora froze. Flexed her fingers at her side as she stared at the bottle. But she made no move to grab it. Could she?

Thalias stepped closer. "Take it."

Mora's throat bobbed. She reached out hesitantly, swallowing as her fingers wrapped around the flask. All these centuries, and she'd never once held it after she'd been cursed. Hadn't known she could. But it was in her palm, the glass warm and lighter than she remembered. Tears welled up in her eyes, threatening to spill over, but she blinked them away.

"I..." Mora couldn't find the words. Could barely think. She clutched the flask tightly, wondering how long it would be until someone took it from her. This wasn't freedom, but it was the closest she'd come in centuries. "Thank you," she breathed. She could barely meet his eyes. "We're still bound until you've made your wishes, I'm afraid. But... thank you."

"Thalias, is this wise?" Vesryn's voice was quiet and unsure, but he flinched away when Mora's eyes darkened, daring him to try and take this from her. Thalias, however, seemed unfazed, waving Vesryn off.

"You are not to leave Arcadia until I've discovered what She wants with you. Otherwise, I'm not your Keeper. I wish for you to do as you please. For as long as you please."

Mora gasped, her fingers tightening around her flask. She closed her eyes as the frigid sensation of the wish taking hold overwhelmed her, welcoming the bite of pain.

Embers crackled in her veins when Thalias growled. It was a low, predatory rumble. When Mora opened her eyes, she found him towering over her, his expression furious. The purple in his eyes grew brighter somehow, an almost silver glow shining through.

Thalias bared his teeth and Mora stared at those canines. Bared her teeth in return. All while smoke and fire—*her fire*—pooled in her palms.

CHAPTER 45

ZADRIEL

Zadriel's skin burned under the endless torment of the sun—he couldn't believe he missed his cloak. Each breath invited a torrent of dust into his lungs and he could barely endure it. The grit in his windpipe worsened the tightness in his chest. Every shallow inhale hurt.

The quiet thrum of his heart slowed, along with the blood seeping from his wound. Zadriel closed his eyes. Felt the roots of a nearby tree wrapping around his fingers. Their touch was soft, hesitant. It made him smile. Albeit weakly.

He wasn't worthy, but knowing Arcadia still cared for him after all these long years and everything he'd done...

Tears burned in his eyes.

May Mora find her way into Arcadia's arms. May the Mother protect her. If the Forest could offer him that, he could find peace.

Something slammed into Zadriel's stomach and he gagged. Curled into himself and wheezed against the bile burning in his throat.

Another blow landed on his chest and Zadriel's vision went white. Pain lanced down his body and all he could do was moan as blood and vomit dribbled down his chin.

Andras's cold voice washed over him as he said, "I'm going to make you wish you'd never been born."

CHAPTER 46

MORA

"What did you do, Wraith?" Thalias snarled, the sound pure, wild Fae. As it rumbled through the forest, the trees moved with it, bending toward the two of them as if they were the center of Arcadia.

Mora let her smoke spill to the earth and curl around his legs. Loved the way her flames twisted through the glittering obsidian. "*You* made your first wish. That's what it feels like when it takes hold."

"I told you I have no interest in this."

"Aren't Fae supposed to be clever? You said you *wish* for me to do as I please. You have two more wishes left. I'd be more careful with your words if you'd like to avoid using them." Mora attempted to step closer, but her feet wouldn't move. She looked down to find dozens of roots snaking around her boots, tethering her to the earth.

Thalias's laugh was cruel. "You're not as subtle as you think."

"I don't need subtlety."

Mora flexed her fingers and pushed harder against her smoke. It spilled from her pores, enveloping her in its cool embrace. As she was about to give herself over completely, Alina screamed, the sharp sound loud enough to make Mora hesitate.

Where Vesryn once stood was a silver-eyed bear. It opened its maw and roared, the sound vibrating down Mora's spine. Those paws were larger than her face, tipped with claws that could eviscerate in one swipe, and Alina lay helpless beneath it, sparks of defensive magic flying from her bound hands. It would do nothing to stop Vesryn's attack.

"I doubt you could end me," Thalias said, his lips curving into a crooked grin. "But if you'd like to attempt it, my mate will make a meal of your friend."

Mate. Mora knew little about Fae mates. But getting between them could be dangerous.

And he could turn into animals? Such a power was unheard of in Berwick. It was as Zadriel said, Arcadia had magic present-day Halflings couldn't imagine.

Now more smoke than woman, Mora stepped out of her bindings, her glowing amber gaze shining through the darkness and into Vesryn's silver eyes. She took great pleasure watching the bear take a cautious step back.

The smoke faded, Thalias's tethers along with it, and Mora emerged, her curls fluttering in the wind as her power settled. She raised a brow at Thalias. They got what they wanted, she was no longer a threat. For now.

A white light erupted, so bright Mora's eyes burned. She squinted, awed by the sage torrent of leaves twisting around the glow. When it faded, Vesryn stood tall—Fae, as he should be, with those delicately pointed ears. He ran his hands over his braids, adjusting the leather band holding them together.

"You dropped something," he said hesitantly. Was that guilt in his tone?

Vesryn tipped his head and Mora followed his gaze. Her flask laid on the ground, the same roots that held her now curling around it. *Fuck.*

Untethering herself meant losing her flask. Leaving it vulnerable. *Her* vulnerable. As she retrieved the bottle, Mora stared into the trees, wondering what or who stared back. And how long she could keep herself safe from their grasp.

A wall of great weeping willows blocked their path. Their boughs were downturned, light green leaves cascading down the branches like verdant curtains. They'd been walking for hours, through an endless sea of vibrant greens in more shades than Mora imagined possible. But, unlike the other trees, these ones didn't bend to clear the path.

"Please tell me we're almost there," Mora wheezed. Her legs ached, the muscles in her calves protesting more with every step. The flask nearly slipped through her sweaty fingers several times, and she found herself cursing Thalias for giving it to her.

Though Mora would never give it back.

Thalias ran his hand along the delicate foliage. "It's me," he said, softly. "I've brought the... wraith-like creature, and a Halfling who trespassed."

A moment passed in silence before the leaves rustled and parted, allowing them passage. Mora gasped as she took in what they'd been hiding.

The ground gave way to a long drop—Mora felt dizzy as she stared down into the abyss. In the distance she could hear waterfalls plunging into the large, glistening lake at the bottom, the water so blue it was nearly blinding. Colorful lights shimmered on the surface and something called from the waters. It sang a quiet, beckoning song that almost had her stepping closer.

Mora clutched her flask harder. Imagined falling without dissipating, for fear of losing her freedom. The thrum in her chest was near maddening. Would the enormous tree catch her? It grew from an island at the lake's center, the trunk thicker than Frederick's manor... Frederick who met his end in the hardened clutches of a rather large apple tree.

Why did I have to think of Frederick...

Mora took a deep breath, grateful for the clean, earthy air.

Could this be the Mother Tree? Had she found the Spirit? A silver sheen dusted its giant, emerald leaves, no gold in sight. And Mora didn't feel a pull. Anywhere. Hadn't from the moment she entered Arcadia.

If the Spirit was dead, would there be anything left to find?

Lights flickered all along the cliffs and Mora realized they were homes. Some on the uneven, rocky edges of the cliffside, others along the trees growing on the land above. The central tree itself was speckled with lights twirling all the way up to its crown.

Thalias and Vesryn continued forward with Alina sleeping in Vesryn's arms, repositioned so her head rested against his shoulder. Mora opened her mouth to call for them as they neared the cliff's edge. Her words died on her tongue when a thick branch from the central tree bent down, wood groaning as it shifted.

A path was built into the thick bough, with polished wooden frames, intricately carved to feature Fae among the trees. It was covered sporadically in soft splashes of moss and dusted with a silver sheen. A tall, Fae female with swirling black tattoos similar to Vesryn's crossed, holding the hand of an elderly male. His dark gray hair hung down to his chin, and Mora tried not to stare. Were Fae not immortal?

When the elderly Fae stumbled, the female's expression turned solemn. She nodded at Thalias as they walked off the bridge. The look on her face changed when she saw Mora and Alina.

Baring her teeth in a snarl, she quickened her steps. "Let's go, son," she said, as she encouraged the elderly male along.

Mora's brows furrowed. Son?

"Are you coming, Wraith?" Thalias called. He hesitated on the bough, his finger tapping against the railing.

Mora stood frozen, her focus darting from the fantastical city to the waters below and back.

Thalias raised a brow, that ridiculous dimple dancing on his face. She forced her feet forward. Ignored how her limbs shook. And how badly she wanted to bolt back to the cliff's edge and through the willows.

The wood beneath her feet shifted as the branch pulled away from the cliff. Mora stumbled and frantically wrapped her free hand around the railing. Then stared at the long drop.

Down.

Down.

Down.

She gulped. Wanted nothing more than to pull away and curl into a ball on the bridge's surface.

Thalias's chuckle didn't help. Nor did the wicked amusement in his voice when he leaned closer and whispered, "I thought you'd be clever enough not to look down."

CHAPTER 47

MORA

There was nothing undignified about laying on the floor and counting the rings on the ceiling in an attempt to forget the steep plunge outside. The giant tree Thalias called home was safe. That's what Mora kept telling herself. Though she didn't particularly believe it.

What an odd thing, feeling afraid of something as simple as heights. If the thought of the drop outside the window didn't steal her breath, she'd almost find it funny. Instead she clutched her flask against her chest and grappled with an odd mixture of elation and terror.

Finally, she could do almost anything she wanted. But what did that look like? How long could she keep her flask? Mora wasn't naïve enough to think Thalias was her last keeper. It would all go south eventually. It always did.

She'd cling to this reprieve with both hands, for as long as she could. Even if it meant she couldn't dissipate.

How do humans do it? Mora could hardly remember life before. She detested the powerlessness that came with being bound to her Keepers, and yet... this made her feel weak in a new way. Mora didn't like it.

Andras's wish was a problem. It would be foolish to bring the flask when she returned to him.

And Zadriel... he lived in her mind. Her heart sank when she tried to imagine how she could get him away from Andras and fell short. The pendant in her pouch freed him for two weeks. That wasn't enough. Could never be enough.

He may not have lived anyway...

Mora scowled and shook her head. She couldn't accept the idea. But her mind kept whispering the possibility Zadriel died, bloodied and alone in the dirt.

The filigree on her flask dug into her skin as she clutched it tighter. The sting of pain in her palm was at least somewhat distracting. Part of her ached to kill Halvard again. The release calmed her, but it hadn't lasted.

Mora counted the rings on the ceiling again. *One, two, three...*

Thalias's head came into view, snow white hair dangling over his eyes. "Do you think you'll survive?"

Rolling her eyes, Mora rose to her feet, her shoulder knocking his arm as she passed. "The God of Death wouldn't want me," Mora said as she made her way to the living room.

Vesryn sat with a book, while Alina laid out beside him on the long chaise. The poor thing was out cold, her occasional snores filling the room. Vesryn's eyes lifted as Mora approached. He subtly pressed further into the plush cushions. Not subtly enough, however. Mora noted his discomfort and grinned. Made to move closer.

Thalias cut in front of her and sat on Vesryn's lap. While Vesryn wrapped an arm around him and adjusted his grip on his novel, Thalias gave Mora a warning look.

He didn't like when she played with his mate.

"I'm sure someone finds relief in that," Thalias said. "Whose scent lingers on your clothes? He's Fae, yet I don't recognize him."

Mora hesitated. Surely Zadriel was safe among his people? He wanted nothing more than to return home. Spoke of Arcadia with hope and reverence. And yet Mora felt protective. Unsure if she should trust them with so much as his name.

Thalias raised a brow. Fiddled with something in his hands. The brooch, Mora realized, her stomach sinking when he noticed her staring.

Mora couldn't risk him knowing she worried about the powerful relic he held, so she blurted, "His name is Zadriel."

"Zadriel?" Vesryn sat up abruptly, nearly unseating Thalias. The book tumbled from his grip, slamming against the ground. "Did you say Zadriel?"

"Yes, he's—"

"What does he look like?"

Mora frowned at Vesryn's eagerness. Looked to Thalias as if he could explain the desperation in Vesryn's voice. But he crossed his arms and nodded at her to go on.

She cleared her throat. "Zadriel's tall. Taller than you, Thalias, though perhaps slightly shorter than Vesryn. He has raven black hair and black eyes with flecks of gold swirling in the iris. He's strong, with broad shoulders. His arms are covered in scars and—"

"Scars?" Vesryn interrupted, recoiling. Both he and Thalias looked down at the intricate tattoos decorating their skin. Neither had a single blemish.

Guilt punched through her gut and Mora's throat worked. "It's not my story to tell," she said softly, sorrow lacing through her tone.

"We assumed he died," Vesryn whispered.

"You knew him?"

A sad smile curled up on Vesryn's soft face. "He was my first friend. When Vehsa didn't return, we thought... is he ok?"

Tears welled up in Mora's eyes. "I don't know."

"What do you mean, you don't know?"

"Things were bad when I was forced away. I..." Mora's voice broke. "I don't know if he lived."

Thalias frowned. "Is he the one who attempted to mark you?"

"Mark me?" The bruise on her neck thrummed pleasantly when she ran her fingers over it. She couldn't believe it was still there. Mora looked to Thalias, and he tipped his chin in confirmation. "Yes," she breathed, thinking back to the oak tree. To the feeling of being wrapped up in Zadriel.

Thalias's hand rose to the mark on his throat, his face grim. "You'd know if he died."

"Please..." Vesryn bit his lip. Braved her luminous amber gaze. "I've wondered for centuries what happened. Where has he been?"

"A horrific man bound Zadriel to his bloodline," Mora said bitterly. "They'll never release him."

Vesryn covered his mouth, but Mora heard his shuddering breath.

Thalias's eyes flared, a silver glow shining through the starfire at their center. He pressed the brooch into Vesryn's hand and stood. "What of Vehsa, his mother?"

Mora tensed. Something in his tone called to the monster within her, plucking at centuries of rage. Part of her knew he wouldn't like what she said next. "They killed her."

The floor trembled, wood shifting and splintering beneath her feet. Mora stumbled, landing hard on her backside. "*I'm* not the one who killed her," she yelled to Thalias. But it was as if he looked through her and saw nothing but his fury.

The house clattered and groaned, and Alina's eyes snapped open. "What's happening?" she screeched, sitting up too swiftly. The Aegist nearly fell over, thanks to her damned bindings, but Vesryn reached out to steady her.

"Thalias," Vesryn said calmly. He shoved the brooch into his pocket before standing from the chaise. "Calm yourself."

Sprouts popped through the wooden slats, unfurling and crawling over the floor. A hole formed a few feet from where Mora sat and she shrieked. It gave her the perfect view of the waters below. *What have I done to deserve this?* Mora shook her head as she scrambled away, knowing she deserved far worse.

A sneer sullied Thalias's face. And the silver markings on his arms glowed as luminously as his eyes. A root shot through the wall behind her and Mora knew if she did nothing they'd all plummet.

Vesryn lifted his hands and inched closer to his mate. "Sapling, you're tearing our home apart."

Mora eyed her flask. It was too big to fit into her pouch—would that work if she could? The best she could think to do was tuck it into her belt and hope it held.

"As much as I love a show of rage," she grumbled, fumbling with her belt, "this isn't helpful, Thalias. Stop."

The weight of his glare fell upon her, and Mora nearly took a step back. Cocking his head animalistically to the side, Thalias considered her as the room continued to take the brunt of his power. His features hardened, nothing but wrath in his stare.

Saplings sprouted from the walls, their roots eating away at the wood. And a wind billowed throughout the room, stirring up scents of spruce and decay.

Mora slipped on moss, but a branch burst through the wall and caught her before she fell. "Gods fucking damn it," she muttered, while smoke leaked freely from her fingers—Mora didn't call her flames, unwilling to risk burning the place down. The ethereal mist twisted around Thalias's calves and climbed up his legs. The Fae bowed his head, brows furrowing as he watched the cool, black smoke envelop him. A root dove for Mora's feet and she jumped away, unable to hide her smirk when Thalias growled.

Who's not subtle now?

"What are you doing?" Vesryn hissed, hands still up. If he reached out, he could touch Thalias's back.

A nervous laugh was the best Mora could offer. "I don't know."

As the mist swallowed Thalias like a ravenous serpent, the glow in his eyes flickered. He stilled, and his magic slowed.

A bough in the living room shuddered, its leaves unfurling and changing from green, to red, to yellow before falling from its branches. They landed on Alina's head. The girl was hunched in her seat, huddled under the best shield she could manage with her bound wrists. "Is it over?"

Mora held Thalias in place as she eyed the hole in the floor. "Vesryn?"

Vesryn bit his lip and ran a hand down Thalias's back, only to earn a growl. "It's me, Sapling," Vesryn cooed. The soothing tones of his voice did something, because the growl in Thalias's chest shifted to a satisfied purr. But those eyes never cleared.

The greenery twitched, a few plants growing a little bigger, pushing at the cracks in the floorboards. Flashbacks of a manor falling to a ferocious apple tree played out in Mora's mind, and she ran a hand over her face. Perhaps the Gods were real, and this was her punishment. It would be fitting of them to gift her the semblance of freedom only to take it away. *If you exist, you're all bastards.* Mora hoped they could hear her thoughts.

"I thought you'd be clever enough not to lose yourself to your rage," Mora spat at Thalias, hoping to break through his trance. At her command, more of her mist curled around him, climbing up to his neck.

Tendrils broke away and brushed over his cheekbones. Mora blinked. That was... odd.

Thalias thrashed, the pressure of his struggle pushing through the smoke and reverberating up Mora's arms. Her muscles screamed, feet sliding against the ground. Mora pushed back against the onslaught. Then, to her shock, Thalias forced his hand through her dark torrent.

Mora's mouth fell open. Her smoke was impenetrable. Nothing had ever broken through...

Thalias stumbled a few steps, pushing through her smoky assault. Sweat trickled down her brow as she pushed harder against her magic. "Once again, Thalias, it wasn't me."

"You have one of Her flowers," he said, his voice echoing through the room.

Her flowers? Mora touched the soft petals of the gilded daisy Zadriel had tucked in her hair. It had nothing to do with his mother—Zadriel picked it from under his oak. Though, if it calmed Thalias, Mora didn't care. She pulled it from her curls and held it out to him. "You can have it."

Wisps of smoke still clung to him, but it wasn't enough to hold him still. It took more effort than usual, but he managed to reach up and take the flower from her.

Vesryn's thick arms wrapped around Thalias's center, pulling him back into his chest. Thalias tensed, though his hold on the flower remained delicate. "Sapling," Vesryn breathed. "We'll make this right, but you need to calm yourself."

Thalias's eyes widened, an eerie glow pulsing in his gaze. "They killed another," he muttered, voice deadly quiet.

"And if you don't control yourself, you'll kill us all."

The light in Thalias's eyes faded completely, and he became weightless, his head lolling back onto Vesryn's shoulder. As Vesryn lifted his mate into his arms, Thalias held up a shaking hand.

Tension bled from Mora's body as the damage happened in reverse. The saplings shrunk until they slipped through the cracks in the wood. Roots pulled away from the walls. Vines shriveled and flowers died. When Thalias finished, the room was pristine, as if nothing happened.

"I'm sorry," Thalias whispered, resting his head on Vesryn's shoulder. He frowned at the flower before handing it back to Mora. "I lost myself. It won't happen again."

CHAPTER 48

ZADRIEL

For days, all Zadriel knew was agony. He could hardly breathe through it. There was a tightness in his chest and the room twisted around him. Tilting his head to the side, he heaved, bloody bile dripping down his chin.

The putrid smell of his own burning flesh hit him before the sharp pain did. Zadriel let out a gurgling moan as the iron dagger was pulled from his chest. Rough fingers clutched his chin, sliding over spittle and pulling his face up until Andras came back into view. Zadriel blinked, barely able to focus. The fire in the hearth swayed behind Andras's shoulder, but watching it made him nauseous.

He tried to listen to Andras. But all he could hear was the wheeze of his lungs as his breath sawed in and out. Oblivion called. And Zadriel wasn't sure it would let go once he entered its embrace. His eyes drifted closed, but Andras slapped him.

"Did you hear me?" he asked.

The skin on Zadriel's shoulder hissed as Andras tapped the blade against it. Firelight glinted off the gilded daisies on the handle, burning into Zadriel's eyes and he thought of another time. Another life. When the blade was gold, matching its hilt. When its purpose was to the people of Arcadia and his mother's duties to the Mother Tree.

What would Vehsa think if she knew what remained of her ceremonial dagger was used to carve up her son?

Zadriel gritted his teeth. Panted through the agony. And said nothing.

Andras's face twisted into a grimace and he shook his head. Muttered something about being disappointed. Zadriel could hardly make him out, but he did his best to glare up at those blazing azure eyes, the speckle of amber only serving to further ignite his fury.

When Andras pushed the dagger back into his chest, Zadriel didn't have the strength to scream. Though the silent whine spilling from his cracked lips made Andras smirk.

It burned. Burned so much he could hardly remember any other feeling. The skin sizzled and split while Andras moved agonizingly slowly, forcing his way through Zadriel's ribs and into his collapsed lung. The coppery scent of his own blood was overwhelming. Zadriel gagged. Retched again against the burning pain. Droplets of blood and bile splashed onto Andras's cheeks and he paused, his lips curling.

"Was she worth it?" he seethed as he wiped his face on his sleeve.

Red soaked into the bright, royal blue fabric, creating a purple stain. Zadriel stared at it. Held his tongue. What Mora was worth to him was none of Andras's business.

Andras rolled his eyes and walked to the counter. He leaned against it, sipped on a glass of water, and stared out the window toward Arcadia.

A cold sweat broke out across Zadriel's brow and he slumped in his chair. He attempted to grab the edge of the armrests to hold himself up but he couldn't feel his fingers. Couldn't convince them to move.

He was so tired.

When Zadriel gave in to oblivion and closed his eyes, he could have sworn he saw Mora's beautiful face, those fierce amber eyes gleaming as they beheld him.

CHAPTER 49

MORA

*M*ora *was home. Nestled safely against Zadriel's chest. She closed her eyes and nuzzled his shoulder, nearly purring when he ran his hand through her thick curls. He sighed, the sound happy and satisfied, and she couldn't help her grin.*

A great tree with golden leaves watched over them as they rested in a field of gilded daisies.

Zadriel's thumb brushed over the lingering bruise on her neck. "Little Witch, what I wouldn't give to hold you again."

Mora's brows furrowed. "What do you mean? I'm in your arms, aren't I?" She tipped her head back and placed a delicate kiss on his chin.

Zadriel leaned into her embrace, those glittering, onyx eyes staring at her with a longing that made her ache. His smile faltered as he wrapped his arms around her waist. Zadriel took a deep breath before he whispered in his low, soothing voice, "This is a dream, love."

Mora leaned against the balcony, trailing her fingers over the smooth railing as she replayed her dream in her mind. She couldn't sleep. Zadriel's dark tunic hung low on her knees, the soft material tickling her skin. While Thalias provided her with plenty of clothing, she rested in Zadriel's tunic nightly. And every time she closed her eyes, she found him in her dreams.

When she woke she could still feel Zadriel's reassuring touch and the soothing scents of mint and summer rain lingered in her room. It felt visceral. Real. Had she found him like she promised, simply not in this realm? It was like he'd slipped through her fingers. Like she'd abandoned him yet again. Mora needed to know he was ok. To find her way back to him.

But Andras's wish tethered her to Arcadia, its clutches slithering around her bones. She knew there was no way she could leave until she found the Spirit.

Where the hell was it?

Nothing called to her. And leaving this damned treehouse was practically impossible without Thalias or Vesryn. If only she could dissipate without leaving her flask.

Mora scanned the twinkling lights along the cliffside. So long as she didn't look down, she could handle her fear. Mostly. Somber voices from a balcony below drifted up to her ears—it was a funeral, from what she could gather. A woman wailed about the loss of her son, her cries tearing at Mora's heart. And someone played a mournful dirge on the fiddle, the sound curling through the wind and swaying with the leaves.

Mora couldn't fathom losing a child. Part of her wished to know what happened, but it didn't feel right to ask Thalias. There were few children here. And more elderly Fae than she imagined. Were they not immortal, like legend said? Zadriel hadn't aged a day in the last three centuries. It made no sense.

With a sigh, Mora turned back toward the balcony doors leading to her chambers. It was a spacious, round room hugging the trunk of the colossal tree at the chasm's center. The large, soft bed was a blessing. A rare treat for someone who typically rested in a flask. The last bed she'd slept in was at Frederick's Manor. And before that... Mora didn't want to think of it.

She should have known Frederick was different from that act alone. He didn't deserve what she'd done to him...

"Your mind is elsewhere."

Mora jumped, goosebumps erupting along her arms. At her behest, smoke gathered in her palm, the cool magic calming her racing heart. How had someone gotten up here?

Nothing could have prepared her for what she found.

The creature had a beautiful, human-like face with bright yellow eyes and long, flowing, midnight blue hair. But attached to her golden arms were glorious feathers in shades of silver and blue. And beneath her naked breasts was the body of a large bird with long tail feathers fluttering in the light breeze. She clutched the handrail with sharp talons, their treacherous claws digging into the wood.

Mora opened her mouth but couldn't find any words.

The creature seemed unbothered. She studied Mora, twisting her head to the side in a birdlike motion. "Pixies told me you were here, though they did not speak of your beauty."

"What are you?" Mora asked, her voice a soft whisper. She clutched her smoke. Inched further from the balcony.

The creature tilted her head to the other side, an oddly blank expression gracing her fascinating face. "I know what I am. Can you say the same?"

Light flared in those wide, yellow eyes. Mora hissed and lifted her arm, shielding herself as she backed away another step. Tears spilled down her cheeks and her irises burned.

"What do you want?" Mora demanded, pushing harder against her smoke. It spilled down her body, curling over the flask she'd tethered to her belt with a spare strip of leather, before pooling at her feet.

When the creature spoke again, Mora could *feel* the words. They caressed her skin, brushing against her with an eerie fondness as the being practically sang, "I see lifeblood dripping through clenched fingers, vessels bursting in pleading eyes. But you will not wish to be saved. Not in the way he intends."

Lifeblood... did she speak of Zadriel? Was she clairvoyant? Mora wrapped her arms around herself, shivering despite the warm summer air. And yet she dared to hope. "Did you see a beautiful Fae with glittering black eyes and scars along his arms? Is he ok?"

The being stretched her arms wide, ruffling her glittering feathers. Those yellow eyes looked skyward, staring at the moon peeking through the forest's canopy. "You are familiar."

"I asked you a question," Mora said through gritted teeth. She dug her nails into her arms, nearly drawing blood. Pain thrummed in her chest while power thrashed against her ribs. It was harder now, holding back. Thanks to Thalias, the only thing standing in the way of Mora's monstrousness was herself.

The creature was unperturbed. Even when Mora's smoke wrapped around the balcony railing. She simply tucked in her wings and adjusted her feet, stretching out her talons one at a time, before shifting away. "My sisters and I like you."

Mora closed her eyes. Took a slow, deep breath before she tried again. "Did you see Zadriel? Is he safe?"

The weight of the creature's stare returned, its large black pupils threatening to drown any who met their gaze for too long. "You will reunite in blood. Take his hand and end his torment."

"How do I find him?" Mora's voice broke, and new tears—ones born of fear and sorrow—spilled down her cheeks. She clutched Zadriel's tunic. Took comfort in the soft material slipping between her fingers.

The being leaned forward, a spark of amusement in her melodic tone. "He found you."

"I don't understand."

"Not yet. In time you will." Her eyes flicked to the pouch at Mora's hips and the creature clicked her tongue, revealing a mouth full of razor-sharp teeth. Mora gulped before inching back another step. "You are cunning," she said, her voice becoming serious. "It hurts. But he doesn't hate you for it."

Mora's stomach sank. What did she mean? Everything she said was nonsensical, and yet Mora knew she spoke the truth. Simply in riddles. "You're not making sense."

The creature smiled. Or, at least, Mora assumed it was a smile. It was too wide to be comforting and displayed too many sharp teeth to be friendly. "Perhaps you aren't listening." She shrugged before stretching her enormous, iridescent wings once more. She flapped them several times, hopping along the balcony until she'd reached the far end.

"Wait!" Mora ran to the railing. Half considered using her smoke to tether the being in place. Though, after Thalias, she wasn't certain it would hold.

Those luminous eyes found Mora's one last time and her melodious voice filled the air. "Be careful with the cherub."

Then she jumped, spreading her arms wide and dropping from sight. Mora leaned over the edge of the balcony, her fingers tightening around the handrail as she came face to face with the drop, the creature nowhere in sight.

"Please... tell me what I need to do," Mora begged. But if the creature was still listening, she paid her no mind. Mora was left alone with the cool embrace of her smoke and a sinking feeling in her chest.

CHAPTER 50

MORA
300 YEARS AGO

*M*ora clung to her velvet cloak, the warm fabric against her skin a rare luxury. She curled her fingers around the soft material, imagining it shielded her body from Dother's burning gaze. Though he was all she saw as darkness swirled around them.

It was almost like the night they met. Dother held her hand, those calloused fingers scratching her skin as he pulled her along. If Mora closed her eyes, she could picture the decrepit barn. Smell the fresh, spring air. Run, *she wished to yell at her past self.* Run as fast and as far as you can.

Had Dother used a sprite to remind her? Or taunt her? He knew how she felt about them. A simple wish and Mora could have brought him anywhere. Instead, they marched down, down, down the cracked stone steps. Where they were in the castle, she had no idea. Though Mora grew up here, Dother found a secret passage she never explored.

All this time by Dother's side and still she didn't understand him. Couldn't figure out his intentions. He claimed a heroic purpose, but Mora didn't buy it. Heroes didn't curse those who refused them. Didn't murder for a crown. Dother had plans. And she needed to discover what they were.

Dother released her hand and leaned closer. "Not too much farther, Treasure," he whispered, his breath tickling the shell of her ear. Mora flinched. Pulled her cloak tighter around her body and hoped it hid the reaction from his gaze. It was eerie, knowing he could see where they were going while she was essentially blind.

Where is he taking me?

Mora's heart raced while dread burned in her belly. Since he'd cursed her, Dother rarely allowed her to leave his rooms. In her human form at least. She spent a good deal of time trapped in her flask, dangling from his damn belt next to that ugly, red journal.

Human form? *Mora grimaced at the thought. What had become of her? To think of her body as a form... she was losing her gods forsaken mind.*

Dother's fingers feathered over her shoulder, the warmth of his ring somehow radiating through her clothes, and Mora tensed. Nearly slipped on the stone stairs. Dust coated her palm as she gripped the railing.

He chuckled. "You're awfully quiet tonight."

Mora held her tongue.

"Aren't you curious?" he asked, sliding his hand down her arm. "Wouldn't you like to know where we're going?"

The air became damp, each breath laced with a thick, musty odor and something rancid. Nausea bubbled in her belly with every inhale. It was colder here. As if winter touched these walls, her cool caress clinging to the stone season to season. In the distance someone whimpered.

This must be the belly of the castle. Which means...

"The dungeons," Mora whispered to herself, but Dother squeezed her arm, pleased with her answer.

"You've always been brilliant, Mora. I knew you'd figure it out. You'll make an amazing queen one day."

"My mother is queen."

"I can change that. All I need is a yes from those precious lips."

No!

Mora trembled as she screamed the word in her mind, her teeth sinking into her cheek until it bled. But what was the point in saying it out loud? Dother refused to hear her.

As they reached the bottom of the stairs, he threaded their fingers together once more and pulled her closer. "You've been on edge, Treasure. I thought an excursion would do you good."

Mora rolled her eyes. Thanked the gods he hadn't turned to look at her face. She'd been on edge from the moment he'd cursed her. All these long months, she'd held herself together by imagining millions of different ways to end his life. Finally she'd made him bleed. That's what he didn't like.

Mora swallowed. This excursion couldn't be good.

They seemed to walk the entire length of the dungeons, turning right, then left, then right again. Mora was dizzy by the time he stopped and called the sprite back. As the darkness pulled away, the dim lights of the few lit wall sconces elongated their shadows. The whimpers were louder here, mixed with pleas and pained moans that grated against her ears and made her stomach roil harder.

Something tugged her cloak and Mora shrieked. If not for Dother's steely grip, she would have run back to the stairs.

"Get your filthy hands off her," Dother hissed.

Mora looked down in time to watch him stomp on an emaciated, dirt caked hand reaching out from between the bars. A sickening crack was followed by an agonized wail. Whoever grabbed her flinched away, but Mora hadn't missed the unnatural angle of their fingers.

"Dother," she gasped, bile crawling up her throat. "How could you?"

A muscle ticked in his jaw and those azure eyes narrowed. "What have I told you?" His grip tightened, the pressure making Mora's fingers ache. "Call me Cillian."

Mora narrowed her eyes in return, hoping he could see the hatred burning within them. Refusing to say his name was one of the few powers she had. But... "Help them and I will consider it." The words tasted like ash in her mouth.

A weight lifted from her chest when he released her hand. She clenched and unclenched her fist, willing the blood to recirculate. All the while he watched her, the shadow of a grin on his face. Mora couldn't help but feel like she gave in too easily.

Her gaze drifted to her feet, bare and frozen against the grimy, stone floor. Already, the soles were black. Had her parents kept prisoners in these filthy conditions? Did Aedlin know who was down here?

Dother grabbed her chin, forcing her to look back up at him. Something like pity softened his face. A snarl clawed up her throat, but she swallowed it down.

"Would you like to help him?" he asked.

The intensity of his stare gave her pause. Mora's heart raced as she tried to guess the right answer. Was this a test? "Why are we here, Dother?"

His grip on her chin tightened, and he forced her back, inch by inch, until her back pressed against the cool metal bars of the cell. They dug painfully into her spine. And yet she preferred the cold bite of metal to the heat of Dother's body pushed against her front. "Do you want to help him?" he asked again, voice low. Lethal.

The thick, sour scent of citrus saturated Mora's lungs, and she nearly gagged. "I don't trust you."

"Answer the question, Treasure." He slid his hand up her face and caressed her cheek, the softness of his touch so at odds with his harsh tone. The two stared at each other, a heartless wolf and his hapless prey, until he couldn't take it any longer. The soft sweep of his thumb over her cheek was almost loving. Yet Dother's eyes darkened. "Or would you prefer I take care of him?"

The hairs on Mora's arms rose. Was that a threat? Dother brought her here for a reason. What did he want from her? And what did it have to do with whoever wept within the cell at her back? She clutched the cold metal bars, her mind racing. Mora couldn't subject someone to Dother. Even if it meant giving in.

"Can I please help him?" she asked, softly.

Dother's slow smile made her shiver. He stepped back, and she sagged against the bars. Took a few deep breaths, the damp, bitter air somehow better than Dother's sickening scent.

The keys he pulled out of his pocket clinked against one another as he brought them to the cell door. It took several tries to find the right one—Dother swore as he fiddled with the lock—but eventually something clicked and the rusty door squeaked open.

Before Mora could reach the man huddled in the corner, Dother grabbed her arm.

"I wish for no sounds to escape this cell. Then you can go to him."

Ice crawled up her spine, weaving its way through her bones and into her marrow. Mora stiffened—would she ever get used to the feeling? Or find a way around Dother's wishes? She played the words over in her mind, but her heart pounded and the wish's grip tightened against her ribcage, demanding she listen.

The whimpers in the back of the cell didn't help. Nor did the smell—piss and vomit saturated the damp stale air. The more she stared at the small space, the more it felt like the grimy walls pressed against her skin.

Mora's breath quickened, the pressure on her chest unbearable. He's going to lock me in here. *She gasped for air. Recoiled when Dother moved her hair away from her face. "Give in and you'll feel better, Treasure."*

They both knew he wasn't talking about the wish. But Mora still breathed a sigh of relief when she stopped fighting it. Cool smoke dripped down her arms, spilling to the floor and swirling around the room. Once again, they were shrouded in darkness. Only this time Mora could see as much as Dother did. And no one outside these walls would hear a thing.

"What's happening," said a quiet, scratchy male voice. It sounded raw, as if they hadn't had water in ages, yet there was something familiar about it.

Dother released her and Mora slowly made her way toward the sound, cringing when her foot connected with thin, bony flesh. The man scrambled back. Mora's throat ached, but she knelt down, careful not to touch him. "It's ok," she said softly. "I want to help."

381

"Princess?"

Mora squeezed her eyes shut, her lips pressed into a thin line. What had Dother done?

"Recognize her by voice alone?" Dother sounded amused. "Philip, I'm impressed."

"Philip?" Mora's voice broke and tears streamed down her cheeks. She fell into Philip's arms, hating herself when he gasped in pain. "I'm sorry," she said over the lump in her throat. She attempted to pull away, but Philip shushed her before winding an arm around her back. He continued to sniffle, while she sobbed against his chest, her tears staining the thin cotton rags they'd clothed him in.

Philip rested his chin on the crown of her head. "I'm glad you're ok."

For a moment Mora was the girl she'd been before, crumbling in the arms of a man who cared. Philip would have kept her safe if he knew. Clinging to him felt like holding on to the last threads of a life she once had. One she wasn't sure she'd have again.

"Why are you here?" she whispered, too aware of Dother's eyes on her back.

Philip trembled beneath her and she couldn't be sure if it was from fear, the chill in the air, or something worse. Mora could barely make out his face in the darkness, but Philip was gaunt, his red hair a dull, matted mess that fell past his chin. And his skin was so filthy, she couldn't find a single freckle.

"When you disappeared, the king blamed me. It was my job to watch over you. I failed. I've been here ever since..." Philip hissed in pain and Mora's chest ached as fury slammed against her bones like a beast intent on escape.

"Dother, what have you done?" she growled.

Philip sucked in a breath. "What's happening, Mora?"

Dother stepped closer. "Does this reunion not please you?"

Mora couldn't hide the venom in her voice. "Philip doesn't belong here."

"He failed at protecting you."

Philip's grip tightened, and she found herself doing the same, her fingers twisting in his thin cotton rags. "No one could have kept me safe from you."

Dother crouched down behind her and rubbed her back. "You're finally understanding, Treasure. You were always going to be mine."

"What did you do to her?" Philip's raspy voice was livid.

At the same time, Mora seethed, "You punished a man who did nothing."

Dother chuckled. "Would you like to help him?"

"Let him go."

He was quiet for a moment, and Mora's breath quickened. She balled her fists, clinging harder to Philip's clothes.

Dother's hand stilled on her back, his touch too heavy for her to bear, even with her thick cloak. He leaned closer, his breath tickling her cheek. "Say yes."

Anything but that.

Mora couldn't do it. Couldn't give herself to him willingly. She leaned further into Philip's embrace and took a slow breath. What else could she offer? One thing came to mind. "Cillian, please."

Dother hummed. Pushed the hair away from her face. When he leaned in to kiss her cheek, Mora forced herself to remain still. To... let him. She closed her eyes and focused on the feel of Philip's hand on her back. When Dother pulled away, she sagged in Philip's arms, praying to whatever Gods listened—Gods she believed in less and less by the day—he'd let Philip go.

"Are you ok?" Philip whispered.

Guilt stabbed her in the chest. The man was emaciated, sick, with broken fingers twisted at horrific angles, and yet he worried about her. She wasn't worthy of him. Not before and definitely not now.

"She's fine," Dother said, as he ran the rough pad of his thumb over her cheek, gathering her tears. Mora clenched her teeth until her jaw ached to keep herself from whimpering. "I love my name on your lips, Treasure. But that's not the word I'm looking for."

"You know I can't give you that," she said, closing her eyes.

"Can't and won't are different things."

"You can't make me yours, Dother."

His fingers curled, nails digging into her cheek. "Cillian."

"Leave her," Phillip spat before a cough rattled in his chest. Mora attempted to sit up, fearful her weight caused him pain, but Philip's weak grip tightened, holding her to him like he could somehow keep her safe.

Much to Mora's surprise, Dother let her pull away and rest her cheek against Philip's chest. There was a crackling in his lungs. He needed help. "If I agree to call you Cillian, will you let him go?"

"I will when you say yes."

Philip shook his head. "Don't give in to him."

Mora shuddered. She'd been trying so hard, for so long, to deny him. In every way she could. How much longer could she hold on? What would be left of her when—if—she were freed? Her eyes wandered to Dother, looming over them like a vengeful god. Philip weakly rubbed her back before his grip loosened and her heart sank.

They both knew this was goodbye.

Silently, Mora cried on Philip's chest. She couldn't leave him like this. Couldn't go back to that room. To Dother's bed. But, more than anything, she couldn't say yes.

Dother sighed as he stood, moving away from them. He dragged his finger through her smoke near the cell door, and she felt the touch as if it were on her own flesh. It made her skin crawl. Made her wish she could remain here instead of going anywhere with him. If she could take Philip's place, she would.

"Philip... I'm sorry." Mora did her best to wind her arms around him. She squeezed her eyes shut when she felt little more than flesh and bone. The Philip she knew was healthy and strong. Full of life. Dother's sick games took everything from him.

A bright light filled the space, burning Mora's eyes. Philip hissed, and they both raised their arms against it. It was like a sun flare, illuminating the grit between the rock wall, the filth on the floor, and Philip... the gray pallor on his face, his sunken cheeks. It was worse than she'd imagined in the dark.

When the light became bearable Mora looked to Dother. Watched as he rolled a glass orb around in his hand, uncaring about the solar sprite inside.

"Are you ready to take his pain away, Treasure?" Dother asked with bored disinterest.

What?

It was foolish, but hope warmed her chest. Would he let her heal Philip?

"I hope you get what's coming to you," Philip said, voice low, his forehead wrinkling in a way that once meant trouble. But he was too weak to do anything. And too foolish to keep his mouth shut.

Dother chuckled, the sound laced with venom, before prowling toward them. He gripped Mora's cloak and pulled, tearing her from Philip's grip. Mora cried out as he dragged her across the floor, reaching for Philip's hand.

"Leave her alone!" Philip yelled, while Dother forced her to her feet.

His arm wrapped around her center and he smiled down at her. "I assure you, Phillip, I have everything I want."

Mora stared into Philip's dark blue eyes. Memorized the love in that gaze. Would this be the last time someone looked at her like that? Her chest heaved.

Dother's hand trailed up her stomach, over the swell of her breasts and to her neck. "Treasure, this has gone on long enough. I wish for you to put him out of his misery. Now." He kissed her forehead and murmured, "Make it quick, I'd like to return to our rooms."

The wish took hold, its frigid, suffocating influence burrowing into Mora's soul.

No.

No, no, no, no.

I can't.

Power slammed against her chest.

I won't.

Tendrils twisted through her ribs, but she held them back.

Please...

Mora screamed, shaking under the pressure.

"What are you doing to her?" Philip attempted to stand, his thin legs trembling as he pushed himself up the wall.

Dother ignored him. Trailed his thumb up and down Mora's throat. "Give in, Mora. Show Philip how much you've changed."

A rib cracked and Mora wheezed. She wouldn't have remained standing if not for Dother's grip on her throat. She couldn't get enough air. Couldn't fill her lungs. The pressure of the wish on her chest intensified, and the room began to spin.

Onyx mist dripped slowly from her fingers and the pain eased along with it. But there was no relief. Mora slumped against Dother. Tried fruitlessly to stop her magic only to watch as more and more smoke gathered on the floor and crawled toward Philip.

The solar sprite's light burned every second into her memory.

"What's happening?" Philip screeched. He cowered against the wall but there was nowhere to go. And he could hardly move as it was. Philip followed the smoke back to Mora's hands, those dark blue eyes widening. "Mora? What is this? Make it stop."

Frigid obsidian crawled up his legs and Philip jerked, shrieking as it climbed to his chest.

"I can't." Mora's breath hitched. "Cillian, please don't make me do this."

Dother rested his cheek against hers, intent to watch. "It's for the best, Treasure."

Tears streamed down Mora's face when her power wrapped around Philip's throat. It may as well have been her own hands gripping him—she knew his pulse raced, heard every labored breath. Philip's feet kicked uselessly as her smoke lifted him in the air, and Mora clutched Dother's arm, her nails digging into his flesh. The bastard didn't flinch.

"You're a monster," Philip choked out between gasps. And Mora didn't know if he meant Dother... or her.

"She's a beautiful monster," Dother agreed, pulling her closer.

Philip attempted to claw at the dark wisps encircling his neck like an ethereal noose, tearing at his own flesh until he bled instead. His broken fingers were twisted and swollen, each movement no doubt causing horrific pain. And yet he tried so hard to tear himself free.

The vaporous ropes tightened excruciatingly slowly, fueled by the wish but tempered by Mora's desperate attempts to stop it. Philip's wheezing eventually transitioned to a raspy gurgle, the sound so horrendous Mora twisted in Dother's grip and vomited onto the stone floor. The ache in her bones pulsed harder, demanding she make it quick, *as Dother wished.*

It was ridiculous to think she couldn't breathe, when she could hear Philip struggling to pull in the tiniest sips of air. But, no matter how hard she tried, Mora couldn't inhale a single breath. Philip was dying. By her hand. And a piece of her died along with him.

The last of her strength slipped—Mora's glittering smoke constricted against Philip's throat until a thunderous crack filled the room.

Philip stopped struggling.

Stopped wheezing.

Stopped...

As his head fell to the side, his neck bent at a horrific angle, silence filled the room. A silence so loud Mora knew she'd never stop hearing it.

She thrashed in Dother's grip. Screamed so loud the vessels in her eyes burst. When Dother let go she fell, knees cracking against the stone floor. But the pain was a distant echo. Much like the thud of Philip's body dropping to the ground as her mist withdrew and sank back into her skin.

Bloodshot dark blue eyes stared ahead. Watching her as they clouded over. Judging her. Blaming her. Vomit slipped between her fingers and soaked her cloak as she crawled to him. But, when she reached Philip, Mora couldn't bring herself to touch him.

Philip was dead.

Mora did this. Dother made *her do this.*

For a moment, her emotions were so tumultuous she thought she may drown in them. Then Mora felt nothing at all.

CHAPTER 51

ZADRIEL

Fresh air trickled into Zadriel's lungs and with each labored breath his chest burned, the blistering pain unbearable. It was a cool summer night. Yet sweat soaked his skin and his muscles tremored.

In his peripheral, Zadriel could see the blood clinging to his body, drenching his naked chest, sticking to the valleys in his abdomen and staining his breeches. Along with the words Andras carved into him.

Zadriel's stomach revolted, bile crawling up his throat.

Each step through the field brought him closer to Arcadia. Long grass swayed against his legs, while dry weeds crunched under his bare feet, slicing through the soles. He could hardly see his destination—a shadow sprite shrouded him in a hazy darkness—but the sharp, sweet scent of evergreens tickled his nose, and he knew exactly where he was.

An ache stung in his dry throat. Other than a few sips when Andras felt generous, the last drink he had was days ago, under the oak tree with Mora. Exhaustion clung to his sore bones, threatening to drag his body into the ether if he didn't stop. And he wished he could sleep. Find his Little Witch in his dreams.

All he could do was watch. Watch as Andras's blood thrall forced his feet forward. Watch as he edged closer and closer to Mora. Without his volition, his fingers clenched into fists, preparing to fulfill Andras's demands. And Zadriel was powerless to stop it.

CHAPTER 52

MORA

Alina's endless prattling grated on Mora's nerves. Despite being a prisoner, the Aegist grew comfortable with the Fae. Though she had little love in her heart for Mora. After listening to her talk to Vesryn about her affinity for ravens and fascination with their connection to the God of Death for nearly an hour, Mora wasn't fond of her either.

She held her tongue. Busied herself by rolling a blueberry under her finger. The bowl Vesryn placed in front of her was full—Mora couldn't bring herself to eat. Zadriel's scent clung to her hair, lingering from her dreams, and her chest ached with each inhale. It was odd, to be comforted and afraid in the same breath.

Please be ok.

The inability to become ethereal and cure her hunger was also strange. Her stomach growled and Mora grimaced. Relented and lifted the berry to her lips. A sweet flavor danced on her tongue, but she couldn't find it in herself to enjoy it.

At least the cushioned kitchen chair she'd settled in was comfortable. Mora plucked a new berry from the bowl to roll over the polished wooden table and watched Vesryn pretend to listen to Alina in the living room. It was difficult not to laugh when Alina turned to get a drink and Vesryn's eyes darted back to his book. How did the little Aegist have so much to say?

Alina reached for her glass, swearing as she fumbled with her still-bound hands. Green vines, the same color as Vesryn's short sleeved-tunic, wrapped around her wrists, limiting her movements. The cup slipped through her fingers, tumbled over the table, and landed on the floor, a trail of water in its wake.

Vesryn sighed and mumbled, "Mother help me," under his breath. Then closed his book and looked to Alina. "Be more careful, Halfling."

Before he could stand, Mora flicked her wrist, releasing a wave of power. Onyx mist flowed from her hands. It slipped over the mess, curled around the table legs, and slithered onto the wooden top. Not a drop of water left behind. When it reached Alina's cup, it dove in, forcing the vessel upright. As the smoke pulled away, the vessel was once again full. The smoke nudged the cup closer before it twirled in the air and flew back to Mora.

It was amazing how simple it was to use her magic freely. It felt like breathing. Like everything was as it should be.

Though Vesryn clearly disagreed. Blood drained from the Fae's face and he pulled his feet up from the floor, curling them under his body. Watching Vesryn—a tall, muscular Fae covered in swirling black tattoos—cower was no longer amusing. They were surrounded by magical beings and Mora still received nothing but wariness from those she deigned to help.

Mora held his stare and smiled menacingly while a wisp of smoke curled around her fingers.

"Thank you," Alina said quietly. Unsure. Mora's eyes met hers. When she looked at the girl's earnest expression, those wide hazel eyes hesitant but sincere, she remembered a different person with kind green eyes, beautiful red hair, and a splash of lovely freckles across his face.

Mora looked away. Swallowed the lump in her throat and muttered, "You're welcome." Vesryn was right to be wary. She was a stain on the lives of those who grew close to her. Zadriel included.

You're a beautiful monster, Dother's memory whispered in her mind.

Fuck you, Mora whispered back, biting her cheek. The sting helped. One day she hoped to forget his voice. How many centuries would it take?

An awkward silence twisted through the space. Mora busied herself with her berries, playing with them more than eating them, as she gazed at the herb-filled jars lining the countertop. They reminded her of Zadriel's room. Had Andras found him? Had he bled him again? Was Zadriel weak, tired, and alone with no one to feed him chocolates?

"I wouldn't be so clumsy if you'd unbind my hands," Alina grumbled.

Closing his book once more, Vesryn pinched the bridge of his nose, a frown pulling at his full lips. "What will you give me in return?"

Alina bowed her head, those short blonde curls falling over her face. "I don't have anything to trade."

"You could owe me a favor?"

Mora opened her mouth to protest, but Alina spoke too quickly. "Ok."

Mora clenched her fingers, crushing a berry in her fist. "That was very stupid, child."

The scowl she directed at Vesryn was lethal, but, for once, he smiled triumphantly in return. Though it died on his face when Mora pushed away from the table and passed him on the way to her room.

The balcony doors crashed against the wall as Mora threw them open. "Are you there, creature? I have questions for you."

It was a cool summer day, the fresh air soothing her heated skin. But it did nothing for her racing mind. Where was the damn Spirit? At this rate, the bird-creature was her best source of information. Though she feared what Andras would do once his wish was fulfilled, Mora *needed* to do something. To get out of the damned treehouse, finish this, and get back to Zadriel.

And away from Vesryn, before she strangled him for what he'd done.

Mora couldn't explain it. The pain in her chest was an endless dull throb, and every second of not knowing Zadriel's fate was driving her mad.

She rubbed the spot over her heart. Wondered if he did the same.

This is a dream, love.

Mora squeezed her eyes shut and yelled down into the abyss. "Do you hear me creature? Tell me more riddles."

"I'd prefer you call me Thalias."

She flinched, turning to find Thalias standing behind her. Gods damn Fae and their silent feet.

"What do you want?"

That crooked smile graced his lovely face, a glimmer of amusement in those starfire eyes. He straightened his green tunic, a perfect match to Vesryn, and said, "It seems I could ask you the same."

Mora lifted her chin, somehow looking down at Thalias despite his taller frame. "I've been cooped up in your treehouse, high above a chasm, in the middle of the woods, little more than a glorified prisoner. What do you think I want?"

"Riddles, apparently. Did a Galadriah find you?"

Mora's brow rose. "A Galadriah?"

"The creature you're screaming for. If she appeared to be part woman, part bird, and spoke in riddles, that was a Galadriah. They see all time. And tend to only make sense in hindsight."

Mora nodded. Wondered if the creature listened.

Thalias walked to the balcony's edge and looked down. "They tend to sleep during the day. And aren't fond of orders. I'm afraid you're out of luck, Wraith." He turned, propped his elbows on the railing and scrutinized her face. When his gaze traveled down

Zadriel's tunic, he scrunched his nose. "I may be willing to answer questions."

"Let me guess, you'll want something in return."

Thalias nodded, his dimple flirting with his left cheek as he grinned. "You're learning."

What an ass.

Mora leaned against the wall and crossed her arms. "Don't mock me, Thalias. What do you want?"

"Answers. What are you?"

"None of your business."

Thalias tilted his head to the side and really looked at her. "I'm beginning to wonder if you know the answer. And so I come with an offer that may satisfy us both."

Mora hated that Thalias was right. She had no idea what Dother had done. Or what the forest wanted.

I blessed our union with the rarest magic, Dother's memory whispered in her mind.

Mora shivered and clutched Zadriel's tunic. Reminded herself Dother was dead. *Dead, dead, dead.*

Did she want to know what he'd done? Did she want Thalias to know?

"What Fae games are you playing?"

He pushed away from the railing and walked closer, though he stopped at a respectable distance. His expression turned serious. "Join me for a walk. There's someone I want you to meet. Someone who may have answers for both of us."

CHAPTER 53

MORA

How Thalias walked for so long in leather armor without the need to rest, drink, or complain, Mora had no idea. While she knew better than to expect sympathy from any of them, she whined endlessly in her mind.

Did he intend to travel the length of Berwick?

Mora hated herself for accepting his offer. After an hour of walking, she couldn't find the energy to care what she was. Could go another three hundred years without knowing. Her legs felt like jelly and she ached to lay on the cool, forest floor, among the dead leaves and pine needles—they'd stick in her curls, but it hardly mattered.

If only she could dissipate. Mora trailed her fingers over the golden petals on the flask at her hip. "Damn you," she whispered. Though perhaps not quietly enough, judging by the way Thalias's ears twitched.

He and Vesryn held hands as they walked. Rays of soft morning light trickled through the forest canopy, making the thin lines of gold outlining the leaves on their armor glitter. It reminded her of Zadriel's oak.

Oh, to go back to the morning they'd spent together...

Mora took a slow breath. Promised herself she'd track down the Spirit soon and find her way back to him, like she vowed. Yet nothing called to her. And there was no way she could explore Arcadia in its entirety. Already, she was out of breath.

Alina did not share Mora's qualms with the distance. The little Aegist walked by their side, her thin legs keeping up. The pine green pants and long matching cloak Thalias provided suited her well. Mora bled the blue from her sheets to stain her cloak, the memory of her family a needed comfort.

"How far are you taking me, Thalias?" she wheezed.

Thalias looked back, chuckling as sweat trickled down Mora's brow. "As far as it takes," he said, before dismissing her and continuing his relentless pace.

Mora rolled her eyes. *He's no better than the damn Galadriah.*

An elderly Fae passed, clutching her red cloak tightly against her chest. Despite her crooked back and spindly legs, she outpaced Mora easily. Though she startled when she noticed Halflings among their group, dropping her basket to the ground. It popped open, mushrooms and berries rolling in the dirt. She stared at her, her yellow-green eyes wide. If Mora weren't so tired, she'd sneer back. Instead, she took a moment to gasp for breath while Thalias and Vesryn helped gather her things and apologized.

As they continued on, Thalias's demeanor changed. His shoulders slumped and his head bowed, until Vesryn whispered something and offered him a gentle smile. Thalias perked up, though sorrow was still present in those bright eyes. Vesryn pulled him out of his misery.

Watching them made the pain in Mora's chest thrum. She rubbed the spot on her neck, but the pleasant pulse was dull—it couldn't crowd out the near-constant ache. Vesryn wrapped his arm around Thalias, closed his eyes and kissed his forehead, and Mora could no longer watch. She eyed the shadows beneath the trees instead and tried not to let her mind race.

Something fluttered in the darkness. "Is that a sprite?" Mora asked. By the time she blinked, it was gone.

It was Vesryn who turned this time. Though he didn't slow. The male walked backwards, uncaring about the trees and shrubs in his path. Even if they stopped shifting out of the way, Thalias wouldn't allow him to trip. "You saw one?"

"I think so?"

Vesryn furrowed his brows and pushed his long braids behind his pointed ears. "Without an offering of cream and berries, it's rare to see them. They blend in with their elements, seldom revealing themselves."

Thalias stopped, his shoulders tensing. "How do you know what a sprite is, Wraith?" He looked back at her, a dangerous gleam in his eyes.

Alina turned with him, curiosity painting her innocent face.

If only you knew.

A fresh breeze twirled in her long, dark brown curls and Mora heard the memory of a voice she hated more than anything. *They're basically insects.* One of Dother's first lies.

Mora felt her cheeks darken. Regretted her loose tongue. But she shrugged. "Halflings told tales after the Exodus."

Thalias's eyes narrowed and Mora knew he didn't believe her, but he turned away and continued forward. "Keep up. You're slowing us down."

Mora wasn't sure if she should feel relieved or furious—it was going to be a long day.

The forest bent and shifted out of their way with each step, yet Mora still managed to trip. She landed hard on her palms, dirt and pine needles caking her fingernails. The will to get back up was nonexistent—she needed a damned break. Resting her head on the cool forest floor, Mora closed her eyes. Inhaled the earthy scent. Prayed Thalias would leave her behind.

The two Fae snickered while Mora struggled to roll over. At least Alina was kind enough to ask if she was ok. Though Mora didn't answer—she was too busy attempting to catch her breath.

When she opened her eyes, she found Thalias standing above her, that damned crooked smile on his face. Even his dimple seemed to mock her. "Can you stand, or do you need Vesryn to carry you?"

Mora growled. She wrapped her fingers around the wildflowers blooming at his feet, tore them from the earth and attempted to toss them at him, but all she managed to do was cover herself in grass and petals. And the Fae laughed harder. *Bastard.*

"You'll be happy to know we're here."

"Ecstatic," Mora said between breaths. "Where's your friend?"

Thalias smiled. He looked past her to an ancient elm tree, its thick trunk covered in soft swatches of moss and bluish-green lichen. "She'll come out when she's ready."

Whatever the hell that means.

Mora's eyes roved over the tree, searching for lights or signs of a home in its canopy. There were none. It was a normal fucking tree. If Thalias tricked her into trekking through the forest for nothing she'd... think of something to do to him once she caught her breath.

Mora dropped her head back onto the blissfully cool ground when he walked away. Sighed when she realized they'd have to walk all the way back once they were done. *Gods save me.* Perhaps she could live here. It wasn't a bad spot—peeks of clear blue sky crept through the breaks in the trees, and the canopy was a glowing array of emerald, viridian, and sage.

A large black cat with a tuft of white fur on its chest peered down from a thick branch, its glowing green eyes boring into her soul before it jumped to another tree and was out of sight.

Mora shivered. Perhaps this wasn't the best place to settle.

Luminous insects flitted past her, a quiet buzz in the air. They reminded Mora of fireflies, though the light in their abdomens glimmered in an array of pastel colors. It took more energy than she cared to muster, but Mora lifted her hand and reached for the nearest one. Before she could touch it, a yellow-haired pixie flew by, snapped the bug out of the air, and tore it in half, all while making a noise she assumed was a war cry. It shoved the entire thing in its mouth, the accompanying crunching sound grating on her ears.

Mora grimaced. A mistake, apparently. The tiny creature darted closer and gave Mora a toothy grin, bits of glowing insect parts staining its teeth. Then it landed on her chest.

Mora sat up. Received a high-pitched earful when the little thing tumbled into her lap. "Thalias?" Mora called out, unsure what to do. The pixie hissed at her. Bunched the fabric of her now dirt stained white top and tugged. "Thalias, what do I do?"

She scanned the trees, twisting around in search of those she'd accompanied. But Vesryn, Thalias, and Alina were out of sight.

"Is that little one bothering you?"

Mora jumped to her feet at the sound of a cheerful voice she didn't recognize, cool smoke laced with crackling embers twisting around her arms. The pixie clung to the soft, buttery fabric of Mora's tunic. It squawked in annoyance, but she ignored it.

Soft doe-eyes the color of fresh cinnamon with specks of honey watched her. They were aglow, as if lit from within. She towered over Mora. Stood taller than Vesryn.

"Hello," she said, waving a light green hand. The gesture seemed friendly, if not for the curved talons gracing each finger—they looked lethal despite being cracked and textured like bark. Her skin, if you could call it that, appeared to be made out of leaves, though, like her talons, coarse patches of dark brown bark covered parts of her body. Almost like clothes. It hugged her small bosom, caressed some of her round stomach, flowed down her center and over parts of her legs. Her feet were bare, the same beautiful green as her the rest of her skin.

Those cinnamon eyes widened as they flicked to Mora's ember soaked mist. "Please be careful with your fire around my tree."

Her tree? Did she mean the elm?

Mora tensed as she moved closer.

"Be nice, Wraith," Thalias called through the trees.

Had that ass left her to meet this creature alone?

Mora clutched her power but remained still as those taloned hands reached out. She gritted her teeth when they skimmed her belly. The being collected the still-chattering pixie and backed away, her long hair, the color of the darkest pine needles, dragging on the forest floor behind her. Tiny blooms of colorful wildflowers and green leaves peeked through the strands, and little antlers curled up on the sides of her head.

"I know, she *is* scary," she cooed, as the pixie settled in her palm. "But you need to have better manners."

Mora felt her upper lip twitch as she listened. They had no idea how scary she could be. "I can hear you," she huffed.

"Hmm?" the tree-creature hummed in question.

Thalias appeared through the tree line, his fingers trailing over the branches and leaves reaching for him. A tinge of pink bloomed under his alabaster skin and Mora smiled inwardly. Wondered if the walk affected him more than he let on. Though it could be worry painting his face. And if he was worried, perhaps she should be too.

"Hello, Elowyn," he said, as he plucked the pixie from her hand and plopped them on his shoulder.

Elowyn smiled softly, pulling a pink flower from her hair. She leaned down and handed it to the pixie, the tiny thing chirping as it accepted her gift.

Thalias's expression turned serious. "I've been searching for you."

Elowyn straightened to her full height and pursed her lips. "I'm rarely far from my tree. You know that." She ran her talons through her hair, pushing it back to reveal a long, pointed ear that looked like a tapered leaf.

Amusement glimmered in Thalias's eyes when he looked to Mora. To the sweat and dirt stuck to her forehead. "I believe you and Mora have a different definition of far."

Mora grumbled as she used her cloak to clean her brow.

"Mora," Elowyn said slowly, as if tasting the word. "What a pretty name." Her voice lowered. "I've heard you turn into a being of endless, black smoke." She crouched so they were at eye level, her cinnamon gaze flicking back to the power still writhing around Mora's arms.

Mora took a step back and shot Thalias an accusing glance. "I see you've been talking about me."

"Not me, Wraith," Thalias said, shaking his head.

"News travels fast in Arcadia." Elowyn nodded toward the pixie, the flowers in her hair moving with her. "They love to tell tales. And my sisters and I are often watching, though you wouldn't know it." For once, she didn't look innocent. Though Elowyn's doe eyes were still wide, Mora didn't miss the shadow of a grin on her face. Collecting secrets made her happy. Gave her a sense of power.

Elowyn crept closer, ignoring the way Mora's fists clenched. "She's not a wraith."

Thalias dipped his chin. "I know. But her shadowy form makes me think of them."

"The trees like her."

"Do *you* like her?"

"I trust Arcadia's judgment." Elowyn hooked a strand of Mora's hair in her talons and brought it to her nose. Before Mora could pull away, she sniffed it and frowned.

Suddenly, a blast of glittering obsidian slammed into the tree-creature's stomach and sent her flying.

"Don't fucking touch me," Mora seethed through gritted teeth.

Something shifted in the air, a swift breeze whooshing through the trees, accompanying the loud pounding in Mora's ears.

Vesryn ran for Elowyn while Thalias closed in on Mora, backing her against the thick trunk of an old pine. "How dare you attack a dryad."

Those starfire eyes glowed while the silver tattoos on Thalias's arms pulsed. As if in answer, vines crawled from the soil and curled around Mora's dark leather boots.

"Thalias," Elowyn called from where she landed in the brush, Vesryn kneeling at her side. Alina watched from afar, blue magic flickering on her fingertips.

Good idea, little Aegist.

Mora bared her teeth, her hands curling into fists, glittering onyx and glowing embers spilling from her palms. "How dare I?" The wind grew wilder, whipping through Mora and Thalias's hair. Wisps of her smoke joined the torrent, painting the air black. "How dare *you* talk about me as if I'm not here. How dare your friend touch me without asking."

As Thalias stepped closer the pixie shrieked, dove off his shoulder and hid in an old, rotten log. The Fae brought his snarling face to Mora's and growled. "Elowyn is our best chance of understanding what Arcadia wants with you. What you are." Behind him, a tree groaned, the massive trunk nearly doubling over.

"Maybe I don't care," Mora spat. The venom in her voice was almost as thick as the overwhelming scent of blossoms in the air.

Wildflowers crowded Thalias's feet, popping through the soil and accumulating rapidly.

"Thalias," Vesryn called. A warning and a plea.

At the same time, branches curled around Thalias and pulled him away. Mora didn't question it. She pulled her smoke back from the billowing winds, sliced through the vines at her feet, and slipped past him.

"Figure it out without me."

Vesryn halted when Mora neared, his hand on Elowyn's elbow. The dryad's fixed stare was awed and wary, her skin paling to a less vibrant green. "Thalias, can we speak in private?"

"He's all fucking yours," Mora muttered under her breath. She nodded to Alina as she passed, the poor thing huddled under a shield. Watching her cower made Mora smile. Reminded her of Zadriel. She could almost hear his deep, soothing voice grumbling in her ear.

You're unbelievable.

You love my antics, she thought with a wistful sigh.

Mora made her way through the woods, dragging her hand along tree trunks and through soft, fluttering leaves. The wind calmed, along with her thundering heart. And the further she roamed the darker it became. A soothing scent in the air reminded her of fresh summer rain laced with mint, while whispers of a beautiful song danced through the trees. Beckoning her. Calling her home.

Leaning against the soft, papery bark of a birch, Mora closed her eyes and took a slow, deep breath. The scent grew thicker, caressing her hot skin. It reminded her of her dreams. Of the comfort of Zadriel's arms. But there was something else, a coppery aroma tickling her nose. A scent that sometimes lingered on Dother's clothes and saturated the air in Andras's cottage after he bled Zadriel.

The sound of a cracking branch had her eyes snapping open, darting wildly around the forest. She half expected to find that large black cat, eager to devour her soul. Nothing was there, but that sound... it was too close. And Mora felt like she was being watched.

"Thalias?" Mora took a step forward, wondering if he was playing tricks on her. "Thal—"

A hand wrapped around her mouth, squeezing her jaw so tightly it cracked. Mora bucked against her attacker's grip. She tried to shriek, but all that came out was a muffled breath. With a harsh yank, she was pulled into a warm chest, slick with sweat and something else.

Shadows curled around her, blotting out the little light trickling through the trees, while shallow breaths tickled the crown of her head. And that scent, the scent she loved so much, surrounded her. Mora relaxed and the grip on her mouth loosened. Tipping her chin up, she looked into a dark, glittering gaze.

"Zadriel," she breathed, the tightness in her chest easing.

Zadriel didn't react. Mora turned to face him, lost in those midnight eyes. So drunk with relief she didn't notice when his hand slid to her throat. Long fingers curled around her neck and squeezed, cutting off her breath and breaking her heart in one swift motion.

CHAPTER 54

MORA
300 YEARS AGO

*M*ora was numb. Shrouded in apathy. It clung to her ethereal form like a warm embrace to shelter her through her nightmare. The flask was her only safe haven. But Dother never allowed her sanctuary for long.

His call pulled at the thread in her center, tugging until she splashed around Dother's feet, a torrent of obsidian mist that gathered and rose, until a woman appeared. Mora stood naked before him. The way he preferred her.

Citrus and alcohol invaded her nostrils but Mora remained stone-faced. It was an effort not to flinch when he tucked a curl behind her ear. Took all her strength to stand still when he ran his finger along her cheek.

Then he reached her chin and forced her to look up into those bright azure eyes. "I've missed you," he said softly.

Dother watched her for a moment, chewing on his left cheek as his eyes bounced between hers, searching for something. Clearly he found her lacking, judging by the disappointed shake of his head.

Dother's fingers resumed their exploration, running along her throat until he curled them around her neck. "It seems you haven't learned to miss me."

Fury flared in her glowing amber eyes, but she clenched her teeth and said nothing. When Dother squeezed harder, her lungs screamed. Burned. Cried for air. She wheezed in his grip, dug her nails into his hand, and refused to drop her furious gaze.

All she could think of was the light fading from Philip's bloodshot eyes. The last words he'd said through labored gasps.

You're a monster.

Mora's heart raced, pounding against her ribs with such force it almost overshadowed the pain in her lungs. When the room began to spin, she readied herself to dissipate. But Dother let go. Grimaced. Made no effort to steady her as she swayed on her feet.

"Undress me, Treasure."

Mora's trembling fingers tightened into fists and she made no attempt to move. Maintained her unblinking, furious glare despite the black spots dancing in her vision.

Dother sighed through his nose. "I wish *for you to disrobe me, Mora."*

The words crawled over her skin, before the wish's frigid touch sawed through her bones. Mora stepped closer, until her chest pressed firmly against his. Swallowed against the burn in her throat when he offered a cruel smile. The bastard cradled her head, his fingers tangling with her hair, and waited for her to remove his burgundy velvet jacket. Golden buttons glinted in the candlelight, as if they too begged for her attention.

Running her fingers along the edge of the soft fabric, Mora considered his wish. Disrobe me. *She knew he wanted her to undress him with too-slow, nervous fingers, until he grew bored and helped, leading to other unsavory activities. A game he played with her often. But...*

There were plenty of ways to remove someone's clothing.

Mora pictured her intent. Plucking at the magic binding her to Dother's demand, she waited, holding her breath as she braced herself for a sting of pain.

Nothing happened.

Then fire—her fire—pooled in her palm and Mora smirked. Stared Dother in the eye and laughed as she gripped his jacket.

Smoke curled through the air, dull and gray compared to Mora's ethereal form, and Dother's brows furrowed. He coughed. Grimaced when the heat pricked at his skin. Screamed as the flames crawled up his chest.

His shriek rang pleasantly in Mora's ears. When his hands slammed into her shoulders forcing her back, she landed on the bed. For once thankful for the soft bedding. Mora crossed her legs and watched as Dother crumbled to the floor and writhed on the hard, black tiles. His agony her new favorite sound.

As the fabric of his clothing yielded to the flames, the wish's grip on her ribcage eased. And Dother's cries grew louder.

A loud bang came from the sitting room, shouts pulling her focus. Guards slammed against the thick, intricately carved, wooden door to the king's chambers, the concern in their voices flooding the room. It buckled against the stone walls. Mora likely had minutes to enjoy this, at best.

She'd face consequences for her actions later. Though not at their hands. It made no difference how angry Dother was, nor how he decided to punish her. Not as she watched the skin on his arms redden and blister under the heat. Not as she enjoyed the putrid scent of his pain. While it made her stomach sour, it was nothing compared to the suffocating aroma of citrus and herbs she typically endured.

Wood groaned and cracked and the guards' voices grew louder, calling desperately to their king. Mora sighed. She eyed her flask on Dother's bedside table and decided it was time.

Pushing herself off the bed, she knelt by his side, pouting in mock sympathy. "You were right."

Dother made a choking sound, tears spilling down his blood red cheeks.

Mora snickered as she leaned closer and whispered in his ear, "I'm ready to be a monster now."

CHAPTER 55

ZADRIEL

M ora's eyes flared as they trailed over Zadriel's torso. It was dark under the shadow sprite's cover, but he knew she could make out his wounds, caked in blood and oozing pus. Felt a horrific mix of dread and shame as she saw how Andras ruined him.

Andras had taken his time. Pushed Zadriel's body to the limit only to let him rest and somewhat heal before starting again. The torture left a mess of crooked, uneven lacerations across his chest with a permanent reminder—for him and Mora—of what Zadriel was. What he'd always be.

Loyal Dog.

Zadriel's fingers pressed harder against Mora's throat, pulling her focus back to his dead eyes. She clawed at his wrist, her mouth opening and closing as she attempted to breathe. All that came out was a near-silent wheeze. He screamed in the confines of his mind, begging her to see through the blood thrall. But his face was slack, his body no longer his own.

Forgive me, Little Witch.

With his free hand, he reached for the flask hanging from her hip, his soul aching when he felt her flinch away. Mora struggled against his hold, nails digging deeper into his skin. But he couldn't be stopped. No matter how much he wished to end this.

Andras's command hummed in his mind, directing every action. *Bring me the flask. Stop at nothing until you have it.*

Zadriel could still feel the echoes of his muscles tensing from fighting uselessly against the spell. Remembered the pounding in his chest while Andras bound their blood together and took control. He'd taken solace in knowing Halvard was Mora's Keeper—Zadriel had no qualms harming Halvard. Would gladly sit back in his consciousness and watch as he tore the oaf apart. It destroyed him when he realized Mora held her flask and he'd be the one to rip it away from her. Where was the lord?

As his fingers wrapped around the bottle, Mora bucked and Zadriel's back slammed into a tree, its rough bark tearing at his skin. It stung. Added to the symphony of pain echoing throughout his body. Warm blood seeped from the wounds and Zadriel cringed inwardly. He couldn't afford to lose more. Yet he didn't slow.

When he yanked the flask, his muscles screamed in agony, and the strap of leather tethering it to her belt snapped. A frigid feeling curled up his arm, oddly soothing against his heated skin. Mora tensed. Felt it too. He'd experienced this once before, all those weeks ago when he found her flask at the bottom of the lake. It felt like a lifetime ago.

Mora stared up at him, her narrowed, watery eyes an eerie mix of honey and blood. Had it hurt when the vessels burst? Zadriel's heart clenched. Why hadn't she dissipated? He had the flask, she didn't need to endure the pain any longer.

Why are you letting me hurt you, Little Witch?

Something cool encircled his wrists, its soft touch a comfort as it crawled up his arms in a tender caress. If he could, he'd sink into the feeling. Zadriel was exhausted. His teeth chattered. A sheen of sweat coated his skin, and he knew he wasn't healing. His immortal body had taken as much as it could.

The frigid touch hesitated around his biceps, then broke apart into gentle wisps that brushed lovingly over his skin. Zadriel would have purred if he could, it felt so soothing. Until they hardened and pulled. In one swift motion they broke his grip on Mora and sent the flask tumbling to the ground.

Even under a blood thrall, Zadriel's body sagged, the thrum of agony nearly too much.

Mora coughed. Doubled over as she choked on air. Mist slipped from her pores into pools of glittering darkness that slithered up his body. The tethers she'd wrapped around his arms held firm but caused him no pain.

It didn't stop him from lunging for the flask at his feet.

Mora acted fast, pulling against his ethereal tethers until she forced him to his knees.

"I'm sorry," she whispered hoarsely while she weaved her smoke into shackles, binding his arms to his ankles. How was she doing this without a wish?

Zadriel toppled to the ground, jerking against his restraints. Rocks cut into his face and dirt stung his eyes as he writhed in the weeds, inching closer to her flask. Inside his mind he begged Mora to stop him. Prayed the blood thrall ended soon.

Mora's long, elegant fingers curled around the flask. She pulled it away before kneeling beside him and gently cupping his face.

Each breath was a raspy wheeze, but Mora spoke the words Zadriel desperately needed to hear. "It's ok, love. I see you. This isn't your fault."

The squeezing pain he'd felt in his heart since she left eased. Zadriel could smell himself on her, the fresh blend of their scents calming his racing mind. He wished he could tell her how relieved he was to know she was ok. All he could do was savor the feeling of her soft palms on his boiling skin while his body twisted in the dirt.

Mora lifted his head onto her lap and ran her fingers through his matted hair, massaging his scalp. She kept the flask out of reach, hidden by obsidian smoke behind her back.

"It's ok, love," she said again. But Mora's gaze was pained and her throat bobbed—Zadriel knew he wasn't ok. Wondered if he ever would be. She cleared her throat and slackened his bonds. "I'm here. We'll wait this out together."

The world was dark, like a starless night, thanks to the sprite's shadows swirling around them. While Zadriel didn't have control over his body, it was the most peaceful he'd felt in days. Mora spoke of how much she missed him. Of how she'd killed Halvard and a Fae took her flask, but wished her to do as she'd like, freeing her magic. Of how everything would be ok now that they'd found each other. The sound of her voice calmed his racing thoughts.

Something whistled through the air and a new, sharp pain bloomed in Zadriel's shoulder. Agony lanced through him, so potent it felt as if it seeped into his blood. As if he were burning alive in torment. A pained breath left his lips. If he were able, he would have screamed. With every dull beat of his sluggish heart, the suffering grew worse.

Time slowed as Mora blinked, her eyes widening while understanding set in.

"No!" she shrieked, her shaking hands coming to hover around the branch sticking out of his wound.

A pale hand ripped through the shadows shielding them, scattering the sprite to the wind. The white-haired Fae's wild eyes were like fiery pools of sanguine softened by splashes of lavender. He growled when he saw Zadriel, sharp canines glinting as he gritted his teeth.

"I knew I recognized your scent," the furious male hissed.

"Thalias, wait!" Mora's hoarse voice cracked. She laid Zadriel's head on the earth and stood. Lifted her hands and approached Thalias slowly. Her smoke trailed with her, the end of the flickering wisp raising like the head of a viper, ready to strike.

Unfortunately it left her flask vulnerable.

Zadriel lunged for the flask, bellowing internally as the sharp branch embedded in his shoulder shifted. When his fingers slid around the golden filigree, Thalias roared. Power glowed behind his eyes as he raised his hands in the air and the ground beneath Zadriel erupted.

The bones in Zadriel's fingers ached as he squeezed the flask tight. He scrambled back, but it was no use. A maple tree sprouted through the earth, its growing branches twisting around him. They pulled Zadriel into a standing position, squeezing his stomach. Then grew larger, until his toes barely touched the ground.

A bough dipped low and Thalias grabbed it, hurtling over Mora as it lifted, and landing in front of Zadriel. Silver swirls pulsed along his arms as he broke a branch from the tree. He squeezed it in his fist and prowled closer.

"You'll pay for what you did."

Zadriel tensed internally as he readied himself for more pain. Pain he deserved. Though who this male was and how he knew—how anyone knew—surprised him.

"Don't fucking touch him, Thalias," Mora yelled as best she could.

Thalias paid her no heed. He leapt forward, his sharp branch raised and ready to strike, but Mora threw herself in front of him. The wood sliced through her arm. A pained shriek echoed through the trees, and Zadriel could have sworn the Forest quaked in response.

Zadriel didn't think one with skin so fair could pale. He was proven wrong as blood drained from Thalias's face and he stumbled back.

Sparkling crimson streaked down Mora's warm brown skin before dripping to the earth. There were clusters of wildflowers where Thalias once stood, but gilded daisies joined them, pushing through the soil wherever Mora's blood fell.

A dryad ran through the trees, her long, forest green hair dragging behind her. "Thalias, what's happening?"

Before he could answer, she saw them. Daisies Arcadia likely hadn't seen in centuries. Daisies Zadriel knew they'd remember fondly. Miss dearly.

Her taloned hand rose to her lips and a green tinted tear spilled down her cheek. She glanced at Thalias, those cinnamon eyes wide, and nodded.

Thalias pushed his fingers through his white hair with a frustrated growl. Bowing his head, he said, "Mora, I regret hurting you. That wasn't my intention. I know this is hard, but please move, this male needs to be handled."

Zadriel had never seen her eyes glow so brightly. He wondered if his mind played tricks on him when barely visible hints of gold pulsed along the veins in her arms.

"*No one* is touching Zadriel." As she spoke, the wind became ravenous, swirling around them and collecting bits of her smoke.

"Zadriel?" The new, deep voice sounded familiar.

Alina slowly approached, her thin frame appearing smaller next to the tall, broad-shouldered male walking by her side. It had been centuries, but Zadriel recognized his old friend. He hated that this was their reunion. When Vesryn's silver eyes roved over Zadriel's marred chest and widened, Zadriel's stomach twisted. While it wasn't Thalias's intention, he'd put Zadriel's shame on display. A punishment worse somehow than the torture he'd endured.

Vesryn's lower lip trembled. He tried to step closer, but Mora's smoke snapped against his chest with an audible thwack, denting the leaf-like scales at the center of his armor.

"Don't make me hurt you, Vesryn," Mora growled, her expression the personification of wrath.

Alina whimpered at Mora's tone. But she swallowed her fears and stepped closer, until she stood by Vesryn's side. His brows furrowed as he looked down at her, but the Aegist gave him a look that said *trust me* and raised her trembling hands. The shield she summoned was solid. Big enough even the dryad decided to step behind it before it sealed around them.

Some of the tension in Thalias's shoulders eased. Though the scowl on his face remained. "Wraith, return to your flask."

"No," she spat, her dark curls whipping around in the wind.

Thalias gritted his teeth. "I wish..." The Fae paused. Grimaced as if the word tasted off. "I wish for you to return to your flask."

A cold laugh slipped from Mora's throat. "I knew you'd want something eventually."

Thalias's lips pressed into a thin line. "I'd be willing to bargain."

"You aren't my Keeper anymore. And I have no interest in your bargains. But I can make you a promise." Mora gifted him a slow, cruel smile. "If you lay a finger on Zadriel, I will tear Arcadia apart, tree by tree, starting with your house."

"Sapling, leave them," Vesryn called from behind Alina's shield.

"You know I can't do that, darling. Don't you recognize his scent? I couldn't place it before, but it was him... he's the reason."

Vesryn's shocked stare hit Zadriel like a punch in the gut. Then his attention snapped to the lingering bruise on Mora's neck, now little more than a faded yellow.

"The Mother has plans for them."

Thalias crossed his arms and shrugged, tense muscles feathering in his jaw. "He deserves no blessings from the Mother."

Mora clenched her fists and Zadriel felt the branches holding him loosen. "Don't you see the words carved in his chest? Or that he's under a blood thrall, unable to control himself?" She closed her eyes for a moment. Took a slow breath. When her gaze lifted back to Thalias, the wind calmed. "Zadriel is innocent. Whatever sins you believe he committed belong to the bloodline that cursed him."

The tree released him. Zadriel's feet hit the ground, and he felt himself stumble. The strength in his hand waned, his fingers twitching.

Was the blood thrall finally wearing off?

A bough slammed into Zadriel's back. Air whooshed from his lungs and his knees hit the earth, teeth cracking together with such force it radiated through his skull.

The flask slipped through his fingers, plunking onto the grass. And Zadriel collapsed with it.

CHAPTER 56

MORA

Mora roared, her rage echoing through Arcadia with such force every creature in the forest turned their heads to listen. Exploding violently into onyx mist, she crashed to the earth in a ferocious wave, rushing toward Thalias. But he ran with shocking speed.

Bits of smoke pelted Alina's shield and blue light flickered through the darkness. Zadriel grabbed the flask before he tried to stand, his legs trembling, and Mora wondered if the blood thrall waned. What came next would leave him more vulnerable. She had to act fast.

Thalias tackled Zadriel to the ground. "You've caused enough damage, traitor," he seethed as he tore the flask from Zadriel's hands. "I won't let you taint things further."

Mora saw red. Hated the frigid touch of her curse binding her to Thalias once again. How dare he call Zadriel a traitor? All these long years, Zadriel dreamed of returning home. Spoke of Arcadia with reverence. And *this* was the welcome he received?

Fuck this. And fuck Thalias.

When Mora crashed into Thalias, ominous clouds bloomed in the sky. They blotted out the sun and descended the forest into darkness. There were no birds calling from the trees. No glowing insects flying through the air. Not a pixie in sight. It was as if all of Arcadia quieted, watching from the shadows.

Mora twisted around Thalias. He growled and struggled in her hold, but she squeezed harder before she ripped him away from Zadriel and tossed him in the air like he was nothing. Branches bent in an attempt to catch him, but Mora threw Thalias with such force they broke under his weight. *Good.* Each snap was music to her ears.

Thalias hit the ground hard, dirt scattering in the air. And Vesryn screamed. Screamed so loud Mora wondered if he summoned the thunder rumbling in the distance.

Somewhere along the way, Thalias lost the flask. It rolled over roots and pine needles before settling in a cluster of vibrant ferns. They curled around it, dragging it closer.

The wind picked up, plucking leaves from trees and breaking branches. Then lightning struck the earth. It lit up the woods, burning all but Mora's eyes, before darkness reigned again.

Zadriel dragged himself to the flask, dirt coating his wounds. If not for Thalias, Mora could have kept him safe until the blood thrall ended. Now... gods, he felt feverish when she held him before. This could only make things worse. If anything happened to Zadriel, Thalias would pay.

"Don't place a finger on that bottle," Thalias bellowed. He launched himself onto the flask before Zadriel's fingers touched the golden filigree.

Gods damn it.

Mora dove for them but Thalias grabbed Zadriel and rolled out of the way. The flask tumbled with them until a new cluster of ferns pulled it close. Silver-flecked blood seeped from a wound on Thalias's head. It stained his white hair and dripped down his cheek. Yet the injury hadn't slowed him.

Thalias straddled Zadriel, snarling as he slammed a fist into his cheek, so hard Mora felt it. Thunder boomed with the next blow of his fist. As Zadriel's head snapped to the side, the sky wept.

Thalias struck him again, the silver markings on his arms pulsing brightly. "You betrayed us," he said through gritted teeth. "You betrayed your legacy."

Mora pounced. Though, this time, when she tossed him, Thalias was ready. As he flew through the air, a bough was waiting, the damn thing slowing his fall, and placing him gently on his feet. He charged back toward the flask while Zadriel crawled to it.

Smoky tendrils slipped around Thalias's ankles and pulled his feet out from under him. He landed hard on his face. Grunted as he hit the ground. For a moment, Mora wondered if he was done—Thalias laid still, his breath sawing in and out. But then he lifted his head and fury flared in those starfire eyes. Inside, Mora laughed at the dirt caking his cheek. Until Thalias grinned that mocking, crooked grin and flicked his wrist.

A shrub with gleams of silver in its viridian leaves burst through the soil, branches unfurling like a hungry maw. They cut through Mora's mist before twisting around her and snapping shut. She slammed against the bramble. Twirled around furiously when they refused to break. It astounded Mora—nothing could stand against her smoke. At least, nothing outside of this gods forsaken forest. As she pressed against the confines of her woody prison, bits of smoke leaked through. But far too slowly.

Lightning speared the earth, nearly hitting Thalias as he rushed back toward Zadriel.

"Thalias, leave them," Vesryn shouted, pounding his fists against Alina's shield. With each thwack the shield hissed. Sparks of blue erupted and Vesryn's skin burned. But it wouldn't deter him. He dug his feet into the ground, holding himself upright as he took blow after blow.

Alina squeezed her eyes shut and begged Vesryn to stop. Her arms shook but her shield held firm.

"May the Mother save us," Elowyn whispered, sage tears rolling down her cheeks.

Zadriel grabbed the flask as a new wave of thunder rumbled. Mora felt it in her soul. Enjoyed the warmth that came with Zadriel's touch, laced with the cool caress of the curse. Though it didn't hurt like it usually did. She pressed harder against the bramble, cursing Thalias's name in her mind.

Zadriel's blood thrall would end soon and he'd be unable to move. Unable to flee. Unable to defend himself. He needed her.

Let me go, you ridiculous bush.

Mora slammed into the branches over and over again. As she slowly slipped free she could do nothing but watch while Thalias kicked Zadriel in the stomach. Bile spilled over Zadriel's chin, splashing into a growing rain puddle by his face. But his fingers solidified around the bottle.

"You are unworthy of her," Thalias spat. And the rain picked up, crashing upon them in an endless barrage.

Mora howled in her mind. The shrub shriveled, those glittering leaves blackening until they fell to the ground in a rotten heap. She rose like a wave behind Thalias, ready to drown him in a sea of obsidian, but he headbutted Zadriel and snarled before wrapping his fingers around the bottle and tugging.

Zadriel wouldn't let go. Couldn't let go. And as they tugged Mora's flask back and forth, a sharp pain snaked through her. It was like being ripped in half. Her dark, glittering wave contorted and thinned before spasming violently.

Mora's smoke tore a hole in the soil as she writhed, chunks of earth flying through the air. The trees around them bent away and the forest groaned. Boughs snapped and trunks collapsed. It was as if they'd been hit by an invisible cyclone.

Alina squeaked when a branch zapped against her shield, blue light sparking.

The obsidian mist flailed before bursting, and a boom shook the trees. Followed by Mora's agonized screams.

CHAPTER 57

ZADRIEL

Z adriel couldn't bear Mora's shrieks. Ached to end this fight with Thalias and go to her. As her agony rang in his ears, a whole new pain lanced through his chest.

Was it because they both held the flask? Were they tearing her apart as they wrestled over the bottle? He wished he could let go. Even if it pained him to leave her in the hands of someone he didn't know and couldn't trust.

Hold on, Little Witch. Please hold on.

"Thalias, stop," the dryad cried. She stared at the crater. At Mora writhing in its center. Something glittered within it, but Zadriel could hardly make it out as he twisted in the mud with Thalias.

Vesryn growled, the sound one of determination and pain, as he continued to relentlessly fight against Alina's shield.

"What are you doing?" Alina demanded. Sweat dripped down her brow and her shoulders slumped. She couldn't keep this up much longer. "This is the only thing keeping us safe."

"Let me out, Aegist," Vesryn said through gritted teeth. "Thalias needs me."

With one more hard bash, Vesryn managed to smash a hole in Alina's shield. It popped, the sound ringing in Zadriel's ears. Blood dripped from Vesryn's hands, pooling at his feet, but he pushed on. Nothing would stop him from getting to his mate.

"You will never be worthy, traitor," Thalias said, those cold red and purple eyes boring into Zadriel's as he attempted once again to pull the flask away. Mora's pained screams grew louder. Inside, Zadriel screamed with her.

If he could, he'd flinch at those words. His eyes stung and his throat ached. It joined the orchestra of pain thrumming through his body. Would he ever be worthy? Of her? Of Arcadia? Of anything?

Light flashed and leaves spun in a vortex around it. When they settled, a large stag with moonlight eyes and a majestic crown of antlers raced toward them. Vesryn bellowed as he crashed into Thalias, forcing him away. His fingers slipped from the flask while Zadriel managed to hold on.

Mora's cries died along with the wind. Though her jagged breathing didn't ease Zadriel's worries.

He clutched the flask, his body relaxing in the mud while rain drops splattered on his boiling skin. It stung as it trickled through his wounds, collecting blood and dirt alike. There was fire in his veins. The burn far more potent than usual. It bled into his muscles and seeped into his skin until all he felt was the blaze. The blood thrall waned and his bones screamed—Zadriel thanked the Mother he was already on the ground.

The flask slipped through his fingers and his head lolled to the side. A muddy puddle soaked his cheek, though he didn't mind. Its cool caress felt nice against his skin.

As his eyes grew heavy Zadriel noticed the daisies. Dozens upon dozens of them poking out from the crater. Their golden petals swayed in the breeze, and in the distance he could have sworn he heard his mother sing.

CHAPTER 58

MORA

Everything hurt. Down to the marrow in Mora's bones. But the warm ache in her heart bothered her most. With each beat she felt a tug, one that grew more and more urgent.

Her legs wobbled as she forced herself to stand. Why in the name of the gods were there so many daisies? Blood dripped from her nose and the damned things reached for it, drinking it like wine. With each drop, a new gilded flower sprouted. Mora didn't have time to ask questions. Or to feel any sympathy when she crushed them under her feet—it would be impossible to take a step otherwise.

Pulling herself from the crater, she cursed the slippery, wet dirt threatening to tug her back in. And the rain slamming down from the heavens. As she crawled onto the grass, she searched for Zadriel. Squinted through the water gathering on her lashes. Through the downpour, she heard Thalias and Vesryn arguing.

"Why did you do that?" Thalias asked. His voice was soft but anger weaved through it.

Vesryn sighed. "Look around you, Sapling. Arcadia's furious. And you were losing yourself."

"I never once lost control."

"Didn't you? Whether you like it or not, the Mother has plans for him."

Thalias growled and dragged his hands through his soaked hair. "Then why does this feel so wrong?"

"I don't know, Sapling. Perhaps Mora—"

"Where's Zadriel?" Mora seethed as she neared.

Vesryn glanced to the right and Mora followed his gaze.

No, no, no, no.

Mora was running before she'd made the choice to move, but her boots slid on the wet earth and sent her sprawling. She grunted when she hit the ground. Her palms slid through mud, sharp pieces of stone and wood slicing her skin. Hissing against the sting, she muttered, "Fuck this," then tore at the invisible tether in her chest. Lightning streaked through the sky. It disturbed the darkness and illuminated the forest floor as she exploded into mist. It was then Mora truly saw him.

Zadriel lay in a puddle at the base of a weather worn birch, the flask discarded at his side. Thunder rumbled as Mora waited for him to breathe.

Oh gods, was he...?

The trees were too close, brushing against her as she weaved through them. It felt as if Arcadia constricted around her—the squeezing pain in her center was too much.

When his chest rose and fell slowly, Mora felt the tiniest sliver of relief. But it wasn't enough. Her obsidian smoke caressed him, curling together until Mora materialized. Tears spilled from her bright, amber eyes as she hovered over him, unsure what to do.

"I'm here, love," she whispered, her voice breaking. "I'm here."

Zadriel's midnight gaze was lifeless. New bruises bloomed on his already mangled chest and stomach, and Thalias had made a mess of his face. She was going to fucking kill him.

Mora cupped Zadriel's cheek. The metallic aroma of blood tainted by the putrid scent of infection burned in her nostrils. Despite the cool rain, he was burning up. Magic slammed against her ribs, stealing her breath, and her heart thundered.

She could heal him. Would it be enough? It had to be enough...

"I'm sorry if this hurts," she said, before kissing his forehead. Her throat bobbed as she placed her trembling hand on his chest. Scabs scratched her skin while pus and blood gathered on her palm. Mora closed her eyes and took a shuddering breath.

Glittering obsidian spilled from her palms and over his wounds. Would its cool touch help? Was she soothing his pain or fueling the torment?

Mora choked on a sob.

Cracks festered in Zadriel's ribs and scars marred his lungs. Mora nearly gagged. Andras hadn't simply carved those awful words into Zadriel. He'd stabbed him over and over. Judging by the different stages of healing, the bastard took his time.

Then he sent him after your flask, with no food or water, and an infection festering in his wounds.

Mora's tears joined the rain splashing against Zadriel's face. "I'm so sorry, Zadriel."

Her rage was a living thing. An intense, pounding pressure thrashing in her chest. It wanted to crack open her ribs and spill out into the world, drowning it in darkness and reigning terror upon anyone who'd dared to even smile at Andras.

One day she would end him.

Mora's smoke weaved Zadriel back together, one laceration at a time. She tipped her head back and let the rain kiss her face while she grappled with what Zadriel endured. Alone.

A hand clapped her shoulder, shattering her concentration. Mora didn't need to open her eyes to know who it was.

She shrugged off his touch. "Leave me, Thalias."

"We need to talk."

Mora glared up at him. Blood and dirt stained his hair and ran down his wet brow. But, unlike Zadriel, Thalias healed. And he had the nerve to interrupt her? The look on her face turned monstrous. "No. Zadriel needs me to heal him, and you need to get as far away from me as you can."

Thalias sighed and shared a look with Vesryn. His mate nodded, water dripping from his long braids. Behind him, Alina and Elowyn huddled under a shield. Blue sparks jumped in the air with each drop of rain. Alina watched Vesryn, a frown pulling on her lips, while Elowyn's wide eyes bounced from Mora to Thalias and back.

"I can heal him," Vesryn said quietly, avoiding Mora's gaze.

Mora's voice dipped low. "Stay. Back." She lifted her hand, smoke spilling from her fingers. Hoped they took the monster lurking in her gaze seriously.

Vesryn gulped. Traced the dent in his leather armor. "Thalias?"

Thalias's eyes narrowed with warning and the wind howled in Mora's ears while thunder boomed. He stepped in front of Vesryn, shielding him. Mora had no desire to fight. Hated every gods damned second they wasted. *Why can't they leave me alone?*

"Vesryn won't hurt him, Wraith."

That doesn't mean you *won't.* "Spare me your Fae bullshit, Thalias."

"I acted rashly, and I regret that." Thalias scrubbed a hand down his face. "There are things you don't understand. Things we need to discuss."

"What I understand is you blame Zadriel for things he couldn't control," Mora growled, fire lacing her smoke. "And you intended to kill him for it."

Thalias paled before backing into his mate's embrace.

"Mora," Vesryn pleaded. He wrapped an arm around Thalias's stomach and backed them both up a step.

Thalias kissed Vesryn's cheek and squeezed his hand. "Speak with me and Vesryn will heal Zadriel."

Mora's fingers curled while fire and shadows rippled over her fist. "Then what?"

"He cannot be allowed near you."

"No."

Thalias pulled away from Vesryn's grasp, eying Mora's power warily. "If it pleases you, I'll banish him from Arcadia. He can leave unharmed." The Fae knelt in front of her and offered his hand, as if she'd fucking take it.

Mora laughed, the sound bitter and cold. "You think that pleases me?"

Thalias dropped his hand to his side and took a frustrated, weary breath. Around him, vines poked out from the soil. "Be reasonable, Mora."

"Speak for your gods damned self."

A muscle feathered in Thalias's jaw. Leaves unfurled as the vines grew—they slid through puddles, brushing against Mora's royal blue cloak as they passed. And Thalias's gaze flicked to something behind her.

Within a breath, Mora knew exactly what Thalias intended.

"Don't make me do this, Wraith."

Rage flared in her eyes. "Don't make an enemy of me, Thalias."

A wave of obsidian rushed to her flask, slicing through the vines. But more and more erupted from the soil.

Thalias stood and pushed his soaked hair away from his face. Mora felt when vines grew behind her wall of obsidian and wrapped around the flask. Thalias closed his eyes. Grimaced. Those silver tattoos pulsing on his arms glowed in the low light, flaring when he looked at her. "I'm sorry. Truly, I am. But—"

Before Mora could launch herself at him, a branch curled around Thalias's mouth, cutting him off. A shocked squeak escaped his lips as roots, vines, ferns and branches wrapped around him and lifted him off the ground.

Thalias struggled against their grasp. His legs kicked, and he clawed at the bough wrapped around his center. The howling wind grew stronger. But it accomplished nothing.

Mora was stone-faced, her glowing amber glare fixed on his wide eyes. The Fae wheezed as twigs curled around his neck. If things were different, Mora may have been amused. But with each of Zadriel's slow, labored breaths, Mora's pulse quickened.

When it was clear Thalias was no longer a problem, she made her way to her flask. Mora's smoke slid over her shoulders, trailing behind her like a cape cut from the darkest night sky.

As she tore her flask free from the clutch of Thalias's vines, Vesryn called her name.

"Mora, please." His voice shook. "Please let Thalias go."

Mora felt nothing as she watched Vesryn tear at the plants twisting around his mate. With every branch he tore away, three more grew to take its place. Thalias's cheeks reddened, his legs kicking desperately. His wild eyes were so wide the whites nearly swallowed his vibrant, crimson irises.

Mora knelt beside Zadriel and got to work tethering her flask to his belt. Her smoke weaved vines together, looping them around the bottle's neck and securing it in place. When she was sure it would stay, Mora pulled at the tether in her chest and readied herself to take Zadriel away.

She was more smoke than woman when she turned. Furious amber eyes swept over Thalias as she promised Vesryn, "That isn't me."

CHAPTER 59

THALIAS

Mora and Zadriel were gone, yet Thalias still dangled in Arcadia's wrathful embrace. He felt numb. Hissed against the prickling sensation in his limbs. She held him too tightly—branches and vines tore at his skin, and he could barely suck in enough air.

Vesryn gave up his fruitless attempts to free Thalias and instead held his hand. "What can I do, Sapling?"

Nothing.

His mate frowned. *Are you certain?*

It was difficult, but Thalias managed to nod. Bark scraped his throat, but it simply added to the thrum of discomfort he felt everywhere. They could only wait. At least the weather calmed, though they were soaked to the bone. Thalias shivered. Water dripped incessantly from his hair and down his cheeks, and he could do nothing but endure its startling, icy touch.

"The trees don't want to let go," Elowyn said with a frown, wildflowers drooping in her hair. She came closer, staring up at him with those sad doe eyes. Her brow scrunched, and she ran a talon along one of the boughs. Leaves shuddered under her touch, but the branch held firm. "Mother won't hear me."

"That tree's your mother?" Alina asked. She'd kept her distance. Though the little Aegist no longer huddled under a shield. Whether it was the lack of Mora or the now clear skies that convinced her to come out, Thalias wasn't certain. All he knew was he envied her dry cloak.

"No, silly. The tree's one of her children. Like I am. Like all Arcadian's are."

Alina blinked. "... ok?"

The dryad's smile gentled. "I still hear Mother's song."

Vesryn pressed his lips together, frustration darkening his brown cheeks. "As much as we all love the Mother, can we focus on Thalias, please?"

Whether Vesryn liked it or not, this *was* about the Mother. Thalias sighed through his nose. Arcadia made Her decision, and he had to respect it, but the pain in his chest at Her visceral reaction against him cut deep.

So many things made sense now.

The branch around Thalias's mouth shifted to curl on his crown like a leafy diadem. The tip patted his head and Thalias couldn't help the shadow of a smile twitching on his lips. It was an apology. One he wasn't ready to accept. But Arcadia was determined—a light breeze saturated with the crisp, refreshing aroma of the Forest curled in his nostrils, a small comfort he couldn't help but savor. Arcadia loosened Her hold on him, and Thalias took a greedy, deep breath.

He tipped his head up, blinking against the sunlight shining down on him through the Forest canopy. "Why did you choose her?" he asked quietly, knowing Arcadia wouldn't answer.

CHAPTER 60

ZADRIEL

Light trickled through the window, caressing Zadriel's face. It was an unwelcomed intrusion—sleep held him in a gentle embrace and Zadriel had no interest in escaping. He groaned. Attempted to shield his eyes only to discover his arm wouldn't budge. A soft breath fluttered on his chest and Zadriel braved the sunlight.

Witnessing Mora sleeping was worth the sting in his eyes. She'd curled herself around him like she could keep him tethered to this world. And perhaps she had. Mora's head rested on his shoulder while her arm fell across his stomach, their legs tangled together. A grin tugged on his lips and he pushed a few stray curls away from her face. Mother Divine, she was beautiful. It almost hurt to look at her.

As her chest rose and fell slowly, Zadriel watched her face for signs of nightmares. It seemed nothing haunted her dreams today. She was relaxed. Peaceful. At home resting by his side. He felt tempted to roll over and pull her into his arms, but he wasn't *that* big an ass. Mora rarely found peace—Zadriel wouldn't be the one to take it from her.

Where were they?

Though he didn't recognize the bed they slept in, or the light green sheets covering them, they were still in Arcadia. The round room with rings on the ceiling told him the Forest grew them a home in the bosom of a tree. Almost like the one he once shared with his mother.

The memory of her screams crowded his mind.

Zadriel squeezed his eyes shut and took a deep breath.

Then Mora murmured something in her sleep, snuggling closer, and Zadriel allowed himself another small smile. Now wasn't the time for grief. He should cherish this moment—quiet comforts were a luxury, and surely wouldn't last. He threaded his fingers in Mora's soft, curly hair and inhaled her delicious scent. A kiss of mint still saturated her crackling ember and pine aroma.

Zadriel's grin widened. His Little Witch wore his tunic.

He couldn't help his satisfied hum. The warm, soothing feeling he always enjoyed in her presence curled around his heart and he couldn't have asked for more. This moment was perfect.

Except... Could it be a dream?

His breathing quickened. Zadriel stared up at the natural wood, waiting for it to fade into a thatched ceiling that sloped too low. The echoes of Andras's dagger burned in his chest along with the phantom scents of blood and vomit. Sweat beaded on his brow as his gaze jumped around the room. There were peeks of Arcadia between ivy curtains. And Mora's flask sat on a simple wooden table by the bed, along with a full glass of water, and a handful of blueberries.

No golden leaves decorated the walls—hints of the Mother Tree nowhere to be found. The dreams he had while Andras tortured him hadn't been like this. This was real.

Which meant...

The scars on his chest were warm to the touch. As he trailed his fingers over the thick ridges that came together to spell *Loyal Dog,* Zadriel's breath hitched. There was no pain. The wounds healed. But he felt ugly. Ruined.

Mora bolted upright. "Thank the gods, you're awake." Her brows furrowed and dark circles painted the skin beneath her eyes. "What hurts?"

Her hands trembled as they hovered over his stomach, his chest, his forehead, each touch barely a whisper against his skin. It was as if she had no idea what to check or how to touch him.

"I'm ok," Zadriel said, though he almost laughed. *You were just sleeping* on *me, Little Witch. Your hands won't hurt.* Nothing ached as he sat up. Each breath unburdened, every movement his own. But unshed tears stung his eyes when he truly looked at what Andras had done.

Mora's bright amber eyes brimmed with tears of her own. "Please, tell me what hurts."

A pallor cooled the golden undertones in her skin. How long had she watched over him? The last thing Zadriel remembered was her pained screams while Thalias fought him for the flask. Then there was only darkness.

Without Mora, he wouldn't be alive. She'd defended him. Protected him.

Thalias was right, Zadriel wasn't worthy of her. But, for once in his life, he intended to be selfish.

Zadriel swallowed. Continued his exploration of the jagged scars Andras carved into his flesh. "Nothing hurts. Why doesn't anything hurt?"

"I healed you. Cleaned you up and fed you when you were lucid enough to eat—a horrific experience, I assure you—made sure you had water, and..." Mora's attention flicked to his neck.

A small, glass vial warmed his skin and he could feel the thrum of power inside. "Andras's pendant," Zadriel whispered, rolling it around between his fingers. Two streams of blood chased each other around and around endlessly inside.

A timer counted down in Zadriel's head. Two weeks. Less. How many days had he lost?

Tick.

Tick.

Tick.

The skin on his scarred arms itched as he imagined what Andras would do when he returned empty-handed. There was no way he'd bring Mora's flask with him. Considering the state he was in, he doubted Andras expected him to succeed. But after Halvard took Mora and Zadriel punched him—he still couldn't believe he'd done that—Andras lost it. Normally Zadriel assumed the power flowing through his veins kept his life safe. But he'd barely survived. Would he make it through another round?

How much time would he and Mora have together?

Zadriel gathered Mora in his arms and hugged her close. "I've missed you, Little Witch."

"All I've thought about is finding the damned Spirit and getting back to you," Mora replied, gently hugging him back. She rested her head on his shoulder and pressed a soft kiss to his throat. "Until recently, I hadn't felt a pull toward anything."

"Until recently?"

"From the moment I brought you here, there's been a tug in my chest." Mora bit her lip and looked out the window, her dark brows furrowing. "It doesn't hurt, but I'm sure it will get more insistent with time."

The idea of finding what was left of the Mother Tree and bringing it to Andras made Zadriel want to scream. Every part of him hated this. But there was no stopping the threads of fate. What Zadriel did centuries ago—what Cillian made him do—led to this.

And Mora needed him.

He nuzzled her hair and took a deep breath of heavenly embers, lavender, and pine. "We can search together."

Mora pulled away to look into his midnight eyes, her face scrunched with concern. "I won't make you do that."

When she laid her hand on Zadriel's chest he flinched. Heat flooded his face, all the way to the graceful tips of his ears, and he found he could no longer hold her gaze.

"What's wrong?" Mora asked, gently stroking her thumb over his scars.

Zadriel stared at Mora's pouch, discarded on the floor with her Arcadian clothing and his mother's belt. He wished a spare tunic was down there with them.

"I'm ruined," he said, so quietly he wondered if he only thought it.

Mora's soft touch froze, and a breath caught in her throat. "What do you mean, ruined?"

"Andras made sure of it."

She cupped his cheek and brought his gaze back to her face. "No one could ruin you, love."

Mora kissed him. A slow brush of her lips that left him feeling lighter. It soothed the cracks in his soul while lulling his racing heart back to a steady beat. Then she leaned down and did the same to every jagged letter Andras carved into his skin. Zadriel shuddered. Tears flowed down his cheeks as her lips grazed over the raised flesh with reverence.

When she was done, Mora pulled him close again. Her breath fluttered against his lips as she said, "There is nothing anyone could do to make you anything less than perfect in my eyes."

"I love you," Zadriel whispered.

Mora's lips parted and something flared in her amber gaze.

"When I look at you, I can hardly breathe." His black eyes sparkled as more tears, happier tears, fell, and her soft fingers were already there to catch them. "You're an exquisite force of nature and I will never understand why the Mother thought I was a worthy mate."

Time slowed. Mora watched him silently, her fingers frozen against his cheeks. "Mate?"

Zadriel stilled—why had he blurted it out like that? Every time he'd imagined telling her... it hadn't gone like this.

Clearing his throat, he offered Mora what he hoped was a reassuring smile. All while praying to the Mother, the Gods, and any being who would listen, he could fix this.

"Your soul calls to mine, Little Witch." He threaded their fingers together and brought their hands to rest over his heart. Could she sense the way his blood sang for her? "When you're near, I feel the comfort and warmth of our bond in my chest. For a long time,

I cursed the feeling. The moment I saw you in the alleyway three hundred years ago I realized what you were to me... what we could never be.

"When Cillian died, any hope for a better life died with him. It was easy to be angry with you. To blame you for the way things were. Then Andras found you and you showed me what a fool I've been. Tore down every wall I tried to erect. I'm not worthy of you, Little Witch. I'm not sure I ever will be. But I will never stop trying."

Mora continued to caress his face. A few times, she opened her mouth to speak, only to close it again. Seconds expanded into what felt like hours as he waited, mind racing.

Would she reject him? Was he foolish to hope?

When Mora finally found the words, her soft voice shook. "If you're unworthy, Zadriel, then I am woefully undeserving. But I don't care. The Fates themselves wouldn't dare try and pull me away from you." Mora's soft smile was a mixture of joy and grief that threatened to crush him. "I'd forgotten what it was like, to love and be loved. To feel safe with someone. All I've had are shreds of haunted memories. But, since I've left Eden, I've thought of you with every breath, saw your face every time I've closed my eyes, felt the echo of your touch on my skin. You've embedded yourself in my soul, and I do not wish for you to leave. You make me want to *live,* for the first time in centuries. I know little of mates or Arcadian traditions, but even if the Mother hadn't tethered our souls together, I'd still ask that you be mine."

Tears gathered on her lashes as she leaned her brow against his and closed her eyes.

"Don't cry," Zadriel said gently, before nuzzling her nose. That soothing, warm feeling expanded in his ribcage and he could hardly believe this was real. Yet there she was, gracing him with her heart. Something he knew didn't come easy. For either of them. Though he'd gladly hand her his on an iron platter if it pleased her. "I vow to be yours for as long as you'll have me."

Mora's eyes flew open as he pledged himself to her. "Of course I'll have you," she breathed.

A sweet, floral aroma curled in the air and gilded daisies sprouted along the walls, cushioned by an array of golden leaves. They curled around the window frame and dangled from the ceiling. And, for a moment, hints of gold pulsed along the veins in Mora's arms.

Within a heartbeat, they collided. Zadriel hauled her against him and Mora wrapped her legs around his waist. He sucked on her decadent bottom lip before trailing kisses along her jaw.

"I vow to be yours," Mora said as she ran her fingers through his hair. The words were like a prayer.

A warm shiver ran up Zadriel's spine, the pleasant feeling curling around his bones. He purred against her throat, nipping her skin until he was sure it bruised. The temptation to sink his teeth in and mark her was nearly too much to deny, but he needed her to say yes first. They'd discuss it later.

He forced himself to pull away and trailed his tongue up to her ear before nibbling on her lobe. "You vowed yourself to me, but can I have all of you?" His eyes strayed to her swollen lips, eagerly watching for the answer.

Mora's desire coursed through him, tangling with his own. The call of her emotions was much stronger than before, when their bond was weak and unwanted, and all they felt was animosity. The blood he'd given her under the oak tree helped things along. One day, when they marked one another, he'd get more than flashes of feelings. The thread connecting their souls would solidify into something they could always feel. Always follow. And she'd become his beacon.

"Are you well enough?" she asked, her voice a breathy whisper.

Zadriel thanked the gods he was well, because denying her—denying himself—was a pain he couldn't bear. "Thanks to you, I'm better than I've been in centuries." She leaned into his touch when he ran his thumb over her plump lower lip. Already so responsive. Gods, he wanted her. Needed her. "Can I have you? I want to hear you say yes."

"Yes, Zadriel. Please," Mora murmured before pressing her lips to his.

Her plea was his undoing.

Without warning, Zadriel flipped Mora onto her back. Mora giggled as she bounced on the mattress, her dark hair fanning around her like a halo—she looked like a goddess and Zadriel would gladly worship at her altar.

Zadriel ran his tongue along the seam of her lips until she opened for him. His hard length pressed painfully against his breeches—he ached to claim her—but he planned to take his time. To savor every moment.

Slipping his hand up her bare thigh, he paused when he met the soft, generous curve of her rear. Mother Divine, she was perfect. He squeezed, pulling her more firmly against him as he ground his length into her heat. A pleased growl rumbled in his chest when Mora automatically curled her legs around him. He needed to get her out of his damned tunic.

Trailing his fingers along the edge of her undergarments, he followed the seam toward her core. Mora squirmed under his touch, her nails digging into his back as he edged his way closer. For the first time in his long life he found himself wishing for scars—those were marks he'd wear proudly.

When he reached her center, he found her already soaking. Zadriel groaned. Cursed his trousers and their now too tight laces. "Have I told you how perfect you are, Little Witch?" he asked, as he ran a finger up her wet slit. The most adorable, little moan slipped through her lips when he circled that sensitive bundle of nerves between her thighs.

"I'd be happy to hear you tell me again," she breathed, her cheeks beautifully flushed.

Mora pouted when he removed his hand, and Zadriel chuckled. "Patience, love." Sucking on his fingers, he couldn't help but groan again at her perfect taste. Gods, he needed her now. He contemplated tearing her undergarments off. But part of him wanted to make her squirm first.

His Little Witch had no interest in taking things slowly. A cloud of soft, onyx smoke enveloped them, the cool mist soothing his heated skin. He felt the fabric beneath his fingers dissipate, followed by his tunic. His incredulous laugh was hardly arousing, but he couldn't help it. Mora was adorably unbelievable.

Her magic hesitated around his waist, coils of midnight slipping around his breeches.

"May I?" she asked.

"You can take anything you want from me."

The material expanded as her smoke weaved into the fabric itself, pulling it apart thread by thread. In mere seconds, his pants were gone, and they were both perfectly, gloriously naked.

Zadriel smiled as he laughed, the sound light and full of joy. Joy he couldn't remember feeling in ages. It was overwhelming. But he'd gladly drown in the feeling.

He pressed a kiss to her lips and murmured, "That was quite the trick, Little Witch."

"I have many," she said sweetly.

"I plan to discover every last one."

Though first he wanted to discover *her*.

Zadriel's gaze trailed over every inch of her exposed skin as he lifted up on his knees. Warm rays of sun trickled through the window and danced on her body, adding a golden glow to her brown skin. Lust and adoration filled her glowing amber eyes and he could hardly catch his breath.

Mora nibbled on her lush bottom lip and he found himself envious. Eager to sink his own teeth into it. Though he was also tempted to give her full breasts his attention—Zadriel dragged a thumb over one of her nipples, the skin a richer, darker brown, and licked his lips as it hardened under his touch.

"Gods, you're beautiful," he said before running his tongue along the same path his thumb had taken, then nipping the sensitive flesh. She gasped as he moved to her other breast, the sound music to his ears.

Mora whimpered as his lips trailed down the curve of her breast to her ribs. "I could say the same of you," she said as she ran her fingers through his hair.

Zadriel grinned against her soft stomach before kissing along the dip of her belly button, intent on making his way to the delicious, wet heat begging for his attention. He offered each of her thighs a gentle kiss before throwing her left leg over his shoulder, spreading her wide.

For a moment, he simply admired the sight of her, soaked and ready for him. Her scent was intoxicating, and he inhaled it greedily, the satisfied rumble in his throat purely Fae. It pleased him greatly when she shuddered in response. She was his. His to touch. His to lick. His to fuck. His to love. And he was wholly hers in return.

The first slow drag of his tongue through her exquisite wetness elicited the most delicious moan. "Oh gods, Zadriel." His name on her lips was a breathy plea and a demand. One he was happy to fulfill.

She jerked beneath him, but he placed a hand against her abdomen to steady her. Gods indeed. Tonight he intended to be her god. To answer her every prayer. Mora's sharp, sweet taste exploded on his tongue and he knew he could easily feast on her all day if she'd allow it.

Zadriel unleashed himself. He plunged his tongue into her opening and nuzzled that sensitive bundle of nerves. Mora bucked, moaned, begged, all the while squirming against his mouth. She grinded against his tongue as she pulled harder on his hair and he loved the sweet sting. Felt tempted to grow it longer so she could tug harder in the future.

Dragging his tongue up, he sucked on her sensitive nub while thrusting two fingers into her center, curling them against a spot he knew would make her see stars.

"Fuck, Zadriel, please," Mora cried, her breathing quickening. "Please, gods, don't stop."

That's it, Little Witch. Lose yourself in me.

The sting in his scalp lessened when one of her hands wandered to the sheets, clutching them tightly as she writhed. He continued to swirl his tongue and added a third finger, working her higher and higher.

It didn't take long for the symphony of her pleasure to reach a crescendo, a beautiful blend of pants, moans and sighs. Her back arched, body tensing and thighs trembling as she succumbed to the building pressure. Zadriel released her stomach, spreading her open wider with his thumbs as he feasted.

"You taste like paradise," he groaned against her thigh, not lifting his head when she sagged against the mattress. His Little Witch was a panting mess, but he knew she could give him more.

CHAPTER 61

MORA

"Ah, Zadriel, *I can't*," Mora panted as a delectable pressure rose up inside her once more.

The male was ravenous, pushing her into frenzy after frenzy with his skilled tongue. It was as if he could never get enough. Like he'd been starved and she was all the sustenance he needed. Mora felt like she was losing her damn mind as her body tensed once again, though she'd gladly go mad if it meant being worshiped like this.

When he pulled away, Mora sagged against the mattress, drowning in the oddest feeling of relief and disappointment.

"You, my beautiful mate, can give me one more," he breathed before grazing his teeth over her taut bud. Then he closed his mouth around it and sucked.

"Oh gods, oh gods, *oh gods*," Mora cried, loud enough she imagined all of Arcadia heard. Her back bowed off the bed, nonsensical sounds spilling from her lips as pleasure like she'd never imagined erupted within her. It felt as if it would go on forever. Mora clamped her eyes shut and saw stars, a constellation of ecstasy that reminded her of Zadriel's eyes.

The sheets were a mess, half torn from the bed, and Mora could hardly catch her breath—she was enraptured by bliss. Unsure if she'd ever come back down.

Then the bed shifted as Zadriel crawled over her and she practically leapt to meet him, eager for his lips to be on hers. She tasted herself on his tongue and some feral part of her soul purred. It fed the warm feeling thrumming with her heart. She needed him. To be surrounded by him. Full of him. Consumed by him.

Zadriel's hard length prodded at her slick entrance, slipping against sensitive flesh, and she couldn't wait a moment longer. His heat sliding through her made her jolt—gods, he'd made a mess of her. And it seemed he wasn't done—Zadriel teased her, coating himself in her slick as she shuddered beneath him.

Mora dug her nails into his shoulders and whimpered.

Zadriel chuckled. "Do you want my cock, Little Witch?"

"Please," she gasped, rubbing herself against him. How was he so patient?

Mora squeezed his firm biceps, admiring the way they flexed under her grip, and readied herself. But Zadriel hesitated, a playful, crooked grin on his face.

"Such lovely manners." He nipped her bottom lip. "I like having you at my mercy."

Mora pouted. "Please," she breathed again.

Zadriel kissed along her jaw until he reached her throat. Those sharp teeth grazed her skin, sending exquisite shivers down her spine.

"Beg me again," he whispered, shifting his hips and sliding over her sensitive folds. "I like hearing it."

Gods damn him.

Mora wrapped her legs around his waist in a fruitless attempt to pull him into her. But he clicked his tongue and stilled. Zadriel was too strong. Even his perfect ass was sculpted, like some heavenly being plucked Mora's fantasies from her mind and carved Zadriel out of marble just for her. Which, frankly, was the least they owed her for the last three centuries. If only he'd give in and fuck her.

Mora hissed when he made a shallow thrust, barely entering her before pulling back.

"Do you intend to drive me mad?" she asked, as she ran her hands over his broad shoulders and down his lean back. He felt so warm against her cool palms.

Zadriel huffed out an amused breath and ran his nose along hers. "Only with need."

His grin faltered when Mora narrowed her eyes.

Before he could blink, cool wisps of glittering black smoke curled around his abdomen and tossed him onto his back.

Zadriel sat up, chuckling as he attempted to scramble toward her, but Mora's power forced him back onto the mattress. When his head hit the pillow, wisps of smoke crawled down his biceps. They wrapped around his wrists and Zadriel's eyes darkened. He ran his tongue over his teeth while his arms were pulled above his head, secured to the bedposts by glittering obsidian.

Mora clicked her tongue as she straddled him. "Who's at whose mercy?" Her fingers trailed over Andras's pendant—it seemed to be working, her mate clearly *very* comfortable. She wondered what she could do to help him if she had more of Andras's blood—a wondering she filed away for later.

Mora grabbed the hemp tethering it to his neck and tugged, forcing him to lift his head. The want in those obsidian eyes did things to her, and she was aching to feel him, but first...

"Do you want me?"

"Yes," he breathed, his breath tickling her lips.

"Then say *please.*"

"Please," he begged, his cheeks flushed, inky black hair perfectly mussed. He looked beautiful like this. Happy, passionate, wanting. In love. A part of himself few, if any, experienced.

Perhaps this was what it meant to be mates. To share a boundless sense of joy. One that could never be found elsewhere. Never be understood by another.

Mora couldn't wait another moment. Lowering herself onto him, she sighed as his every glorious inch filled her in a way she'd never experienced. Dear gods, nothing felt like this before. Her body stretched perfectly around him, thanks to Zadriel's earlier attention. Then he bucked his hips, forcing himself impossibly deeper, and a needy moan spilled from Mora's throat—even tied up, he couldn't be controlled.

"Fuck," Zadriel panted, and Mora found herself staring at those sharp canines. She wanted them back against her throat. Needed them to draw blood. It was the strangest feeling, but the thought alone was enough to make her whimper and roll her hips faster.

Those long fingers flexed as Zadriel tugged at his ethereal bindings—he was dying to touch her. And Mora wanted it. Needed those hands sliding over every inch of her body. But she'd keep him at her mercy a little longer.

Mora spread her legs wider, giving him a better view of how he filled her so perfectly. Then she swirled her fingers where he'd once swirled his tongue. "Gods," she hissed. The sensation was intense as she rode him. Mora felt herself rising toward another peak, her body growing taut. She threw her head back, her long curls tickling her sensitive skin as her moans grew louder.

"I love the way you sing for me, Little Witch." Zadriel's deep voice was thick with want and it broke her resolve.

Onyx wisps tore away from the bedpost and slid over Zadriel's body, caressing his sweat slicked skin. He rose immediately, his hands curling around her thighs and guiding her legs to wrap around his lower back. He was much deeper like this. Filling her so deliciously her toes curled.

The tension in Mora's core tightened. "Zadriel," she whined, her back bowing.

He clutched her waist in a bruising grip and guided her movements, bringing her down on him harder.

"That's it, Mora, take what you need," he growled.

Zadriel's low voice was like honey, the perfect contrast to his rough touch. She buried her head in the crook of his neck, getting drunk off his minty scent, and quickened her movements. The scrape of her teeth over his skin made him shiver and his grip on her tightened. Somehow he grew harder. Dear gods. Mora nipped at his skin, reveling in the sounds of his pleasure.

"You feel so fucking good," he gritted out. His hands slid to her rear, squeezing the flesh in his palms as he guided her up and down his thick length. "Come for me, just like this. I want to watch you fall apart while you ride me."

Mora was right on the edge, her inner muscles clenching around him. And the way he groaned in her ear... she loved that low rumble. It made her impossibly wetter.

It felt like she was being consumed by him. Like drowning in a state of euphoria. It coated her skin, filled her lungs and swam through her veins. Those lust filled midnight eyes watched her and Mora had never felt so safe, wanted, and cherished.

Zadriel met her thrusts, his slick chest sliding against hers as the sound of their bodies coming together created the filthiest symphony. Yet she wanted him closer. Her smoke shuddered as it trailed up his corded back and pulled him further into her embrace. Mora wrapped her arms around his neck and threaded her fingers through his hair.

She kissed him desperately. "I love you," she whispered against his lips. Zadriel hummed in response, the satisfied sound curling in Mora's ears like beautiful music.

A cool wisp of smoke slid between them, gliding over Zadriel's muscled abs until it settled between her thighs. It curled, circling the sensitive bundle of nerves she'd abandoned, and Mora jolted, bucking wildly in Zadriel's lap. The cold touch felt too good. Yet she hadn't told it to do that...

"Holy gods!" she cried, squeezing her eyes shut. She was so fucking close.

"Give me those beautiful eyes." Zadriel's voice was rough, the demanding words spilling out through panted breaths as he chased his own euphoria.

When Mora didn't listen, he ran a hand up her back, collecting her hair and wrapping it around his fist. He tugged just hard enough to pull her neck back, so she stared up at him. His glittering onyx eyes glowed brighter than she'd ever seen as he watched her—it was like staring into the night sky.

"There you are." He traced her lips with his tongue. "Come for me, Little Witch."

Her smoke combined with his powerful thrusts pushed Mora over the edge. "*Zadriel!*" Her entire body went taut as insurmountable pleasure built in her core. Then it unraveled and Mora fell into ecstasy. She wasn't aware of the noises she made, or the way she ran her nails down Zadriel's back.

His lips crashed into hers and the room spun. Mora landed on the rumpled green sheets with Zadriel on top of her, the male completely undone. He chased his own pleasure, groaning between ravenous kisses. When his lips trailed to her throat, Mora cried out, the pressure inside of her twisting and coiling once more.

"Please, please, *please*. I... I need..."

Those sharp teeth clamped down in a bruising bite, the delicious pinch not quite what she needed—what she couldn't believe she needed—but it was enough. He growled as he bit her, his thrusts quickening, and Mora screamed his name. Her core spasmed around him again, and she dug her nails so deeply into his back she was sure he bled. But Mora couldn't stop herself as the tension within her exploded. Zadriel joined her, groaning against her throat. His thrusts became ragged before he planted himself deep and stilled, flooding her with warmth.

It felt as if their shared pleasure danced in her chest. Mora could hardly understand it. As she lay beneath him, marveling in the tandem beats of their hearts, she couldn't untangle her bliss from his own. His adoration wrapped around her until it tumbled beneath her skin to twirl with her smoke. This was home. *He* was home.

When he released her neck, they stared at one another, sharing their breaths. Zadriel's midnight eyes sparkled, like pools of starlight she would gladly lose herself in.

"I love you," he whispered. And the words made her soul sing.

CHAPTER 62

MORA

Golden petals fluttered as they fell from the ceiling like glittering drops of rain. They tickled Mora's bare skin and glinted in Zadriel's inky black hair, like a gilded flower crown. Mora smiled softly. She'd love to see pixies make him one someday.

The flowers wilted while their stems slowly disappeared into the treehouse's walls. They'd bloomed when Zadriel vowed himself to her, the same flowers that filled the crater in the forest, that calmed Thalias when he'd lost his mind... that grew in the presence of her blood. It had to be related to her curse. But *he* was the last person Mora wanted to think about. This moment was too precious to sully.

A petal landed on Zadriel's cheek, the gold sparkling against his light, olive tan, and Mora brushed it away. She held her breath when his lashes fluttered, but he didn't stir. Zadriel slept with Mora draped over his chest, wrapped in his warm embrace, yet she couldn't convince herself to join him and rest. She was busy marveling at his perfect face. Replaying the hours they'd been consumed by an overwhelming need for one another.

It had been a frenzy—she was almost surprised he'd given her the opportunity to rest. Whenever she caught her breath Zadriel needed to steal it once again. Wild fucking turned to slow, passionate lovemaking, sweet murmurs, giggles, and declarations of forever. Memories she'd always cherish.

Mora rested her head on Zadriel's chest and listened to the steady beat of his heart. What did he see in his dreams? Were they peaceful? Did they mirror the ones she had while they were apart?

Apart.

Mora cringed.

How long until they were forced apart again?

Melancholy flooded her mind. *You ruined the moment, Mora*, she thought with a sigh.

You've ruined everything.

Of course Lillian's ghost decided to haunt her now. Mora closed her eyes and willed the echoes of her shame to go away, at least for a few more hours. She snuggled closer to Zadriel, breathing in his comforting scent while she memorized the warm feeling of his skin against hers. The slow, rhythmic sounds of his breathing. The weight of his arms curled around her back. May this memory haunt her instead. May she never stray from him for long.

An idea formed in her mind. A flicker of hope. A dream. One Zadriel wouldn't like... but Mora needed to convince him.

Zadriel's long legs shifted as he stirred. He pulled her closer and placed a soft kiss on her crown. "I could get used to waking like this."

So could she.

Two streams of blood danced inside Andras's pendant, but it would inevitably come to an end. And if Mora didn't find a way out in time, Zadriel would go back. Or suffer endlessly. She couldn't allow either.

Her palm pressed against his new scars as she lifted herself up to look at him, and Zadriel flinched.

Fuck.

Fury threatened to consume her. Mora's power rumbled in her chest, the monstrous smoke begging to be set loose, and her heart thundered along with it.

One day, I'll make Andras pay.

Zadriel's dark eyes watched her knowingly. Those perfect lips dipped into a frown and he asked, "What are we going to do?"

His fear coated her throat, so potent it almost felt like her own. Mora swallowed past it. "You won't be going back to him." It was a promise. Foolish, perhaps. But she intended to keep it.

Zadriel's fingers threaded with hers and he absentmindedly traced his scars, his gaze growing distant. "I have no choice, Little Witch. Once the enchantment on this pendant expires, I'll either return to his side or lose myself to the pain."

Mora wriggled in his grip until they were face to face, her amber eyes ablaze. "I'll find a way."

"I'm sure you'll try," Zadriel said with a sad smile.

He squeezed her hand and Mora thought of the Galadriah. *Take his hand and end his torment.* Whatever the hell that meant. Gods damned creature and her riddles. Though Mora was certain she spoke of Zadriel—there had to be a way.

"Will you go back?" Zadriel's jaw tensed as he waited for the answer he already knew.

Mora stared through the cracks in the ivy curtain to the forest outside. The sun had long since fallen from the sky, leaving Arcadia in a misty evening haze. Wherever the Spirit lingered, it didn't feel far. And once she found it...

Mora swallowed. "I have to."

"We can hide your flask and go back together."

"No. You won't be going back, Zadriel. I'll find a way."

Zadriel graced her with a soft kiss that ended far too quickly. "If we can save me, we can save you too, Little Witch. We'll find our way through this together." He dragged his free hand up her back until he found the bruise he'd made on her throat. When he brushed his thumb over it Mora shivered and a comforting warmth pulsed in her chest. "We need to talk about this."

"Hmm?" Mora barely heard him. She was too busy leaning into his touch and enjoying the feeling, her anxiety melting away.

"Remember when I gave you my blood?"

"How could I forget?" she mumbled, memories of the sweet, coppery taste dancing on her tongue.

"And how I said it wasn't *that* kind of blood magic?"

Mora's brows furrowed. "Yes..."

"It's a type of blood magic. The first kind. Something sacred among Arcadians." Zadriel took a breath, those endless eyes boring into Mora's soul. A wistfulness laced his tone, nearly breaking her heart. "Before the Exodus, the only blood magic that existed was between mates. Among other things, it's a way to deepen what's already there."

"I don't understand?" Mora's stomach dropped. She was certain of her feelings. Made vows knowing—loving—that it was her choice. Was she a fool?

Zadriel kept moving his thumb over her throat, his soft touch a comfort despite Mora's racing thoughts. "Think of your blood as a well of power, one that carries the essence of who you are. Your magic, your lifeforce, your heart's desires. Your mate won't have access to that well if you don't wish to share it." Zadriel moved their clasped hands over his heart, sighing happily as her warm fingers settled above it. "You may feel a warm sort of comfort whenever they're near, and if their emotions are strong enough, they may affect you. But until you exchange blood, the bond isn't complete."

"You tricked me into completing the bond?"

Zadriel laughed through his nose. "I told you you'd regret tasting my blood back at the manor, didn't I?"

Mora scowled. Before she could retort, Zadriel continued.

"You have every right to be angry with me, Little Witch. If it helps, I tricked you into strengthening our bond, not completing it. I needed to heal you, and the only way I could was by letting you dip into my well so I could share my lifeforce. But I didn't want to burden you with what we are. It wasn't the right time." Zadriel sighed and rubbed his thumb over the bruise once more. "Fae tend to mark our mates here when we take that step. And intentions matter. You would be aware and accepting, and you'd have to mark me too. This sort of blood magic is often carnal and passionate and would leave a scar. One that would never fade and can't be affected by other magic."

The tension knotting her shoulders released its hold, and the chattering in her mind slowed. Mora took a breath. Was she angry?

Should she be? Zadriel warned her about their connection strengthening before giving her his blood. Though he kept the depth of their connection a secret.

Mora thought of the marks Thalias and Vesryn bore on their throats, and the bruise on her own that refused to fade when she dissipated into smoke. This would be something no one, not even her curse—not even Dother—could take away from her.

Already, she vowed to be his. And yet... There was something about this that made her throat tighten and her eyes sting. Gods, she didn't want to cry. For the first time in ages, Mora felt a flicker of who she once was, the young woman who dreamed of the freedom to choose love over everything life expected of her. Perhaps her soul always knew Zadriel was out there waiting.

Mora released a shuddering breath. "What happens after that?"

Zadriel wiped away a tear with his thumb and kissed the tip of her nose. "In some ways, we'd become extensions of one another. You'd feel me in your chest as steadily as the air in your lungs and the thrum of your heart. You'd know my emotions. Feel the space between us like a thread that could lead you home to my arms. With a simple thought, you could speak to me, mind to mind. Unless we were separated by too great a distance."

"You might not like knowing my feelings."

"I'm sure I could handle them." The smile died on his face and Zadriel's voice became grim. "It may help us with Andras. He knows, by the way. I lost myself when Halvard took you and..." Zadriel looked down at his chest and grimaced. "Andras wasn't happy."

When Mora sat up, golden petals tumbled from her curls and landed on the rumpled green sheets. As she stared at them now, all she saw was the filigree decorating her flask, as if reminders of her curse laid all around her, souring the sliver of peace she'd found.

"Fuck Andras," she hissed.

"He'll never stop, Mora. As long as he breathes, there will be no peace for us."

I can fix that. Mora smiled. It was beautifully monstrous and Zadriel didn't need to hear her to know what she thought.

"He'll never stop until what? He becomes Dother?" she asked, flicking a petal off her arm.

"Andras hopes to surpass him. To fulfill a destiny Cillian's father imagined for their bloodline." Zadriel ran a hand through his hair and more petals scattered against the pillows. "They intend to create a Berwick where Halflings rule with a Dother as their King. Cillian came close. They've spent centuries trying to get back what they lost. Andras has read Cillian's journal his whole life, preparing for the day he'd find you and get what he needs to take the throne."

Azure eyes flashed in her mind. *Be my queen and this ends now.*

No. No, no, no, no.

The sheets turned black, and the walls pressed against Mora's skin. She couldn't breathe. Every gasp for air left her choking on citrus.

He's dead, he's dead, he's dead.

Mint and summer rain curled around her and the bed shifted. Zadriel scooped her into his arms and Mora didn't balk—she clung to his shoulders while he tore her from the hell in her mind.

"You're safe. It's ok," he whispered, rocking them back and forth. "We don't need to talk about it."

"Yes, we do," she said quietly, burying her head in the crook of Zadriel's shoulder. "Can you stop calling him... by his first name."

Each quick breath filled her lungs with Zadriel's scent. It helped. Mora melted into him, allowing the safety of his hold to ground her.

"Of course," he said as he rested his cheek on her head. "Whatever you need."

"He wanted me to give him everything, and when I wouldn't, he took it. He took..." Mora's voice broke, and she choked on a sob. "He took so much, Zadriel. But he could never get me to give in. I wouldn't even give him his name. And I never will."

"And now neither will I." Zadriel held her tighter and kissed her crown.

"Want to know the worst part?"

"I'll hear whatever you wish to share, Little Witch."

Mora closed her eyes and took a calming breath. Zadriel's hand cradling the back of her head was the comfort she needed to go on. "I became a monster, like he said I would. It was the only way to survive him. To survive all of this. I have some regrets, but the blood staining my hands is rarely a burden. And I sometimes wonder if that means he won." It was a truth she rarely allowed herself to think, better yet, say out loud.

Zadriel surprised her when he asked, "Did he suffer when you ended him?" The wild edge in his low, rumbling voice told her he'd resurrect the man if he could and cause him endless agony.

Mora smiled. She could still remember how Dother's warm blood coated her skin, enveloping her in an armor promising pain to any who touched her again. "Yes."

"Then he didn't win, Little Witch, I promise you that."

Mora shifted in his hold so she could watch his face. "Is he the reason Thalias hates you?"

WISH

A muscle feathered in Zadriel's cheek as he clenched his jaw and Mora hated herself for forcing him to face his shame. Yet it couldn't be helped—they both needed to face their demons if they intended to find a way through this. They watched each other for a moment before Zadriel sighed and wiped away the tears staining her cheeks. His gentle touch so at odds with the simmering mixture of devastation and fury churning in his dark gaze.

"Thalias has every right to hate me. They all do. You might not be fond of me either once you know."

Mora turned so she could kiss his palm. Her lips found one of the few scars peppering the skin there and another piece of her heart broke. "You didn't have a choice, love."

"The funny thing is you already saw what I did."

"What?"

Zadriel curled his arm around her back, holding her to him as he reached for her flask. The glass scraped against the wood when he pulled it off the bedside table and Mora smiled softly, thinking of her mother—she was always so precious about furniture. Gods, she wished things turned out differently.

"When Andras made his wish, you said you watched a great tree burn." Zadriel laid the flask on the bed, cushioning in a pile of gilded petals. Shame flooded his face as he ran a finger over the filigree. "That's what Dother made me do."

"You killed the Mother Tree?"

Zadriel's breath hitched. "I'm a loyal dog, remember?"

Power rumbled under Mora's skin at the reminder of Zadriel's torture, bits of smoke seeping through her pores. "Andras doesn't get to decide who you are, Zadriel. None of them do."

"Since I was eight, Little Witch, I've learned to comply or suffer. I wish I had half your will, but I became obedient. It was the only way *I* could survive." His deep voice wavered and Mora reached for his hand, threading their fingers together. The cool smoke curling in her palm brushed over his warm skin in comforting circles. "When Brennan pushed Dother to move forward with their plans, I told myself it wasn't what Dother wanted. That he did this to please his father."

Zadriel took a deep breath through his nose. "They couldn't do it without me. I often wonder if that's why they took me in the first place. Dother knew how I felt about betraying my people, so he promised to set me free once he was done in Moldenna. And he swore the shadow sprite's cloak prevented anyone from knowing it was me. I had no reason to doubt him.

When we returned, I was a mess. I didn't eat for days. Dother could barely convince me to leave the shade of my oak tree. I knew what I did to my people. Though I never imagined the pain I'd cause you."

Mora's smoke stilled. "What do you mean?"

A tear spilled down Zadriel's cheek. "I stole the Mother Tree's sap. I plucked Her leaves, tore Her branches and cut out Her heart. I ripped Her daisies from the earth and helped Dother set Her aflame so no one else could bond with Arcadia." Zadriel picked up the flask with his free hand and held it between them, staring at the golden filigree. "Everything he used to curse you, I gave him."

An ache thrummed in Mora's chest and she couldn't be sure if it was his or her own. But she felt sick. "Did you know what he planned to do to me?"

"No. Dother intended to use what we stole to empower himself." His upper lip curled, and he tossed the flask back on the bed. "Everything changed when he met you."

I didn't know these would be yours when I took them.

Mora shook her head, cringing at the memory of Dother's voice, until a deeper, smoother voice swept through and pushed it away. *You don't deserve these.*

"That's why you were so angry when you held my flask," she whispered, more to herself.

Zadriel swept a stray curl away from her forehead. "I was angry with myself, Little Witch. And furious I had to retrieve you. I wanted nothing to do with a mate I couldn't have and the woman who killed what I believed was my only chance at freedom. And then you called me Keeper..." Zadriel shook his head. "I'm so sorry."

Mora smirked and her smoke curled around his wrist. "I'm sure you can convince me to forgive you."

Zadriel pressed his brow against hers and closed his eyes, "I'm willing to grovel."

"I doubt Thalias will be happy when he learns the Mother Tree was used to curse me. I wonder if he already knows?"

A growl rumbled in Zadriel's throat. "He certainly wanted your flask."

"I need to make sure he doesn't get it. That no one gets their hands on it again."

"What can I do to help?"

Mora took a deep breath and met his gaze, her smoke churning around his wrist. She desperately needed him to agree. It was the only way she could use her powers freely without fear of losing her flask. And the one thing keeping them together. "I need you to keep it."

"What?" Zadriel's glittering midnight eyes flared, and the blood drained from his face. He gripped her hand tighter. "Mora, I can't. Andras will take it from me. Even when I refuse, he'll use blood magic to force my hand."

"You aren't going back to him, love." Mora reached for her flask, disturbing its bed of gilded petals—why did they grow for her? She intended to bombard Zadriel with questions later. "I can barely function with it on me. And I can't have it end up in the wrong hands." She pressed the flask to Zadriel's chest, ready to beg if that's what it took. "You are the *only* one I trust, Zadriel. The only one who makes me feel safe. *Please*."

Mora nearly sagged when Zadriel's fingers curled around the bottle, but he made no move to take it from her. "What if—"

Pressing her fingers to his soft lips, Mora shushed him before he finished his thought. "Andras will *never* touch you again."

Zadriel's throat bobbed, but he took the flask and nodded before placing it back on the bed. "I love you," he breathed, pressing a soft kiss on her lips. It was a slow, gentle kiss full of fear and yearning.

Mora expected him to pull her closer. Kiss her harder. But when he pulled away, there was a cautious look in his eyes. One that had her holding her breath.

"There's something else you should know."

"What?" she asked, doing her best to ignore the dread sinking its teeth into her heart.

Zadriel's grip on her tightened, but before he could speak, someone banged on the front door.

"Come out, Wraith. We need to talk."

CHAPTER 63

MORA
300 YEARS AGO

A ngry voices spilled through the windows, the symphony of bitterness pressing uncomfortably in Mora's ears. It had been this way for ages. When she peeked outside, she caught glimpses of the horde—a siege of furious villagers bolstered by noblemen who stoked their prejudice and fear. Though the nobles' real interest lay in regaining their Indentured.

Regardless, they all wanted Dother's head.

The man paced his bedroom, muttering to himself while Mora watched from her perch at the end of his bed. She smoothed her velvet skirt, admiring the soft, navy fabric. It was a simple dress. One she chose because of its long sleeves and high neckline. The weight soothed the tightness in her chest. Though the leather pouch Dother forced her to wear was a horrific reminder of how naïve she'd once been. Even when he allowed her to dress, the bastard needed to have a piece of himself clinging to her.

Mora's fingers curled into fists. Would there come a day when she'd be free of his suffocating presence?

"We're almost out of food," he said suddenly.

Mora blinked. Was he talking to her? She held his stare, stone-faced, daring him to say what he really wanted. Those blinding blue eyes made her stomach churn. But Mora grew better at hiding her discomfort. And things changed between them since she'd learned to twist wishes.

Pain and fear were powerful motivators. He'd taught her that. And she was glad to return the favor. Finding ways to burn him was her favorite method—from igniting his clothes, to boiling his bathwater—but simple tricks, like forcing him to kiss frogs or drink curdled milk, were also entertaining.

There were many nights Mora couldn't win. Horrific nights where his wishes were too cleverly worded and she had no choice but to endure. But the game changed. Dother could no longer predict how Mora would react, or what harm may come to him when he uttered the words I wish.

It made him hesitant. Afraid. And Mora fucking loved it.

Dother sighed and began pacing again, the soles of his brown leather shoes clacking against the dark tiles. The crowd beyond the castle walls grew louder, their words coalescing into a single, unintelligible voice filling the room and pounding in Mora's ears. As she cringed, Dother stopped in front of his writing desk and snatched up an empty sprite flask. He snarled as he threw it across the room. Glass crashed against the wall, raining on the bedside table and littering the floor.

Mora laughed. A cruel, amused snicker Dother grew accustomed to. "Did that make you feel better?"

He scowled and pushed messy tendrils of chocolate brown hair away from his forehead. "I need your help, Treasure," he said slowly.

"Make a wish then," she taunted.

Dother's eyes narrowed. "You have no desire to help your mother?"

Mora winced. It was one of the few strings Dother could pull. A final piece of her heart yet to shrivel into a festering, black husk. But Dother taught her the wrong lesson with Philip. Never again would she allow herself to hope for good intentions. Dother had none.

Mora schooled her features and examined her nails. "If you want my help, you'll need to wish for it." Her eyes flicked up to his, sparkling with amusement. "I'd recommend you hurry. Once you run out of food, you may find your guards aren't as loyal as you hoped."

Dother chewed on his left cheek. "Not long ago, you claimed you'd never be a monster."

Mora tensed. He was right. Every day another piece of who she was slipped away. She looked to the ornate mirror hanging above Dother's dresser, not recognizing the woman who stared back. Mora hadn't aged a day. Though there was an eerie glow in her eyes and a harshness to her features that hadn't been there before. This woman looked haunted. Dangerous. Monstrous.

The thing that scared her most was she liked it.

She crossed her arms. "I'm surprised you aren't happier you were right."

Dother came closer and Mora squeezed her arms tighter, begging her hands to stop trembling. Could he see it? Gods, she hoped he hadn't noticed.

He grabbed her chin, his ugly ring digging into Mora's flesh, and made her look up at him. "I'll force your hand if I must."

Mora smiled slowly. "Go on then."

"I wish..." Dother paused. His brows furrowed, and he released her before swearing under his breath. "You'll be the death of me, woman."

If only.

He swiped his journal off his desk and nearly tipped over the ink when he grabbed a quill. "Give me a moment," he muttered, before scribbling his wish on paper.

Dother wrote and rewrote the same demand, worded differently with each attempt. When he'd practically filled an entire page, he nodded to himself and cleared his throat, not lifting his blue eyes from the journal.

"I wish for you to find a way to restock our food stores without causing an unnecessary eruption of violence. You are to enter Moldenna, remain unseen, and return once you have enough food for everyone within these walls, guards included, for at least tonight. And you are to find a long-term solution to keep us fed while we wait this out. I expect you to behave."

His wish feasted on Mora's bones, but she didn't flinch. Instead she stood and offered Dother her most sinister smile. "Your wish is my command," she said, with a mocking bow, before she gave herself to the smoke.

A bitter frost painted the alley walls and a dense layer of fresh snow piled on the ground. It fell from the sky, thick snowflakes gathering in Mora's hair and sticking to her lashes. The chill sank through her dress and clung to her skin. Yet she withstood it, soaking in the frigid cold and watching her breath puff in the air.

Mora hadn't been outside since... before. Hadn't felt wind on her cheeks or smelled fresh air. She shivered as she stared at the dark sky. How much time had passed?

More than a year.

It was autumn when Dother tore her father down and plucked his crown from the ashes. Autumn when he married her mother. Autumn when he destroyed Mora's life.

Did you honestly believe I'd let you go, Treasure?

Mora shrieked at the memory and balled her fist, slamming it against the brick wall. A sharp pain shot through her hand, but she continued to scream and punched the rough surface until her knuckles were shredded and bleeding. Mora didn't stop until she was leaning against the wall, clutching her hand and gasping for breath.

"I made it so easy for him," *she whispered between clenched teeth. Blood dripped from her knuckles, the gold-streaked sanguineous drops staining the snow with her misery. Part of her wondered if she should care. If someone could use her blood against her.*

What more could they do to me? *Mora wondered with a shrug. Though she still kicked the snow, burying the mess.*

Something scratched her shoulder, and Mora stilled. Dother wished for her to remain unseen. Where was the warning someone approached? The bite of pain as magic squeezed her ribs? It tickled her skin again, and Mora spun on her feet. But it was simply the branches of a scraggly tree growing through cracks in the cobblestones. It clung to life, encased in a shimmering coat of ice. When it swayed toward her again, brushing against her face, Mora could have sworn it attempted to comfort her.

I've lost my mind.

Mora clenched her fists only to gasp. The skin on her knuckles split further, adding to the throbbing ache. "Enough of this," she muttered, tearing at the thread in her chest.

A torrent of glittering onyx splashed against the snow and slipped down the road. Mora knew—hated—where she was going. She didn't stop until she reached a building with gray stone walls she'd never forget.

The tavern. Where it all began.

There were too many ghosts here, eager to haunt her. Memories of Dother's glittering eyes and his amused smile when she told him her fake name—he knew exactly who she was, the bastard. And the revelry that descended into madness. Mora would have laughed if she could. A fist fight was hardly worth panicking over now.

As she passed the alley, Mora remembered the sharp blade dancing on her throat and the Fae who held it. Gods damn him. To this day, when she closed her eyes she could remember his intoxicating scent. Sometimes when Dother and his suffocating citrus became too much, she thought of mint and summer rain wrapped in delicious pine. It helped, and she hated it. Hated that she loved it. Hated the Fae for working with the man who destroyed her. Hated everything.

I'm glad he burned.

Mora seeped under the crack in the tavern door and rematerialized in a shadowy corner. The space was quiet. Empty. With tables pressed against the walls and stools resting on their surfaces. None of the candles were lit and the acrid scent of smoke hung in the air. As she made her way across the room, it all played out in her mind, a horrific scene in slow motion. The dashing rogue and the foolish princess who thought herself cunning. Calamity taking her into his arms with a charming smile. And she'd leaned willingly, gratefully into his touch. Until he'd consumed her whole and made her nothing more than a shadow in a flask.

His unwilling mistress.

His monster.

His.

And here she was, fulfilling his desire yet again. At least this one allowed for fresh air and fewer bruises...

Where there was a tavern, there was food, and she intended to steal any she could find. While the owners hadn't wronged her, she could think of no one better to target. It wasn't justice. But she'd met Dother here, and this felt akin to revenge. That was good enough for her.

Despite her detestation for this place, she recalled the savory scent of roasted herring permeating the air that night. Back then, Mora hadn't taken a single bite of the meats, cheeses, and breads they'd offered, and barely sipped on their bitter, golden ale. Now she'd scarf it all down and demand seconds. Dother rarely fed her unless it was part of his games. Dissipating into smoke cured her of her hunger, but she'd do anything for a delicious meal. Would kill for a handful of chocolates.

As Mora passed the bar and neared the alcove leading to the kitchen, the floorboards above her creaked and a door swung open.

"I don't care if there's been more drunken violence, Henry, we can't afford to keep the doors closed."

The second man, presumably Henry, walked over to the balcony overlooking the tavern. Mora crept closer to the kitchen, hoping they didn't come down.

"They nearly beat a man to death and lit a table on fire. We can't afford to watch this place burn to the ground. What would you have me do?"

"Kill the damn king so this madness will end," the first voice said calmly, joining his companion on the balcony.

Henry huffed out a humorless laugh. "I'd lose my head before I lifted a finger against him."

"Well, I pray someone gets their hands on him soon."

"It's been months, William. This won't end soon. Even if they remove him, what then? They don't want Queen Aedlin on the throne either." Henry sighed. "Things are going to get bloody. I think we should head to Eldenna."

William drummed his fingers on the old wooden handrail. "And what of this place? The life we've made here?"

"Look around you, lamb. Moldenna isn't safe. The guards have abandoned us in favor of protecting the castle."

Guilt bubbled in Mora's stomach. This no longer felt like vengeance for meeting Dother. It was simply another wrong in a list of too many wrongs. And now Mora was the monster prowling in the dark.

She forced herself forward, slipping into the kitchen. The smell of fresh bread and vinegar wafted in the air. An odd blend, yet Mora didn't hate it. And she hadn't been wrong—the tavern had a healthy stock of food.

Crooked shelves lined the back wall, each overstuffed with root vegetables piled high in bowls. How they held so much, Mora couldn't be sure. One shove and the shelving would topple. Beneath them, pickled eggs lined the worn counter, and a rather large, freshly plucked chicken sat on an old, cracked cutting board.

It wouldn't last Dother long, but this would do for now.

Mora plucked a jar from the counter, tilting it to and fro as she leaned against the wall. Off-white eggs bobbed in a yellowish brine. Hardly appetizing. But perhaps if she left a few behind, along with a handful of vegetables, those men would be ok?

Henry was right to abandon Berwick. If she could, Mora would run up those stairs and beg them to take her too. But it was pointless. Even if she could handle the suffocating grip of a wish unfulfilled, one touch, one whisper to that gods forsaken flask, and she'd be pulled back into Dother's vile arms.

The voices neared and Mora set the jar down before allowing herself to come undone, inky black smoke spilling from her pores. One sweep around the room and she'd disappear into the night, taking their food with her.

"I'm sorry," she said quietly, her body fading to mist.

As they neared, William asked, "Do you think they'll reinstate the Laws?"

"Depends," Henry said with a chuckle. "Will the next king wish to keep his head?"

"Har, har, very funny, lamb."

Henry's tone dipped low. "Of course they will. That's what this madness is about, isn't it? If the fire last night scared you, imagine having people who could burst into flames at will roaming around the city. My cousin in Reverie said a Halfling froze their neighbor solid when he caught him squatting in their chicken coup. People like that can't be left unattended."

The tension in Mora's heart eased. Halflings deserved a better world. While she hated to agree with Dother, it was wrong to imprison those who were born with magic. Her parents were right to force a change. Even if their reasons were selfish... and their actions not enough.

William was silent for a moment. "What of the king? Will they send him to a cloister? Or simply take his head?"

"Only the Gods know, Will. Either way, the sooner this ends, the sooner things can hopefully go back to normal."

Cruel amusement danced in Mora's chest as she twisted through the shadows and fled into the night.

Indeed.

Dother wanted a solution. And Mora found it hiding in the dark corners of the tavern where he'd first set his sights on conquering her.

CHAPTER 64

THALIAS

"I know you're there, Wraith." Thalias rapped his fist against the simple wooden door for the third time. Normally, he'd have Arcadia rip it open for him. But he knew She wouldn't listen.

A branch bent down and caressed Thalias's cheek, but he clenched his jaw and pulled away. It followed him, lingering by his side, as he leaned his head against the soft moss and lichen clinging to the doorframe like garland.

They won't come out, he thought to Vesryn.

"Patience," his mate said aloud. Vesryn sauntered up to him and wrapped his arms around his waist.

The soft linen of Vesryn's deep green cloak brushed against Thalias's arm. They left their leathers at home—Mora needed to know they'd come in peace.

Thalias closed his eyes and traced the grooves in the bark. Arcadia grew Mora and Zadriel a small cottage in a great oak and he wondered, "...Is this cottage like Vehsa's?"

"It is," Vesryn said. He brushed a soft kiss on the pointed tip of Thalias's ear. "Though the home she and Zadriel shared was bigger. And closer to the Mother Tree."

"I can't believe She's forgiven him." Thalias turned in Vesryn's embrace, searching for comfort in those moonlight eyes. "*I* can't forgive him," he said quietly.

Vesryn pulled him closer and trailed a finger up the silver markings swirling on Thalias's arm. A pleasant shiver followed his touch, all the way to the seam of Thalias's short, green sleeves. "There are many things we don't know, Sapling," Vesryn said softly. "I know that's hard for you to accept."

"I doubt Mora will accept things either," Thalias muttered.

"I'm sure we can make her understand." Elowyn emerged from the thicket of trees cradling the cottage, Alina trailing behind, careful not to step on the dryad's long hair.

In the distance, several other dryads peeked around the greenery, hidden in the evening shadows. Though they couldn't hide from Thalias. When he focused, he could feel them. Like he felt Arcadia, Her song swimming in his blood and flooding his mind.

The moment Thalias stepped away from Vesryn's embrace, dryads ducked back into their hiding places. Thalias smirked as they disappeared. He knew they were always watching—no matter where you were in Arcadia, a dryad wasn't far, though they rarely showed themselves. Only Elowyn braved those who wished to speak with her—the Mother made her more curious than her sisters. She'd been a friend to Thalias from the moment he was born. Though that didn't mean she listened well.

"What are you doing here?" Thalias demanded. "It's not safe for you to be near Mora... or me. Not until we figure this out."

Thalias's cheeks heated, staining his fair skin a humiliating shade of red. He and Mora made a mess of the Forest fighting over Zadriel, and her flask. Thank the Mother they hadn't destroyed the wrong tree and killed a dryad. He couldn't allow any harm to come to them. Especially Elowyn.

Thalias took a breath and moved closer to his friend. "I told you to stay away, Elowyn." His voice softened. "I need you to watch over the Aegist while Vesryn and I take care of things."

Thalias's heart raced and Arcadia responded. Roots pushed through the soil and curled around Elowyn's leg, tugging at her limb in a gentle attempt to lead her away. Those cinnamon eyes narrowed as she stared at the roots snaking over her flesh. For the first time, Elowyn bared her teeth at Thalias. "I'm meant to be here!"

"Elowyn, you saw what happened when Mora and I disagreed." He gestured toward the roots curling around her calf. "I can hardly control it now. You and your sisters need to distance yourselves."

When Elowyn curled her talons and flicked her hand the roots around her leg hesitated, but they didn't let go. Instead they seized, warring between her command and his.

"*You* need to remember why you're here," she hissed, the flowers in her hair unfurling.

Her words hit him like a blow, and Thalias prowled closer. "I have *never* forgotten my purpose."

Would he ever be enough? Did they not see how much he'd given Arcadia?

Vesryn stepped between them, his hand resting on Thalias's firm stomach. "That's not fair Elowyn," Vesryn said, his voice quiet and soothing, but with an edge of warning.

Elowyn blinked a few times before tilting her head to the side. "A lot of things aren't fair." Her voice wobbled, and she looked away, staring longingly into the brush. "Mother still sings to me. It's quiet, but we hear it, my sisters and me. You know I need to be here."

Vesryn's soothing voice flooded Thalias's mind. *I'll watch them.* He turned and cupped Thalias's cheek, a soft expression on his beautiful face.

Thalias threaded his fingers through Vesryn's and leaned into his warm touch. *Elowyn shouldn't risk herself. And you have enough to worry about, darling.*

If someone told you to stay behind, you'd follow along too.

Vesryn gave him a knowing look and Thalias grimaced. He was right. Nothing would have kept him away.

"What happened to your mother?" Alina asked, her quiet voice uncertain.

The Halfling brushed a hand against the bark on Elowyn's arm, and it was difficult for Thalias to hold back his sneer. He ground his teeth so hard his jaw ached. Perhaps it was a mistake, bringing the Halfling outside and leaving her with Elowyn. What if she tainted the Forest like her ancestors had? Would he regret his mercy?

The flowers in Elowyn's hair drooped, and the soft smile on her face held no joy. "She died."

Understanding flashed in Alina's eyes. "I'm sorry."

"Thank you, little Aegist." Elowyn ran her fingers through the Halfling's short, blonde curls, but her rough talons tore through tangles. Alina flinched. The dryad's face remained serene, oblivious.

"Mother's roots run deep. They hold my tree in Her embrace and I know She's still with us."

Thalias watched Alina's face. She nodded and smiled as she and Elowyn spoke. A tightness rose in his chest, drowning his fury. Thalias didn't like it. Hardly understood it. There should be no pity or concern for Halfling's in his heart—they took so much from Arcadia.

Flames licked up Mother Tree's flesh and Arcadia screamed. Screamed so loud Her people screamed with Her. Thalias roared louder than them all.

Thalias growled, the animalistic sound startling Alina and Elowyn. They backed away, blue magic sparking in Alina's trembling hands. Thalias ran his tongue over his sharp teeth and cocked his head to the side. *Try me Aegist.*

The wind picked up, and he clenched his eyes shut. Mother spare him. He was losing his mind. Vesryn reached out but Thalias shrugged him away. Tearing his dark green shirt free from his trousers, he wiped the sweat from his brow, wincing at the memory of burning flesh knitting together. Wildflowers grew in the wake of his steps as he rushed back to the door and smashed his fist on the wood. The sound was so loud Vesryn winced.

I'm fine, Thalias thought to his mate. Though he couldn't hide the bitterness from his tone.

It's ok if you're not, Sapling.

Warmth spread through Thalias's chest. He inhaled deeply, grateful for his mate's crisp autumn scent, caressed with hints of Thalias's spruce—that pleased him greatly.

I love you. Thalias smiled as he thought it. Felt Vesryn's adoration in return.

Mora and Zadriel's muffled voices reached the door and Thalias hit the wood again. "For the love of the Mother, will you *please* come?"

"Ask a little nicer and I'll consider it," Mora yelled from the other side.

As Thalias growled, a branch above groaned and the wind howled. He raked a hand through his white hair and gave Vesryn a pleading look.

"We've come in peace, Mora," Vesryn called through the door, his voice somehow loud and gentle. That was Vesryn's nature, as strong and patient as a towering oak. He pulled his hair back into a bun, securing his long braids with a loose leather band.

Thalias raised a brow. *Are we preparing for battle?*

I hope not, Vesryn responded, and Thalias felt his mate's pulse flutter.

Me neither.

Although... Thalias pursed his lips and looked to the Aegist, watching with Elowyn from the shadows. Perhaps peace wasn't the right way to motivate Mora.

Vesryn bit his lip. *You're up to something.*

Thalias snickered as he grinned. It was the crooked grin Vesryn loved, his dimple dancing on his left cheek. "What did you say would happen if I harm the girl, Wraith? I'll learn how wonderful it is to be in your company?"

Thalias stalked toward Alina. The wind followed him, twisting in his hair and rattling the trees as he passed. His starfire eyes glowed bright, a promise of mayhem in their depths.

Alina scurried away, hiding behind Elowyn's tall frame. "What do you want?" Blue light flickered and branches cracked beneath her feet with every clumsy step.

"Thalias?" Elowyn chirped. She closed the distance between them and rested a taloned hand on Thalias's chest. "What are you doing?"

"Motivating Mora to open the door." He peered around Elowyn at the Aegist's paling face.

The dryad's cinnamon eyes widened. "You wouldn't."

"I'll stop when she comes out."

Alina gulped and took another step back. "Whatever you're planning, please keep me out of it." A vine snaked around her ankle and the child shrieked, raising her hands. Sparks danced on her fingers and a dome of blue light surrounded her, but the earth writhed under her feet. And it listened to *him*.

"Mora won't come out for me," she pleaded, kicking at the plants slithering up her shoes.

"Oh, I think she will." The silver markings on Thalias's arms pulsed. But when he tried to step around Elowyn, she pushed against his chest.

"Leave her, Thalias."

The door smacked against the thick trunk of Mora and Zadriel's cottage and Thalias smiled triumphantly.

He winked at the Aegist, earning a scowl in return, and the plants released her. "I told you she—"

A ball of glittering onyx mist slammed into Thalias's side, its cold grip squeezing his ribs. Within a breath it lifted Thalias off the ground and sent him hurling through the air.

Mother damn me. Thalias should have been ready. His heart thundered as he stretched his fingers out, calling to the trees.

Branches snapped against his skin, leaving stinging cuts in their wake, until a nearby maple bent to catch him. But there wasn't enough time. Thalias slammed into the rough bark, air whooshing from his lungs. As he slid down the trunk, blood soaked the back of his tunic but at least the roots grabbed him and slowed his fall.

"Sapling!" Vesryn raced toward his mate. "Are you all right?" He knelt by his side, his gentle hands cupping his face.

Thalias nodded, despite the ache in his bones. He couldn't help but chuckle as he leaned against the maple tree. "Mora didn't lie," he said between gasps. "Her company is *wonderful*."

Vesryn shook his head, but the shadow of a smile crept up his face. Warmth followed his touch, slipping over Thalias's skin in a gentle caress. Vesryn's healing magic was soothing, and Thalias found himself closing his eyes and leaning into his mate's touch.

"Would you like some of my blood, Sapling?"

Thalias's eyes flared. "When we return home tonight, I want all of you."

Vesryn's lips found his, the kiss gentle and full of longing, but it was cut short when the damned Wraith cleared her throat.

"I'm here. What the hell do you want?" Mora seethed. An air of authority weaved through her low voice. It sounded more regal than the eldest among the Fae.

Thalias pushed his white hair away from his eyes and gave Vesryn one final peck on the lips before he looked to Mora. She tipped her chin up and curled her smoke covered fingers.

Mora may as well have been Arcadia's queen in her gown; a light green dress with a train trailing behind her. Gilded daisy petals decorated the bodice and the long, flowing sleeves. Zadriel walked out behind her and rested a hand on her shoulder. He looked well.

Unfortunately. Though he was barefoot and wore the same dark breeches from before, his tunic matched Mora, with gilded daisy petals along the collar.

Thalias suppressed his growl. Their mixed scents wafted in the air and his stomach churned. While they bore fresh bruises on their throats, the bond wasn't yet complete. *Thank the Mother.*

No fear or shame painted Zadriel's features. Instead, he watched Mora, his soft gaze glued to her face. *Her* rage, however, hit Thalias like another physical blow, rousing the beast in his chest, and he tensed, holding his furious magic at bay.

Mora crossed her arms. "I'm beginning to think you *want* me to hate you."

"I—" Something glinted on Zadriel's belt, and Thalias's red eyes flared, silver churning within the purple at their center. It was the flask, tethered in place by a strip of light green fabric. How dare he carry pieces of the Mother Tree? Zadriel had no right to touch *anything* that came from Her, Mora included.

Leaves rattled in the wind as Vesryn helped him stand. The Druid eyed the canopy, his dark brows furrowing, but Thalias squeezed his hand. It took a few calming breaths, but the winds died down.

"No, Wraith," Thalias said, careful with his tone. "I'm not here to fight."

Mora glanced sidelong at Zadriel and shifted so he was behind her. Her short stature did little to hide him—Zadriel towered over her.

Thalias lifted his hands. "We need to talk."

"And you threatened Alina to get me to come out?" Mora mocked. "I expected someone as ancient as you to have more patience."

Thalias chuckled. "I'm the youngest among us, if we don't take the Halfling into consideration."

"The Halfling I told you not to harm," Mora spat. Trickles of smoke fell from her hands and gathered at her feet.

Thalias hated to admit it, but Mora was his equal when it came to magic. Another fight could be disastrous if Arcadia didn't intervene. Phantom aches prickled the surface of Thalias's skin—he knew who She'd pick.

"I haven't touched her." He gestured toward Alina, who still cowered under her shield. Mora followed his gaze, her eyes racking over the Halfling.

She huffed. "Because I opened the door." They glared daggers at one another and Thalias felt saplings twisting in the dirt, waiting to be called to the surface. "And you tried to kill my mate."

I was a fool to come here. Thalias tensed and the Forest tensed with him. If Mora's smoke neared again, he'd be ready. He knew better than to send Arcadia after her, but he called to the giant roots anchoring their cottage to the ground in case he needed a barrier.

"Can you two not fight?" Elowyn pleaded. She came closer, dragging the Aegist along with her. How she convinced Alina to drop her shield, he didn't know.

"I second that," Alina said with a sigh. "I've had enough terrorizing to last me a lifetime."

Regret flashed in Mora's eyes, so quickly Thalias wondered if he imagined it. She reached back to grab the end of Zadriel's tunic, as if he were her anchor. When Zadriel's hand found hers, he ran his thumb in slow circles and some of the tension left Mora's body.

"Say what you need to say, then leave us," Mora ground out as she leaned into Zadriel's chest.

The traitor wrapped an arm around her waist, his focus never leaving Thalias. When Thalias's upper lip twitched, Zadriel pulled Mora closer, violence glittering in those black eyes. The press of Thalias's power against his ribs was overwhelming, but he curled his fists and withstood it, barely affecting the breeze.

"It's complicated," Thalias said, as calmly and firmly as he could. His gaze found Vesryn, silver eyes soft and encouraging. He nodded, and Thalias looked back to Mora. "Can we speak alone?"

Mora's lips pressed together, and she shook her head. "I'm not leaving Zadriel alone with any of you."

"Is he unable to fend for himself?" Thalias asked. He grinned mockingly at Zadriel, snickering as a muscle feathered in his jaw.

"If you intend to be an ass, I'll be excusing myself," Mora retorted.

Zadriel lifted his chin. "We'll hear you together, or not at all."

Tell them, Vesryn said to him alone. *There are no secrets between mates.* The Druid returned to Thalias's side and slipped an arm around his waist.

Thalias's mind spun so quickly he could hardly follow a thought. Days had passed and still he couldn't think of what to say.

Would Mora listen? The Wraith loved to be difficult. And there were centuries to discuss—where should he begin?

Thalias's heart was in his throat, and a familiar ache rose in his chest, one that was rarely far away. His hands shook and clouds darkened the night sky, consuming the stars and concealing the heavens. A splash of rain hit his cheek, the drops spilling down his face like Arcadia's tears.

"I..." Thalias stepped closer, his mate by his side. "I need your blood."

Zadriel's growl rumbled through the space. He snarled, his nostrils flaring, and all Thalias saw was pure, lethal rage. Within a blink, Zadriel was in his face. His chest heaved with each breath and his low voice rumbled in Thalias's ears. "Choose your next words very carefully."

CHAPTER 65

ZADRIEL

Zadriel couldn't help the way his hands shook, or the quake in his heart. The scars along his arms burned, echoes of pain enveloping his skin, as he remembered every swipe of that damned blade. Every helpless moment locked in the suffocating grip of a blood thrall. Mora couldn't be controlled in the same way. But the idea of someone taking Mora's blood and doing Mother knew what with it... He'd never allow it. Couldn't condemn her to a similar fate.

Another growl rumbled in his throat.

Thalias lifted his chin, a silver glow emanating from his sanguine eyes. "You of all people will come to understand why this is necessary."

As he spat the words, the soil shifted beneath Zadriel's feet. Saplings and vines slithered below the surface, enticed by the call of Thalias's magic. Zadriel didn't care. Let Thalias try and bring all of

Arcadia down upon him. It would do nothing to sway his mind or move his body.

Soft ivy leaves tickled his bare feet as vines crawled out from the earth and reached for his ankles. Zadriel eyed them with disdain. When his gaze flicked back to Thalias, the Fae had the nerve to smirk. A dimple appeared on his left cheek, and Zadriel flexed his fingers. The temptation to slam his fist into it was nearly too difficult to deny.

"Not this again." Elowyn sighed. She muttered something to Alina, but the pounding in Zadriel's ears drowned them out.

"Does this act of aggression make you feel like a worthy mate?" Thalias asked. Those silver tattoos seemed to writhe under his skin, the markings not unlike the golden ones that once graced Zadriel's mother's arms. "Because we both know that will never be the case."

"Thalias, don't," Vesryn breathed, shaking his head. He saw the look in Zadriel's eyes before Thalias did and shifted to move between them. But not fast enough.

Zadriel didn't think before he lunged. Vines dug into his shins, nearly breaking the skin as he grabbed Thalias's tunic and tugged him closer. A fire saturated his veins. Though it paled in comparison to the expanding, searing pain in his scars. He clenched his teeth until his jaw cracked.

Was he going mad? Mora was more than capable of protecting herself, and yet he couldn't calm himself. Couldn't stop picturing her arms, scarred and bloody. *She can't scar,* he reminded himself. Though that hardly mattered. Perhaps, physically, she was unblemished, but Mora bore as many scars as he did. They simply hid from the eyes. Made their marks on her soul instead. If he could help it, no one would hurt her like that ever again.

"Let me make something *very* clear, Thalias," he seethed, uncaring when the male bared his teeth. Vesryn moved closer, but his mate shook his head and the Druid stilled. "The only one who gets to decide if I'm worthy is Mora. And *you* don't have *any* rights to her. Don't even *think* about claiming any part of her. She owes you nothing." Zadriel dipped his head closer, his deep voice growing lethally quiet. "Her blood is hers alone and the only one she will share it with, if she so chooses, is *me*. Her mate."

"Be rational, Zadriel," Vesryn pleaded.

Zadriel glanced sidelong at him. "Rational?" He huffed a cold, bitter laugh. "Would you be rational if someone asked for *your* mate's blood?"

Vesryn flinched. The knowing look in his eyes said it all. Of course he wouldn't be happy—blood sharing between mates was sacred. A symbol of their trust. A deepening of their connection. The audacity of Thalias to request Mora share such an intimate part of herself with him... Zadriel's lips peeled back, flashing his sharp canines.

When Thalias opened his mouth to speak, Zadriel had no interest in whatever excuses he had to offer. He shoved him away. Hard. Thalias stumbled, nearly tripping over a root that shifted away too slowly, but Vesryn was there to catch him.

"Zadriel," Vesryn hissed, a sharpness to his tone.

Those moonlight eyes narrowed, flicking to Zadriel's face. It was difficult not to cringe at the fury emanating in that stare. Despite his endless *need* to protect Mora, he regretted it was his old friend's mate that awoke the wild, protective part of his Fae nature. It simply wasn't enough to stop him. Would never be enough.

So many things had changed since they were children. Too many things.

Vesryn shook his head, a frown pulling at his full lips, before he tore his gaze away and fussed over Thalias.

Zadriel watched them, wondering if this would end in yet another brawl. His knuckles cracked as he clenched his fist—at least, this time, they were more evenly matched. *I dare you,* he thought, when Thalias stood, that glowing gaze eyeing him warily.

The endless pounding of Zadriel's heart was near maddening. Until a cool, soothing smoke slid over his back, its delicate touch leaving pleasant shivers in its wake. Zadriel took a breath. Tension bled from his body the more Mora enveloped him in her power. It slipped over his shoulders, dripping to the ground and pooling at his feet. The glittering obsidian writhed there. Waiting.

"Remove your vines, Thalias," Mora demanded. She stepped away from the treehouse and moved to Zadriel's side, her light green train dragging through Thalias's wildflowers. A tide of crackling embers, florals, and pine with a generous splash of mint curled in Zadriel's nostrils. He took another slow, deep breath.

The white-haired male rolled his eyes, but his fingers flexed and the ivy sank back into the soil.

A smirk graced Mora's beautiful face. She looked up at Zadriel, amusement sparkling in her amber eyes before her gaze wandered down his body, slowly taking him in. Warmth spread over his heart, then traveled lower. Zadriel's lips twitched upward. That was *her* desire dancing between them. His Little Witch was enjoying this.

The beast pacing in his chest calmed. Curse the Mother—Zadriel wanted nothing more than to abandon this needless argument and take Mora back to their bed. To spend another day learning all the sounds she made as he explored her with his tongue. He intended to do just that once they were done here.

"What is this about?" Mora asked as she slid her hand up Zadriel's back, following the path of her smoke.

Zadriel glared at Thalias, a low growl escaping his throat.

Silver continued to bleed through Thalias's irises, overtaking the lavender at their center. Leaves twitched above and the churning beneath the soil quickened. Every muscle in Zadriel's body tensed, readying for a fight. But Thalias closed his eyes and pinched the bridge of his nose. After a deep breath, the Forest calmed.

"It would be easier if I showed you," Thalias said, pleading eyes—now back to their sanguine and lavender shade—shifting to Mora. "At least listen to what I have to say before you make any rash decisions." His gaze flitted back to Zadriel, a sneer sullying his handsome face. Zadriel was more than happy to sneer back.

Unfortunately, his Little Witch seemed to be in a giving mood. "Fine." She sighed. "Show me whatever it is you think will convince me to help you. Though I suggest you not get your hopes up."

Zadriel ground his teeth, certain this wouldn't end well. But, as Mora made to follow Thalias, he grabbed her hand. It didn't matter where he led them, Zadriel would follow his mate toward certain doom, so long as they could remain together.

Zadriel braced himself as they walked an old, worn trail he remembered all too well. Centuries passed, and still he could walk it with his eyes closed. This was the last place he expected Thalias to take them.

Though, as they neared Arcadia's center, Zadriel's understanding grew, along with his fury. He opened his mouth to tell Thalias exactly what he thought of his plans, but they passed through a rotten pile of bramble, and Zadriel faced his sins.

The world stopped. Zadriel's breath caught in his lungs and he trembled under the weight of his self-hatred. A crushing feeling in his chest nearly squeezed the life from his heart, and he almost wished it succeeded.

Zadriel stared at the husk of the once great Mother Tree, its rotten wood bleached and covered in remnants of char. A cool breeze brushed against his cheeks, smothering him in the scents of mold and decay. But he didn't cringe when the rot hit his nose.

Nothing grew.

What was once a breathtaking field of glittering, gilded daisies, poking up through the greenery and wildflowers, was bare. Even the trees surrounding the circular meadow were bent and gnarled, their branches devoid of leaves.

The quiet was the worst part. There were no pixies fluttering through the air, no birds chirping their songs, no signs of life at all. Only death wandered here.

And it was Zadriel's fault.

If shame were a physical thing, it would wrap Zadriel in an eternal embrace, seeping into his flesh until they became one.

His gaze flitted across the meadow, staring at the rotten remains of The Mother Tree—his family's pride and joy. Their *great purpose*. The breeze tousled his hair and Zadriel could have sworn he heard something. Like quiet remnants of an ancient song dancing in the wind. One he recognized from childhood days spent parading through the daisies while his mother worked.

Zadriel's throat bobbed. Was it Vehsa? Did her ghost haunt this place? Had she found her way home? He'd always hoped she'd moved to the next realm to be with his father... but Brennan kept so many pieces of her for his enchanting. All Zadriel could do was bury the scraps of his mother Dother stole in a shallow grave under the oak tree in Eden. It wasn't enough. Would never be enough.

Tears streamed down Zadriel's face as the song grew louder. Everything faded. Everything except Mora's soft hand in his. All that remained was him and her and the memories of who he once was. He could almost smell the herbaceous air and feel the tickle of grass and daisy petals against his legs.

When he blinked, the husk of the Mother Tree was back to Her healthy brown, though gilded sap stained the grooves in the bark. And there was his mother, with her long black hair and golden eyes, beautiful, gilded markings flowing up her arms. She sang in the old tongue. The language of trees. A language Zadriel began learning before he was ripped from this life. She looked at him, smiling while a tree branch with golden leaves rested on her shoulder.

The whole of Arcadia heard his mother's song, captivated by the soothing tones of her voice. And when she finished, the Forest sang back. Leaves rustled in the wind, pixies hummed, even the wildest creatures living in shadows called back to her. Vehsa unsheathed her gilded blade from her belt—the same belt Mora now wore—and sliced through the Mother's bark. As he stared at the daisies on the handle a burning pain stung his arms, as if the Dothers sliced through his flesh. Golden sap rose to the surface like blood to a wound and Vehsa caught it in a wooden bowl. The Mother Tree's Lifeblood.

Blood Zadriel stole. A life he ended.

Zadriel would never be like his mother. Could never fulfill the role Arcadia intended for him. He swallowed against the ache in his throat, his lower lip wobbling. He didn't deserve Vehsa's song. But those golden eyes invited him to try, and something churned in his chest, magic he rarely acknowledged demanding to be set free.

Mora squeezed his hand but he couldn't pull his eyes away from his mother. He found himself aching to memorize every line on her face. And the love he saw in her gaze. Zadriel shuddered, that squeezing feeling around his heart nearly too much.

Vehsa nodded and gave Zadriel another encouraging smile. He closed his eyes, ignoring the weight of his grief, and reached for the power in his chest. It was more alive than it had been in centuries. Yet all he sensed was Mora.

She was everything.

Zadriel treasured the warmth of her hand in his, though she seemed so far away. With every beat of his traitorous heart, he felt her. But he didn't feel the Mother Tree. There was nothing left—no daisies or sap for him to call upon. The Mother was dead. He betrayed Her and damned his people. Damned Mora.

The ache in his heart didn't matter. Not when Thalias stared at Mora as if she were Arcadia's salvation. Zadriel understood it. Could only imagine how her blood might help Arcadia's children. But he didn't care.

They wouldn't bleed her. They wouldn't lay a finger on her. And if that damned him, so be it.

CHAPTER 66

MORA

Mora ached to move. To pace around the decaying corpse of the Mother Tree until she could no longer feel her pounding heart or the weight of Zadriel's grief pressing against her chest. But he clung to her hand, as if he feared she may disappear the moment he released it. Mora stared at his beautiful face, her heart aching as his bottom lip quivered. She squeezed his hand before lifting it to press a kiss to his knuckles. But Zadriel didn't move. Didn't acknowledge her at all. It was as if he were lost in his own haunted memories.

Something Mora understood well.

Zadriel wasn't the only one who mourned. Elowyn and Vesryn both gazed at the dead meadow with wide, watery eyes and furrowed brows, while Alina stood silently at their side. Mora imagined Alina had as many, if not more, questions than she did. Likely bit her tongue to hold them at bay.

Thalias looked away, glaring at Zadriel when he thought Mora wasn't looking. Though his features softened when he caught her watching him, hope glittering in those starfire eyes.

"I take it this is the Mother Tree?" Mora asked. The pull in her chest was gone, once again. But she knew she was in the right place.

"What's left of Her," Thalias said bitterly.

Mora tensed, waiting for him to say something about Zadriel, but Thalias only glared in his direction, teeth bared in a silent snarl. Zadriel paid him no mind. He focused instead on the twisted, leafless branches of the Mother Tree. His palms grew clammy, tremoring in Mora's grip, while tears slid down his cheeks. But as Zadriel's breathing slowed, a warm feeling spread through Mora's skin. It pooled in her palm before sliding up her arm and settling in her chest. The beat of Mora's heart calmed and her nerves settled.

Mora swayed in Zadriel's direction, half considering leaning against his shoulder and resting. Until Thalias narrowed his eyes.

"I assume you have questions?" he asked, crossing his arms. The silver tattoos winding around his fingers and following his veins until they snaked under his sleeves seemed alive, pulsing more than before.

Mora blinked. What was she doing? She shifted on her feet, grimacing as black rot crunched under her shoes and the scents of decay filled her nose.

"What does my blood have to do with the corpse of a tree?"

"Everything." A sad smile appeared briefly on Thalias's lips.

The warmth in Mora's chest thrummed and her eyes felt heavy. She squeezed Zadriel's hand again, but still, he didn't move.

Elowyn came closer, reaching for Mora's hand before she thought better of it and let her arm fall to her side. "This is your Mother too," she said, gesturing toward the once giant Mother Tree. Tears stained her green cheeks, but her voice was awed. Hopeful.

Mora furrowed her brows. "My mother was a human named Aedlin."

The dryad tilted her head to the side, her long, pine green hair catching on the dead plants at her feet. "That was your human mother. You haven't been human for a long time."

What the hell did that mean? Dother's curse hadn't changed who her mother was. He took so much, he couldn't take that too. Mora clenched her jaw and curled her fingers, but another pulse of warmth filled her body and she relaxed.

She opened her mouth, unsure what to say, but Vesryn interrupted. "That won't mean anything to her, Elowyn." He glanced to Mora, his eyes widening for a moment, until Thalias gave him a look.

What was that about?

Thalias's attention shot briefly toward Zadriel's hand and his upper lip curled, but he quickly schooled his features. "What do you know of the Mother Tree, Wraith?"

"Dother killed it and used what he stole to curse me." Mora's fingers clenched in Zadriel's hold. But the warm feeling emanating from his touch intensified, her skin tingling pleasantly.

"Dother couldn't have acted alone. Only Zadriel could—"

Ah, there was her familiar rage. Mora lifted a finger and silenced him with a click of her tongue. "Careful, Thalias. I won't stay if you finish that thought."

Thalias prowled closer, dead weeds crunching under his boots—even his wildflowers wouldn't grow here. "I speak the truth." He gestured at the decay all around them, as if Mora hadn't noticed.

"You speak of something you don't understand."

"This is all very sad," Elowyn said, her eyes bright with fresh, green tinted tears.

Vesryn frowned up at the dryad before patting her back, careful of the flowers peeking out through the silky strands of her long, pine green hair. He looked back toward the Mother Tree, searching for Alina. The Aegist's eyes were far away, her head tilted as if she were listening for something.

Mora heard it too. Something curled through the breeze, the musical tone so quiet she wondered if she imagined it.

"What else do you know of the Mother Tree?" Thalias asked cautiously. As she focused on him the music disappeared.

Mora searched her mind. All she wanted to do was curl up with Zadriel and rest—it was nearly impossible to concentrate. And this place felt so... familiar. "I know that it—"

"She."

Once again, Thalias cut through her calm.

"That *she* was the source of all magic. And everything in Arcadia can be traced back to it." Thalias cleared his throat and Mora rolled her eyes. "You know I meant her."

"Does anyone hear that?" Alina asked.

Thalias ignored her and crossed his arms, his face stony as he once again gazed at Mora and Zadriel's entwined hands.

Vesryn's moonlight eyes bore into hers. "Do you know where Her magic came from?"

Mora shook her head.

"Her sap," Elowyn said. "It created the entire Forest."

"Early Fae were born of the Mother Tree Herself," Thalias added. "The first of Her children became the Keepers of Arcadia. One to tend the Tree, and the other to tend Her children."

Mora's brows furrowed. "Keepers?"

Thalias smirked, that infuriating dimple appearing on his left cheek. "Yes, Keepers. And mates. One saw and understood all magic and helped teach Arcadians how to use their gifts. The other spoke to the Mother Tree. She could call forth and prepare Her sap, so the rest of us could drink it, connect with Arcadia, and reach our full potential."

The memory of Zadriel explaining Fae magic in Eden came back to Mora.

We can *be more.*

Can be. Not are.

Thalias lifted his arm, displaying his silver tattoos. "Arcadians have drops of the Mother Tree's sap in our blood, simply by nature. It's what gives us the well of power we're born with. If we drink Her sap, we become more. What we're meant to be. Without it, our magic is stunted and we live mortal lives. Before, when we came of age, the Keeper prepared the sap for us so we could bond to Arcadia's endless well of power and live eternally in Her embrace."

It reminded Mora of what Zadriel shared about the mate bond and Arcadian's sacred blood magic. Fae drank the Mother Tree's sap like blood and connected to her well. And, in bonding with her, they became the powerful creatures humans knew them to be.

Alina wandered closer. "Why was the sap prepared?"

Quiet music floated through the air again and Zadriel's thumb brushed over Mora's skin, sending warm shivers up her spine. Mora leaned against his shoulder and listened—she could have sworn she heard a voice. It beckoned to her, the song almost as lovely as the one in Frederick's garden. Though this one didn't wrap around her heart and promise paradise. It didn't feel like home.

"Mora?" Vesryn's voice sounded far away. And, if Mora squinted, she could almost see golden leaves fluttering along the bent, decaying boughs of the Mother Tree. It reminded her of her dreams.

Thalias sighed and a burst of wind hit her face.

"Hey!" Mora's cheeks burned. Her power thrummed under her skin and she took a step toward Thalias, intent on retaliating with her smoke. But Zadriel's grip tightened, stilling her.

Thalias took a breath and continued with his lecture. "The sap was pure, raw magic. The Keeper prepared it to suit our specific gifts. To drink it straight from the Tree had unpredictable effects, twisting the body and mind in irreversible ways. Only Her Keepers could consume it raw. And their child."

"Where are they now?"

Elowyn's cinnamon eyes softened. "They're gone."

Mora was almost afraid to ask. "What happened?"

"Humans," Thalias spat. "We made the mistake of allowing them in, breeding with them and creating Halflings."

Mora sneered at Thalias. For someone who wanted to win her over, he wasn't doing a great job. "Need I remind you *I* am a Halfling."

Thalias waved his hand dismissively.

"You're more than that," Elowyn chirped.

Thalias's lips twitched upward. "I'm getting to that, Elowyn."

"Then get to it," Mora demanded.

It was Vesryn who continued. "Halflings, as you know, can sometimes have power, thanks to their Fae ancestry. But the sap in their blood is diluted, which makes them weaker than Fae. Many weren't happy about that." He reached for Thalias's hand, threading their fingers together. That one touch grounded Thalias—tension bled from his shoulders.

Mora's brows furrowed, and she glanced back at the rotten husk of the Tree. "Did they not become more powerful when they drank the sap?"

Vesryn's gaze drifted to his boots. "Arcadia wouldn't allow it."

"That hardly seems fair."

A muscle tensed in Thalias's jaw. "Don't worry, Wraith, some rebelled and found their own way to be powerful. Their Enchanters bastardized blood magic, twisting our sacred traditions to bond to and control other creatures. Starting with sprites."

Mora didn't miss the accusation in his tone. He hadn't forgotten how she'd noticed a sprite, and knew what shrouded Zadriel from sight when he arrived. Mora ground her teeth and toed the remains of a blackened daisy. Did he think she was guilty of blood magic? She opened her mouth to ask him, but he spoke first.

"When Alaius, the Keeper of Arcadia's children, was found dead and mutilated, his mate's fury awoke a rage in the Forest that still echoes through the leaves. And Arcadia forced the humans and Halflings out."

The Exodus. Mora's stomach dropped. Thalias said *some* rebelled and yet *all* Halflings were forced out of the forest and faced hell in Berwick. It wasn't fair. But if she found Zadriel dead...

I'd destroy everything.

Mora tensed, her pulse pounding in her ears, and the beast in her chest thrashed against her ribs. Then the wind picked up, that voice growing louder. And Zadriel's warm fingers twitched in her hand.

He was here. He was safe. Mora took a slow breath and relaxed. "What happened to the other Keeper?"

"Eight years later, she and her son disappeared." Thalias sneered. "Decades after that, her son returned and burned down the Mother Tree."

"Oh gods," Mora whispered.

The Keepers of Arcadia were Zadriel's parents.

Bile burned in her throat and her mind raced, digging through every mention Zadriel made of his parents and himself. Why hadn't he told her?

And Thalias. Mora would never forget the animalistic look on his face when she confirmed Vehsa's death. The cracking of wood while plants tore the room apart still haunted her nightmares. But she assumed he'd lost his damned mind and nearly plunged them into the chasm because he was furious another *Fae* was murdered. It was so much more than that.

"Only Vehsa could prepare the sap so we may consume it. Zadriel should have been our savior, but he destroyed what hope remained."

"Thalias," Vesryn admonished, his round cheeks darkening.

Mora was too lost in Zadriel's grief to be angry. It slipped over her body like a second skin and she found she could hardly breathe. Both his parents died violently. Leaving him alone to navigate horrors even she couldn't imagine. And then his captors forced him to destroy his legacy and leave an endless stain on his soul.

As her heartbeat intensified, bucking against her ribcage, Zadriel growled. Mora wished she could bring people back from the dead, if only to kill Dother again. And again. And again.

Fuck.

Mora looked up at Zadriel. He was stock still, fury painting every inch of his perfect face, and the flecks of gold in his eyes glowed. Since they'd entered the clearing, he hadn't looked away from the Mother Tree's remains. Hadn't spoken a word.

Mora tugged on his hand. "Zadriel?"

Vesryn worried his bottom lip. "Without Vehsa and the Mother Tree, we can't connect to Arcadia…"

"Our children are dying, Mora." Thalias breathed.

Mora swallowed, knots twisting in her stomach. What had Dother done?

"Every child born after Vehsa's death ages and dies," Vesryn said, his voice hoarse.

Silver flared in Thalias's eyes, saturating his irises. "I'm not enough to save them."

Wind twisted through the clearing, tearing through decaying plant matter and snapping branches from the Mother Tree. It sang to the fury rooted in Mora's heart. But on the tail of Thalias's breeze was that song, stronger than before, and Mora no longer knew how she felt.

"Thalias tried to grow a new tree," Vesryn said, rubbing his mate's back. "It became a safe haven, our new home. But it did not replace the Mother."

"Our Mother is gone. And so is Her sap." Elowyn dragged her feet as she approached Thalias, offering him a quick hug. The glow in Thalias's eyes dimmed slightly, and he leaned into her embrace.

"Not gone," Thalias whispered, his bright gaze lifting to Mora's. "It simply resides elsewhere."

"I don't understand," Mora muttered.

The warmth of Zadriel's touch spread through her. Thalias's red eyes flicked down to their entwined hands and this time Mora followed. A gasp slipped through her lips. Lines of gold traced the veins on their fingers and flowed up their arms, thrumming with the tandem beats of their hearts.

It was like her dream in Eden...

Mora peered up at Zadriel, who'd closed his eyes and tipped his head back. "Zadriel," she breathed, pulling at his hand. Those pointed ears twitched at the sound of her voice.

Thalias kissed Vesryn's knuckles before he pulled away and came closer. "Do you know why your flask is covered in remnants of the Mother Tree? Why nature heeds your call? Why gilded daisies bloom in the wake of your blood?"

Why did his tone put her on edge? There was a threat in those words. Not of violence, but of something she knew she wouldn't like.

"I don't know what Dother did to me."

"Does anyone else hear singing?" Alina asked again. She tipped her head up, searching the empty night sky for the source, but only the stars stared back.

The ethereal voice grew louder, the sound so inviting. Soothing. It shifted, deeper tones weaving through the air and calling to Mora. *This* was a song she would follow into the unknown.

"What about him?" Thalias made no attempt to hide his disdain as he flicked his fingers toward Zadriel. "Do you know why you feel so attached to the traitor? Why he cares so deeply for you?"

Mora bared her teeth. "Don't call him that, Thalias."

"He's all that remains of the Keepers, Mora. And The Mother Tree's sap, raw and pure, runs through your veins."

Mora felt Thalias's eyes on her face, but her racing mind was far away.

It's fitting I gift the woman who has my heart with such powerful relics. That I bind us in blood and bless our union with the rarest magic.

The rarest magic. What the fuck had Dother done to her?

Memories of a golden liquid sloshing around in her flask and a sweet, burnt sugar taste on her tongue nearly made her gag. Gods, nothing made sense. And yet Thalias raised his brows, waiting for her to speak.

There was one thing Mora knew with certainty. "Zadriel's my mate. He loves me."

His devotion saturated her blood. Mora felt it with every breath. Even now, when the memory of Dother's voice echoed in her ears, Zadriel's presence calmed her. She could breathe through it, comforted by the warm feeling emanating from his touch.

Thalias shook his head, something like pity staining his features. "I can't deny the mate bond. But Zadriel loves the false tree you've allowed him to keep on his belt. He loves the call of your blood."

"Stop it!" Mora screamed, something in her snapping. She snarled as she broke the distance between them, tugging Zadriel along. Fae couldn't lie. Though that didn't mean they told the truth. And she was fucking done.

Obsidian smoke flowed down her arm, its frigid touch leaving goosebumps in its wake... but Mora hadn't summoned it. It curled around Zadriel's forearm, the wispy tendrils covering his scars. Mora flexed her hand, calling it back.

"Zadriel?" Mora asked, louder this time. She tore her hand from his grasp and it was as if she'd broken a spell.

Zadriel blinked, and the glow faded from his dark eyes, along with the song on the winds. "She was here," he whispered, more to himself. Then he shifted, reaching for Mora's wrist. His brows furrowed as he stared at the fading gold staining their fingers and the smoke around his arm. "What's happening?" he asked, voice thick with grief.

Mora didn't answer. Her mist wouldn't return to her, no matter how hard she tried. The pounding in Mora's ears was maddening. She flexed her fingers, feeling for the power curling around Zadriel's skin, but there was nothing. As if it wasn't part of her at all.

"Mora," Thalias said, his voice softer than before. He backed up a step and Mora found herself grateful. Until she looked up at him again and found reverence in his gaze. "You are the Heart of Arcadia. Your blood may save us."

Zadriel sucked in a breath, his fingers stilling around her wrist. But Mora barely breathed. The meadow felt smaller. Like the glass of her flask pressing against her skin. She wanted to flee into the forest, leaving all but Zadriel behind.

Whatever Thalias thought Mora was, she had no interest. Already, she'd spent centuries as a relic passed around by greedy men. This sounded like another prison.

"How would you know?" Mora hissed, staring with Zadriel as her smoke snaked further up his arm.

The dark wisps settled, and he ran a finger through them. Zadriel's throat bobbed as he looked back at Mora and opened his mouth to speak, but Thalias interrupted.

"I didn't know until Elowyn confirmed it. But I can *feel* it, Wraith. I have since the moment we met."

Mora's head spun. She wished she were back in the treehouse with Zadriel, curled up in the sheets she now wore as a dress. She clenched her fists, focusing on the nip of pain as her nails dug into her palm. "Why the hell would there be something between us?"

Thalias crossed his arms and watched Mora silently. A muscle ticked in his jaw while he assessed her, struggling with some internal debate. He looked back at Vesryn, whose silver eyes softened. He offered a small, encouraging smile and nodded.

Thalias sighed. He pushed his white hair back and stared up at the stars. "I was born here. Birthed in a raging fire, fully formed by the hands of Death." He hesitated. "But I was never enough alone."

Thalias offered Mora his hand, his eyes pleading. As she reached to take it, Zadriel released her wrist, but he didn't stray. If it weren't for the cool touch of her stolen smoke, she would have relaxed into his chest when he wrapped an arm around her waist. Zadriel was tense. Ready for a fight. But Mora saw the desperation in Thalias's eyes. Whatever he had to say, she needed to hear it.

She rested her hand in his, his touch cold against her heated skin. The fading gold on her fingers was so much like the silver on his. Their markings pulsed as she touched him, the colors deepening.

"When the Mother Tree was dying She took what remained of Her lifeforce and created a vessel so Arcadia may survive." Thalias took a deep breath. "You are Her Heart, Mora. And I am Her Spirit."

CHAPTER 67

MORA

The silence following Thalias's confession was loud. Even the breeze died, as if it too waited on bated breath to see what happened next.

Mora squeezed her eyes shut, shaking against the onslaught of magic twisting around her bones. It demanded she act. That she fulfill Andras's wish. Thalias cocked his head to the side, his white brows furrowing. And Mora hated herself.

Why did it have to be this way?

Leaning into Zadriel's embrace, she tipped her head back and found her panic mirrored in his midnight eyes. Had he known about Thalias? Did he know about her?

Zadriel's lips pressed into a thin line and he shook his head. Yet Mora couldn't be sure if it was an answer or if he was begging her to fight. To leave one piece of the home he loved so much untouched by the Dothers' greedy hands.

Her smoke—his smoke, it seemed—writhed on his arm like an ethereal tattoo, and so many questions flooded her mind.

How did he steal bits of her power? Was their bond real? Or his love...?

Tears welled in Mora's eyes, but she blinked them away. It felt like something squeezed her heart. If it weren't for the rising pain in her ribs and the horrific business she had to attend to, Mora would demand Zadriel explain himself. That he tell her everything.

When she tore her gaze away from his, she regretted it immediately. No matter how confusing her emotions were, his eyes were home. And without them...

How was she going to face what came next?

The rotten remains of Arcadia's Mother Tree stood behind Thalias like an ill omen, its colossal trunk twisting oddly. As if the tree had curled inward while it burned. Thalias was born here, surrounded by flames as death reigned all around him.

It explained so much.

With each furious beat of her heart, Mora could have sworn one of the broken branches twitched. Gods, she hated this. Didn't want it. And yet she couldn't look away.

He loves the call of your blood.

Mora rubbed the spot over her heart with her free hand, hating Thalias's words. Hating the doubt they fostered.

They could have her blood. They could take it all. Thalias, Zadriel, and this whole damned forest could tear the stolen magic from her bones. She didn't care.

Mora was tired. Tired of the constant manipulations. Tired of fighting. Tired of endless solitude. She'd only ever been worth what she could offer. Power. They could fucking have it all.

Then Zadriel's voice, low and soft and full of awe, pushed back against the pain.

I love you.

I vow to be yours for as long as you'll have me.

Mora wished she could talk to him. Wished she had time to understand.

But it was too late. Her hesitation agitated the one wish holding any power. Demand twisted tighter around her bones, cracks forming along the surface, and Mora wheezed against the pain. Her hand slipped from Thalias's. She balled her fists, holding on with all her might, but time wasn't on their side.

Thalias frowned. "Nothing to say, Wraith?"

Cool tendrils of obsidian mist leaked from her fingers, dripping onto the blackened earth. Mora took one last look at the death and rot permeating what was once a beautiful meadow, a pang of guilt twisting in her gut—The Mother Tree's blood may not stain her hands, but it rushed through her veins.

Her gaze skirted over Elowyn, Alina, and Vesryn. In another life, perhaps they could have been friends. But Mora knew this would be the last time they looked at her without hatred in their eyes.

Her lower lip quivered when she looked up at Zadriel once more. He kissed her forehead and Mora took a deep breath, filling her lungs with his scent. Before she pulled away, he held her tighter, hugging her to his body. Then Zadriel let her go.

Mora offered Thalias a sad smile. She reached for his hand and Thalias arched a brow but didn't move away.

"I'm sorry," she said, her pleading eyes on him, but her voice loud enough for all to hear.

Before anyone could move, Mora burst into smoke. A gasp barely escaped Thalias's lips as she pulled him into her obsidian embrace and tore him away from Arcadia.

CHAPTER 68

VESRYN

Vesryn watched Thalias's red eyes go wide as Mora burst into a horrifying cloud of sparkling obsidian. His heart galloped in his chest, but he swallowed his fear and moved toward them, tensing as he readied for another senseless fight.

Within a blink, they were gone.

Elowyn and Alina stared incredulously at the spot Mora and Thalias had been moments ago. But Zadriel watched Vesryn, a pained look in his dark, glittering eyes.

"Thalias?" Vesryn breathed. Rotten branches and weeds crunched under his feet when he took another step, nearing where Thalias once stood. "Thalias?" he cried out, louder this time, the sound echoing through the dead, empty space.

He was gone.

Dropping to his knees, Vesryn fisted the black remains of what was once a proud meadow of gilded splendor. In his chest, he could feel the pull of the bond he and Thalias shared and knew a vast distance stretched between them. It was further than they'd ever been from one another. He tried to speak to him, mind to mind, but the distance was too vast. Wherever his mate was, he was no longer in Arcadia.

The ache in his shattering heart was too much, each crack threatening to break him. Squeezing his fists tight, he didn't flinch when aged wood pierced his flesh. Warm blood pooled in his palm but the dull sting helped him focus.

Mora took Thalias.

I'm sorry.

Those were her final words before she tore him away. What sinister deeds was she apologizing for? What were her plans for him?

Vesryn was a fool. When Thalias told him what she was, he felt hope for the first time in centuries. How quickly it deflated into a festering pile of despair.

A gust of wind swept through the dead meadow, twisting through Vesryn's braids and cooling his heated skin. As if Arcadia released a long exhale after holding Her breath. Was She furious? Or had Mora stained Her heart so black Arcadia no longer cared what happened to Her people?

Closing his eyes, he tipped his head back and released a shuddering breath as the cool breeze caressed his face. Those thoughts could wait. For now, finding Thalias was all that mattered.

A hard, taloned hand pat his shoulder, pulling him from his spiraling thoughts, and he heard Elowyn's joints creak as she knelt beside him.

"Where is he?" he asked, voice breaking. Elowyn squeezed his shoulder in an attempt to calm him, her hard grip pinching his skin, but she didn't answer. Like him, she had no idea where Thalias had gone. But...

Vesryn swiftly stood, knocking the poor dryad over as he marched toward Zadriel. "Where is he!" It wasn't a question.

Zadriel's black eyes widened, and he took a step back.

"There's no need for violence," Elowyn pleaded as she righted herself.

At the same time Zadriel said, "Mora didn't have a choice."

Vesryn didn't care *why* Mora did what she did. His lips peeled back in a snarl. "Where is he?"

"She didn't want to do this."

"WHERE IS HE!" Vesryn's voice boomed throughout all of Arcadia.

Zadriel gave him a pitying look. "He's with the same person who had me, Ves."

The rot in the air was too heavy, its scent saturating Vesryn's lungs. With each quick gasp he felt as if he were drowning in it. His eyes raked over the scars on Zadriel's arms, years of pain etched into his skin.

Thalias was with a Halfling who had a fondness for blood magic.

Vesryn shoved his hand in his cloak pocket and worried the brooch Thalias gave him. It was warm, the enchantment weaved into the trinket eager to be used. Thalias wasn't certain what it could do—the blood stained golden leaf was enough to give him pause. They intended to bury it under the Mother Tree today. To put this tainted piece of Her to rest. But now... Vesryn clutched it tighter. Would it mean anything to the man who had his mate? Could he trade it or—Vesryn swallowed—use it to get him back?

I'll find you, Sapling. It hardly mattered what he needed to do, Vesryn would give anything to get to Thalias.

"Mora took him to Andras?" Alina asked, her hazel eyes darting between Vesryn and Zadriel. She pursed her lips, her brows lowering as confusion painted her young face.

Vesryn ground his teeth and Alina paled as she stared at his sharp canines, likely remembering how much longer they were when he shifted into a bear. It was tempting, the need to shift into something bigger. Part of him ached to tear everything to shreds. He prowled closer to Zadriel, herding him toward the Mother Tree.

"We should go," Elowyn said quietly. Her eyes never left Vesryn as she clutched Alina's arm and led her into the brush.

When Zadriel's back pressed against the blackened trunk, he lifted his hands. "I'm sorry." The dark smoke he'd somehow collected awakened. Whispers of onyx curled around Zadriel's forearm, snaking down to his hand and twisting over his fingers. "And I know Mora's sorry too."

Vesryn's gaze flicked to the flask at Zadriel's hip, a plan forming in his mind. White light glowed on his deep, umber-brown skin as he shoved Zadriel against the rotten trunk, and decayed plant matter spun around them. His jaw ached as his teeth elongated, but he welcomed the pain.

Before the bear took over, Vesryn leaned closer. His rumbling voice was lethal as he said, "You aren't sorry, Zadriel. But you will be."

CHAPTER 69

MORA
300 YEARS AGO

"I'm back," Mora declared, materializing in Dother's sitting room. Her bounty fell to the floor, raw chicken splatting against the dark tiles. One jar of pickled eggs shattered, brine splashing against Dother's white trousers, and Mora covered her mouth, muffling her laughter.

Dother was less amused. His eyes widened as he took in the mess. "Are you mad?" he hissed, shoes crunching over broken glass as he prowled toward her.

Mora didn't shrink back. In fact, she met him halfway, enjoying the squish of pickled eggs under her black leather shoes.

"You didn't tell me where you wanted the food, Dother."

WISH

The metal of his ring bruised her flesh as he wrapped his fingers around her wrist. Mora ignored the black void inside, though it twisted in its casing to look up at her. Gods, she hated that thing.

"You know this isn't what I wanted, Treasure." Dother pulled her into his chest, the citrus and herb musk on his royal blue tunic too much.

Mora's fingers splayed on his hard stomach as she pushed away from his hold. He barely allowed her an inch. But it was better than nothing. She smiled up at him innocently, ignoring the way her heart quaked in her chest. "Do you wish for me to fix it?"

Dother's lips twisted at the thought, and he glanced at his journal—it sat open on one of the opulent white chairs he'd pulled away from the window. The angry mob still screamed outside the castle walls. When he looked back, the fire in his azure eyes stole the breath from Mora's lungs, and the velvet material covering her wasn't enough. She could feel the weight of his body on hers. The heat of his breath in her ears. It made her think of sticky black sheets on her back. And how it felt when he—

She took a shuddering breath, and the bastard grinned.

"I should make you get on your hands and knees and clean like a servant."

"Then wish it so," Mora said bitterly.

With a sigh, Dother spun on his heels, lifting Mora in his arms and marching toward his bedroom. Chunks of eggs scattered in the air as she kicked and shrieked.

"Fight me all you like, Treasure. This ends with me inside you."

Mora screeched when he tossed her onto his bed, soft furs and silky blankets breaking her fall. She blew her curls away from her face as she lifted herself up on her forearms. "Only if you're careful with your words," she spat.

525

His eyes narrowed but Mora glared back. She hoped his heart galloped in his chest too. Prayed he saw the monster he'd created prowling behind her glowing amber eyes and regretted what he'd done.

The furious chants of the townsfolk broke the silence, the sound growing louder, and Dother ran to the window. Whatever he saw caused the blood to drain from his face. Mora shifted on the bed, but before her feet could touch the ground Dother turned.

"Do not leave our bed," he seethed.

Mora fisted the sheets and bared her teeth. "Your bed, Dother. There is no us."

"THERE WILL ALWAYS BE AN US!" He turned away from the horrific sight outside the castle and slammed his fist on his writing desk, papers and trinkets tumbling to the floor. Mora's heart squeezed when a water sprite bounced around in their spherical flask, slamming against the glass.

Her shoes smacked against the black tiles as she jumped off the bed. Before she could reach the sprite, Dother collided with her. They tumbled to the ground, her dress tearing in his steely grip. Cool air danced along her exposed ribs and Mora's breathing quickened.

"Get off me!" she screamed, slamming her hands against his chest.

"No." Dother's laugh was bitter. "What did you intend to do with the sprite, Treasure?"

Save it, Mora thought. But she remained silent, gazing at her flask, tipped over on the floor with the rest of Dother's things.

"What did you intend to do?"

"Fuck you, Dother," she snarled, tearing at the thread in her chest. Smoke bled from her pores, enveloping her in its cool embrace. Dother rolled off her, reaching for her flask. But Mora didn't care. They could

play this game all night if he wished... or until *he wished. Even a second in her flask was a reprieve. And she was almost—*

A horrific pressure stabbed through her, the sudden agony so severe Mora sputtered in the air. Glittering mist seized before compressing, her body coming together with such force she saw stars.

Mora plunged to the floor, slamming against the tiles. Her bones screamed on impact, and an errant piece of glass from the pickle jar lodged into her cheek. A pained moan tried to escape her, but cold liquid bubbled out from behind her lips instead. It puddled around her face, joining the bits of egg littering the floor.

Mora writhed, trying again and again to gasp for air. All she could do was choke. Something tore through her lungs, an icy blaze raging more and more with each attempted breath.

Dother knelt by her side, clutching her flask so tightly his fists were white. Water splashed against the crystal as he shook it in front of her face. She could have sworn she glimpsed the sprite, its wings fluttering against the glass.

"I did not dismiss you," he said smugly.

The icy burn in her chest felt endless. It didn't matter how much she coughed and wheezed, water flooded her body like an ocean raging inside her mouth, her esophagus, her stomach, her lungs. Black spots danced in her vision while Mora clawed at her throat, moaning piti-fully.

"Shh," Dother cooed.

He pulled her into his lap and ran his hands through her curls, un-caring about the water spilling from her lips and soaking his trousers. The shadow of a smile danced on his face as he watched her. Mora gagged. The room spun and all she could hear was the horrific sound of water sloshing in her ears.

"You've given me no choice, Mora. Your antics have gotten out of hand and it's time you face consequences."

Dother looked at her expectantly, those cold blue eyes fixed on her face as if she were supposed to answer. Instead, she whimpered, more cold liquid dribbling down her chin.

Patting her cheek, he pulled her closer, settling her head on his shoulder. "Next time you decide to act out, Treasure, remember this moment."

Mora's vision darkened. Dother's wicked kiss on her forehead was the last thing she felt before the water pulled her under.

Mora woke with a start, gasping for air. A phantom ache throbbed in her lungs while the memory of churning water echoed in her ears. At least she could breathe. Each inhale came quicker than the last as she caught her bearings.

Gods, she was in Dother's bed. Bile clawed up her throat as she dealt with his overpowering scent. It cocooned her, along with a pile of silks and furs. They pooled around her waist as she sat up and pressed her hand to her still damp chest. Her heart thrashed against her ribcage, but at least she was clothed. The torn navy fabric hung awkwardly at her side, cool air nipping at her skin, but the long skirt twisted around her legs, hiding most of her from Dother's touch.

He lay at her side, grumbling in his sleep as the bed dipped. When she moved his grip on her hip tightened. He didn't wake, however. A small mercy. Part of her wished to escape to her flask, to turn to mist and curl up somewhere no one could touch her. But the memory of water flooding her lungs was too fresh. Dother would do it again if she disobeyed.

Besides, she had a plan. A foolish one, perhaps. And if it didn't go well, Mora imagined she'd contend with something much worse than drowning. But she needed to try.

It was dark; orange embers barely clung to life in the fireplace. And her ribs ached, pain radiating like a heartbeat, along with a horrific sting in her cheek.

Oh gods, the glass!

Mora touched her cheek, expecting to find sharp fragments. The skin was tender—she hissed as she dragged her fingers over the wound—but it scabbed over and was cleaned. Dother would expect her thanks for his kindness.

Mora's eyes flicked over to him, sleeping soundly by her side. A lifetime ago she would watch him sleep like this in a different room. Covered in different sheets. Considering vastly different things. That Mora would have run her fingers through his hair, worrying about the future. She would have admired the way his skin glowed in the moonlight. She would have leaned down to kiss him and enjoyed a few more moments in his presence. That Mora invited a monster into her bed.

That Mora was dead.

She took one more slow, deep breath, praying to whatever Gods listened—though she believed in none of them—and forced herself to speak.

"Dother," *she hissed in the darkness, cringing when her hands met his warm, naked flesh.*

Mora shook him lightly. It would be smarter to let him sleep in case she failed. But, more than anything, she needed to see the look in his eyes if—when—she won.

"Dother, wake up."

He mumbled something incoherent before fisting her dress and pulling her closer. Mora twisted in his grip, pushing against him until he rolled onto his back. The bastard still wouldn't release the torn velvet fabric at her side, ripping it more as he settled. Goosebumps rose on her exposed stomach. But the cold wasn't what made her tremble.

Mora swallowed, half considering pulling away and attempting to sleep. Or perhaps escaping to her flask and facing the consequences tomorrow. But she slid her palms up his sternum, finding the soft, slow thud of his heart, and pictured her intent.

"Dother. I found a solution to your food problem."

He sucked in a breath, stirring beneath her. "What?" he mumbled.

"I know how to fix everything," she whispered, plucking at the magic binding her to his wish.

He blinked before wiping the sleep from his eyes. Though his other hand never released her dress.

"Go on," he said with a yawn.

Her fingers twitched, aching to curl into a fist, but Mora forced herself to remain still.

"When I was out gathering food—"

"The food you ruined," he muttered, scowling. His hand traveled down her side until it rested on her rear.

Mora's eyes flared, and she leaned closer. "Wish for me to fix it."

Dother sighed, shaking his head. "Have you learned nothing tonight? Do you need me to force another sprite into your flask to teach

you some manners? I was thinking fire may be a good motivator." He
squeezed her flesh in a bruising grip.

Sweat coated Mora's palms and her body tensed. She'd braced herself for pain, wondering if the wish would disagree with her interpre-
tation, but she wasn't ready for Dother. "Can we move on," she hissed
through gritted teeth.

"So long as you behave."

Mora rolled her eyes. "I snuck into the tavern."

"The one where we met?" Dother finally sounded awake. His fingers
trailed up her dress, back to the tear he'd made. She managed not to
flinch when he softly traced her ribs. "I remember that place fondly."

Fondly. Mora almost scoffed. If she could go back to that night,
she would never have left the castle. That night was the beginning of
Mora's end, and she'd walked willingly into the arms of her doom. If
only she'd listened to Philip and stayed home.

Dother would have come for you anyway.

Mora knew it. Though it didn't stop the endless what ifs from
flitting through her mind. Was there a reality where her father and
Philip lived and Mora wasn't cursed? Or did her own failings not
matter—was this what the Fates wanted for her?

If so, damn them all. And damn Dother with them.

Another slow breath helped ease the tension in her body. Mora
cleared her throat. "I heard the owners speaking about the uprising,
and their wishes for things to return to normal. And I realized something."

"Oh?"

Mora considered his wish for her to find a way to keep them fed until
the siege ended. No pain came as she imagined her solution. Instead of
a crushing feeling in her chest, the air tasted fresher, and though her

heart raced, Mora felt lighter than she had in ages. She grinned as cool smoke gathered in her palms and curled around her fingers until it slid over her fingernails.

"It's simple," she said, bending so their breath mingled.

Something flashed in Dother's eyes and his hand stilled. He pressed back into the pillow, his azure eyes trailing over every inch of her face. "What are you up to, Treasure?"

"I'm ending this." Before Dother could blink, Mora plunged her smoke deep into his chest.

Dother screamed, the sound bouncing off the stone walls, but she pressed harder, reveling in the hot blood coating her fingertips.

"What the fuck are you doing?!" he bellowed, thrashing and rolling violently.

Mora laughed, the deranged sound bubbling out of her chest. It danced around the room, chasing his screams like a beast on the hunt while she stared at his blood. She'd intended to watch Dother's face. To memorize every minute twitch while he suffered. But she couldn't shift her gaze. This felt like a dream, and Mora feared it would disappear if she looked away.

Dother struck, his fist slamming into her temple, and black spots crowded Mora's vision. She swayed, nearly toppling over. But her smoke twisted around Dother's sternum, slipping through blood and piercing tissue until it clutched bone, anchoring her in place. When his fist crashed into her nose, Mora's head spun and bile churned in her stomach. Blood dripped down her face, joining the pool on his chest. But she didn't stop.

"It's over." Mora sneered down at him.

"You bitch!"

Dother shifted, flipping them over. Blood rained down from his chest, coating her throat, her face, her hair. She was soaked in his agony. Mora grinned while he scrambled, his hands slipping through blood as he attempted to remain upright.

"You die, the siege ends and food stores return," Mora hissed as his hand wrapped around her throat. A loud crack echoed through the room as his bones splintered, the sound so vile Mora nearly gagged.

"Stop," he begged on a shuddering breath. His free hand wrapped around her wrist, his grip bruising as he tried to force her away, but her mist rooted in his chest. And he knew better than anyone, it was impossible to stop a wish from being fulfilled.

"I'm giving you what you wanted," Mora wheezed, praying his grip would weaken. Her face pounded, and the blood from her nose ran down her throat as Dother forced her head back.

The color drained from his face while more blood soaked into Mora's dress. "I never wanted this," he panted.

Mora scoffed. "Neither did I, but that didn't stop you."

His heart raced, slamming against Mora's smoke as it edged closer. Dother's grip weakened. "You'll be cursed forever."

Mora froze, the weight of his words settling over her. She knew. There was no escaping what he'd done. The room shrank, walls pressing against her skin like teeth, the coppery air too thin. Mora shook as she attempted to hide her panic. What would happen when someone new got their hands on her flask? She couldn't do this again. Wouldn't do this again.

I will survive it.

Mora wasn't the same woman Dother cursed over a year ago. If future Keepers intended to use her, she would make them bleed.

And, unlike Dother, others could only make three wishes. Unless they were his blood, but, as far as she knew, Dother had no living relatives.

"And you'll never touch me again," she spat, pushing harder against her smoke.

Dother gasped. "You'll never be rid of me, not truly." His hands slipped, and he landed on top of her, warm blood pooling between them.

Mora ignored his words. She thrashed beneath him until she was able to roll them over. The moonlight trickling through the window slipped over his pale skin, the color nearly drained. Her power snaked around his heart. It fluttered under the mist's touch, and Dother quivered along with it. His eyes closed, and while he'd reached up once more to grip her wrist, his hold was weak, fingers cold and clammy.

"He'll... find you someday," he breathed as she pulled back, snapping the arteries tethering his heart in place.

"Who?" she asked. But it was too late. The smoke slipped away, leaving Dother's wet, too-warm heart in her palm. It convulsed, the damn thing still beating, spitting blood in the air.

Mora sat frozen, unable to breathe, as she fixated on it. Dother lay, unmoving, beneath her, and yet she still trembled, waiting for him to sit up and strangle her until the darkness took her once more. And when she woke, he'd force her to—

No. Never again.

"He's dead," she whispered to herself. "He's dead, he's dead, he's dead."

Mora kept saying it. Repeating it to herself over and over like a chant. A promise. Dother was dead. He'd never hurt her again. And, no matter what came next, no one else would either. Not like this.

Her gaze fixed on the still-beating red organ resting in her palm. Blood soaked her curls, her dress, the sheets. It stuck to her skin, staining most of her body, and yet she didn't feel dirty. It felt like armor. Like Dother's death enveloped her and, in a way, set her free. Mora was powerful, painted in his agony.

The pounding in her ears was so loud Mora didn't hear the footsteps marching across Dother's sitting room to the bedroom. By the time the knob rattled and the door creaked open, it was too late. She jumped at the sound, inadvertently crushing Dother's heart in her fist.

Amber eyes met hers as she destroyed the last living piece of Dother, untethering herself from him. The flask called, its demanding song undeniable, and the cold caress of smoke slowly tore her apart, piece by piece.

It wasn't the unknown that horrified her. It was those wide, terrified eyes staring at her blood stained flesh and the dead man lying beneath her.

"Mora?" the woman whispered, trembling as blood dripped down Mora's face and onto Dother's cooling body.

Mora opened her mouth to speak, but it was too late—the flask pulled harder, a pain building in her chest that she didn't have the energy to fight. She came undone, fading into an ethereal cloud of obsidian.

The last thing she heard as she slipped away was her mother's horrified scream.

CHAPTER 70

THALIAS

A furious wind spun around Thalias and all he knew was darkness and the cool caress of Mora's smoke.

And Vesryn... he could *feel* his mate's panic. It gripped his heart, squeezing until he could hardly take it. Yet, somehow, it was worse when distance dulled the sensation to little more than a distressing throb. To know Vesryn's pain was better than barely feeling him at all.

As he stared at the gold flecks glittering in the darkness, Thalias realized he could no longer feel the endless network of roots cuddling in the soil. He couldn't sense the branches stretching towards the sun, or leaves fluttering in the breeze. The pain, the joy, the hunger of Arcadia... it was gone.

Quiet like Thalias had never known settled over him until it grew so heavy he was certain he would suffocate.

CHAPTER 71

MORA

Mora followed the pull of Andras's wish to an unfamiliar room. It was pristine, with white walls and rows of ivory bookshelves, filled to the brim with books and ledgers. And the smell of fresh paint permeated the air. Mora did her best to be gentle with Thalias, curling on the floor before rematerializing. He appeared beside her, huddled on the hardwood, those wild eyes widening as he took in the lines and knots in the wood flooring.

"Where have you taken me?" Thalias demanded.

Mora couldn't meet his eyes. She grimaced, shaking her head as she looked around, searching for Andras. She could *feel* him—he was nearby. But where was he hiding? "I don't know where we are, Thalias. It's the *who* you should concern yourself with."

And the fact that I can't save you.

Andras's wish that she not interfere with his dominion over the Spirit of Arcadia sealed Thalias's fate. No matter what happened next, her hands were tied.

"And that would be?"

Mora swallowed, hating the tightness in her chest. "Andras."

Thalias's brows furrowed. He pursed his lips, his red eyes growing distant as he searched his memory. "Alina said you belong to him."

"Alina doesn't know what she's talking about," Mora muttered as she neared the fireplace. Its white marble mantle was trimmed with gold, every inch carved to display glimpses of Arcadia. Hiding among the alabaster trees were Fae of all types, playing around the fire. And above the mantle...

"But he was your Keeper?" Thalias asked.

Mora ground her teeth and stared at Halvard's face. The portrait was grand, the work of a skilled painter who'd made Halvard's long auburn hair look almost real. And the smug sneer, it was perfect. No redness stained his cheeks, his porcelain skin unblemished, like it was when Mora first saw him in Frederick's library. His gray eyes were bright, though they didn't look kind. They watched her, as if he judged her and found her lacking.

"The artist captured his scowl perfectly."

Mora turned, her arm knocking against Thalias's side.

"Andras," she hissed, offering him a scowl of her own.

Andras watched them from across the large room, a smug grin on his face. He sat at an ivory desk, Dother's journal open on its surface. Mora could have sworn she saw her name on the page. There were rough drawings stained with splotches of ink, one of which looked so much like her flask. Mora clenched her jaw as she stared at the familiar scrawl—she recognized Dother's writing well.

Andras pushed the journal aside before rising from his plush white leather chair. "Tell me," he said, cold amusement sparkling in those bright, blue eyes. "Did Halvard scream when you killed him?"

Mora blinked. "How did you know?"

Beside her, Thalias tensed, his nostrils flaring. The silver on his arms glowed dimly and Mora braced herself for an onslaught of furious plants. But nothing happened.

As Andras rounded the desk, he dragged a finger over its intricate gilded detailing. Swirling, golden vines and leaves decorated the edges, coming together in the middle to create a beautiful tree. Its branches and roots curved toward one another, resembling a circle. Thalias snarled when he saw it, his cheeks flushing—there were too many symbols of Arcadia in this room.

Had Halvard's obsession with power and status sparked an interest in Arcadia? Did Andras use that against him? Mora sighed inwardly. She should have questioned him before she took his life.

"I knew he wouldn't last a day with you." Andras chuckled. "I'm still furious he took your flask, but we both know it's only a matter of time before I get it back."

He watched them, those azure eyes igniting the furious beat of Mora's heart. Andras looked so much like he did at Frederick's party, regal and impeccably dressed in a crisp cotton shirt and royal blue waistcoat with a silver trim... he looked too much like Dother.

You'll never be rid of me.

The scent of citrus pushed through the overwhelming aroma of fresh paint and Mora's stomach twisted.

He's dead, he's dead, he's dead. She clenched her fist and kept the panic off her face.

Mora lifted her chin. "It took centuries for your family to find me. I wouldn't be so sure of myself if I were you."

A muscle ticked in Andras's jaw and he narrowed his eyes. It helped to focus on the amber splotch in his left iris. The firelight illuminated the color like a splash of honey in a sea of azure and tension bled from Mora's body. *He's not Dother.*

Andras twisted his ring, jostling the pearly white gem inside. It twisted in its casing until the dark iris pointed toward Thalias, as if it saw him.

Thalias's lip curled as he stared at it. "What have you done, Wraith?"

"I'm sorry," she whispered.

Andras fixed his cravat and adjusted his waistcoat, then pushed away from the desk. Before he came closer, he grabbed a golden paperweight off the corner—it almost looked like a large seed, made from gilded leaves plastered one on top of the other. Leaves from the Mother Tree, like the ones decorating Mora's flask.

"You must be the Spirit of the Forbidden Forest," Andras said as he neared Thalias, fiddling with the golden trinket. "Cillian had theories on what shape it would take after the tree was dealt with."

A silver glow flared in the center of Thalias's eyes and he bared his teeth.

"Something wrong, Fae?"

Thalias flexed his fingers, those silver markings pulsing. When nothing happened, he sniffed the air and grimaced. "Iron." He spat out the word like it tasted awful on his tongue.

Andras nodded, tossing the paperweight up in the air and catching it. "I couldn't be sure what Mora would bring to my door." He shrugged. "Protecting myself against Fae was a needed precaution.

Powdered iron and the bones of a Keeper helped me enchant the paint so you can't use your power in the manor. Or chateau, as the late Halvard called it."

"You kept Vehsa's bones?" Thalias sneered, the markings on his arms glowing as luminously as his eyes. But no roots pushed through the floorboards, and no branches shot through the arched windows.

"I intend to do far more interesting things with yours." Andras's eyes narrowed as his gaze raked over Mora. "Cillian was brilliant, but his obsession with *her* blinded him to the possibilities."

The hairs on the back of Mora's neck stood at the sound of that damn name. She squeezed her fingers into fists to hide the way they trembled. Thalias growled, the sound low and predatory. Before he could make a move toward Andras, Mora stepped in front of him.

"As if you didn't proposition me," she snarled. "You're no better than he was."

"I plan to use you, Mora, nothing more." Andras stepped closer and reached for Mora's chin, but she slapped his hand away. Fury flared in those azure eyes, but Mora didn't cower. "I offered to make things easier for you, and more entertaining for us both. We could have worked together and enjoyed something more..." Andras rolled the gilded trinket around his palm as he considered his words. "...carnal. Instead, you've made it clear I need to break you, like my ancestors broke Zadriel. It's not ideal. But it's your choice."

The memory of Zadriel's pained gasps while they cut him crowded her mind and Mora bared her teeth. Andras sounded proud. Proud his ancestors abused an eight-year-old Fae into submission. The pounding in her ears was maddening. And the pressure in her chest threatened to steal her breath.

541

SARA FLANAGAN

"You will *never* touch Zadriel again," Mora growled. She thought of Dother's last breath. Of his blood soaking her skin and enveloping her in death. There was no end to how monstrous she'd become if it meant handing Zadriel the same revenge.

Andras laughed. The low sound made the power in her chest thrash harder.

"I see he found you. You're welcome for the reminder, by the way."

"Careful, Andras. I've considered how I'll carve you up in return. And you can't make me heal you this time."

Andras frowned and absentmindedly touched his cheek. Mora may have erased the wound, but pain had a way of leaving a mental scar. One no magic could tear from your memory. He shook his head, tendrils of chocolate brown hair tickling his brow. "I hoped Zadriel would influence you to behave. I did you both a kindness in reminding you of his place." With a sigh, he tapped his ring against a golden leaf, his eyes growing distant. "Clearly, that hasn't worked. But he'll need to return to me eventually. And when he does..."

Mora's blood froze. "When he does, what?"

Andras clapped her on the shoulder, smirking when she flinched. "Make sure to return with him, flask in hand." He shook the paperweight in front of her face as if it were her flask. "Or I may find I no longer have use for him."

The pinch of his grip on her shoulder faded and Mora's vision went red. There was nothing but violence in her mind when she broke the distance between them and snarled in his face. "Lay another finger on Zadriel and I will show you anguish like you couldn't imagine. I'll grind *your* bones to powder and paint myself in your agony. You will *beg* me to end you."

542

Andras shoved her away. "I'm not idiotic enough to make a wish that would allow you to harm me."

"Foolish Halfling," Thalias muttered.

Andras's gaze snapped to Thalias, and he smiled. It was smug. Triumphant. So much like Dother's smile the day he'd cursed her. Mora's stomach dropped.

"It's time you left me with my prize, Mora. I'm sure I'll see you soon."

"What will you do with him?" Mora asked, a lump forming in her throat.

Before Andras could answer, Thalias's roar echoed through the room. He lunged for Andras, tackling him to the floor. The crack of Andras's head against the hardwood followed, the sound so loud Mora grinned. Thalias didn't offer him a moment to breathe—he righted himself and slammed his fist against Andras's face. Blood coated Thalias's knuckles. More spattered his cheeks, the red stark against his alabaster skin. Mora watched with envy, wondering if she'd feel as powerful covered in Andras's blood as she did when Dother's enveloped her.

With a sigh, she backed away until she leaned against the wall. It was pathetic—Andras was no match for the Fae, even without his magic. She wondered if her guilt for Thalias was misplaced. If perhaps they'd be leaving together shortly.

If only she could help... Andras's wish wouldn't allow it—magic twisting around her bones as she dreamt of joining the brawl, as if the wish waited for her to step out of line.

The wish was too carefully worded, Mora hadn't found a way around it. It was likely Andras prepared the wording months, if not years, in advance. Damn Dother's journal. Mora chewed her lip, wondering how it found its way from the castle to a living relative. Had Zadriel retrieved it? There were so many things she needed to ask him.

Something twisted in her heart when she thought of him. Of them. Of the venom Thalias spat, still pooling in her mind.

Now's not the time.

Mora dug her nails into her forearms and returned her focus to the fight in time to watch Thalias wrap his hand around Andras's neck. He lifted the man off the floor, pulling him closer until their noses nearly touched. Despite the enchantment in the walls cutting Thalias off from his abilities, there was deadly power in his voice. "You aren't worthy of the magic my ancestors gave you, Halfling. And I will make certain you never use it to harm my people again."

Redness bloomed in Andras's cheeks as the man choked. They reddened further when Mora cackled, the color so bright against his fading tan. Her fingers twitched and Mora wished it were her hand wrapped around Andras's throat. Or Zadriel's beautiful fingers choking the life from him. She'd happily watch him take his revenge. Regardless of what happened next, every piece of her wanted that for him.

Andras swung his fist, slamming the sharp edges of the trinket's gilded leaves into Thalias's cheek. The Fae hissed, baring his canines. And those cold red and purple eyes filled with pure, violent rage.

But all Mora saw was the silver flecked blood staining the golden leaves. And the smile on Andras's face.

"Thalias, no!" Mora screamed.

CHAPTER 72

MORA

Mora flinched when Andras dropped the paperweight, the golden leaves clattering against the floor. The sound grated in her ears. But the sight of the leaves unfurling, revealing a hollow center stained with Thalias's blood, had Mora holding her breath.

Quiet music curled through the air. It was the same gentle voice from the clearing, only this song was morose, the sound pushing against Mora's skin as if urging her away. She pressed harder against the wall. For the first time in her long life, the magic within her re-coiled, burrowing deeper into her chest. With every shallow breath, the song grew louder.

Thalias released Andras's neck and fell to the floor screaming. The sound of it was awful, but she forced herself to listen. He scrambled away from the trinket, his breathing ragged, spittle running down his chin. Blood began dripping from his nose.

"Thalias!" Mora tried to run to him, but it was as if a trembling, ethereal fist clutched her ribcage and squeezed the moment she made the choice to intervene. A wheeze spilled from her lips and she nearly doubled over, wincing. Black spots danced in her vision. The pressure didn't ease until she managed to make it back to the wall.

All she could do was catch her breath and watch. Watch as the blood vessels burst in Thalias's eyes. As he cried between gasps, twisting on the floor. As his bones bent in the wrong directions. Bile burned in Mora's throat, but she refused to look away.

"You're killing him," she cried, tears spilling down her cheeks.

Andras wiped his bloody nose, then sneered at the mess on his hand. He pulled a handkerchief from his breast pocket, barely sparing Mora a glance as he pressed it to the wound. "You, of all people, know he'll be fine. He only needs to give in."

Mora froze. "No," she breathed. "You can't."

"Don't worry, *Treasure*," Andras mocked. "He won't be like you. Cillian used all the materials I needed to recreate your curse." Those bright eyes met hers and Mora swallowed at the sinister gleam sparkling in their depth. "I do, however, wonder what I could accomplish with your blood. Cillian had few notes on the subject. I think he wanted to own you, in all ways. The idea of any part of you attached to an enchantment he'd give to another likely horrified him."

"Fuck you, Andras," Mora spat through clenched teeth.

Andras waved her off before stepping over Thalias and moving toward the fireplace. As he tossed the handkerchief into the fire, Thalias managed to roll over. "Mora, please," he rasped.

Within those frantic, bloodshot eyes, Mora saw visions of herself being torn apart on her old bedroom floor. As he grit his teeth against the pain, the phantom memory of her own bones bending and twisting played in her mind. She could almost feel that first tug in her center, pulling her apart and weaving her back together into something more pliable. Something belonging to Dother. And Mora damned Thalias to a similar fate.

It didn't matter that Andras's wish forced her hand. She did this. And she could do nothing to stop it.

Mora swallowed her tears and clenched her shaking fingers. "I can't help you," she whispered, shaking her head.

Thalias let out a soul-wrenching scream. Pure black smoke, not unlike her own, rose from the trinket and curled around him. He attempted to crawl away from its grasp, but it plastered itself to his skin, enveloping him in shadows. He threw Mora one final pleading look before it swallowed him whole and pulled back. In a blink, he was gone. The morose song ended, and the gilded leaves clicked shut, one by one. It was blissfully, horrifically quiet.

Turning away felt like a betrayal. Dother's chuckle crowded her mind, and when Andras looked back at her, Mora was certain he saw the same silent promise burning in her eyes as Dother had centuries ago.

Andras didn't balk. "You're no longer needed, Mora, return to your flask," he said as he made his way toward the trinket.

The leather of her pouch was soft under her fingers. Mora slid the buckle free. "You aren't my Keeper anymore," she said, slipping her hand inside.

"And you can't do anything to save him. Now, begone." Andras didn't spare her a glance.

Torn, silky fabric gathered in Mora's hand as she thought of emerald stained with gravy and crimson. She clutched it tight in her

SARA FLANAGAN

fist, digging her nails into her palm until it stung, blood rising to the surface.

"Once again you've underestimated me."

Smoke gathered in her palm, bits of onyx dripping to the floor as she pulled her hand free from her pouch. It weaved into the shredded piece of her dress from Frederick's banquet. Thread by thread, the emerald came apart until blood, fresh as the day it dripped from Andras's nose, joined her own.

Something wicked stirred inside her. And she had no desire to cage it. "I'm not too proud to say I'll enjoy hurting you." Mora couldn't hold back the mist spilling from her pores. What Andras saw, a woman dripping in darkness, amber eyes aflame, must have looked every bit like the wraith Thalias compared her to. The man gulped, face paling. He took a step back, but Mora followed. Her glittering smoke gathered behind her, trailing on the floor like an ethereal cape.

"What are you doing?" Andras asked as he skirted the mantle.

Mora tossed the emerald scraps at his feet, revealing two streams of blood, caressed in a strand of smoky onyx, chasing each other around her fist. "Teaching you a lesson." Mora offered a mocking grin. "Your outbursts left me no choice. I hope it was worth it."

Andras recoiled. "You can't kill me, that would go against my wish. You'd be interfering with my dominion over the Spirit."

He was right. A dead man could rule over nothing—his wish that she not interfere protected his life. Unfortunately. But that didn't mean she couldn't hurt him...

"I'm not interfering." There was nothing human about Mora's cold laugh. "All this time with Dother's journal, and you learned nothing." Mora's blood devoured his, and Andras moaned pitifully.

His limbs shook as he staggered, tripping over his feet and tumbling to the floor, knees slamming against the hardwood. Andras gasped in pain. And Mora cackled.

As the sanguineous tether wrapped in darkness settled around Mora's wrist, his spine arched painfully. Mora knelt by his side. "I will always find a way to fight back."

Andras's throat worked. But when he opened his mouth, no words came out. Tears gathered on his lashes, the azure in his eyes shining too brightly. Mora had half a mind to dig them out of his skull, but it would likely kill him and his wish truly wouldn't allow it. Pity.

"Give me your hand," Mora demanded, grinning as he complied. His movements were stiff. Unnatural. So much like Zadriel when Andras tortured him this way. Mora squeezed his palm, knowing it must have stung, but the bastard couldn't react. She eyed that eerie ring, the black void inside staring back. It seemed like a fitting enough trinket for Zadriel—a gift and a promise. A reminder his suffering was over.

Glittering onyx crawled from Mora's fingers to twist around Andras's wrist. She called to her fire and sent a blaze wrapping around her smoke. Andras could do nothing as his flesh bubbled, blisters erupting, then cooling under the smoke's frigid caress. It coiled tighter. And the nauseatingly sweet smell of burning flesh assaulted Mora's nostrils.

"Watch," Mora said, a thrill shooting through her.

Andras looked down, wide, watery eyes glued to his wrist. A quiet moan bubbled in his throat as her smoke sawed through muscle, fire cauterizing the wound.

"How does it feel to be powerless?" Mora asked. White bone peeked through pink flesh and charred bits of muscle. Despite the blood thrall, Andras's breathing turned ragged. His heart battered against his chest, loud enough Mora could hear, and she hummed, enjoying its frantic beat. "Because I can do so much worse. Leave Zadriel and me alone, unless you'd like to learn how monstrous I can be."

Blood soaked into Andras's white breeches and Mora's dress, though the splashes of crimson suited her well. "A word of advice," she said with a low laugh. "Take good care of Thalias." With her free hand, Mora fisted his cravat, tugging until Andras fell against her. As his head lolled on her shoulder, she breathed in his ear, "Or you, like Dother, may wake to find the monster you created tearing your heart from your chest."

As smoke cut through bone, Mora jerked her hand, tearing his wrist free. She turned it around in her grasp before using it to pat Andras on the cheek twice. "Good boy," she mocked.

Pushing Andras aside, Mora eyed his raw, severed wrist. It was blistered and oozing. And hopefully horrifically painful. She shoved her prize into her pouch, smiling as she imagined how she'd use his blood. Would Zadriel be happy with what she had in mind?

Mora tipped her head back and took a deep, satisfying breath, then stood. There was one more thing she wanted to take from Andras.

As she walked to the ivory desk, Andras sat on the floor, stone-faced and unmoving except for the rise and fall of his chest. It would be hours before he could move. Thank the gods. Mora stared at the cracked leather of Dother's journal for far too long, fingers twisting at her side. She didn't want to touch it. To hold a piece of him. But it contained too many secrets to leave in Andras's possession. Secrets she may need to know... did she *want* to know?

Mora didn't give herself another moment to think as she swiped it off the desk. It felt wrong in her hands. And as her heart thrummed in her chest, she half considered feeding it to her flames. Perhaps someday.

Before she gave herself to her mist's ethereal embrace, Mora looked back. The gilded trinket caging Thalias glinted in the fire-light, and the beast in her chest roared. She bared her teeth, her glowing amber gaze fixing on Andras one final time.

"Andras," she cooed, the command of the blood thrall echoing in her voice. "You have my permission to scream now."

A song of pained bellows rang pleasantly in Mora's ears as she flew from the manor.

CHAPTER 73

THALIAS

Thalias's skull pounded, pain throbbing along with his heart. He took an experimental breath, relieved he could fill his lungs, though they still ached. Shouldn't he be healing? Or did Andras's enchanted walls dampen that as well?

Instead of a pristine, white room, polished perfectly to distract from human inferiority, Thalias was surrounded by gold. Gold so bright his eyes watered. The floor beneath him was hard, and the ceiling rose into a pointed dome, the structure tapered as if it was constructed out of... leaves.

Impossible.

Spinning on his heels, he found no windows, no doors, no escape. Nothing but stolen pieces of Arcadia weaved together and enchanted to swallow its Spirit whole.

How could a Halfling accomplish this? It must be the ring.

Something shifted and Thalias felt whispers of Arcadia. He couldn't understand how, but it pushed against the deafening silence and he welcomed the feeling. He closed his eyes. Leaned into the familiar embrace. A warmth radiated in his chest and as he inhaled he could nearly taste the fresh, earthy air. Until acrid smoke poisoned his tongue.

Thalias stilled, visions of flames burning behind his eyes. He reached out to Arcadia for comfort but... something was off. This wasn't the Forest Thalias knew. She felt like a ghost—Her cold touch slipped through his body and twisted all around him.

"Hello, Thalias," a soft, feminine voice said behind him.

Thalias was greeted by sad, golden eyes, and a tight, joyless smile. Long, silky black hair fell to her waist, the delicate points of her ears sticking out between the strands.

He didn't know her... but she looked so much like her son.

"Vehsa?"

EPILOGUE

MORA

A dark cloud descended upon Eden, careening through the fields and stirring up dirt lining the roads. Animals fled to the far edges of their pastures and there were screams as villagers ran to the nearest buildings. Mora laughed inwardly. As if a door would stop her.

Fortunately for them, their houses would remain standing. Part of her ached to crash through every structure, tearing the village apart until it wept. Until it felt every ounce of pain the Dothers caused her and Zadriel. But Zadriel's plea for mercy weighed on her mind. For him, Eden would survive.

It wasn't long before she found a familiar door, brown chipped paint peeling back against her onslaught. She dove beneath the crack, spilling into the kitchen. New wooden chairs with the same curved backs and arms sat around a matching table, but they shat-

tered when Mora slammed into them, a rain of splinters and kindling clattering to the floor.

Mora twisted into the cramped pantry—Zadriel's room. The
scents of mint and summer rain hung in the air, and she couldn't
help but feel lighter. Gods, she missed him. Ached for him. Hated
the doubt in her head and the pain in her heart. Spinning through
the space, Mora pulled Zadriel's things into her ethereal embrace,
along with the contents of Andras's shelves. The clink of blood
vials and sprite flasks and the squeak of the pixie had her smiling
internally.

Mora sped back through the kitchen and crashed into Andras's
room. A furious wind flew at her back, tearing black sheets from
Andras's large bed as papers spun in the air.

A torrent of obsidian landed, shrinking back to reveal Mora,
fury glowing in her amber eyes. Though smoke trailed behind her,
holding her stolen goods. Mora pushed her curls away from her face,
searching for a parchment and quill. She found them on the floor,
along with a jar of toppled ink, the black liquid slowly saturating
Andras's plush, white rug. Mora snorted. He wouldn't be happy.
She ran her fingers over her pouch and laughed quietly. He wouldn't
be happy about many things.

It had been ages since Mora wrote a note, but she remembered her
lessons well—each letter was elegant, fit for royal eyes. May it add to
the mockery. Folding the sheet, she placed it delicately on the bed
before dropping an empty blood vial on top.

As she walked through the kitchen Mora ran her hand along the
wall, through the thin curtains, and over the counter. Flames trailed
behind, following the path of her fingers until an inferno feasted on
the cottage.

Once outside, Mora inhaled the late summer air, the fresh scent made better by embers and brimstone. As Andras's house fell, she hummed an old song. One that reminded her of a time long since passed. One that made her think of her mother.

The smoke cleared too quickly. And all that remained was a pile of charred wood, Andras's bed, and Mora's message.

She lingered a moment, too many emotions swelling in her chest. But as the sun crawled over the horizon, she burst into smoke and rushed toward Arcadia, ash twirling in the air behind her.

Andras had plans for her. For them all. But Mora had plans of her own.

She would be his undoing. His end.

BONUS SCENE

CHAPTER 1 -ZADRIEL'S POV
FINDING MORA

Scents of embers, lavender, and pine curled in the air, flirting with Zadriel's senses and coaxing a warmth to bloom over his heart. He grimaced. Cursed himself when he realized he took a single step toward the source.

Mother damn me.

Mora's scent was different from before, and yet he knew it was her. Sparks ignited in his soul and every part of him screamed *mine*. Though his mind yelled *no* in response.

Peering through a patch of scraggly, winter-warn trees, he spied the manor. Red bricks framed the opulent home. Sunlight glinted off the bay windows, blocking his view of what awaited inside—not that he'd be allowed to set foot in such a place. But Zadriel found himself curious.

A branch leaned down to pat his shoulder, the leaf buds peppering its surface catching the soft fabric of Zadriel's black cloak. He stepped away, ignoring the tightness in his chest, and searched the grounds. There wasn't much to see—spring barely held Berwick in her hands. Though some of the garden bloomed generously, much to Zadriel's surprise.

And there, standing stark still in the middle of it, clinging to a rose bush, was Mora.

Zadriel sucked in a breath. She was as beautiful as he remembered. Dark brown curls fell to her waist, tickling her turquoise gown, and the sun kissed her warm brown skin. It coaxed the golden undertones to the surface, lending her an almost ethereal glow. And those eyes... his heart fluttered, and Zadriel hated himself for it. They were the same stunning honeyed amber burned into his memory. Yearning and fury twisted in his gut as he watched her. When her gaze lifted, raw magic shone in its depth.

Arcadia's magic—Mora didn't deserve it.

The pounding of his heart no longer held a trace of yearning in its furious tempo. He wanted nothing more than to turn away. To lie to Andras and tell him Mora was, once again, gone by the time they'd arrive. But he couldn't.

Damn his nature. Damn the Fates for leading him here, back to her. Damn his Fae instincts for desiring her so badly, despite everything she'd done.

The Little Witch condemned him to another three centuries of suffering.

Tracing his fingers over his arm, he followed the map of scars that had grown larger since Mora killed Cillian. A phantom burn echoed in the wake of his touch. It helped. The more sensible parts of his mind awakened when he felt that ache. Zadriel spent too many years staring out toward Arcadia, dreaming of a home he'd never return to. Cursing Mora's name. She wasn't a worthy mate.

Why did she have to be here? After three centuries of searching to no avail he'd hoped they'd never cross paths again. He'd travel all over this gods forsaken island, over and over, with whichever Dother held his leash at the time. When the rumors proved true, they'd arrive too late, finding only misery. Mora had a track record. Except for the rare occasion, those she didn't kill suffered in other horrific ways. Though it was never enough to give any of the Dothers pause. And clearly not enough to stop generations of nobles from making wishes.

Now he had to face her.

Face the woman who'd burned him.

The woman who'd damned him.

The woman who called to his soul, despite the hatred he'd harbored in his heart.

His mate.

Mother damn us both.

If Andras knew... would he have sent Zadriel here? Would he find a way to use their bond to his benefit? The man was controlling and obsessive. More interested in Cillian and their family's so-called destiny than any who came before him. Brennan would have loved him.

Mora gasped for breath, her eyes darting over the gardens, wide and frantic, and Zadriel froze.

Had she seen him?

He curled his fingers around the seam of his dark cloak, pulling it tighter around his body. Andras had given him a shadow sprite in case he found need of it—it rested in Zadriel's pocket. The spherical flask felt heavy against his thigh. He did his best not to think of the tiny creature inside. If he could manage, he'd prefer not to use it.

More than anything, he wished to set it free. But Andras would find out. Zadriel wasn't skilled enough in the art of deceit to think he could fool him. If he returned without the sprite, there would be questions.

When Mora's attention shifted to her palm, Zadriel released his grip on his cloak. Thank the gods, she hadn't noticed him.

"Yet," he muttered to himself. A heavy sigh escaped his lips as he grappled with the idea of facing her. It would happen soon enough.

She took a breath, picked up her skirt, and wandered through the gardens, trickles of her stolen power spilling from her fingers. A low growl rumbled in Zadriel's chest. The few birds in the trees quieted at the sound, but a brazen red squirrel chattered in response. He turned a bored look toward the creature before baring his teeth. A tiny being like that wouldn't be the one to out him. It clamped its mouth shut and skittered up the tree, leaving Zadriel to chuckle under his breath.

When Mora exploded into a cloud of glittering, obsidian mist, all Zadriel saw was his sins. Within a blink he was back in Arcadia, coughing against an onslaught of onyx smoke. Choking on his own self-hatred as Cillian took his hand and pulled him away. The sound of Arcadia's people screaming while their Mother Tree died rang in his ears.

A sound he'd never forget. No matter how many centuries passed.

Perhaps he didn't deserve to go home.

Perhaps this fate was all he was worthy of.

A wave of darkness curled through the trees, rustling their branches. He had no interest in being caught—Zadriel backed away until his boots found the soft, muddy bank of the lake. Tipping his head back, he watched as the world awakened under her touch. Leaves unfurled from their buds, the cluster of trees no longer a mess of naked branches looming among pines. Before his eyes, it became a sea of viridian and sage. Something about it soothed the tension in his shoulders. Branches bent in her direction as she spun away, aching to touch the creature that held whatever pieces of the Mother Tree Cillian weaved into her soul with his enchanting. A curse Zadriel didn't fully understand. Though he'd played a hand in it.

I should go, he thought, finding himself unable to turn away. Not as he watched those wisps of obsidian come together through the trees, shrinking back until Mora emerged. Her smile was radiant. A grin attempted to take purchase on his face, but he smothered it.

No.

Gods, he hated her.

Hated this.

Hated... himself.

That warmth in Zadriel's chest spread, along with a hum in his blood. He rubbed the spot over his heart, hoping for relief. He couldn't help but move closer, slipping through the trees until he'd reached the edge. One last look, he promised himself. One more and then he'd find Andras and face whatever hell came next.

He couldn't help the way his dark gaze roamed over her face, delighting in how her eyes lit up as she took in her work, before slipping lower. Down her frame. Snagging on the curve of her waist.

Curse the Mother, this wasn't going to be easy.

Her smile grew as she backed away, toward the manor. Watching her like this brought him back to another time. When he was young. When he had scraps of hope to cling to. When he followed her home to the castle, furious Cillian's scent clung to her skin. It had taken every ounce of his strength not to roar when Cillian muttered his plans that day as he prepared to race to the castle, pulling on one of the few luxurious outfits he owned. Despite all odds, Zadriel had found his mate. The woman he'd been sent to kidnap. Someone he could never have. And then his brother slept with her and intended to find a way to make her his wife.

It was a reminder of his place, if nothing else. Of his lot in life. At least there was a chance of returning to Arcadia back then.

Now he had nothing. All because of her.

Branches swayed in his direction once more, bending down to soothe him. They brushed his cheek, soft, new leaves pulling on his hood. Zadriel swallowed and kept his head down. He didn't deserve their adoration. He was no Keeper of Arcadia.

Readying himself to leave, he looked up at Mora one final time, unable to deny the flutter in his heart when his eyes found her face. When his gaze lifted to her luminous eyes, he found her staring back.

Zadriel stilled.

Her lips parted, and a warm shiver ran up his spine. As they watched one another, he swore he heard whispers of a beautiful song twisting through the winds. One that hummed along the tether binding their souls. And, despite his own muddled feelings, the wild part of his mind, the part unable to deny their bond, beckoned. *Come to me, Little Witch. Come home.*

What in the name of the gods was wrong with him? Zadriel shook his head, freeing himself from the spell, and turned away. The heat in his chest twisted into something pained, begging him to turn back. To run to Mora and pull her into his arms. But that was foolish. His instincts were wrong.

Even if she hadn't killed Cillian and destroyed any chance Zadriel had at freedom, he couldn't have her. It was smarter to walk away. To hate her. To deny the Fates and whatever destiny they thought to weave. They had never done right by him anyway. The only thing in this world Zadriel could trust was himself.

Yet, he couldn't help one final look back.

ACKNOWLEDGEMENTS

Oh goodness, where do I even begin? I'm feeling so much gratitude for every single soul who's been by my side in one way or another as I've crafted Mora and Zadriel's story – I'm sure I could write an entire book of thank yous! But I'll do my very best to keep this short(ish) and sweet.

To my incredible beta readers, thank you for being the best cheerleaders all while helping me make Wish everything it deserves to be. I couldn't have asked for a more amazing team!

To my ARC readers, thank you bunches for diving into Wish and giving this debut author a chance. Your excitement, your enthusiasm, your reviews, it means everything and has a greater impact than you know. You've given Wish the most incredible welcome into the world and I am forever thankful.

To my street team, the Keepers of the Flask – I still can't get over you! Many of you hadn't read Wish when you decided to help hype up my debut. The fact that all of you took a chance on me and decided to bring your amazing, positive energy to the team is the most beautiful thing and I am truly so thankful to have you by my side.

To my sensitivity readers, Ritika and Lwazi, I cannot stress enough how important your work is and how appreciative I am for everything you've done to help make Wish what it needs to be.

To my editor, chapter art and map designer, Whitney of New Ink Book Services, I adore you. Thank you for somehow taking my words and making them real with your artistic talent. Plus, the polish you've given Wish with your knowledge of the written word is everything.

To my proofreader, Vanessa of Veerie Edits, you are a darling! Thank you for making Wish sparkle, giving it the final touches it needed, and for being one of the sweetest people in the universe.

To my cover designer, Gigi of Hey Gigi Creatives, you are my freaking hero! I will never get over this cover. Ever. Thank you for taking my vision and bringing it to life with a cover that's beyond my wildest dreams!

To Adrien, my love. I'm forever grateful I get to journey through life with you by my side, and, as you know, I plan on finding you in the next one and all the ones that come after. Thank you for encouraging and supporting all of my dreams, for listening to me talk endlessly about Wish, for reading everything, analyzing chapters and letting me poke your brain. I'd be lost without you. I love you so much, and I couldn't have asked for a better partner. Thank you for being you, and for being mine.

To my parents, Anne and Louis, thank you for fostering my whimsical soul. For encouraging my imagination and listening to all of my stories. For taking me on adventures, and filling my childhood with nature, books, music and art. And, most of all, thank you for your endless faith in me. You have never doubted any of my dreams and I have achieved so many things thanks to your love and encouragement. All of your support throughout this author journey means the world. I couldn't have asked for better parents and I love you both with all of my heart.

To Melani, Amanda and Breanna, thank you all for being my big sisters. For always cheering me on and being there for the big moments (and the little ones—how would little me have made it without you?) I love you all so, so much. All your support throughout this author journey means everything.

To my in-laws, Ginette and Bob, thank you for raising the man of my dreams, and for being such kind, wonderful, supportive people. You make my life richer and I am so thankful.

To Maryann, thank you for being excited about this from the very first day. And thank you for seeing Zadriel immediately. He was worth restructuring everything for, eh? I can never thank you enough for all of your support. I love you bunches!

To Jaclyn, I love and adore you so much! And I am forever grateful we became friends. Thank you for your help, your encouragement and all the laughs. Everything! Thank the gods (Von) we found each other. I am so excited to hold Between the Moon and Her Night in my hands, and I know I will have an entire bookshelf dedicated to you one day.

To Tracy, I know you would have been so excited about this! I hope you know how much I miss you. You're forever in my heart and I will always treasure the time we had together.

To Rachel, thank you for being the sweetest, most supportive soul. You are a gem and I adore you!

To Haydn, Celaena, Angela, Juno, Jess and Hope, I am forever glad this journey brought me to you. You are all such talented authors and beautiful people. Your friendship means the world and I adore you all so much.

Thank you to Stephanie Leblanc, Alannah Russell, Caitlin Tarr, Mary Bordage, Haven Greenlaw, Kaitlyn Hillebrand, Courtney Mussatt, Alexis Hrinik, Siara Manning, and so many others I'm sure I've missed and will kick myself for not listing. You've all helped and supported me in so many ways. You have no idea how much I appreciate you!

To my family and friends, I am so lucky to be surrounded by so much love! Thank you for being a part of my life and for every word of encouragement you've shared throughout this adventure.

And to you, lovely reader, thank you, thank you, thank you. This dream of mine couldn't happen without you. Whether you've been excitedly waiting for Wish since the very first teaser or are joining in right now, thank you for giving this debut author a chance and diving into Mora and Zadriel's story.

Wish couldn't have happened without all of you. From the bottom of my heart, thank you all so much.

Love,

Sara

ABOUT THE AUTHOR

S ara Flanagan grew up running through the forest and swimming in the ocean. She has a slight obsession with chocolate
that may or may not bleed into her books. A sucker for a good story,
Sara is happy to consume them in novels, games and music. When
she isn't writing or reading you'll likely find her spending time in
nature, playing guitar, gaming or painting. She lives in the Canadian
Maritimes with her wonderful husband, Adrien, and their adorable
cat, Kiwi.

Sara writes fantasy romance with dark themes and a generous
pinch of spice. She loves exploring morally grey characters and
weaving in exciting plot twists and devastating revelations. It's her
greatest hope that you laugh, rage, cry and kick your feet along with
her as you read her books.

Obsessed with Wish and dying for more?
Stay up to date and connect with Sara here:

instagram.com/saraflanaganbooks
tiktok.com/@saraflanaganbooks
facebook.com/saraflanaganbooks
saraflanaganbooks.com

Made in the USA
Middletown, DE
10 January 2025

69271186R00345